"STRIKEBREAKER" by Isaac Asimov—While studying the people of an isolated planetoid, an Earth sociologist seeks to mediate in a most unusual strike. But can he find a final solution without changing the way the whole world thinks?

"THE MILE LONG SPACESHIP" by Kate Wilhelm—Captured by warlike aliens, would he prove the savior or betrayer of his world?

"THE CAGE" by A. Bertram Chandler—Marooned on a distant world beyond the reach of civilization, imprisoned in an alien zoo, how can they prove their intelligence to their keepers?

"SOLDIER" by Harlan Ellison—What place is there for a soldier from the future in a past world in search of peace?

Explore alien worlds and future destinies in—

ISAAC ASIMOV PRESENTS THE GREAT SF STORIES 19

ISAAC ASIMOV

PRESENTS

THE GREAT SF STORIES

#19

(1957)

EDITED BY ISAAC ASIMOV AND MARTIN H. GREENBERG

DAW BOOKS, INC.

DONALD A. WOLLHEIM, PUBLISHER

1633 Broadway, New York, NY 10019

First Printing, February 1989

1 2 3 4 5 6 7 8 9

PRINTED IN THE U.S.A.

ACKNOWLEDGMENTS

CONTENTS

Introduction 9

STRIKEBREAKER
Isaac Asimov 15

OMNILINGUAL
H. Beam Piper 33

THE MILE-LONG SPACESHIP
Kate Wilhelm 89

CALL ME JOE
Poul Anderson 103

YOU KNOW WILLIE
Theodore R. Cogswell 149

HUNTING MACHINE
Carol Emshwiller 157

WORLD OF A THOUSAND COLORS
Robert Silverberg 167

LET'S BE FRANK
Brian W. Aldiss 187

THE CAGE
A. Bertram Chandler 199

THE EDUCATION OF TIGRESS McCARDLE
C. M. Kornbluth 215

THE TUNESMITH
Lloyd Biggle, Jr. 229

A LOINT OF PAW
Isaac Asimov 281

GAME PRESERVE
  Rog Phillips   285
SOLDIER
  Harlan Ellison   305
THE LAST MAN LEFT IN THE BAR
  C. M. Kornbluth   335

INTRODUCTION

In the world outside reality it was an explosive year as Great Britain joined the club of thermonuclear powers and the United States tested its first intercontinental ballistic missile (ICBM) while the International Atomic Energy Agency was established.

In 1957 Harold Macmillan replaced Anthony Eden as Prime Minister of Great Britain, largely because of the defeat suffered the previous year as a result of the Suez fiasco. Israel was forced by the United States to withdraw from the Sinai and rely on American promises that attacks on her territory would cease and that shipping to her Gulf port of Elat would not be harmed.

On a more pacific note, the so-called "Six" signed the Treaty of Rome, which gave impetus to the formation of the Common Market in Europe. Chinese leader Chou En-lai visited the Soviet Union in what turned out to be a futile attempt to prevent the further deterioration of USSR-Chinese relations. The struggle for supremacy in the Soviet Union after the death of Stalin *still* continued, as power contenders Molotov and Malenkov were formally stripped of their posts. In the United States, a power struggle of a different sort continued as the AFL-CIO battled against criminals and corruption; a struggle that saw Jimmy Hoffa and his Teamsters Union driven from membership in the parent organization.

Words like "Beat" came into common usage, as President Eisenhower used Federal troops to protect the rights of black students attending formerly all-white schools in Little Rock, Arkansas. Hurricane Audrey killed over five hundred people in coastal Louisiana and Texas. But the highlight of the year for many of us was the successful launching of Sputniks I and II, the first man-made objects to orbit the Earth. This achievement, attained during the International Geophysical Year of 1957, coupled with the failure of the United States to get a satellite in orbit, set the stage for a great debate in this country about the state of American science and education.

Some of the top songs of 1957 were Elvis Presley's "All Shook Up" and "Jailhouse Rock"; "Tonight" and "Maria," both from the smash Broadway hit *West Side Story*; "Seventy-Six Trombones," from Broadway's *The Music Man*; and Pat Boone's (pop music's answer to Elvis) "Love Letters in the Sand."

In 1957 Andrew Wyeth painted *Brown Swiss* while Chagall produced his famous *Self-Portrait* as the number of cities in the world with populations over 1,000,000 grew to seventy-one.

Outstanding books of the year included *The Wapshot Chronicle* by John Cheever; *Gimpel the Fool* by Isaac Bashevis Singer; *Kids Say the Darndest Things!* (he always talked that way) by Art Linkletter; *By Love Possessed* by James Gould Cozzens; *Compulsion* by Meyer Levin; and *Theory of Criticism* by Northrop Frye. Albert Camus won the Nobel Prize for Literature; while Richard Wilbur's *Things of the World* won the Pulitzer Prize for Poetry.

Sports headlines of 1957 included the Milwaukee

Braves' great seventh game win over the New York Yankees to win the World Series; Iron Liege, with Willie Hartack aboard, winning the Kentucky Derby; the Detroit Lions demolishing Marty's Cleveland Browns to win the NFL title; Carmen Basilio taking the World Middleweight crown from Sugar Ray Robinson; Ted Williams hitting an incredible .388 to lead the majors in batting and Hank Aaron winning the home run crown with a decent 44. Auburn was the NCAA football leader. But the really big and horrible sports event of 1957 was the decision to move the Brooklyn Dodgers and New York Giants to Los Angeles and San Francisco, respectively—a decision that still brings tears to millions of fans.

It was a great year for movies—films to you serious types—*Paths of Glory*, directed by Stanley Kubrick; Billy Wilder's *Witness for the Prosecution*; the Academy-Award winning *The Bridge Over the River Kwai*; Marilyn Monroe in *The Prince and the Showgirl*; Henry Fonda in *Twelve Angry Men*; and (wasn't she something) Brigitte Bardot in Roger Vadim's *And God Created Woman*. The ill-fated Rock Hudson was the number one box-office draw in the World.

Television continued to boom as such popular shows as *Perry Mason, Maverick, Leave It To Beaver*, (leave *what* to Beaver?), *Wagon Train, Have Gun, Will Travel,* and *American Bandstand* hit the airwaves.

Nobelium, the 102nd element, was discovered. The Asian Flu appeared. Hula Hoops and Frisbees became popular. Ford introduced the Edsel, a car that would live in infamy.

Death took Diego Rivera, Dorothy L. Sayers, Charles Pathé, Jean Sibelius, John Von Neumann (who some consider to be the greatest mind of the twentieth century), Christian Dior, Jimmy Dorsey, Admiral Richard E. Byrd, Erich von Stroheim,

Arturo Toscanini, Ezio Pinza, Sholem Asch, and even Humphrey Bogart.

Mel Brooks was Mel Brooks.

In the real world it was another outstanding year as a goodly number of excellent science fiction novels and collections were published (some of which had been serialized years before in the magazines), including *Earthman's Burden* by Poul Anderson and Gordon R. Dickson, *The Naked Sun* and *Earth is Room Enough* by one Isaac Asimov, *The Hunger and Other Stories* by the tragic Charles Beaumont, *Rogue in Space* by Fredric Brown, *The Deep Range* and *Tales From the White Hart* by Arthur C. Clarke, *Cycle of Fire* by Hal Clement, *They'd Rather Be Right* by Mark Clifton and Frank Riley, *The Cosmic Puppets* by Philip K. Dick, *Occam's Razor* by the vastly underrated David Duncan, *The Green Odyssey* by Philip Jose Farmer, *The Third Level* by Fritz Leiber, *Colonial Survey* by Murray Leinster, *The Shores of Space* by Richard Matheson, *Doomsday Morning* by C. L. Moore, *Star Born* by Andre Norton, *The Winds of Time* by Chad Oliver, *Slave Ship* and *The Case Against Tomorrow* by Frederik Pohl, *The Shrouded Planet* by "Robert Randall" (Robert Silverberg and Randall Garrett), *Wasp* by Eric Frank Russell, *Pilgrimage to Earth* by Robert Sheckley, the greatly influential *On the Beach* by Nevil Shute, *Master of Life and Death* by Robert Silverberg, *Big Planet* by Jack Vance, *Empire of the Atom* and *The Mind Cage* by A. E. van Vogt, *Those Idiots From Earth* by Richard Wilson, and *The Midwich Cuckoos* by John Wyndham.

More wondrous things were happening in the real world as two more writers made their maiden voyages into reality: J. F. Bone with "Survival Type" in March; and the wonderful David R. Bunch with "Routine Emergency" in December.

New magazines continued to take off in 1957,

including the terrific *Venture Science Fiction*, edited by Robert P. Mills; *Saturn, The Magazine of Science Fiction*, edited by Donald A. Wollheim; and *Space Science Fiction Magazine*, edited by Lyle Kenyon Engel, who later became famous as one of the first book "packagers" in the United States, but this attempt did not last out the year. In addition, Chicago area fans established Advent Press, which is still actively publishing books about the field.

The real people gathered together for the fifteenth time as the World Science Fiction convention (the Loncon) was held in London, marking the first occasion that the Worldcon was held outside of the North American continent. However, this Convention chose not to award Hugos to writers or artists, but instead gave the coveted statuette to *Astounding Science Fiction* as the best American magazine, to *New Worlds* as the best British magazine, and to *Science-Fiction Times* as the best fanzine.

The year 1957 saw the release of a number of science fiction films, some good, some awful, including *The Abominable Snowman of the Himalayas, The Amazing Colossal Man, Attack of the Crab Monsters, Beginning of the End*, the chilling *The Black Scorpion, The Curse of Frankenstein*, the awful *The Cyclops, The Deadly Mantis, Enemy From Space, The Giant Claw, I Was a Teenage Frankenstein* and its brother, *I Was a Teenage Werewolf*, the excellent *The Incredible Shrinking Man, Kronos, The Monolith Monsters*, the Japanese *Rodan*, the very effective *20 Million Miles to Earth, The 27th Day*, and *X the Unknown*.

Let us travel back to that honored year of 1957 and enjoy the best stories that the real world bequeathed to us.

STRIKEBREAKER

BY ISAAC ASIMOV (1920–   )

SCIENCE FICTION STORIES
JANUARY (AS "MALE STRIKEBREAKER")

Considering that there is a general impression to the effect that I am a monster of vanity and arrogance (the impression is quite false, but never mind), I suppose it's useless to expect that people won't think I deliberately choose to include my own stories in these "best of" volumes.

Well, I don't. Marty does. He consults me on the others, but he doesn't on mine and there's an agreement that I must trust his judgment with respect to that.

But I'm glad he picked this one. It's one of those stories that you write and think a lot of and yet nothing ever happens to it. (Oh, well, it's been anthologized three times that I know of before this, but that somehow doesn't strike me as enough.)

In any case, Marty says he chose it because he's a professor of political science who specializes in terrorism. (He once said so in a loud voice in a crowded restaurant. "What is your specialty, Professor Greenberg?" "Oh, I specialize in terrorism." I expected half a dozen people to make a citizen's arrest at once, but no one budged.)

In a way, "Strikebreaker" is an example of terror-

*ism, but a very odd example as you will see when
you read it.*

*By the way, when it first appeared in magazine
form, the editor, my good friend Robert W. Lowndes,
decided to change the name to "Male Strikebreaker."
It seems a peculiarly inept title change and I never
found out why. (IA)*

Elvis Blei rubbed his plump hands and said, "Self-
containment is the word." He smiled uneasily as he
helped Steven Lamorak of Earth to a light. There
was uneasiness all over his smooth face with its
small wide-set eyes.

Lamorak puffed smoke appreciatively and crossed
his lanky legs.

His hair was powdered with gray and he had a
large and powerful jawbone. "Home grown?" he
asked, staring critically at the cigarette. He tried to
hide his own disturbance at the other's tension.

"Quite," said Blei.

"I wonder," said Lamorak, "that you have room
on your small world for such luxuries."

(Lamorak thought of his first view of Elsevere
from the spaceship visiplate. It was a jagged, airless
planetoid, some hundred miles in diameter—just a
dust-gray rough-hewn rock, glimmering dully in the
light of its sun, 200,000,000 miles distant. It was the
only object more than a mile in diameter that cir-
cled that sun, and now men had burrowed into that
miniature world and constructed a society in it. And
he himself, as a sociologist, had come to study the
world and see how humanity had made itself fit into
that queerly specialized niche.)

Blei's polite fixed smile expanded a hair. He said,
"We are not a small world, Dr. Lamorak; you
judge us by two-dimensional standards. The surface
area of Elsevere is only three quarters that of the
State of New York, but that's irrelevant. Remem-

ber, we can occupy, if we wish, the entire interior of Elsevere. A sphere of 50 miles radius has a volume of well over half a million cubic miles. If all of Elsevere were occupied by levels 50 feet apart, the total surface area within the planetoid would be 56,000,000 square miles, and that is equal to the total land area of Earth. And none of these square miles, Doctor, would be unproductive."

Lamorak said, "Good Lord," and stared blankly for a moment. "Yes, of course you're right. Strange I never thought of it that way. But then, Elsevere is the only thoroughly exploited planetoid world in the Galaxy; the rest of us simply can't get away from thinking of two-dimensional surfaces, as you pointed out. Well, I'm more than ever glad that your Council has been so cooperative as to give me a free hand in this investigation of mine."

Blei nodded convulsively at that.

Lamorak frowned slightly and thought: He acts for all the world as though he wished I had not come. Something's wrong.

Blei said, "Of course, you understand that we are actually much smaller than we could be; only minor portions of Elsevere have as yet been hollowed out and occupied. Nor are we particularly anxious to expand, except very slowly. To a certain extent we are limited by the capacity of our pseudo-gravity engines and Solar energy converters."

"I understand. But tell me, Councillor Blei—as a matter of personal curiosity, and not because it is of prime importance to my project—could I view some of your farming and herding levels first? I am fascinated by the thought of fields of wheat and herds of cattle inside a planetoid."

"You'll find the cattle small by your standards, Doctor, and we don't have much wheat. We grow yeast to a much greater extent. But there will be some wheat to show you. Some cotton and tobacco, too. Even fruit trees."

"Wonderful. As you say, self-containment. You recirculate everything, I imagine."

Lamorak's sharp eyes did not miss the fact that this last remark twinged Blei. The Elseverian's eyes narrowed to slits that hid his expression.

He said, "We must recirculate, yes. Air, water, food, minerals—everything that is used up—must be restored to its original state; waste products are reconverted to raw materials. All that is needed is energy, and we have enough of that. We don't manage with one hundred percent efficiency, of course; there is a certain seepage. We import a small amount of water each year; and if our needs grow, we may have to import some coal and oxygen."

Lamorak said, "When can we start our tour, Councillor Blei?"

Blei's smile lost some of its negligible warmth. "As soon as we can, Doctor. There are some routine matters that must be arranged."

Lamorak nodded, and having finished his cigarette, stubbed it out.

Routine matters? There was none of this hesitancy during the preliminary correspondence. Elsevere had seemed proud that its unique planetoid existence had attracted the attention of the Galaxy.

He said, "I realize I would be a disturbing influence in a tightly-knit society," and watched grimly as Blei leaped at the explanation and made it his own.

"Yes," said Blei, "we feel marked off from the rest of the Galaxy. We have our own customs. Each individual Elseverian fits into a comfortable niche. The appearance of a stranger without fixed caste is unsettling."

"The caste system does involve a certain inflexibility."

"Granted," said Blei quickly; "but there is also a certain self-assurance. We have firm rules of inter-marriage and rigid inheritance of occupation. Each man, woman and child knows his place, accepts it, and is accepted in it; we have virtually no neurosis or mental illness."

"And are there no misfits?" asked Lamorak.

Blei shaped his mouth as though to say no, then clamped it suddenly shut, biting the word into silence; a frown deepened on his forehead. He said, at length, "I will arrange for the tour, Doctor. Meanwhile, I imagine you would welcome a chance to freshen up and to sleep."

They rose together and left the room, Blei politely motioning the Earthman to precede him out the door.

Lamorak felt oppressed by the vague feeling of crisis that had pervaded his discussion with Blei.

The newspaper reinforced that feeling. He read it carefully before getting into bed, with what was at first merely a clinical interest. It was an eight-page tabloid of synthetic paper. One quarter of its items consisted of "personals": births, marriages, deaths, record quotas, expanding habitable volume (not area! three dimensions!). The remainder included scholarly essays, educational material, and fiction. Of news, in the sense to which Lamorak was accustomed, there was virtually nothing.

One item only could be so considered and that was chilling in its incompleteness.

It said, under a small headline: *DEMANDS UN-CHANGED: There has been no change in his attitude of yesterday. The Chief Councillor, after a second interview, announced that his demands remain completely unreasonable and cannot be met under any circumstances.*

Then, in parentheses, and in different type, there

was the statement: *The editors of this paper agree that Elsevere cannot and will not jump to his whistle, come what may.*

Lamorak read it over three times. *His* attitude. *His* demands. *His* whistle.

Whose?

He slept uneasily, that night.

He had no time for newspapers in the days that followed; but spasmodically, the matter returned to his thoughts.

Blei, who remained his guide and companion for most of the tour, grew ever more withdrawn.

On the third day (quite artificially clock-set in an Earthlike twenty-four hour pattern), Blei stopped at one point, and said, "Now this level is devoted entirely to chemical industries. That section is not important—"

But he turned away a shade too rapidly, and Lamorak seized his arm. "What are the products of that section?"

"Fertilizers. Certain organics," said Blei stiffly.

Lamorak held him back, looking for what sight Blei might be evading. His gaze swept over the close-by horizons of lined rock and the buildings squeezed and layered between the levels.

Lamorak said, "Isn't that a private residence there?"

Blei did not look in the indicated direction.

Lamorak said, "I think that's the largest one I've seen yet. Why is it here on a factory level?" That alone made it noteworthy. He had already seen that the levels on Elsevere were divided rigidly among the residential, the agricultural and the industrial.

He looked back and called, "Councillor Blei!"

The councillor was walking away and Lamorak pursued him with hasty steps. "Is there something wrong, sir?"

Blei muttered, "I am rude, I know. I am sorry. There are matters that prey on my mind—" He kept up his rapid pace.

"Concerning *his* demands."

Blei came to a full halt. "What do *you* know about that?"

"No more than I've said. I read that much in the newspaper."

Blei muttered something to himself.

Lamorak said, "Ragusnik? What's that?"

Blei sighed heavily. "I suppose you ought to be told. It's humiliating, deeply embarrassing. The Council thought that matters would certainly be arranged shortly and that your visit need not be interfered with, that you need not know or be concerned. But it is almost a week now. I don't know what will happen and, appearances notwithstanding, it might be best for you to leave. No reason for an Outworlder to risk death."

The Earthman smiled incredulously. "Risk death? In this little world, so peaceful and busy. I can't believe it."

The Elseverian councillor said, "I can explain. I think it best I should." He turned his head away. "As I told you, everything on Elsevere must recirculate. You understand that."

"Yes."

"That includes—uh, human wastes."

"I assumed so," said Lamorak.

"Water is reclaimed from it by distillation and absorption. What remains is converted into fertilizer for yeast use; some of it is used as a source of fine organics and other by-products. These factories you see are devoted to this."

"Well?" Lamorak had experienced a certain difficulty in the drinking of water when he first landed on Elsevere, because he had been realistic enough to know what it must be reclaimed from; but he had conquered the feeling easily enough. Even on Earth, water was reclaimed by natural processes from all sorts of unpalatable substances.

Blei, with increasing difficulty, said, "Igor Ragusnik is the man who is in charge of the industrial processes immediately involving the wastes. The position has been in his family since Elsevere was first colonized. One of the original settlers was Mikhail Ragusnik and he—he—"

"Was in charge of waste reclamation."

"Yes. Now that residence you singled out is the Ragusnik residence; it is the best and most elaborate on the planetoid. Ragusnik gets many privileges the rest of us do not have; but, after all—" passion entered the Councillor's voice with great suddenness, "we cannot *speak* to him."

"What?"

"He demands full social equality. He wants his children to mingle with ours, and our wives to visit— Oh!" It was a groan of utter disgust.

Lamorak thought of the newspaper item that could not even bring itself to mention Ragusnik's name in print, or to say anything specific about his demands. He said, "I take it he's an outcast because of his job."

"Naturally. Human wastes and—" words failed Blei. After a pause, he said more quietly, "As an Earthman, I suppose you don't understand."

"As a sociologist, I think I do." Lamorak thought of the Untouchables in ancient India, the ones who handled corpses. He thought of the position of swineherds in ancient Judea.

He went on, "I gather Elsevere will not give in to those demands."

"Never," said Blei, energetically. "Never."

"And so?"

"Ragusnik has threatened to cease operations."

"Go on strike, in other words."

"Yes."

"Would that be serious?"

"We have enough food and water to last quite a while; reclamation is not essential in that sense. But the wastes would accumulate; they would infect the planetoid. After generations of careful disease control, we have low natural resistance to germ diseases. Once an epidemic started—and one would—we would drop by the hundreds."

"Is Ragusnik aware of this?"

"Yes, of course."

"Do you think he is likely to go through with his threat, then?"

"He is mad. He has already stopped working; there has been no waste reclamation since the day before you landed." Blei's bulbous nose sniffed at the air as though it already caught the whiff of excrement.

Lamorak sniffed mechanically at that, but smelled nothing.

Blei said, "So you see why it might be wise for you to leave. We are humiliated, of course, to have to suggest it."

But Lamorak said, "Wait; not just yet. Good Lord, this is a matter of great interest to me professionally. May I speak to the Ragusnik?"

"On no account," said Blei, alarmed.

"But I would like to understand the situation. The sociological conditions here are unique and not to be duplicated elsewhere. In the name of science—"

"How do you mean, speak? Would image-reception do?"

"Yes."

"I will ask the Council," muttered Blei.

They sat about Lamorak uneasily, their austere and dignified expressions badly marred with anxiety. Blei, seated in the midst of them, studiously avoided the Earthman's eyes.

The Chief Councillor, gray-haired, his face harshly wrinkled, his neck scrawny, said in a soft voice, "If in any way you can persuade him, sir, out of your own convictions, we will welcome that. In no case, however, are you to imply that we will, in any way, yield."

A gauzy curtain fell between the Council and Lamorak. He could make out the individual councillors still, but now he turned sharply toward the receiver before him. It glowed to life.

A head appeared in it, in natural color and with great realism. A strong dark head, with massive chin faintly stubbled, and thick, red lips set into a firm horizontal line.

The image said, suspiciously, "Who are you?"

Lamorak said, "My name is Steven Lamorak; I am an Earthman."

"An Outworlder?"

"That's right. I am visiting Elsevere. You are Ragusnik?"

"Igor Ragusnik, at your service," said the image, mockingly. "Except that there is no service and will be none until my family and I are treated like human beings."

Lamorak said, "Do you realize the danger that Elsevere is in? The possibility of epidemic disease?"

"In twenty-four hours, the situation can be made normal, if they allow me humanity. The situation is theirs to correct."

"You sound like an educated man, Ragusnik."

"So?"

"I am told you're denied of no material comforts. You are housed and clothed and fed better than anyone on Elsevere. Your children are the best educated."

"Granted. But all by servo-mechanism. And motherless girl-babies are sent us to care for until they grow to be our wives. And they die young for loneliness. Why?" There was sudden passion in his voice. "Why must we live in isolation as if we were all monsters, unfit for human beings to be near? Aren't we human beings like others, with the same needs and desires and feelings. Don't we perform an honorable and useful function—?"

There was a rustling of sighs from behind Lamorak. Ragusnik heard it, and raised his voice. "I see you of the Council behind there. Answer me: Isn't it an honorable and useful function? It is *your* waste made into food for *you*. Is the man who purifies corruption worse than the man who produces it?— Listen, Councillors, I will *not* give in. Let all of Elsevere die of disease—including myself and my son, if necessary—but I will not give in. My family will be better dead of disease, than living as now."

Lamorak interrupted. "You've led this life since birth, haven't you?"

"And if I have?"

"Surely you're used to it."

"Never. Resigned, perhaps. My father was resigned, and I was resigned for a while; but I have watched my son, my only son, with no other little boy to play with. My brother and I had each other, but my son will never have anyone, and I am no longer resigned. I am through with Elsevere and through with talking."

The receiver went dead.

The Chief Councillor's face had paled to an aged yellow. He and Blei were the only ones of the group left with Lamorak. The Chief Councillor said, "The man is deranged; I do not know how to force him."

He had a glass of wine at his side; as he lifted it to his lips, he spilled a few drops that stained his white trousers with purple splotches.

Lamorak said, "Are his demands so unreasonable? Why can't he be accepted into society?"

There was momentary rage in Blei's eyes. "A dealer in excrement." Then he shrugged. "You are from Earth."

Incongruously, Lamorak thought of another unacceptable, one of the numerous classic creations of the medieval cartoonist, Al Capp. The variously-named "inside man at the skonk works."

He said, "Does Ragusnik really deal with excrement? I mean, is there physical contact? Surely, it is all handled by automatic machinery."

"Of course," said the Chief Councillor.

"Then exactly what is Ragusnik's function?"

"He manually adjusts the various controls that assure the proper functioning of the machinery. He shifts units to allow repairs to be made; he alters functional rates with the time of day; he varies end production with demand." He added sadly, "If we had the space to make the machinery ten times as complex, all this could be done automatically; but that would be such needless waste."

"But even so," insisted Lamorak, "all Ragusnik does he does simply by pressing buttons or closing contacts or things like that."

"Yes."

"Then his work is no different from any Elseverian's."

Blei said, stiffly, "You don't understand."

"And for that you will risk the death of your children?"

"We have no other choice," said Blei. There was enough agony in his voice to assure Lamorak that the situation was torture for him, but that he had no other choice indeed.

Lamorak shrugged in disgust. "Then break the strike. Force him."

"How?" said the Chief Councillor. "Who would

touch him or go near him? And if we kill him by blasting from a distance, how will that help us?"

Lamorak said, thoughtfully, "Would you know how to run his machinery?"

The Chief Councillor came to his feet. "I?" he howled.

"I don't mean *you,*" cried Lamorak at once, "I used the pronoun in its indefinite sense. Could *someone* learn how to handle Ragusnik's machinery?"

Slowly, the passion drained out of the Chief Councillor. "It is in the handbooks, I am certain—though I assure you I have never concerned myself with it."

"Then couldn't someone learn the procedure and substitute for Ragusnik until the man gives in?"

Blei said, "Who would agree to do such a thing? Not I, under any circumstances."

Lamorak thought fleetingly of Earthly taboos that might be almost as strong. He thought of cannibalism, incest, a pious man cursing God. He said, "But you must have made provision for vacancy in the Ragusnik job. Suppose he died."

"Then his son would automatically succeed to his job, or his nearest other relative," said Blei.

"What if he had no adult relatives? What if all his family died at once?"

"That has never happened; it will never happen."

The Chief Councillor added, "If there were danger of it, we might, perhaps, place a baby or two with the Ragusniks and have it raised to the profession."

"Ah. And how would you choose that baby?"

"From among children of mothers who died in childbirth, as we choose the future Ragusnik bride."

"Then choose a substitute Ragusnik now, by lot," said Lamorak.

The Chief Councillor said, *"No! Impossible!* How can you suggest that? If we select a baby, that baby is brought up to the life; it knows no other. At this point, it would be necessary to choose an adult and subject him to Ragusnik-hood. No, Dr. Lamorak, we are neither monsters nor abandoned brutes."

No use, thought Lamorak helplessly. *No use, unless—*

He couldn't bring himself to face that *unless* just yet.

That night, Lamorak slept scarcely at all. Ragusnik asked for only the basic elements of humanity. But opposing that were thirty thousand Elseverians who faced death.

The welfare of thirty thousand on one side; the just demands of one family on the other. Could one say that thirty thousand who would support such injustice deserved to die? Injustice by what standards? Earth's? Elsevere's? And who was Lamorak that he should judge?

And Ragusnik? He was willing to let thirty thousand die, including men and women who merely accepted a situation they had been taught to accept and could not change if they wished to. And children who had nothing at all to do with it.

Thirty thousand on one side; a single family on the other.

Lamorak made his decision in something that was almost despair; in the morning he called the Chief Councillor.

He said, "Sir, if you can find a substitute, Ragusnik will see that he has lost all chance to force a decision in his favor and will return to work."

"There can be no substitute," sighed the Chief Councillor; "I have explained that."

"No substitute among the Elseverians, but I am not an Elseverian; it doesn't matter to me. *I* will substitute."

*   *   *

They were excited, much more excited than Lamorak himself. A dozen times they asked him if he was serious.

Lamorak had not shaved, and he felt sick, "Certainly, I'm serious. And any time Ragusnik acts like this, you can always import a substitute. No other world has the taboo and there will always be plenty of temporary substitutes available if you pay enough."

(He was betraying a brutally exploited man, and he knew it. But he told himself desperately: *Except for ostracism, he's very well treated. Very well.*)

They gave him the handbook and he spent six hours, reading and re-reading. There was no use asking questions. None of the Elseverians knew anything about the job, except for what was in the handbook; and all seemed uncomfortable if the details were as much as mentioned.

"Maintain zero reading of galvanometer A-2 at all times during red signal of the Lunge-howler," read Lamorak. "Now what's a Lunge-howler?"

"There will be a sign," muttered Blei, and the Elseverians looked at each other hang-dog and bent their heads to stare at their finger-ends.

They left him long before he reached the small rooms that were the central headquarters of generations of working Ragusniks, serving their world. He had specific instructions concerning which turnings to take and what level to reach, but they hung back and let him proceed alone.

He went through the rooms painstakingly, identifying the instruments and controls, following the schematic diagrams in the handbook.

There's a Lunge-howler, he thought, with gloomy satisfaction. The sign did indeed say so. It had a semi-circular face bitten into holes that were obviously designed to glow in separate colors. Why a "howler" then?

He didn't know.

Somewhere, thought Lamorak, *somewhere wastes are accumulating, pushing against gears and exits, pipelines and stills, waiting to be handled in half a hundred ways. Now they just accumulate.*

Not without a tremor, he pulled the first switch as indicated by the handbook in its directions for "Initiation." A gentle murmur of life made itself felt through the floors and walls. He turned a knob and lights went on.

At each step, he consulted the handbook, though he knew it by heart; and with each step, the rooms brightened and the dial-indicators sprang into motion and a humming grew louder.

Somewhere deep in the factories, the accumulated wastes were being drawn into the proper channels.

A high-pitched signal sounded and startled Lamorak out of his painful concentration. It was the communications signal and Lamorak fumbled his receiver into action.

Ragusnik's head showed, startled; then slowly, the incredulity and outright shock faded from his eyes. *"That's* how it is, then."

"I'm not an Elseverian, Ragusnik; I don't mind doing this."

"But what business is it of yours? Why do you interfere?"

"I'm on your side, Ragusnik, but I must do this."

"Why, if you're on my side? Do they treat people on your world as they treat me here?"

"Not any longer. But even if you are right, there are thirty thousand people on Elsevere to be considered."

"They would have given in; you've ruined my only chance."

"They would *not* have given in. And in a way,

you've won; they know now that you're dissatisfied. Until now, they never dreamed a Ragusnik could be unhappy, that he could make trouble."

"What if they know? Now all they need do is hire an Outworlder anytime."

Lamorak shook his head violently. He had thought this through in these last bitter hours. "The fact that they know means that the Elseverians will begin to think about you; some will begin to wonder if it's right to treat a human so. And if Outworlders are hired, they'll spread the word that this goes on upon Elsevere and Galactic public opinion will be in your favor."

"And?"

"Things will improve. In your son's time, things will be much better."

"In my son's time," said Ragusnik, his cheeks sagging. "I might have had it now. Well, I lose. I'll go back to the job."

Lamorak felt an overwhelming relief. "If you'll come here now, sir, you may have your job and I'll consider it an honor to shake your hand."

Ragusnik's head snapped up and filled with a gloomy pride. "You call me 'sir' and offer to shake my hand. Go about your business, Earthman, and leave me to my work, for I would not shake yours."

Lamorak returned the way he had come, relieved that the crisis was over, and profoundly depressed, too.

He stopped in surprise when he found a section of corridor cordoned off, so he could not pass. He looked about for alternate routes, then startled at a magnified voice above his head. "Dr. Lamorak, do you hear me? This is Councillor Blei."

Lamorak looked up. The voice came over some sort of public address system, but he saw no sign of an outlet.

He called out, "Is anything wrong? Can you hear me?"

"I hear you."

Instinctively, Lamorak was shouting. "Is anything wrong? There seems to be a block here. Are there complications with Ragusnik?"

"Ragusnik has gone to work," came Blei's voice. "The crisis is over, and you must make ready to leave."

"Leave?"

"Leave Elsevere; a ship is being made ready for you now."

"But wait a bit." Lamorak was confused by this sudden leap of events. "I haven't completed my gathering of data."

Blei's voice said, "This cannot be helped. You will be directed to the ship and your belongings will be sent after you by servomechanisms. We trust—we trust—"

Something was becoming clear to Lamorak. "You trust *what?*"

"We trust you will make no attempt to see or speak directly to any Elseverian. And of course we hope you will avoid embarrassment by not attempting to return to Elsevere at any time in the future. A colleague of yours would be welcome if further data concerning us is needed."

"I understand," said Lamorak, tonelessly. Obviously, he had himself become a Ragusnik. He had handled the controls that in turn had handled the wastes; he was ostracized. He was a corpse-handler, a swineherd, an inside man at the skonk works.

He said, "Good-bye."

Blei's voice said, "Before we direct you, Dr. Lamorak—. On behalf of the Council of Elsevere, I thank you for your help in this crisis."

"You're welcome," said Lamorak, bitterly.

OMNILINGUAL

BY H. BEAM PIPER (1904–1964)

ASTOUNDING SCIENCE FICTION
FEBRUARY

H. Beam Piper was a railroad engineer, a gun collector, and a tragic figure in the history of science fiction. Beset by personal and financial problems, and too proud to ask his many friends for help, he took his own life. This tragedy is compounded by the fact that his major works were largely unpublished in book form during his lifetime; indeed, it was only in the 1970s that his clever, well-plotted adventure stories achieved the popularity they deserved.

His "Federation" series of books featuring the "Fuzzies," prototypical cutesy aliens, are his most important legacy to the field, and include Little Fuzzy *(1962),* Junkyard Planet *(1963),* Space Viking *(1963), and* The Other Human Race *(1964), but I prefer the short stories in* The Worlds of H. Beam Piper *(1983).*

"Omnilingual" is his most famous shorter work and deservedly so. It may also be the finest story about archeological linguistics ever published. (MHG)

I love puzzle stories; I'm convinced that everyone does, even though they seem to have gone out of fashion now. Fifty years ago, in the heyday of the British murder mysteries, the most successful myster-

33

ies were puzzles in which all the clues were carefully laid out with just enough misdirection to keep the reader looking in the wrong direction. Then the detective would point out the solution and you would be delighted. (If you outguessed him, the story was a failure.)

Even a science fiction story can be a good puzzle story. Ross Rocklynne used to write them very well when I was a youngster and he kept me fascinated.

One of the very best puzzle stories in the science fiction field is the one you're about to read. And it's a good puzzle and a potentially real-life puzzle. If there was a long-dead civilization on Mars and it left writing behind, how do you read it? We can read ancient unknown languages by getting hints from modern languages that have descended from them or from translations that may exist in other ancient languages we do know. But there are no such hints available for Martian. (I'm not giving anything away. This is the situation the story starts with.)

When I first read the story back in 1957, I didn't outguess Beam, but that didn't make me happy. It filled me with wild regret. I should have. To this day I think of "Omnilingual" as the story whose ending I didn't foresee, but should have.

Oh, well, if you have never read the story, perhaps you can do better than I did. (IA)

Martha Dane paused, looking up at the purple-tinged copper sky. The wind had shifted since noon, while she had been inside, and the dust storm that was sweeping the high deserts to the east was now blowing out over Syrtis. The sun, magnified by the haze, was a gorgeous magenta ball, as large as the sun of Terra, at which she could look directly. To-night, some of that dust would come sifting down from the upper atmosphere to add another film to what had been burying the city for the last fifty thousand years.

The red loess lay over everything, covering the streets and the open spaces of park and plaza, hiding the small houses that had been crushed and pressed flat under it and the rubble that had come down from the tall buildings when roofs had caved in and walls had toppled outward. Here where she stood, the ancient streets were a hundred to a hundred and fifty feet below the surface; the breach they had made in the wall of the building behind her had opened into the sixth story. She could look down on the cluster of prefabricated huts and sheds, on the brush-grown flat that had been the waterfront when this place had been a seaport on the ocean that was now Syrtis Depression; already, the bright metal was thinly coated with red dust. She thought, again, of what clearing this city would mean, in terms of time and labor, of people and supplies and equipment brought across fifty million miles of space. They'd have to use machinery; there was no other way it could be done. Bulldozers and power shovels and draglines; they were fast, but they were rough and indiscriminate. She remembered the digs around Harappa and Mohenjo-Daro, in the Indus Valley, and the careful, patient native laborers—the painstaking foremen, the pickmen and spademen, the long files of basket men carrying away the earth. Slow and primitive as the civilization whose ruins they were uncovering, yes, but she could count on the fingers of one hand the times one of her pickmen had damaged a valuable object in the ground. If it hadn't been for the underpaid and uncomplaining native laborer, archaeology would still be back where Wincklemann had found it. But on Mars there was no native labor; the last Martian had died five hundred centuries ago.

Something started banging like a machine gun,

four or five hundred yards to her left. A solenoid jackhammer; Tony Lattimer must have decided which building he wanted to break into next. She became conscious, then, of the awkward weight of her equipment, and began redistributing it, shifting the straps of her oxy-tank pack, slinging the camera from one shoulder and the board and drafting tools from the other, gathering the notebooks and sketchbooks under her left arm. She started walking down the road, over hillocks of buried rubble, around snags of wall jutting up out of the loess, past buildings still standing, some of them already breached and explored, and across the brush-grown flat to the huts.

There were ten people in the main office room of Hut One when she entered. As soon as she had disposed of her oxygen equipment, she lit a cigarette, her first since noon, then looked from one to another of them. Old Selim von Ohlmhorst, the Turco-German, one of her two fellow archaeologists, sitting at the end of the long table against the farther wall, smoking his big curved pipe and going through a looseleaf notebook. The girl ordnance officer, Sachiko Koremitsu, between two droplights at the other end of the table, her head bent over her work. Colonel Hubert Penrose, the Space Force CO, and Captain Field, the intelligence officer, listening to the report of one of the airdyne pilots, returned from his afternoon survey flight. A couple of girl lieutenants from Signals, going over the script of the evening telecast, to be transmitted to the *Cyrano*, on orbit five thousand miles off planet and relayed from thence to Terra via Lunar. Sid Chamberlain, the Trans-Space News Service man, was with them. Like Selim and herself, he was a civilian; he was advertising the fact with a white shirt and a sleeveless blue sweater. And Major Lindemann, the engineer officer, and one of his assistants, arguing over some plans on a drafting board. She hoped, drawing a pint of hot water to wash her hands and sponge off her face, that they were doing something about the pipeline.

She started to carry the notebooks and sketchbooks over to where Selim von Ohlmhorst was sitting, and then, as she always did, she turned aside and stopped to watch Sachiko. The Japanese girl was restoring what had been a book, fifty thousand years ago; her eyes were masked by a binocular loup, the black headband invisible against her glossy black hair, and she was picking delicately at the crumbled page with a hair-fine wire set in a handle of copper tubing. Finally, loosening a particle as tiny as a snowflake, she grasped it with tweezers, placed it on the sheet of transparent plastic on which she was reconstructing the page, and set it with a mist of fixitive from a little spraygun. It was a sheer joy to watch her; every movement was as graceful and precise as though done to music after being rehearsed a hundred times.

"Hello, Martha. It isn't cocktail time yet, is it?" The girl at the table spoke without raising her head, almost without moving her lips, as though she were afraid that the slightest breath would disturb the flaky stuff in front of her.

"No, it's only fifteen-thirty. I finished my work, over there. I didn't find any more books, if that's good news for you."

Sachiko took off the loup and leaned back in her chair, her palms cupped over her eyes.

"No, I like doing this. I call it micro-jigsaw puzzles. This book, here, really is a mess. Selim found it lying open, with some heavy stuff on top of it; the pages were simply crushed." She hesitated briefly. "If only it would mean something, after I did it."

There could be a faintly critical overtone to that.

As she replied, Martha realized that she was being defensive.

"It will, some day. Look how long it took to read Egyptian hieroglyphics, even after they had the Rosetta Stone."

Sachiko smiled. "Yes, I know. But they did have the Rosetta Stone."

"And we don't. There is no Rosetta Stone, not anywhere on Mars. A whole race, a whole species, died while the first Crô-Magnon cave-artist was daubing pictures of reindeer and bison, and across fifty thousand years and fifty million miles there was no bridge of understanding.

"We'll find one. There must be something, somewhere, that will give us the meaning of a few words, and we'll use them to pry meaning out of more words, and so on. We may not live to learn this language, but we'll make a start, and some day somebody will."

Sachiko took her hands from her eyes, being careful not to look toward the unshaded lights, and smiled again. This time Martha was sure that it was not the Japanese smile of politeness, but the universally human smile of friendship.

"I hope so, Martha; really I do. It would be wonderful for you to be the first to do it, and it would be wonderful for all of us to be able to read what these people wrote. It would really bring this dead city to life again." The smile faded slowly. "But it seems so hopeless."

"You haven't found any more pictures?"

Sachiko shook her head. Not that it would have meant much if she had. They had found hundreds of pictures with captions; they had never been able to establish a positive relationship between any pictured object and any printed word. Neither of them said anything more, and after a moment Sachiko replaced the loup and bent her head forward over the book.

Selim von Ohlmhorst looked up from his notebook, taking his pipe out of his mouth.

"Everything finished, over there?" he asked, releasing a puff of smoke.

"Such as it was." She laid the notebooks and sketches on the table. "Captain Gicquel's started airsealing the building from the fifth floor down, with an entrance on the sixth; he'll start putting in oxygen generators as soon as that's done. I have everything cleared up where he'll be working."

Colonel Penrose looked up quickly, as though making a mental note to attend to something later. Then he returned his attention to the pilot, who was pointing something out on a map.

Von Ohlmhorst nodded. "There wasn't much to it, at that," he agreed. "Do you know which building Tony has decided to enter next?"

"The tall one with the conical thing like a candle extinguisher on top, I think. I heard him drilling for the blasting shots over that way."

"Well, I hope it turns out to be one that was occupied up to the end."

The last one hadn't. It had been stripped of its contents and fittings, a piece of this and a bit of that, haphazardly, apparently over a long period of time, until it had been almost gutted. For centuries, as it had died, this city had been consuming itself by a process of auto-cannibalism. She said something to that effect.

"Yes. We always find that—except, of course, at places like Pompeii. Have you seen any of the other Roman cities in Italy?" he asked. "Minturnae, for instance? First the inhabitants tore down this to repair that, and then, after they had vacated the city, other people came along and tore down what was left, and burned the stones for lime, or crushed them to mend roads, till there was nothing left but the foundation traces. That's where we are fortunate; this is one of the places where the Martian race perished, and there were no barbarians to come later and destroy what they had left." He puffed slowly at his pipe. "Some of these days, Martha, we are going to break into one of these buildings and find that it was one in which the last of these people died. Then we will learn the story of the end of this civilization."

And if we learn to read their language, we'll learn the whole story, not just the obituary. She hesitated, not putting the thought into words. "We'll find that, sometime, Selim," she said, then looked at her watch. "I'm going to get some more work done on my lists, before dinner."

For an instant, the old man's face stiffened in disapproval; he started to say something, thought better of it, and put his pipe back into his mouth. The brief wrinkling around his mouth and the twitch of his white mustache had been enough, however; she knew what he was thinking. She was wasting time and effort, he believed; time and effort belonging not to herself but to the expedition. He could be right, too, she realized. But he had to be wrong; there had to be a way to do it. She turned from him silently and went to her own packing-case seat, at the middle of the table.

Photographs, and photostats of restored pages of books, and transcripts of inscriptions, were piled in front of her, and the notebooks in which she was compiling her lists. She sat down, lighting a fresh cigarette, and reached over to a stack of unexamined material, taking off the top sheet. It was a photostat of what looked like the title page and contents of some sort of a periodical. She remembered it; she had found it herself, two days before, in a closet in the basement of the building she had just finished examining.

She sat for a moment, looking at it. It was readable, in the sense that she had set up a purely arbitrary but consistently pronounceable system of phonetic values for the letters. The long vertical symbols were vowels. There were only ten of them; not too many, allowing separate characters for long and short sounds. There were twenty of the short horizontal letters, which meant that sounds like -ng or -ch or -sh were single letters. The odds were millions to one against her system being anything like the original sound of the language, but she had listed several thousand Martian words, and she could pronounce all of them.

And that was as far as it went. She could pronounce between three and four thousand Martian words, and she couldn't assign a meaning to one of them. Selim von Ohlmhorst believed that she never would. So did Tony Lattimer, and he was a great deal less reticent about saying so. So, she was sure, did Sachiko Koremitsu. There were times, now and then, when she began to be afraid that they were right.

The letters on the page in front of her began squirming and dancing, slender vowels with fat little consonants. They did that, now, every night in her dreams. And there were other dreams, in which she read them as easily as English; waking, she would try desperately and vainly to remember. She blinked, and looked away from the photostated page; when she looked back, the letters were behaving themselves again. There were three words at the top of the page, over-and-underlined, which seemed to be the Martian method of capitalization. *Mastharnorvod Tadavas Sornhulva*. She pronounced them mentally, leafing through her notebooks to see if she had encountered them before, and in what contexts. All three were listed. In addition, *masthar* was a fairly common word, and so was *norvod,* and so was *nor,* but -*vod* was a suffix and nothing but a suffix. *Davas,* was a word, too, and *ta-* was a common prefix; *sorn* and *hulva* were both common words. This language, she had long ago decided, must be something like German; when the Martians had needed a new word, they had just pasted a couple of existing words together. It would probably turn out to be a grammatical horror. Well, they had published magazines, and one of them had been called *Mastharnorvod Tadavas Sornhulva.* She wondered if it had been something like the *Quarterly Archaeological Review,* or something more on the order of *Sexy Stories.*

A smaller line, under the title, was plainly the issue number and date; enough things had been found numbered in series to enable her to identify the numerals and determine that a decimal system of numeration had been used. This was the one thousand and seven hundred and fifty-fourth issue, for Doma, 14837; then Doma must be the name of one of the Martian months. The word had turned up several times before. She found herself puffing furiously on her cigarette as she leafed through notebooks and piles of already examined material.

Sachiko was speaking to somebody, and a chair scraped at the end of the table. She raised her head, to see a big man with red hair and a red face, in Space Force green, with the single star of a major on his shoulder, sitting down. Ivan Fitzgerald, the medic. He was lifting weights from a book similar to the one the girl ordnance officer was restoring.

"Haven't had time, lately," he was saying, in reply to Sachiko's question. "The Finchley girl's still down with whatever it is she has, and it's something I haven't been able to diagnose yet. And I've been checking on bacteria cultures, and in what spare time I have, I've been dissecting specimens for Bill Chandler. Bill's finally found a mammal. Looks like a lizard, and it's only four inches long, but it's a real warm-blooded, gamogenetic, placental, viviparous mammal. Burrows, and seems to live on what pass for insects here."

"Is there enough oxygen for anything like that?" Sachiko was asking.

"Seems to be, close to the ground." Fitzgerald got the headband of his loup adjusted, and pulled it down over his eyes. "He found this thing in a ravine down on the sea bottom— Ha, this page seems to be intact; now, if I can get it out all in one piece—"

He went on talking inaudibly to himself, lifting the page a little at a time and sliding one of the transparent plastic sheets under it, working with minute delicacy. Not the delicacy of the Japanese girl's small hands, moving like the paws of a cat washing her face, but like a steam-hammer cracking a peanut. Field archaeology requires a certain delicacy of touch, too, but Martha watched the pair of them with envious admiration. Then she turned back to her own work, finishing the table of contents.

The next page was the beginning of the first article listed; many of the words were unfamiliar. She had the impression that this must be some kind of scientific or technical journal; that could be because such publications made up the bulk of her own periodical reading. She doubted if it were fiction; the paragraphs had a solid, factual look.

At length, Ivan Fitzgerald gave a short, explosive grunt.

"Ha! Got it!"

She looked up. He had detached the page and was cementing another plastic sheet onto it.

"Any pictures?" she asked.

"None on this side. Wait a moment." He turned the sheet. "None on this side, either." He sprayed another sheet of plastic to sandwich the page, then picked up his pipe and relighted it.

"I get fun out of this, and it's good practice for my hands, so don't think I'm complaining," he said, "but, Martha, do you honestly think anybody's ever going to get anything out of this?"

Sachiko held up a scrap of the silicone plastic the Martians had used for paper with her tweezers. It was almost an inch square.

"Look; three whole words on this piece," she crowed. "Ivan, you took the easy book."

Fitzgerald wasn't being sidetracked. "This stuff's absolutely meaningless," he continued. "It had a meaning fifty thousand years ago, when it was written, but it has none at all now."

She shook her head. "Meaning isn't something that evaporates with time," she argued. "It has just as much meaning now as it ever had. We just haven't learned how to decipher it."

"That seems like a pretty pointless distinction," Selim von Ohlmhorst joined the conversation. "There no longer exists a means of deciphering it."

"We'll find one." She was speaking, she realized, more in self-encouragement than in controversy.

"How? From pictures and captions? We've found captioned pictures, and what have they given us? A caption is intended to explain the picture, not the picture to explain the caption. Suppose some alien to our culture found a picture of a man with a white beard and mustache sawing a billet from a log. He would think the caption meant, 'Man Sawing Wood.' How would he know that it was really 'Wilhelm II in Exile at Doorn?' "

Sachiko had taken off her loup and was lighting a cigarette.

"I can think of pictures intended to explain their

captions," she said. "These picture language-books, the sort we use in the Service—little line drawings, with a word or phrase under them."

"Well, of course, if we found something like that," von Ohlmhorst began.

"Michael Ventris found something like that, back in the Fifties," Hubert Penrose's voice broke in from directly behind her.

She turned her head. The colonel was standing by the archaeologists' table; Captain Field and the airdyne pilot had gone out.

"He found a lot of Greek inventories of military stores," Penrose continued. "They were in Cretan Linear B script, and at the head of each list was a little picture, a sword or a helmet or a cooking tripod or a chariot wheel. That's what gave him the key to the script."

"Colonel's getting to be quite an archaeologist," Fitzgerald commented. "We're all learning each others' specialties, on this expedition."

"I heard about that long before this expedition was even contemplated." Penrose was tapping a cigarette on his gold case. "I heard about that back before the Thirty Days' War, at Intelligence School, when I was a lieutenant. As a feat of cryptanalysis, not an archaeological discovery."

"Yes, cryptanalysis," von Ohlmhorst pounced. "The reading of a known language in an unknown form of writing. Ventris' lists were in the known language, Greek. Neither he nor anybody else ever read a word of the Cretan language until the finding of the Greek-Cretan bilingual in 1963, because only with a bilingual text, one language already known, can an unknown ancient language be learned. And what hope, I ask you, have we of finding anything like that here? Martha, you've been working on these Martian texts ever since we landed here—for the last six months. Tell me, have you found a single word to which you can positively assign a meaning?"

"Yes, I think I have one." She was trying hard not to sound too exultant. "*Doma*. It's the name of one of the months of the Martian calendar."

"Where did you find that?" von Ohlmhorst asked. "And how did you establish—?"

"Here." She picked up the photostat and handed it along the table to him. "I'd call this the title page of a magazine."

He was silent for a moment, looking at it. "Yes. I would say so, too. Have you any of the rest of it?"

"I'm working on the first page of the first article, listed there. Wait till I see; yes, here's all I found, together, here." She told him where she had gotten it. "I just gathered it up, at the time, and gave it to Geoffrey and Rosita to photostat; this is the first I've really examined it."

The old man got to his feet, brushing tobacco ashes from the front of his jacket, and came to where she was sitting, laying the title page on the table and leafing quickly through the stack of photostats.

"Yes, and here is the second article, on page eight, and here's the next one." He finished the pile of photostats. "A couple of pages missing at the end of the last article. This is remarkable; surprising that a thing like a magazine would have survived so long."

"Well, this silicone stuff the Martians used for paper is pretty durable," Hubert Penrose said. "There doesn't seem to have been any water or any other fluid in it originally, so it wouldn't dry out with time."

"Oh, it's not remarkable that the material would have survived. We've found a good many books and papers in excellent condition. But only a really vital culture, an organized culture, will publish magazines, and this civilization had been dying for hundreds of years before the end. It might have been a thousand years before the time they died out completely that such activities as publishing ended."

"Well, look where I found it; in a closet in a cellar. Tossed in there and forgotten, and then ignored when they were stripping the building. Things like that happen."

Penrose had picked up the title page and was looking at it.

"I don't think there's any doubt about this being a magazine, at all." He looked again at the title, his lips moving silently. *"Mastharnorvod Tadavas Sornhulva.* Wonder what it means. But you're right about the date—*Doma* seems to be the name of a month. Yes, you have a word, Dr. Dane."

Sid Chamberlain, seeing that something unusual was going on, had come over from the table at which he was working. After examining the title page and some of the inside pages, he began whispering into the stenophone he had taken from his belt.

"Don't try to blow this up to anything big, Sid," she cautioned. "All we have is the name of a month, and Lord only knows how long it'll be till we even find out which month it was."

"Well, it's a start, isn't it?" Penrose argued. "Grotefend only had the word for 'king' when he started reading Persian cuneiform."

"But I don't have the word for month; just the name of a month. Everybody knew the names of the Persian kings, long before Grotefend."

"That's not the story," Chamberlain said. "What the public back on Terra will be interested in is finding out that the Martians published magazines, just like we do. Something familiar; make the Martians seem more real. More human."

*   *   *

Three men had come in, and were removing their masks and helmets and oxy-tanks, and peeling out of their quilted coveralls. Two were Space Force lieutenants; the third was a youngish civilian with close-cropped blond hair, in a checked woolen shirt. Tony Lattimer and his helpers.

"Don't tell me Martha finally got something out of that stuff?" he asked, approaching the table. He might have been commenting on the antics of the village half-wit, from his tone.

"Yes; the name of one of the Martian months." Hubert Penrose went on to explain, showing the photostat.

Tony Lattimer took it, glanced at it, and dropped it on the table.

"Sounds plausible, of course, but just an assumption. That word may not be the name of a month, at all—could mean 'published' or 'authorized' or 'copyrighted' or anything like that. Fact is, I don't think it's more than a wild guess that that thing's anything like a periodical." He dismissed the subject and turned to Penrose. "I picked out the next building to enter; that tall one with the conical thing on top. It ought to be in pretty good shape inside; the conical top wouldn't allow dust to accumulate, and from the outside nothing seems to be caved in or crushed. Ground level's higher than the other one, about the seventh floor. I found a good place and drilled for the shots; tomorrow I'll blast a hole in it, and if you can spare some people to help, we can start exploring it right away."

"Yes, of course, Dr. Lattimer. I can spare about a dozen, and I suppose you can find a few civilian volunteers," Penrose told him. "What will you need in the way of equipment?"

"Oh, about six demolition-packets; they can all be shot together. And the usual thing in the way of lights, and breaking and digging tools, and climbing equipment in case we run into broken or doubtful stairways. We'll divide into two parties. Nothing ought to be entered for the first time without a qualified archaeologist along. Three parties, if Martha can tear herself away from this catalogue of systematized incomprehensibilities she's making long enough to do some real work."

She felt her chest tighten and her face become stiff. She was pressing her lips together to lock in a furious retort when Hubert Penrose answered for her.

"Dr. Dane's been doing as much work, and as important work, as you have," he said brusquely. "More important work, I'd be inclined to say."

Von Ohlmhorst was visibly distressed; he glanced once toward Sid Chamberlain, then looked hastily away from him. Afraid of a story of dissension among archaeologists getting out.

"Working out a system of pronunciation by which the Martian language could be transliterated was a most important contribution," he said. "And Martha did that almost unassisted."

"Unassisted by Dr. Lattimer, anyway," Penrose added. "Captain Field and Lieutenant Koremitsu did some work, and I helped out a little, but nine-tenths of it she did herself."

"Purely arbitrary," Lattimer disdained. "Why, we don't even know that the Martians could make the same kind of vocal sounds we do."

"Oh, yes, we do," Ivan Fitzgerald contradicted, safe on his own ground. "I haven't seen any actual Martian skulls—these people seem to have been very tidy about disposing of their dead—but from statues and busts and pictures I've seen, I'd say that their vocal organs were identical with our own."

"Well, grant that. And grant that it's going to be impressive to rattle off the names of Martian notables whose statues we find, and that if we're ever able to attribute any place names, they'll sound a lot better than this horse-doctors' Latin the old astronomers splashed all over the map of Mars," Lattimer said. "What I object to is her wasting time on this stuff, of which nobody will ever be able to read a word if she fiddles around with those lists till there's another hundred feet of loess on this city, when there's so much real work to be done and we're as shorthanded as we are."

That was the first time that had come out in just so many words. She was glad Lattimer had said it and not Selim von Ohlmhorst.

"What you mean," she retorted, "is that it doesn't have the publicity value that digging up statues has."

For an instant, she could see that the shot had scored. Then Lattimer, with a side glance at Chamberlain, answered:

"What I mean is that you're trying to find something that any archaeologist, yourself included, should know doesn't exist. I don't object to your gambling your professional reputation and making a laughing stock of yourself; what I object to is that the blunders of one archaeologist discredit the whole subject in the eyes of the public."

That seemed to be what worried Lattimer most. She was framing a reply when the communication-outlet whistled shrilly, and then squawked: "Cocktail time! One hour to dinner; cocktails in the library, Hut Four!"

The library, which was also lounge, recreation room, and general gathering-place, was already crowded; most of the crowd was at the long table topped with sheets of glasslike plastic that had been wall panels out of one of the ruined buildings. She poured herself what passed, here, for a martini, and carried it over to where Selim von Ohlmhorst was sitting alone.

For a while, they talked about the building they had just finished exploring, then drifted into reminiscences of their work on Terra—von Ohlmhorst's in Asia Minor, with the Hittite Empire, and hers in Pakistan, excavating the cities of the Harappa Civilization. They finished their drinks—the ingredients were plentiful; alcohol and flavoring extracts synthesized from Martian vegetation—and von Ohlmhorst took the two glasses to the table for refills.

"You know, Martha," he said, when he returned, "Tony was right about one thing. You are gambling your professional standing and reputation. It's against all archaeological experience that a language so completely dead as this one could be deciphered. There was a continuity between all the other ancient languages—by knowing Greek, Champollion learned to read Egyptian; by knowing Egyptian, Hittite was learned. That's why you and your colleagues have never been able to translate the Harappa hieroglyphics; no such continuity exists there. If you insist that this utterly dead language can be read, your reputation will suffer for it."

"I heard Colonel Penrose say, once, that an officer who's afraid to risk his military reputation seldom makes much of a reputation. It's the same with us. If we really want to find things out, we have to risk making mistakes. And I'm a lot more interested in finding things out than I am in my reputation."

She glanced across the room, to where Tony Lattimer was sitting with Gloria Standish, talking earnestly, while Gloria sipped one of the counterfeit martinis and listened. Gloria was the leading contender for the title of Miss Mars, 1996, if you liked big bosomy blondes, but Tony would have been just as attentive to her if she'd looked like the

Wicked Witch in "The Wizard of Oz," because Gloria was the Pan-Federation Telecast System commentator with the expedition.

"I know you are," the old Turco-German was saying. "That's why, when they asked me to name another archaeologist for this expedition, I named you."

He hadn't named Tony Lattimer; Lattimer had been pushed onto the expedition by his university. There'd been a lot of high-level string-pulling to that; she wished she knew the whole story. She'd managed to keep clear of universities and university politics; all her digs had been sponsored by nonacademic foundations or art museums.

"You have an excellent standing; much better than my own, at your age. That's why it disturbs me to see you jeopardizing it by this insistence that the Martian language can be translated. I can't, really, see how you can hope to succeed."

She shrugged and drank some more of her cocktail, then lit another cigarette. It was getting tiresome to try to verbalize something she only felt.

"Neither do I, now, but I will. Maybe I'll find something like the picture-books Sachiko was talking about. A child's primer, maybe; surely they had things like that. And if I don't, I'll find something else. We've only been here six months. I can wait the rest of my life, if I have to, but I'll do it sometime."

"I can't wait so long," von Ohlmhorst said. "The rest of my life will only be a few years, and when the *Schiaparelli* orbits in, I'll be going back to Terra on the *Cyrano*."

"I wish you wouldn't. This is a whole new world of archaeology. Literally."

"Yes." He finished the cocktail and looked at his pipe as though wondering whether to re-light it so soon before dinner, then put it in his pocket. "A whole new world—but I've grown old, and it isn't for me. I've spent my life studying the Hittites. I can speak the Hittite language, though maybe King Muwatallis wouldn't be able to understand my modern Turkish accent. But the things I'd have to learn, here—chemistry, physics, engineering, how to run analytic tests on steel girders and beryllosilver alloys and plastics and silicones. I'm more at home with a civilization that rode in chariots and fought with swords and was just learning how to work iron. Mars is for young people. This expedition is a cadre of leadership—not only the Space Force people, who'll be the commanders of the main expedition, but us scientists, too. And I'm just an old cavalry general who can't learn to command tanks and aircraft. You'll have time to learn about Mars. I won't."

His reputation as the dean of Hittitologists was solid and secure, too, she added mentally. Then she felt ashamed of the thought. He wasn't to be classed with Tony Lattimer.

"All I came for was to get the work started," he was continuing. "The Federation Government felt that an old hand should do that. Well, it's started, now; you and Tony and whoever come out on the *Schiaparelli* must carry it on. You said it, yourself; you have a whole new world. This is only one city, of the last Martian civilization. Behind this, you have the Late Upland Culture, and the Canal Builders, and all the civilizations and races and empires before them, clear back to the Martian Stone Age." He hesitated for a moment. "You have no idea what all you have to learn, Martha. This isn't the time to start specializing too narrowly."

They all got out of the truck and stretched their legs and looked up the road to the tall building with the queer conical cap askew on its top. The four little figures that had been busy against its wall climbed into the jeep and started back slowly, the smallest of them, Sachiko Koremitsu, paying out an electric cable behind. When it pulled up beside the truck, they climbed out; Sachiko attached the free end of the cable to a nuclear-electric battery. At once, dirty gray smoke and orange dust puffed out from the wall of the building, and, a second later, the multiple explosion banged.

She and Tony Lattimer and Major Lindemann climbed onto the truck, leaving the jeep standing by the road. When they reached the building, a satisfyingly wide breach had been blown in the wall. Lattimer had placed his shots between two of the windows; they were both blown out along with the wall between, and lay unbroken on the ground. Martha remembered the first building they had entered. A Space Force officer had picked up a stone and thrown it at one of the windows, thinking that would be all they'd need to do. It had bounced back. He had drawn his pistol—they'd all carried guns, then, on the principle that what they didn't know about Mars might easily hurt them—and fired four shots. The bullets had ricochetted, screaming thinly; there were four coppery smears of jacket-metal on the window, and a little surface spalling. Somebody tried a rifle; the 4000-f.s. bullet had cracked the glasslike pane without penetrating. An oxyacetylene torch had taken an hour to cut the window out; the lab crew, aboard the ship, were still trying to find out just what the stuff was.

Tony Lattimer had gone forward and was sweeping his flashlight back and forth, swearing petulantly, his voice harshened and amplified by his helmet-speaker.

"I thought I was blasting into a hallway; this lets us into a room. Careful; there's about a two-foot drop to the floor, and a lot of rubble from the blast just inside."

He stepped down through the breach; the others began dragging equipment out of the trucks—shovels and picks and crowbars and sledges, portable flood-lights, cameras, sketching materials, an extension ladder, even Alpinists' ropes and crampons and pick-axes. Hubert Penrose was shouldering something that looked like a surrealist machine gun but which was really a nuclear-electric jackhammer. Martha selected one of the spike-shod mountaineer's ice axes, with which she could dig or chop or poke or pry or help herself over rough footing.

The windows, grimed and crusted with fifty mil-lennia of dust, filtered in a dim twilight; even the breach in the wall, in the morning shade, lighted only a small patch of floor. Somebody snapped on a floodlight, aiming it at the ceiling. The big room was empty and bare; dust lay thick on the floor and reddened the once-white walls. It could have been a large office, but there was nothing left in it to indicate its use.

"This one's been stripped up to the seventh floor!" Lattimer exclaimed. "Street level'll be cleaned out, completely."

"Do for living quarters and shops, then," Linde-mann said. "Added to the others, this'll take care of everybody on the *Schiaparelli*."

"Seem to have been a lot of electric or electronic apparatus over along this wall," one of the Space Force officers commented. "Ten or twelve electric outlets." He brushed the dusty wall with his glove, then scraped on the floor with his foot. "I can see where things were pried loose."

The door, one of the double sliding things the Martians had used, was closed. Selim von Ohlmhorst tried it, but it was stuck fast. The metal latch-parts had frozen together, molecule bonding itself to mol-ecule, since the door had last been closed. Hubert

Penrose came over with the jackhammer, fitting a spear-point chisel into place. He set the chisel in the joint between the doors, braced the hammer against his hip, and squeezed the trigger-switch. The hammer banged briefly like the weapon it resembled, and the doors popped a few inches apart, then stuck. Enough dust had worked into the recesses into which it was supposed to slide to block it on both sides.

That was old stuff; they ran into that every time they had to force a door, and they were prepared for it. Somebody went outside and brought in a power-jack and finally one of the doors inched back to the door jamb. That was enough to get the lights and equipment through; they all passed from the room to the hallway beyond. About half the other doors were open; each had a number and a single word, *Darfhulva*, over it.

One of the civilian volunteers, a woman professor of natural ecology from Penn State University, was looking up and down the hall.

"You know," she said, "I feel at home here. I think this was a college of some sort, and these were classrooms. That word, up there; that was the subject taught, or the department. And those electronic devices, all where the class would face them; audio-visual teaching aids."

"A twenty-five-story university?" Lattimer scoffed. "Why, a building like this would handle thirty thousand students."

"Maybe there were that many. This was a big city, in its prime," Martha said, moved chiefly by a desire to oppose Lattimer.

"Yes, but think of the snafu in the halls, every time they changed classes. It'd take half an hour to get everybody back and forth from one floor to another." He turned to von Ohlmhorst. "I'm going up above this floor. This place has been looted clean up to here, but there's a chance there may be something above," he said.

"I'll stay on this floor, at present," the Turco-German replied. "There will be much coming and going, and dragging things in and out. We should get this completely examined and recorded first. Then Major Lindemann's people can do their worst, here."

"Well, if nobody else wants it, I'll take the downstairs," Martha said.

"I'll go along with you," Hubert Penrose told her. "If the lower floors have no archaeological value, we'll turn them into living quarters. I like this building; it'll give everybody room to keep out from under everybody else's feet." He looked down the hall. "We ought to find escalators at the middle."

The hallway, too, was thick underfoot with dust. Most of the open rooms were empty, but a few contained furniture, including small seat-desks. The original proponent of the university theory pointed these out as just what might be found in classrooms. There were escalators, up and down, on either side of the hall, and more on the intersecting passage to the right.

"That's how they handled the students, between classes," Martha commented. "And I'll bet there are more ahead, there."

They came to a stop where the hallway ended at a great square central hall. There were elevators, there, on two of the sides, and four escalators, still usable as stairways. But it was the walls, and the paintings on them, that brought them up short and staring.

They were clouded with dirt—she was trying to imagine what they must have looked like originally, and at the same time estimating the labor that would be involved in cleaning them—but they were still distinguishable, as was the word, *Darfhulva*, in golden letters above each of the four sides. It was a moment before she realized, from the murals, that she had at last found a meaningful Martian word. They were a vast historical panorama, clockwise around the room. A group of skin-clad savages squatting around a fire. Hunters with bows and spears, carrying the carcass of an animal slightly like a pig. Nomads riding long-legged, graceful mounts like hornless deer. Peasants sowing and reaping; mud-walled hut villages, and cities; processions of priests and warriors; battles with swords and bows, and with cannon and muskets; galleys, and ships with sails, and ships without visible means of propulsion, and aircraft. Changing costumes and weapons and machines and styles of architecture. A richly fertile landscape, gradually merging into barren deserts and bushlands—the time of the great planetwide drought. The Canal Builders—men with machines recognizable as steam-shovels and derricks, digging and quarrying and driving across the empty plains with aquaducts. More cities—seaports on the shrinking oceans; dwindling, half-deserted cities; an abandoned city, with four tiny humanoid figures and a thing like a combat-car in the middle of a brush-grown plaza, they and their vehicle dwarfed by the huge lifeless buildings around them. She had not the least doubt; *Darfhulva* was History.

"Wonderful!" von Ohlmhorst was saying. "The entire history of this race. Why, if the painter depicted appropriate costumes and weapons and machines for each period, and got the architecture right, we can break the history of this planet into eras and periods and civilizations."

"You can assume they're authentic. The faculty of this university would insist on authenticity in the *Darfhulva*—History—Department," she said.

"Yes! *Darfhulva*—History! And your magazine

was a journal of *Sornhulva!*" Penrose exclaimed.
"You have a word, Martha!" It took her an instant
to realize that he had called her by her first name,
and not Dr. Dane. She wasn't sure if that weren't a
bigger triumph than learning a word of the Martian
language. Or a more auspicious start. "Alone, I
suppose that *hulva* means something like science or
knowledge, or study; combined, it would be equivalent
to our 'ology. And *darf* would mean something like
past, or old times, or human events, or chronicles."

"That gives you three words, Martha!" Sachiko
jubilated. "You did it."

"Let's don't go too fast," Lattimer said, for once
not derisively. "I'll admit that *darfhulva* is the Martian word for history as a subject of study; I'll admit
that *hulva* is the general word and *darf* modifies it
and tells us which subject is meant. But as for
assigning specific meanings, we can't do that because we don't know just how the Martians thought,
scientifically or otherwise."

He stopped short, startled by the blue-white light
that blazed as Sid Chamberlain's Kliegettes went
on. When the whirring of the camera stopped, it
was Chamberlain who was speaking:

"This is the biggest thing yet; the whole history of
Mars, stone age to the end, all on four walls. I'm
taking this with the fast shutter, but we'll telecast it
in slow motion, from the beginning to the end.
Tony, I want you to do the voice for it—running
commentary, interpretation of each scene as it's
shown. Would you do that?"

Would he do that! Martha thought. If he had a
tail, he'd be wagging it at the very thought.

"Well, there ought to be more murals on the
other floors," she said. "Who wants to come downstairs with us?"

Sachiko did; immediately, Ivan Fitzgerald volunteered. Sid decided to go upstairs with Tony Lattimer,

and Gloria Standish decided to go upstairs, too. Most of the party would remain on the seventh floor, to help Selim von Ohlmhorst get it finished. After poking tentatively at the escalator with the spike of her ice axe, Martha led the way downward.

The sixth floor was *Darfhulva*, too; military and technological history, from the character of the murals. They looked around the central hall, and went down to the fifth; it was like the floors above except that the big quadrangle was stacked with dusty furniture and boxes. Ivan Fitzgerald, who was carrying the floodlight, swung it slowly around. Here the murals were of heroic-sized Martians, so human in appearance as to seem members of her own race, each holding some object—a book, or a test tube, or some bit of scientific apparatus, and behind them were scenes of laboratories and factories, flame and smoke, lightning-flashes. The word at the top of each of the four walls was one with which she was already familiar—*Sornhulva*.

"Hey, Martha; there's that word," Ivan Fitzgerald exclaimed. "The one in the title of your magazine." He looked at the paintings. "Chemistry, or physics."

"Both," Hubert Penrose considered. "I don't think the Martians made any sharp distinction between them. See, the old fellow with the scraggly whiskers must be the inventor of the spectroscope; he has one in his hands, and he has a rainbow behind him. And the woman in the blue smock, beside him, worked in organic chemistry; see the diagrams of long-chain molecules behind her. What word would convey the idea of chemistry and physics taken as one subject?"

"*Sornhulva*," Sachiko suggested. "If *hulva's* something like science, *sorn* must mean matter, or substance, or physical object. You were right, all along,

Martha. A civilization like this would certainly leave
something like this, that would be self-explanatory."

"This'll wipe a little more of that superior grin off
Tony Lattimer's face," Fitzgerald was saying, as
they went down the motionless escalator to the
floor below. "Tony wants to be a big shot. When
you want to be a big shot, you can't bear the possibility of anybody else being a bigger big shot, and
whoever makes a start on reading this language will
be the biggest big shot archaeology ever saw."

That was true. She hadn't thought of it, in that
way, before, and now she tried not to think about
it. She didn't want to be a big shot. She wanted to
be able to read the Martian language, and find
things out about the Martians.

Two escalators down, they came out on a mezzanine around a wide central hall on the street level,
the floor forty feet below them and the ceiling thirty
feet above. Their lights picked out object after object below—a huge group of sculptured figures in
the middle; some kind of a motor vehicle jacked up
on trestles for repairs; things that looked like
machine-guns and auto-cannon; long tables, tops
littered with a dust-covered miscellany; machinery;
boxes and crates and containers.

They made their way down and walked among
the clutter, missing a hundred things for every one
they saw, until they found an escalator to the basement. There were three basements, one under another, until at last they stood at the bottom of the
last escalator, on a bare concrete floor, swinging the
portable floodlight over stacks of boxes and barrels
and drums, and heaps of powdery dust. The boxes
were plastic—nobody had ever found anything made
of wood in the city—and the barrels and drums
were of metal or glass or some glasslike substance.
They were outwardly intact. The powdery heaps

might have been anything organic, or anything containing fluid. Down here, where wind and dust could not reach, evaporation had been the only force of destruction after the minute life that caused putrefaction had vanished.

They found refrigeration rooms, too, and using Martha's ice axe and the pistol-like vibratool Sachiko carried on her belt, they pounded and pried one open, to find dessicated piles of what had been vegetables, and leathery chunks of meat. Samples of that stuff, rocketed up to the ship, would give a reliable estimate, by radio-carbon dating, of how long ago this building had been occupied. The refrigeration unit, radically different from anything their own culture had produced, had been electrically powered. Sachiko and Penrose, poking into it, found the switches still on; the machine had only ceased to function when the power-source, whatever that had been, had failed.

The middle basement had also been used, at least toward the end, for storage; it was cut in half by a partition pierced by but one door. They took half an hour to force this, and were on the point of sending above for heavy equipment when it yielded enough for them to squeeze through. Fitzgerald, in the lead with the light, stopped short, looked around, and then gave a groan that came through his helmet-speaker like a foghorn.

"Oh, no! *No!*"

"What's the matter, Ivan?" Sachiko, entering behind him, asked anxiously.

He stepped aside. "Look at it, Sachi! Are we going to have to do all that?"

Martha crowded through behind her friend and looked around, then stood motionless, dizzy with excitement. Books. Case on case of books, half an acre of cases, fifteen feet to the ceiling. Fitzgerald, and Penrose, who had pushed in behind her, were talking in rapid excitement; she only heard the sound of their voices, not their words. This must be the main stacks of the university library—the entire literature of the vanished race of Mars. In the center, down an aisle between the cases, she could see the hollow square of the librarians' desk, and stairs and a dumb-waiter to the floor above.

She realized that she was walking forward, with the others, toward this. Sachiko was saying: "I'm the lightest; let me go first." She must be talking about the spidery metal stairs.

"I'd say they were safe," Penrose answered. "The trouble we've had with doors around here shows that the metal hasn't deteriorated."

In the end, the Japanese girl led the way, more catlike than ever in her caution. The stairs were quite sound, in spite of their fragile appearance, and they all followed her. The floor above was a duplicate of the room they had entered, and seemed to contain about as many books. Rather than waste time forcing the door here, they returned to the middle basement and came up by the escalator down which they had originally descended.

The upper basement contained kitchens—electric stoves, some with pots and pans still on them—and a big room that must have been, originally, the students' dining room, though when last used it had been a workshop. As they expected, the library reading room was on the street-level floor, directly above the stacks. It seemed to have been converted into a sort of common living room for the building's last occupants. An adjoining auditorium had been made into a chemical works; there were vats and distillation apparatus, and a metal fractionating tower that extended through a hole knocked in the ceiling seventy feet above. A good deal of plastic furniture of the sort they had been finding everywhere in the city was stacked about, some of it broken up, apparently for reprocessing. The other rooms on the street floor seemed also to have been devoted to manufacturing and repair work; a considerable industry, along a number of lines, must have been carried on here for a long time after the university had ceased to function as such.

On the second floor, they found a museum; many of the exhibits remained, tantalizingly half-visible in grimed glass cases. There had been administrative offices there, too. The doors of most of them were closed, and they did not waste time trying to force them, but those that were open had been turned into living quarters. They made notes, and rough floor-plans, to guide them in future more thorough examination; it was almost noon before they had worked their way back to the seventh floor.

Selim von Ohlmhorst was in a room on the north side of the building, sketching the position of things before examining them and collecting them for removal. He had the floor checkerboarded with a grid of chalked lines, each numbered.

"We have everything on this floor photographed," he said. "I have three gangs—all the floodlights I have—sketching and making measurements. At the rate we're going, with time out for lunch, we'll be finished by the middle of the afternoon."

"You've been working fast. Evidently you aren't being high-church about a 'qualified archaeologist' entering rooms fist," Penrose commented.

"Ach, childishness!" the old man exclaimed impatiently. "These officers of yours aren't fools. All of them have been to Intelligence School and Criminal Investigation School. Some of the most careful amateur archaeologists I ever knew were retired soldiers or policemen. But there isn't much work to be done. Most of the rooms are either empty or like this one—a few bits of furniture and broken trash and scraps of paper. Did you find anything down on the lower floors?"

"Well, yes," Penrose said, a hint of mirth in his voice. "What would you say, Martha?"

She started to tell Selim. The others, unable to restrain their excitement, broke in with interruptions. Von Ohlmhorst was staring in incredulous amazement.

"But this floor was looted almost clean, and the buildings we've entered before were all looted from the street level up," he said, at length.

"The people who looted this one lived here," Penrose replied. "They had electric power to the last; we found refrigerators full of food, and stoves with the dinner still on them. They must have used the elevators to haul things down from the upper floor. The whole first floor was converted into workshops and laboratories. I think that this place must have been something like a monastery in the Dark Ages in Europe, or what such a monastery would have been like if the Dark Ages had followed the fall of a highly developed scientific civilization. For one thing, we found a lot of machine-guns and light auto-cannon on the street level, and all the doors were barricaded. The people here were trying to keep a civilization running after the rest of the planet had gone back to barbarism; I suppose they'd have to fight off raids by the barbarians now and then."

"You're not going to insist on making this building into expedition quarters, I hope, colonel?" von Ohlmhorst asked anxiously.

"Oh, no! This place is an archaeological treasure-house. More than that; from what I saw, our technicians can learn a lot, here. But you'd better get this floor cleaned up as soon as you can, though. I'll have the subsurface part, from the sixth floor down, airsealed. Then we'll put in oxygen generators and power units, and get a couple of elevators into service. For the floors above, we can use temporary airsealing floor by floor, and portable equipment; when we have things atmosphered and lighted and heated, you and Martha and Tony Lattimer can go to work systematically and in comfort, and I'll give you all the help I can spare from the other work. This is one of the biggest things we've found yet."

Tony Lattimer and his companions came down to the seventh floor a little later.

"I don't get this, at all," he began, as soon as he joined them. "This building wasn't stripped the way the others were. Always, the procedure seems to have been to strip from the bottom up, but they seem to have stripped the top floors first, here. All but the very top. I found out what that conical thing is, by the way. It's a wind-rotor, and under it there's an electric generator. This building generated its own power."

"What sort of condition are the generators in?" Penrose asked.

"Well, everything's full of dust that blew in under the rotor, of course, but it looks to be in pretty good shape. Hey, I'll bet that's it! They had power, so they used the elevators to haul stuff down. That's just what they did. Some of the floors above here don't seem to have been touched, though." He paused momentarily; back of his oxy-mask, he seemed to be grinning. "I don't know that I ought to mention this in front of Martha, but two floors above we hit a room—it must have been the reference library for one of the departments—that had close to five hundred books in it."

The noise that interrupted him, like the squawking of a Brobdingnagian parrot, was only Ivan Fitzgerald laughing through his helmet-speaker.

Lunch at the huts was a hasty meal, with a gabble of full-mouthed and excited talking. Hubert Penrose and his chief subordinates snatched their food in a huddled consultation at one end of the table; in the afternoon, work was suspended on everything else and the fifty-odd men and women of the expedition concentrated their efforts on the University. By the middle of the afternoon, the seventh floor had been completely examined, photographed and sketched, and the murals in the square central hall covered with protective tarpaulins, and Laurent Gicquel and his airsealing crew had moved in and were at work. It had been decided to seal the central hall at the entrances. It took the French-Canadian engineer most of the afternoon to find all the ventilation-ducts and plug them. An elevator-shaft on the north side was found reaching clear to the twenty-fifth floor; this would give access to the top of the building; another shaft, from the center, would take care of the floors below. Nobody seemed willing to trust the ancient elevators, themselves; it was the next evening before a couple of cars and the necessary machinery could be fabricated in the machine shops aboard the ship and sent down by landing-rocket. By that time, the airsealing was finished, the nuclear-electric energy-converters were in place, and the oxygen generators set up.

Martha was in the lower basement, an hour or so before lunch the day after, when a couple of Space Force officers came out of the elevator, bringing extra lights with them. She was still using oxygen-equipment; it was a moment before she realized that the newcomers had no masks, and that one of them was smoking. She took off her own helmet-speaker, throat-mike and mask and unslung her tank-pack, breathing cautiously. The air was chilly, and musty-acrid with the odor of antiquity—the first Martian odor she had smelled—but when she lit a cigarette, the lighter flamed clear and steady and the tobacco caught and burned evenly.

The archaeologists, many of the other civilian scientists, a few of the Space Force officers and the two news-correspondents, Sid Chamberlain and Gloria Standish, moved in that evening, setting up cots in vacant rooms. They installed electric stoves and a refrigerator in the old Library Reading Room, and put in a bar and lunch counter. For a few days, the place was full of noise and activity, then, gradually, the Space Force people and all but a few of the civilians returned to their own work. There was still the business of airsealing the more habitable of the buildings already explored, and fitting them up in readiness for the arrival, in a year and a half, of the five hundred members of the main expedition. There was work to be done enlarging the landing field for the ship's rocket craft, and building new chemical-fuel tanks.

There was the work of getting the city's ancient reservoirs cleared of silt before the next spring thaw brought more water down the underground aquaducts everybody called canals in mistranslation of Schiaparelli's Italian word, though this was proving considerably easier than anticipated. The ancient Canal Builders must have anticipated a time when their descendants would no longer be capable of maintenance work, and had prepared against it. By the day after the University had been made completely habitable, the actual work there was being done by Selim, Tony Lattimer and herself, with half a dozen Space Force officers, mostly girls, and four or five civilians, helping.

They worked up from the bottom, dividing the floor-surfaces into numbered squares, measuring and listing and sketching and photographing. They packaged samples of organic matter and sent them up to the ship for Carbon-14 dating and analysis; they opened cans and jars and bottles, and found that everything fluid in them had evaporated, through the porosity of glass and metal and plastic if there were no other way. Wherever they looked, they found evidence of activity suddenly suspended and never resumed. A vise with a bar of metal in it, half cut through and the hacksaw beside it. Pots and pans with hardened remains of food in them; a leathery cut of meat on a table, with the knife ready at hand. Toilet articles on washstands; unmade beds, the bedding ready to crumble at a touch but still retaining the impress of the sleeper's body; papers and writing materials on desks, as though the writer had gotten up, meaning to return and finish in a fifty-thousand-year-ago moment.

It worried her. Irrationally, she began to feel that the Martians had never left this place; that they were still around her, watching disapprovingly every time she picked up something they had laid down. They haunted her dreams, now, instead of their enigmatic writing. At first, everybody who had moved into the University had taken a separate room, happy to escape the crowding and lack of privacy of the huts. After a few nights, she was glad when Gloria Standish moved in with her, and accepted the newswoman's excuse that she felt lonely without somebody to talk to before falling asleep. Sachiko Koremitsu joined them the next evening, and before going to bed, the girl officer cleaned and oiled her pistol, remarking that she was afraid some rust may have gotten into it.

The others felt it, too. Selim von Ohlmhorst developed the habit of turning quickly and looking behind him, as though trying to surprise somebody or something that was stalking him. Tony Lattimer, having a drink at the bar that had been improvised from the librarian's desk in the Reading Room, set down his glass and swore.

"You know what this place is? It's an archaeological *Marie Celeste*!" he declared. "It was occupied right up to the end—we've all seen the shifts these people used to keep a civilization going here—but what was the end? What happened to them? Where did they go?"

"You didn't expect them to be waiting out front, with a red carpet and a big banner, *Welcome Terrans*, did you, Tony?" Gloria Standish asked.

"No, of course not; they've all been dead for fifty thousand years. But if they were the last of the Martians, why haven't we found their bones, at least? Who buried them, after they were dead?" He looked at the glass, a bubble-thin goblet, found, with hundreds of others like it, in a closet above, as though debating with himself whether to have another drink. Then he voted in the affirmative and reached for the cocktail pitcher. "And every door on the old ground level is either barred or barricaded from the inside. How did they get out? And why did they leave?"

The next day, at lunch, Sachiko Koremitsu had the answer to the second question. Four or five electrical engineers had come down by rocket from the ship, and she had been spending the morning with them, in oxy-masks, at the top of the building.

"Tony, I thought you said those generators were in good shape," she began, catching sight of Lattimer. "They aren't. They're in the most unholy mess I ever saw. What happened, up there, was that the supports of the wind-rotor gave way, and weight snapped the main shaft, and smashed everything under it."

"Well, after fifty thousand years, you can expect something like that," Lattimer retorted. "When an archaeologist says something's in good shape, he doesn't necessarily mean it'll start as soon as you shove a switch in."

"You didn't notice that it happened when the power was on, did you," one of the engineers asked, nettled at Lattimer's tone. "Well, it was. Everything's burned out or shorted or fused together; I saw one busbar eight inches across melted clean in two. It's a pity we didn't find things in good shape, even archaeologically speaking. I saw a lot of interesting things, things in advance of what we're using now. But it'll take a couple of years to get everything sorted out and figure what it looked like originally."

"Did it look as though anybody'd made any attempt to fix it?" Martha asked.

Sachiko shook her head. "They must have taken one look at it and given up. I don't believe there would have been any possible way to repair anything."

"Well, that explains why they left. They needed electricity for lighting, and heating, and all their industrial equipment was electrical. They had a good life, here, with power; without it, this place wouldn't have been habitable."

"Then why did they barricade everything from the inside, and how did they get out?" Lattimer wanted to know.

"To keep other people from breaking in and looting. Last man out probably barred the last door and slid down a rope from upstairs," von Ohlmhorst suggested. "This Houdini-trick doesn't worry me too much. We'll find out eventually."

"Yes, about the time Martha starts reading Martian," Lattimer scoffed.

"That may be just when we'll find out," von Ohlmhorst replied seriously. "It wouldn't surprise me if they left something in writing when they evacuated this place."

"Are you really beginning to treat this pipe dream of hers as a serious possibility, Selim?" Lattimer demanded. "I know, it would be a wonderful thing, but wonderful things don't happen just because they're wonderful. Only because they're possible, and this isn't. Let me quote that distinguished Hittitologist, Johannes Friedrich: 'Nothing can be translated out of nothing.' Or that later but not less distinguished Hittitologist, Selim von Ohlmhorst: 'Where are you going to get your bilingual?' "

"Friedrich lived to see the Hittite language deciphered and read," von Ohlmhorst reminded him.

"Yes, when they found Hittite-Assyrian bilinguals." Lattimer measured a spoonful of coffee-powder into his cup and added hot water. "Martha, you ought to know, better than anybody, how little chance you have. You've been working for years in the Indus Valley; how many words of Harappa have you or anybody else ever been able to read?"

"We never found a university, with a half-million-volume library, at Harappa or Mohenjo-Daro."

"And, the first day we entered this building, we established meanings for several words," Selim von Ohlmhorst added.

"And you've never found another meaningful word since," Lattimer added. "And you're only sure of general meaning, not specific meaning of word-elements, and you have a dozen different interpretations for each word."

"We made a start," von Ohlmhorst maintained. "We have Grotefend's word for 'king.' But I'm going to be able to read some of those books, over there, if it takes me the rest of my life here. It probably will, anyhow."

"You mean you've changed your mind about going home on the *Cyrano?*" Martha asked. "You'll stay on here?"

The old man nodded. "I can't leave this. There's too much to discover. The old dog will have to learn a lot of new tricks, but this is where my work will be, from now on."

Lattimer was shocked. "You're nuts!" he cried. "You mean you're going to throw away everything you've accomplished in Hittitology and start all over again here on Mars? Martha, if you've talked him into this crazy decision, you're a criminal!"

"Nobody talked me into anything," von Ohlmhorst said roughly. "And as for throwing away what I've accomplished in Hittitology, I don't know what the devil you're talking about. Everything I know about the Hittite Empire is published and available to anybody. Hittitology's like Egyptology; it's stopped being research and archaeology and become scholarship and history. And I'm not a scholar or a historian; I'm a pick-and-shovel field archaeologist—a highly skilled and specialized grave-robber and junk-picker—and there's more pick-and-shovel work on this planet than I could do in a hundred lifetimes. This is something new; I was a fool to think I could turn my back on it and go back to scribbling footnotes about Hittite kings."

"You could have anything you wanted, in Hittitology. There are a dozen universities that'd sooner have you than a winning football team. But no! You have to be the top man in Martiology, too. You can't leave that for anybody else—" Lattimer shoved his chair back and got to his feet, leaving the table with an oath that was almost a sob of exasperation.

Maybe his feelings were too much for him. Maybe he realized, as Martha did, what he had betrayed. She sat, avoiding the eyes of the others, looking at the ceiling, as embarrassed as though Lattimer had flung something dirty on the table in front of them. Tony Lattimer had, desperately, wanted Selim to go home on the *Cyrano*. Martiology was a new field; if Selim entered it, he would bring with him the reputation he had already built in Hittitology, automatically stepping into the leading role that Lattimer had coveted for himself. Ivan Fitzgerald's words echoed back to her—when you want to be a big shot, you can't bear the possibility of anybody else being a bigger big shot. His derision of her own efforts became comprehensible, too. It wasn't that he was convinced that she would never learn to read the Martian language. He had been afraid that she would.

Ivan Fitzgerald finally isolated the germ that had caused the Finchley girl's undiagnosed illness. Shortly afterward, the malady turned into a mild fever, from which she recovered. Nobody else seemed to have caught it. Fitzgerald was still trying to find out how the germ had been transmitted.

They found a globe of Mars, made when the city had been a seaport. They located the city, and learned that its name had been Kukan—or something with a similar vowel-consonant ratio. Immediately, Sid Chamberlain and Gloria Standish began giving their telecasts a Kukan dateline, and Hubert Penrose used the name in his official reports. They also found a Martian calendar; the year had been divided into ten more or less equal months, and one of them had been Doma. Another month was Nor, and that was a part of the name of the scientific journal Martha had found.

Bill Chandler, the zoologist, had been going deeper and deeper into the old sea bottom of Syrtis. Four hundred miles from Kukan, and at fifteen thousand feet lower altitude, he shot a bird. At least, it was a something with wings and what were almost but not quite feathers, though it was more reptilian than avian in general characteristics. He and Ivan Fitzgerald skinned and mounted it, and then dissected the carcass almost tissue by tissue. About seven-eighths of its body capacity was lungs; it certainly breathed air containing at least half enough oxygen to support human life, or five times as much as the air around Kukan.

That took the center of interest away from archaeology and started a new burst of activity. All the expedition aircraft—four jetticopters and three wingless airdyne reconnaissance fighters—were thrown into intensified exploration of the lower sea bottoms, and the bio-science boys and girls were wild with excitement and making new discoveries on each flight.

The University was left to Selim and Martha and Tony Lattimer, the latter keeping to himself while she and the old Turco-German worked together. The civilian specialists in other fields, and the Space Force people who had been holding tape lines and making sketches and snapping cameras, were all flying to lower Syrtis to find out how much oxygen there was and what kind of life it supported.

Sometimes Sachiko dropped in; most of the time she was busy helping Ivan Fitzgerald dissect specimens. They had four or five species of what might loosely be called birds, and something that could easily be classed as a reptile, and a carnivorous mammal the size of a cat with birdlike claws, and a herbivore almost identical with the piglike thing in the big *Darfhulva* mural, and another like a gazelle with a single horn in the middle of its forehead.

The high point came when one party, at thirty thousand feet below the level of Kukan, found breathable air. One of them had a mild attack of *sorroche* and had to be flown back for treatment in a hurry, but the others showed no ill effects. The daily newscasts from Terra showed a corresponding shift in interest at home. The discovery of the University had focused attention on the dead past of Mars; now the public was interested in Mars as a possible home for humanity. It was Tony Lattimer who brought archaeology back into the activities of the expedition and the news at home.

Martha and Selim were working in the museum on the second floor, scrubbing the grime from the glass cases, noting contents, and grease-penciling numbers; Lattimer and a couple of Space Force officers were going through what had been the administrative offices on the other side. It was one of these, a young second lieutenant, who came hurrying in from the mezzanine, almost bursting with excitement.

"Hey, Martha! Dr. von Ohlmhorst!" he was shouting. "Where are you? Tony's found the Martians!"

Selim dropped his rag back in the bucket; she laid her clipboard on top of the case beside her.

"Where?" they asked together.

"Over on the north side." The lieutenant took hold of himself and spoke more deliberately. "Little room, back of one of the old faculty offices—conference room. It was locked from the inside, and we had to burn it down with a torch. That's where they are. Eighteen of them, around a long table—"

Gloria Standish, who had dropped in for lunch, was on the mezzanine, fairly screaming into a radio-phone extension:

". . . Dozen and a half of them! Well, of course they're dead. What a question! They look like skeletons covered with leather. No, I do not know what they died of. Well, forget it; I don't care if Bill Chandler's found a three-headed hippopotamus. Sid, don't you get it? We've found the *Martians!*"

She slammed the phone back on its hook, rushing away ahead of them.

Martha remembered the closed door; on the first survey, they hadn't attempted opening it. Now it was burned away at both sides and lay, still hot along the edges, on the floor of the big office room in front. A floodlight was on in the room inside, and Lattimer was going around looking at things while a Space Force officer stood by the door. The center of the room was filled by a long table; in armchairs around it sat the eighteen men and women who had occupied the room for the last fifty millennia. There were bottles and glasses on the table in front of them, and, had she seen them in a dimmer light, she would have thought that they were merely dozing over their drinks. One had a knee hooked over his chair-arm and was curled in foetuslike sleep. Another had fallen forward onto the table, arms extended, the emerald set of a ring twinkling dully on one finger. Skeletons covered with leather, Gloria Standish had called them, and so they were— faces like skulls, arms and legs like sticks, the flesh shrunken onto the bones under it.

"Isn't this something!" Lattimer was exulting. "Mass suicide, that's what it was. Notice what's in the corners?"

Braziers, made of perforated two-gallon-odd metal cans, the white walls smudged with smoke above them. Von Ohlmhorst had noticed them at once, and was poking into one of them with his flashlight.

"Yes; charcoal. I noticed a quantity of it around a couple of hand-forges in the shop on the first floor. That's why you had so much trouble breaking in; they'd sealed the room on the inside." He straightened and went around the room, until he found a ventilator, and peered into it. "Stuffed with rags. They must have been all that were left, here. Their power was gone, and they were old and tired, and all around them their world was dying. So they just came in here and lit the charcoal, and sat drinking together till they all fell asleep. Well, we know what became of them, now, anyhow."

Sid and Gloria made the most of it. The Terran

public wanted to hear about Martians, and if live Martians couldn't be found, a room full of dead ones was the next best thing. Maybe an even better thing; it had been only sixty-odd years since the Orson Welles invasion-scare. Tony Lattimer, the discoverer, was beginning to cash in on his attentions to Gloria and his ingratiation with Sid; he was always either making voice-and-image talks for telecast or listening to the news from the home planet. Without question, he had become, overnight, the most widely known archaeologist in history.

"Not that I'm interested in all this, for myself," he disclaimed, after listening to the telecast from Terra two days after his discovery. "But this is going to be a big thing for Martian archaeology. Bring it to the public attention; dramatize it. Selim, can you remember when Lord Carnarvon and Howard Carter found the tomb of Tutankhamen?"

"In 1923? I was two years old, then," von Ohlmhorst chuckled. "I really don't know how much that publicity ever did for Egyptology. Oh, the museums did devote more space to Egyptian exhibits, and after a museum department head gets a few extra showcases, you know how hard it is to make him give them up. And, for a while, it was easier to get financial support for new excavations. But I don't know how much good all this public excitement really does, in the long run."

"Well, I think one of us should go back on the *Cyrano*, when the *Schiaparelli* orbits in," Lattimer said. "I'd hoped it would be you; your voice would carry the most weight. But I think it's important that one of us go back, to present the story of our work, and what we have accomplished and what we hope to accomplish, to the public and to the universities and the learned societies, and to the Federation Government. There will be a great deal of work that will have to be done. We must not allow

the other scientific fields and the so-called practical
interests to monopolize public and academic support. So, I believe I shall go back at least for a
while, and see what I can do—"

Lectures. The organization of a Society of Martian Archaeology, with Anthony Lattimer, Ph.D.,
the logical candidate for the chair. Degrees, honors;
the deference of the learned, and the adulation of
the lay public. Positions, with impressive titles and
salaries. Sweet are the uses of publicity.

She crushed out her cigarette and got to her feet.
"Well, I still have the final lists of what we found in
Halvhulva—Biology—department to check over. I'm
staring on Sornhulva tomorrow, and I want that
stuff in shape for expert evaluation."

That was the sort of thing Tony Lattimer wanted
to get away from, the detail-work and the drudgery.
Let the infantry do the slogging through the mud;
the brass-hats got the medals.

She was halfway through the fifth floor, a week
later, and was having midday lunch in the reading
room on the first floor when Hubert Penrose came
over and sat down beside her, asking her what she
was doing. She told him.

"I wonder if you could find me a couple of men,
for an hour or so," she added. "I'm stopped by a
couple of jammed doors at the central hall. Lecture
room and library, if the layout of that floor's anything like the ones below it."

"Yes. I'm a pretty fair door-buster, myself." He
looked around the room. "There's Jeff Miles; he
isn't doing much of anything. And we'll put Sid
Chamberlain to work, for a change, too. The four
of us ought to get your doors open." He called to
Chamberlain, who was carrying his tray over to the
dish washer. "Oh, Sid; you doing anything for the
next hour or so?"

"I was going up to the fourth floor, to see what Tony's doing."

"Forget it. Tony's bagged his season limit of Martians. I'm going to help Martha bust in a couple of doors; we'll probably find a whole cemetery full of Martians."

Chamberlain shrugged. "Why not. A jammed door can have anything back of it, and I know what Tony's doing—just routine stuff."

Jeff Miles, the Space Force captain, came over, accompanied by one of the lab-crew from the ship who had come down on the rocket the day before.

"This ought to be up your alley, Mort," he was saying to his companion. "Chemistry and physics department. Want to come along?"

The lab man, Mort Tranter, was willing. Seeing the sights was what he'd come down from the ship for. She finished her coffee and cigarette, and they went out into the hall together, gathered equipment and rode the elevator to the fifth floor.

The lecture hall door was the nearest; they attacked it first. With proper equipment and help, it was no problem and in ten minutes they had it open wide enough to squeeze through with the floodlights. The room inside was quite empty, and, like most of the rooms behind closed doors, comparatively free from dust. The students, it appeared, had sat with their backs to the door, facing a low platform, but their seats and the lecturer's table and equipment had been removed. The two side walls bore inscriptions: on the right, a pattern of concentric circles which she recognized as a diagram of atomic structure, and on the left a complicated table of numbers and words, in two columns. Tranter was pointing at the diagram on the right.

"They got as far as the Bohr atom, anyhow," he said. "Well, not quite. They knew about electron shells, but they have the nucleus pictured as a solid mass. No indication of proton-and-neutron structure. I'll bet, when you come to translate their scientific books, you'll find that they taught that the atom was the ultimate and indivisible particle. That explains why you people never found any evidence that the Martians used nuclear energy."

"That's a uranium atom," Captain Miles mentioned.

"It is?" Sid Chamberlain asked, excitedly. "Then they did know about atomic energy. Just because we haven't found any pictures of A-bomb mushrooms doesn't mean—"

She turned to look at the other wall. Sid's signal reactions were getting away from him again; uranium meant nuclear power to him, and the two words were interchangeable. As she studied the arrangement of the numbers and words, she could hear Tranter saying:

"Nuts, Sid. We knew about uranium a long time before anybody found out what could be done with it. Uranium was discovered on Terra in 1789, by Klaproth."

There was something familiar about the table on the left wall. She tried to remember what she had been taught in school about physics, and what she had picked up by accident afterward. The second column was a continuation of the first: there were forty-six items in each, each item numbered consecutively—

"Probably used uranium because it's the largest of the natural atoms," Penrose was saying. "The fact that there's nothing beyond it there shows that they hadn't created any of the transuranics. A student could go to that thing and point out the outer electron of any of the ninety-two elements."

Ninety-two! That was it; there were ninety-two items in the table on the left wall! Hydrogen was Number One, she knew; One, *Sarfaldsorn*. Helium was Two; that was Tirfaldsorn. She couldn't remember which element came next, but in Martian it was *Sarfalddavas. Sorn* must mean matter, or substance, then. And *davas;* she was trying to think of what it could be. She turned quickly to the others, catching hold of Hubert Penrose's arm with one hand and waving her clipboard with the other.

"Look at this thing, over here," she was clamoring excitedly. "Tell me what you think it is. Could it be a table of the elements?"

They all turned to look. Mort Tranter stared at it for a moment.

"Could be. If I only knew what those squiggles meant—"

That was right; he'd spent his time aboard the ship.

"If you could read the numbers, would that help?" she asked, beginning to set down the Arabic digits and their Martian equivalents. "It's decimal system, the same as we use."

"Sure. If that's a table of elements, all I'd need would be the numbers. Thanks," he added as she tore off the sheet and gave it to him.

Penrose knew the numbers, and was ahead of him. "Ninety-two items, numbered consecutively. The first number would be the atomic number. Then a single word, the name of the element. Then the atomic weight—"

She began reading off the names of the elements. "I know hydrogen and helium; what's *tirfalddavas,* the third one?"

"Lithium," Tranter said. "The atomic weights aren't run out past the decimal point. Hydrogen's one plus, if that double-hook dingus is a plus sign; Helium's four-plus, that's right. And lithium's given as seven, that isn't right. It's six-point-nine-four-oh. Or is that thing a Martian minus sign?"

"Of course! Look! A plus sign is a hook, to hang

things together; a minus sign is a knife, to cut something off from something—see, the little loop is the handle and the long pointed loop is the blade. Stylized, of course, but that's what it is. And the fourth element, *kiradavas;* what's that?"

"Beryllium. Atomic weight given as nine-and-a-hook; actually it's nine-point-oh-two."

Sid Chamberlain had been disgruntled because he couldn't get a story about the Martians having developed atomic energy. It took him a few minutes to understand the newest development, but finally it dawned on him.

"Hey! You're reading that!" he cried. "You're reading Martian!"

"That's right," Penrose told him. "Just reading it right off. I don't get the two items after the atomic weight, though. They look like months of the Martian calendar. What ought they to be, Mort?"

Tranter hesitated. "Well, the next information after the atomic weight ought to be the period and group numbers. But those are words."

"What would the numbers be for the first one, hydrogen?"

"Period One, Group One. One electron shell, one electron in the outer shell," Tranter told her. "Helium's period one, too, but it has the outer—only—electron shell full, so it's in the group of inert elements."

"*Trav, Trav. Trav's* the first month of the year. And helium's *Trav, Yenth; Yenth* is the eighth month."

"The inert elements could be called Group Eight, yes. And the third element, lithium, is Period Two, Group One. That check?"

"It certainly does. *Sanv, Trav; Sanv's* the second month. What's the first element in Period Three?"

"Sodium, Number Eleven."

"That's right; it's *Krav, Trav.* Why, the names of the months are simply numbers, one to ten, spelled out."

"*Doma's* the fifth month. That was your first Martian word, Martha," Penrose told her. "The word for five. And if *davas* is the word for metal, and *sornhulva* is chemistry and/or physics, I'll bet *Tadavas Sornhulva* is literally translated as: 'Of-Metal Matter-Knowledge,' Metallurgy, in other words. I wonder what *Mastharnorvod* means." It surprised her that, after so long and with so much happening in the meantime, he could remember that. "Something like 'Journal,' or 'Review,' or maybe 'Quarterly.' "

"We'll work that out, too," she said confidently. After this, nothing seemed impossible. "Maybe we can find—" Then she stopped short. "You said 'Quarterly.' I think it was 'Monthly,' instead. It was dated for a specific month, the fifth one. And if *nor* is ten, *Mastharnorvod* could be 'Year-Tenth.' And I'll bet we'll find that *masthar* is the word for year." She looked at the table on the wall again. "Well, let's get all these words down, with translations for as many as we can."

"Let's take a break for a minute," Penrose suggested, getting out his cigarettes. "And then, let's do this in comfort. Jeff, suppose you and Sid go across the hall and see what you find in the other room in the way of a desk or something like that, and a few chairs. There'll be a lot of work to do on this."

Sid Chamberlain had been squirming as though he were afflicted with ants, trying to contain himself. Now he let go with an excited jabber.

"This is really it! *The* it, not just it-of-the-week, like finding the reservoirs or those statues or this building, or even the animals and the dead Martians! Wait till Selim and Tony see this! Wait till

Tony sees it; I want to see his face! And when I get this on telecast, all Terra's going to go nuts about it!" He turned to Captain Miles. "Jeff, suppose you take a look at that other door, while I find somebody to send to tell Selim and Tony. And Gloria; wait till she sees this—"

"Take it easy, Sid," Martha cautioned. "You'd better let me have a look at your script, before you go too far overboard on the telecast. This is just a beginning; it'll take years and years before we're able to read any of those books downstairs."

"It'll go faster than you think, Martha," Hubert Penrose told her. "We'll all work on it, and we'll teleprint material to Terra, and people there will work on it. We'll send them everything we can . . . everything we work out, and copies of books, and copies of your word-lists—"

And there would be other tables—astronomical tables, tables in physics and mechanics, for instance —in which words and numbers were equivalent. The library stacks, below, would be full of them. Transliterate them into Roman alphabet spellings and Arabic numerals, and somewhere, somebody would spot each numerical significance, as Hubert Penrose and Mort Tranter and she had done with the table of elements. And pick out all the chemistry textbooks in the Library; new words would take on meaning from contexts in which the names of elements appeared. She'd have to start studying chemistry and physics, herself—

Sachiko Koremitsu peeped in through the door, then stepped inside.

"Is there anything I can do—?" she began. "What's happened? Something important?"

"Important?" Sid Chamberlain exploded. "Look at that, Sachi! We're reading it! Martha's found out how to read Martian!" He grabbed Captain Miles by the arm. "Come on, Jeff; let's go. I want to call the others—" He was still babbling as he hurried from the room.

Sachi looked at the inscription. "Is it true?" she asked, and then, before Martha could more than begin to explain, flung her arms around her. "Oh, it really is! You are reading it! I'm so happy!"

She had to start explaining again when Selim von Ohlmhorst entered. This time, she was able to finish.

"But, Martha, can you be really sure? You know, by now, that learning to read this language is as important to me as it is to you, but how can you be so sure that those words really mean things like hydrogen and helium and boron and oxygen? How do you know that their table of elements was anything like ours?"

Tranter and Penrose and Sachiko all looked at him in amazement.

"That isn't just the Martian table of elements; that's *the* table of elements. It's the only one there is," Mort Tranter almost exploded. "Look, hydrogen has one proton and one electron. If it had more of either, it wouldn't be hydrogen, it'd be something else. And the same with all the rest of the elements. And hydrogen on Mars is the same as hydrogen on Terra, or on Alpha Centauri, or in the next galaxy—

"You just set up those numbers, in that order, and any first-year chemistry student could tell you what elements they represented," Penrose said. "Could if he expected to make a passing grade, that is."

The old man shook his head slowly, smiling. "I'm afraid I wouldn't make a passing grade. I didn't know, or at least didn't realize, that. One of the things I'm going to place an order for, to be brought on the *Schiaparelli*, will be a set of primers in chemistry and physics, of the sort intended for a bright child of ten or twelve. It seems that a Martiologist has to learn a lot of things the Hittites and the Assyrians never heard about."

Tony Lattimer, coming in, caught the last part of the explanation. He looked quickly at the walls and, having found out just what had happened, advanced and caught Martha by the hand.

"You really did it, Martha! You found your bilingual! I never believed that it would be possible; let me congratulate you!"

He probably expected that to erase all the jibes and sneers of the past. If he did, he could have it that way. His friendship would mean as little to her as his derision—except that his friends had to watch their backs and his knife. But he was going home on the *Cyrano*, to be a big shot. Or had this changed his mind for him again?

"This is something we can show the world, to justify any expenditure of time and money on Martian archaeological work. When I get back to Terra, I'll see that you're given full credit for this achievement—"

On Terra, her back and his knife would be out of her watchfulness.

"We won't need to wait that long," Hubert Penrose told him dryly. "I'm sending off an official report, tomorrow; you can be sure Dr. Dane will be given full credit, not only for this but for her previous work, which made it possible to exploit this discovery."

"And you might add, work done in spite of the doubts and discouragements of her colleagues," Selim von Ohlmhorst said. "To which I am ashamed to have to confess my own share."

"You said we had to find a bilingual," she said. "You were right, too."

"This is better than a bilingual, Martha," Hubert Penrose said. "Physical science expresses universal facts; necessarily it is a universal language. Heretofore archaeologists have dealt only with pre-scientific cultures."

THE MILE-LONG SPACESHIP

BY KATE WILHELM (1928–)

ASTOUNDING SCIENCE FICTION
APRIL

*It's a pleasure to welcome the very talented Kate
Wilhelm to this series. She began publishing in the
science fiction field in 1956, producing about four
stories per year until 1960, when her productivity
increased along with her reputation. Her first novel,*
The Clone, *written with Theodore L. Thomas, appeared in 1965, and she has since published some
twenty novels and story collections in the genre. Much
of her best work of the 1970s appeared in* Orbit, *the
excellent original anthology series edited by her husband, Damon Knight. She has won the Nebula Award
twice, along with a Hugo and several other prizes;
"Forever Yours, Anna" captured the Nebula for best
short story of 1987.*

*Her work is characterized by great power and
clarity, and such outstanding achievements as* The
Clewiston Test *(1976),* Where Late the Sweet Birds
Sang *(1976), and* Welkcome, Chaos *(1983) have
won her a significant following both inside and outside the sf field.*

*"The Mile-Long Spaceship" is the best of her early
stories—in fact, it remains one of her best works, a
landmark in a successful career of more than thirty
years. (MHG)*

Some of our planetary probes were expected to leave the solar system after they had passed near some of the outer planets and fulfilled their function. It was a source of pride to me that the first of these carried a gold-plated plaque that showed a man and woman, giving our size compared to the vessel that was carrying it and enough of a code to indicate our location in space to any advanced intelligences finding the plaque and knowing at least as much about astronomy as we do.

There were some who worried that we might be giving away our location to "the enemy."

I didn't. For one thing, it was very unlikely that the probe would pass anywhere near a star for many millions of years. It was unlikely that any intelligent race of beings would happen to come upon this object in the unimaginable vastness of interstellar space. Even if some day, eons from now, it were discovered, humanity would surely be long gone. Even the solar system itself would be long gone from its indicated position.

And finally it seems to my idealist self that any intelligence advanced enough to find the plaque would be beyond any primitive desire to kill and dominate. Even we, savage and uncivilized as we are, are trying to help threatened species survive, for no other reason than a burgeoning fellow-feeling for all forms of life.

But read Kate's story. (IA)

Allan Norbett shivered uncontrollably, huddling up under the spotless hospital sheet seeking warmth. He stirred fretfully as consciousness slowly returned and with it the blinding stab of pain through his head. A moan escaped his lips. Immediately a nurse was at his side, gently, firmly forcing him back on the bed.

"You must remain completely still, Mr. Norbett.

You're in St. Agnes' Hospital. You suffered a fractured skull in the accident, and surgery was necessary. Your wife is outside waiting to see you. She is uninjured. Do you understand me?''

The words had been spoken slowly, very clearly, but he had grasped only fragments of them.

What accident? The ship couldn't have had an accident. He'd be dead out there in space. And his wife hadn't even been there.

"What happened to the ship? How'd I get back on Earth?" The words came agonizingly, each effort cost much in pain and dizziness.

"Mr. Norbett, please calm yourself. I've rung for your doctor. He'll be here presently." The voice soothed him and a faint memory awakened. The wreck? His wife? HIS WIFE?

"Clair? Where's Clair?" Then the doctor was there and he also was soothing. Allan closed his eyes again in relief as they reassured him about Clair's safety. She would be here in a moment. The other memories receded and mingled with the anaesthetic dreams he'd had. The doctor felt his pulse and listened to his heart and studied his eyes, all the while talking.

"You are a lucky man, Mr. Norbett. That was quite a wreck you were in. Your wife was even luckier. She was thrown clear when the biwheel first hit you."

Allan remembered it all quite clearly now and momentarily wondered how he'd come out of it at all. The doctor finally finished his examination and smiled as he said, "Everything seems perfectly normal, considering the fact that you have been traipsing all over space for the last five days."

"Days?"

"Yes. The wreck was Saturday. This is Thursday. You've been under sedation quite a bit—to help you rest. There was extensive brain injury and absolute quiet was essential. Dr. Barnsdale performed a brilliant operation Saturday night."

Allan had the feeling the doctor was purposely being so loquacious to help him over the hump of the shock of awakening after almost six days. He was in no pain now while he kept his head still, but talking brought its own punishment and he was grateful to the doctor for answering unasked questions. The doctor waited by his side for a second or two, then in a professional tone he told the nurse to bring in Clair.

And again to Allan: "She can only stay a few minutes—less if you begin talking. I'll be in again this afternoon. You rest as much as possible. If the pain becomes severe, tell your nurse. She's instructed to administer a hypo only if you request it." Again he laughed jovially, "Don't let her talk you into it, though. She is really thrilled by that space yarn you've been telling and might want to put you to sleep just to hear more."

Clair's visit was very brief and very exhausting. Afterwards he rested comfortably for nearly an hour before the pain flooded his whole being.

"Nurse."

"Yes, Mr. Norbett?" Her fingers rested lightly on his wrist for a moment.

"The pain—"

"Just try to relax, sir. It will be gone soon." He didn't feel the prick of the needle in his arm. But the pain left him in layers, gradually becoming a light enough load to permit sleep. And the coldness.

Space was so cold. No winds to blow in spurts and gusts, to relieve the cold by their absence, only the steady, numbing same black, empty cold. He turned his head to look over his shoulder and already Earth was indistinguishable among the countless stars and planets. Never had man, he told himself, seen all the stars like this. They were incredibly bright and even as he viewed them, he wondered at the movement of some of them. There was a visible pulsation, sometimes almost rhythmically, other times very erratic. A star would suddenly seem to expand enormously on one side, the protuberance around it glow even more brightly, then die down only to repeat the performance over and over. Allan wished he knew more about astronomy. He had only the most rudimentary knowledge that everyone had since the first spaceship had reached Mars. He had been out of school when space travel had become possible and had never read past the newspaper for the information necessary to understand the universe and its inhabitants.

He shivered again and thought about the advantages of eyeless seeing. There was no pupil to dilate, no retina to burn or damage, no nerves to protest with pain at the brightness of the sight. It was, he decided smugly, much better to be here without his cumbersome body to hamper him. Then he suddenly remembered the ship—the mile-long spaceship. For an instant he sent his mental gaze deep into space all around him, but the ship was nowhere to be seen. He surmised it must still be millions of light-years from Earth. As he visualized it again he slowly became aware that once more he was aboard her and the stars he was seeing were on the giant wall screen.

He watched with interest as one planet after another turned a pale violet and became nearly invisible. He had grown accustomed to the crew of the ship, so paid little heed to them. Their voices were low, monotonous to his ear, never rising or speeding up or sounding indecisive. Completely expressionless, their words defied any attempt to interpret them.

*　　*　　*

"He's back," the telepath announced.

"Good. I was afraid that he might die." The navigator in charge went calmly about his duties of sighting and marking in a complex three-dimensional chart the course of the mighty ship as it ranged among the stars.

"He's recovering from his injury. He still can't receive any impulses from me." The telepath tried again and again to create a picture in the alien mind in their midst. "Futile," he said, "the differences are too great."

"Undisciplined," said the psychologist who had been waiting ever since that first visit by the alien. "A disciplined mind can be reached by telepathy."

"Can you see his world?" This from the astro navigator.

"Only the same intimate scenes of home-life, his work and his immediate surroundings. He is very primitive, or perhaps merely uneducated."

"If only he knew something about astronomy." The navigator shrugged and made a notation on his chart as two more distant planets registered violet.

"The names he associates with stars are these," the telepath probed deeper, "The Dipper, North Star, Mars . . . no, that is one of the planets they have colonized." A wave of incredulity emanated from him, felt by the others of the crew, but not expressed in his voice. "He doesn't know the difference between single stars, clusters, constellations, only that they appear as individual stars to him, and he thinks of them as such."

The navigator's calm voice belied the fury the others felt well out from him. "Look at his sun, perhaps that will give us a hint." They all knew the improbability of this. The telepath began droning what little Allan knew about the sun when the captain appeared through another wall screen.

He was accompanied by the ship's ethnologist,

the expert who could reconstruct entire civilizations from the broken remains of a tool or an object of art, or less if necessary. The captain and his companions made themselves comfortable near the star screen and seemed immediately engrossed in the broken lines indicating the ship's flight in the three-dimensional reproduced outer spaces.

"Is he still here?"

"Yes, sir."

"Is he aware yet that we discovered his presence among us?"

"No, sir. We have made no effort to indicate our awareness to him."

"Very good." The captain then fell silent pondering his particular problem as the ethnologist began adding to the growing list of facts that were known to Allan about Earth.

They would have a complete picture of the present and the past. As complete as the alien's mind and memory could make it. But unless they could locate his planet they might just as well go home and view space-fiction films. This exploration trip had achieved very little real success. Only fourteen planets that could be rated good with some sub-intelligent life, several hundred fair with no intelligence and only one he could conscientiously rate excellent. This mind was of an intelligent, though as yet unadvanced humanoid race. The planet it inhabited met every requirement to be rated excellent. Of this the captain was certain.

Suddenly the telepath announced, "He's gone. He became bored watching the screen. He knows nothing about astronomy; therefore, the course loses its significance to him. He has the vague idea that we're going to a predetermined destination. The idea of an exploration, charting cruise hasn't occurred to him as yet."

"I wonder," mused the captain, "how he reconciles his conscious mind to his subconscious wandering.''

The psychologist answered. "As he begins to awaken other dreams probably mingle with these memories causing them to dim at the edges, thus becoming to his mind at any rate merely another series of especially vivid well-remembered dreams. I believe much of what lies in his subconscious is dream memory rather than fact memory.'' The psychologist didn't smile, or indicate in any fashion the ridicule and sarcasm the others felt as he continued, "He has the memory of being always well fed. He has buried the memory of hunger so far down in his subconscious that it would take a skilled psychologist a long time to call it forth.''

The telepath stirred and started to reply, then didn't. The alien's mind had been like a film, clear and easy to read. Some of the pictures had been disturbing and incomprehensible, but only through their strangeness, not because they were distorted by dream images. The psychologists never could accept anything at face value. Always probing and looking for hidden places and meanings. Just as he did when told of the world democracy existing on Earth.

"Most likely a benign dictatorship. A world couldn't be governed by a democratic government, a small area, perhaps, but not a world.'' Thus spoke the psychologist. But the telepath had been inside Allan's mind, and he knew it could and did work. Not only the planet Earth, but also the colonies on Mars and Venus.

The captain was still pursuing his own line of questioning.

"Has he ever shown any feeling of fear or repulsion toward us?''

"None, he accepts us as different but not to be feared because of it.''

"That's because he believes we are figments of his imagination; that he can control us by awakening."

The captain ignored this explanation advanced by the psychologist. A mind intelligent enough for dreams, could feel fear in the dreams—even a captain knew that. He was beginning to get the feeling that this Earth race might prove a formidable foe when and if found.

"Has he shown any interest in the drive?"

"He assumed we use an atomic drive. He has only the scantiest knowledge of atomics, however. His people use such a drive."

"The fact that the race has atomics is another reason we must find them." This would be the third planet using atomic energy. A young race, an unknown potential. They did not have interstellar travel now, but one hundred fifty years ago they didn't have atomic energy and already they had reached their neighbor planets. It had taken three times as long for the captain's people to achieve the same success. The captain remembered the one other race located in his time that had atomics. They were exploring space in ever widening circles. True they hadn't made any startling advances yet in weapons, they had found decisive bombs and lethal rays and gases unnecessary. But they had learned fast. They had resisted the invaders with cunning and skill. Their bravery had never been questioned, but in the end the aggressors had won.

The captain felt no thrill of satisfaction in the thought. It was a fact, accomplished long ago. The conclusion had been delayed certainly, but it had also been inevitable. Only one race, one planet, one government could have the energy, and the right to the raw materials that made the space lanes thoroughfares. The slaves might ride on the masters' crafts, but might not own or operate their own.

That was the law, and the captain was determined to uphold to the end that law.

And now this. One mind freed from its body and its Earth roaming the universe, divulging its secrets, all but the only one that mattered. How many millions of stars lit the way through space? And how many of them had their families of planets supporting life? The captain knew there was no answer, but still he sought ways of following the alien's mind back to his body.

Allan stirred his coffee slowly, not moving his head. This was his first meal sitting up, now at its conclusion he felt too exhausted to lift his spoon from his cup. Clair gently did it for him and held the cup to his lips.

"Tired, darling?" Her voice was a caress.

"A little." A little! All he wanted was his bed under him and Clair's voice whispering him to sleep. "I don't believe I'd even need a hypo." He was startled that he had spoken the thought, but Clair nodded, understanding.

"The doctor thinks it best to put off having anything if you can. I'll read to you and see if you can sleep." They had rediscovered the joy of reading books. Real leather-bound books instead of watching the three D set, or using the story films. Allan loved to lie quiescent, listening to the quiet voice of his wife rise and fall with the words. Often the words themselves were unimportant, but there was music in listening to Clair read them. They were beautifully articulated, falling into a pattern as rhythmic as if there were unheard drums beating the time.

He tried to remember what the sound of her voice reminded him of. Then he knew. By the very difference in tone and expression he was reminded of the crew of the mile-long spaceship in his dream.

He grinned to himself at the improbability of the dream. Everyone speaking in the same metallic tone, the monotonous flight, never varying, never having any emergency to cope with.

The noises of the hospital dimmed and became obscure and then were lost entirely. All was silent again as he sped toward the quiet lonesome planet he had last visited. There he had rested, gazing at the stars hanging in expanding circles over him. He had first viewed the galaxy from aboard the spaceship. Interested in the spiral shape of it he had left the ship to seek it out at closer range. Here on this tiny planet the effect was startling. If he closed out all but the brightest and largest of the stars there was ring after ring of tiny glowing diamonds hanging directly above him. How many times had he come back? He couldn't remember, but suddenly he thought about the mile-long spaceship again.

"He's back," the telepath never moved from his position, before the sky screen, nor did the astro navigator. Abruptly, however, the panorama went blank and the two moved toward the screen on the opposite wall.

"Is he coming?"

"Yes. He's curious. He thinks something is wrong."

"Good." The two stepped from the screen into a large room where a group watched a film.

The navigator and the telepath seated themselves slightly behind the rest of the assemblage. The captain had been talking, he continued as before.

"Let me know what his reactions are."

"The film interests him. The dimensional effect doesn't bother him, he appears accustomed to a form of three-dimensional films."

"Very good. Tell me the instant something strikes a responsive chord."

The film was one of their educational astronomy

courses for beginners. Various stars were shown
singly and in their constellations and finally in their
own galaxies. Novae and super novae, planets and
satellites appeared. The telepath dug deep into the
alien's memory, but found only an increasing interest, no memories of any one scene. Suddenly the
telepath said,

"This one he thinks he has seen before. He has
seen a similar galaxy from another position, one
that shows the spiral directly overhead."

The captain asked, "Has this one been visible on
the screen from such a position?"

"Not in detail. Only as part of the charted course."
The navigator was making notes as he answered.
"There are only three fixes for this particular effect.
A minor white dwarf with six satellites and two
main sequence stars, satellites unknown."

The captain thought deeply. Maybe only a similar
galaxy, but again maybe he was familiar with this
one.

The orders were given in the same tone he had
used in carrying on the conversation. The alien had
no way of knowing he was the helmsman guiding
the huge ship through space.

The telepath followed the alien's mind as he gazed
raptly at the ever-changing film. Occasionally he
reported the alien's thoughts, but nothing of importance was learned. As before, the departure of the
alien was abrupt.

With the telepath's announcement, "He's gone,"
the film flicked off and normal activity was resumed.

Later the captain called a meeting of the psychologist, the telepath, the chief navigator and the
ethnologist.

"We represent the finest minds in the universe,
yet when it comes to coping with one inferior intellect, we stand helpless. He flits in and out at will,
telling us nothing. We are now heading light-years

out of our way on what might easily prove to be a fruitless venture, merely because you," he held the telepath in his merciless gaze "think he recognized one of the formations." The captain's anger was a formidable thing to feel, and the rest stirred uneasily. His voice, however, was the same monotone it always was as he asked, "And did you manage to plant the seeds in his mind as suggested at our last meeting?"

"That is hard to say. I couldn't tell." The telepath turned to the psychologist for confirmation.

"He wouldn't know himself until he began feeling the desire for more education. Even then it might be in the wrong direction. We can only wait and hope we have hit on the way to find his home planet through making him want to learn astronavigation and astronomy." Soon afterward the meeting adjourned.

Allan was back at work again, with all traces of his accident relegated to the past. His life was well-ordered and full, with no time for schooling. He told himself this over and over, to no avail. For he was still telling himself this when he filled out the registration blank at the university.

"He's here again!" The telepath had almost given up expecting the alien ever again. He kept his mind locked in the other's as he recited as though from a book. "He's completely over his injury, working again, enrolled in night classes at the school in his town. He's studying atomic engineering. He's in the engine room now getting data for something they call a thesis."

Quietly the captain rolled off a list of expletives that would have done justice to one of the rawest space hands. And just as quietly, calmly, and perhaps, stoically, he pushed the red button that began the chain reaction that would completely vaporize the mile-long ship. His last breath was spent in hoping the alien would awaken with a violent headache. He did.

CALL ME JOE

BY POUL ANDERSON (1926–   )

ASTOUNDING SCIENCE FICTION
APRIL

The incredibly prolific and multi-talented Poul Anderson returns to this series with what I consider to be his most powerful story. "Call Me Joe" is simply a thrilling exercise in speculative science and speculative psychology, a most unusual and difficult combination for any writer. It is also (for my money) the best story ever written about Jupiter. Of course we know more about the landscape of Jupiter now than we did when Poul wrote this masterpiece, but I well remember thinking "yes, this is what it is like!" when I first read the story. Everything about "Call Me Joe" felt right and it still does thirty-one years later.

The members of the Science Fiction Writers of America voted it a retrospective Nebula by including it in The Science Fiction Hall of Fame *(1973). (MHG)*

The background to science fiction stories can become outdated. (I was about to say "alas," but this is a good thing, for it indicates that scientific knowledge is advancing and it also means that we science fiction writers can be assured of new backgrounds for new plots.)

In 1957, when this story appeared it was still possi-

ble to think of Jupiter as a world that resembled Earth in some way. It had a much thicker, deeper atmosphere that was very poisonous; tremendous storms; ammonia in place of water; a surface gravity several times what ours was. Nevertheless, under that atmosphere was a solid surface and, conceivably, life. If we could imagine a being far stronger than ourselves and adapted to the cold and the gravity and the horrible chemistry, he might find life tolerable and we might find it admirable.

But then came 1973 and the first probe skimming by Jupiter and we found that Jupiter was almost entirely hydrogen and helium and had no solid surface worth mentioning. It is possible that at the core there is a ball of metal and rock, perhaps even larger than Earth, but it is under tens of thousands of miles of hydrogen and helium. As one sinks through the atmosphere, the temperature rises and quickly becomes far too hot for any form of life as we know it to survive. The gases turn liquid under the unbelievable pressures and become hotter than the surface of the Sun. Jupiter is a world whose structure is not like Earth's in any way.

Just the same, we can take the background as described, even if it has become nothing but fantasy. The story Poul tells remains just as powerful now as in 1957. (IA)

The wind came whooping out of eastern darkness, driving a lash of ammonia dust before it. In minutes, Edward Anglesey was blinded.

He clawed all four feet into the broken shards which were soil, hunched down, and groped for his little smelter. The wind was an idiot bassoon in his skull. Something whipped across his back, drawing blood, a tree yanked up by the roots and spat a hundred miles. Lightning cracked, immensely far overhead where clouds boiled with night.

As if to reply, thunder toned in the ice mountains and a red gout of flame jumped and a hillside came booming down, spilling itself across the valley. The earth shivered.

Sodium explosion, thought Anglesey in the drum-beat noise. The fire and the lightning gave him enough illumination to find his apparatus. He picked up tools in muscular hands, his tail gripped the trough, and he battered his way to the tunnel and thus to his dugout.

It had walls and roof of water, frozen by sun-remoteness and compressed by tons of atmosphere jammed onto every square inch. Ventilated by a tiny smokehole, a lamp of tree oil burning in hydrogen made a dull light for the single room.

Anglesey sprawled his slate-blue form on the floor, panting. It was no use to swear at the storm. These ammonia gales often came at sunset, and there was nothing to do but wait them out. He was tired anyway.

It would be morning in five hours or so. He had hoped to cast an axehead, his first, this evening, but maybe it was better to do the job by daylight.

He pulled a decapod body off a shelf and ate the meat raw, pausing for long gulps of liquid methane from a jug. Things would improve once he had proper tools; so far, everything had been painfully grubbed and hacked to shape with teeth, claws, chance icicles, and what detestably weak and crumbling fragments remained of the spaceship. Give him a few years and he'd be living as a man should.

He sighed, stretched, and lay down to sleep.

Somewhat more than one hundred and twelve thousand miles away, Edward Anglesey took off his helmet.

He looked around, blinking. After the Jovian surface, it was always a little unreal to find himself here again, in the clean quiet orderliness of the control room.

His muscles ached. They shouldn't. He had not really been fighting a gale of several hundred miles an hour, under three gravities and a temperature of 140 Absolute. He had been here, in the almost nonexistent pull of Jupiter V, breathing oxynitrogen. It was Joe who lived down there and filled his lungs with hydrogen and helium at a pressure which could still only be estimated because it broke aneroids and deranged piezoelectrics.

Nevertheless, his body felt worn and beaten. Tension, no doubt—psychosomatics—after all, for a good many hours now he had, in a sense, been Joe, and Joe had been working hard.

With the helmet off, Anglesey held only a thread of identification. The esprojector was still tuned to Joe's brain but no longer focused on his own. Somewhere in the back of his mind, he knew an indescribable feeling of sleep. Now and then, vague forms or colors drifted in the soft black—dreams? Not impossible, that Joe's brain should dream a little when Anglesey's mind wasn't using it.

A light flickered red on the esprojector panel, and a bell whined electronic fear. Anglesey cursed. Thin fingers danced over the controls of his chair, he slued around and shot across to the bank of dials. Yes—there—K-tube oscillating again! The circuit blew out. He wrenched the faceplate off with one hand and fumbled in a drawer with the other.

Inside his mind he could feel the contact with Joe fading. If he once lost it entirely, he wasn't sure he could regain it. And Joe was an investment of several million dollars and quite a few highly skilled man-years.

Anglesey pulled the offending K-tube from its socket and threw it on the floor. Glass exploded. It eased his temper a bit, just enough so he could find a replacement, plug it in, switch on the current again—as the machine warmed up, once again amplifying, the Joeness in the back alleys of his brain strengthened.

Slowly, then, the man in the electric wheelchair rolled out of the room, into the hall. Let somebody else sweep up the broken tube. To hell with it. To hell with everybody.

Jan Cornelius had never been farther from Earth than some comfortable Lunar resort. He felt much put upon that the Psionics Corporation should tap him for a thirteen-month exile. The fact that he knew as much about esprojectors and their cranky innards as any other man alive was no excuse. Why send anyone at all? Who cared?

Obviously the Federation Science Authority did. It had seemingly given those bearded hermits a blank check on the taxpayer's account.

Thus did Cornelius grumble to himself, all the long hyperbolic path to Jupiter. Then the shifting accelerations of approach to its tiny inner satellite left him too wretched for further complaint.

And when he finally, just prior to disembarkation, went up to the greenhouse for a look at Jupiter, he said not a word. Nobody does, the first time.

Arne Viken waited patiently while Cornelius stared. *It still gets me, too,* he remembered. *By the throat. Sometimes I'm afraid to look.*

At length Cornelius turned around. He had a faintly Jovian appearance himself, being a large man with an imposing girth. "I had no idea," he whispered. "I never thought . . . I had seen pictures, but—"

Viken nodded. "Sure, Dr. Cornelius. Pictures don't convey it."

Where they stood, they could see the dark broken rock of the satellite, jumbled for a short way beyond the landing slip and then chopped off sheer. This moon was scarcely even a platform, it seemed, and cold constellations went streaming past it, around it. Jupiter lay across a fifth of that sky, softly ambrous, banded with colors, spotted with the shadows of planet-sized moons and with whirlwinds as broad as Earth. If there had been any gravity to speak of, Cornelius would have thought, instinctively, that the great planet was falling on him. As it was, he felt as if sucked upward; his hands were still sore where he had grabbed a rail to hold on.

"You live here . . . all alone . . . with this?" He spoke feebly.

"Oh, well, there are some fifty of us all told, pretty congenial," said Viken. "It's not so bad. You sign up for four-cycle hitches—four ship arrivals— and believe it or not, Dr. Cornelius, this is my third enlistment."

The newcomer forbore to inquire more deeply. There was something not quite understandable about the men on Jupiter V. They were mostly bearded, though otherwise careful to remain neat; their low-gravity movements were somehow dreamlike to watch; they hoarded their conversation, as if to stretch it through the year and month between ships. Their monkish existence had changed them—or did they take what amounted to vows of poverty, chastity, and obedience, because they had never felt quite at home on green Earth?

Thirteen months! Cornelius shuddered. It was going to be a long cold wait, and the pay and bonuses accumulating for him were scant comfort now, four hundred and eighty million miles from the sun.

"Wonderful place to do research," continued Viken. "All the facilities, hand-picked colleagues, no distractions . . . and of course—" He jerked his thumb at the planet and turned to leave.

Cornelius followed, wallowing awkwardly. "It is very interesting, no doubt," he puffed. "Fascinating. But really, Dr. Viken, to drag me way out here and make me spend a year plus waiting for the next ship . . . to do a job which may take me a few weeks—"

"Are you sure it's that simple?" asked Viken gently. His face swiveled around, and there was something in his eyes that silenced Cornelius. "After all my time here, I've yet to see any problem, however complicated, which when you looked at it the right way didn't become still more complicated."

They went through the ship's air lock and the tube joining it to the station entrance. Nearly everything was underground. Rooms, laboratories, even halls had a degree of luxuriousness—why, there was a fireplace with a real fire in the common room! God alone knew what *that* cost!

Thinking of the huge chill emptiness where the king planet laired, and of his own year's sentence, Cornelius decided that such luxuries were, in truth, biological necessities.

Viken showed him to a pleasantly furnished chamber which would be his own. "We'll fetch your luggage soon and unload your psionic stuff. Right now, everybody's either talking to the ship's crew or reading his mail."

Cornelius nodded absently and sat down. The chair, like all low-gee furniture, was a mere spidery skeleton, but it held his bulk comfortably enough. He felt in his tunic hoping to bribe the other man into keeping him company for a while. "Cigar? I brought some from Amsterdam."

"Thanks." Viken accepted with disappointing casualness, crossed long thin legs, and blew grayish clouds.

"Ah . . . are you in charge here?"

"Not exactly. No one is. We do have one administrator, the cook, to handle what little work of that type may come up. Don't forget, this is a research station, first, last, and always."

"What is your field, then?"

Viken frowned. "Don't question anyone else so bluntly, Dr. Cornelius," he warned. "They'd rather spin the gossip out as long as possible with each newcomer. It's a rare treat to have someone whose every last conceivable reaction hasn't been— No, no apologies to me. 'S all right. I'm a physicist, specializing in the solid state at ultrahigh pressures." He nodded at the wall. "Plenty of it to be observed —there!"

"I see." Cornelius smoked quietly for a while. Then: "I'm supposed to be the psionics expert, but frankly, at present, I've no idea why your machine should misbehave as reported."

"You mean those, uh, K-tubes have a stable output on Earth?"

"And on Luna, Mars, Venus . . . everywhere, apparently, but here." Cornelius shrugged. "Of course, psibeams are always pernickety, and sometimes you get an unwanted feedback when— No. I'll get the facts before I theorize. Who are your psimen?"

"Just Anglesey, who's not a formally trained esman at all. But he took it up after he was crippled, and showed such a natural aptitude that he was shipped out here when he volunteered. It's so hard to get anyone for Jupiter V that we aren't fussy about degrees. At that, Ed seems to be operating Joe as well as a Ps.D. could."

"Ah, yes. Your pseudojovian. I'll have to examine that angle pretty carefully too," said Cornelius. In spite of himself, he was getting interested. "Maybe the trouble comes from something in Joe's biochemistry. Who knows? I'll let you into a carefully guarded little secret, Dr. Viken: psionics is not an exact science."

"Neither is physics," grinned the other man. After a moment, he added more soberly: "Not my brand of physics, anyway. I hope to make it exact. That's why I'm here, you know. It's the reason we're all here."

Edward Anglesey was a bit of a shock, the first time. He was a head, a pair of arms, and a disconcertingly intense blue stare. The rest of him was mere detail, enclosed in a wheeled machine.

"Biophysicist originally," Viken had told Cornelius. "Studying atmospheric spores at Earth Station when he was still a young man—accident crushed him up, nothing below his chest will ever work again. Snappish type, you have to go slow with him."

Seated on a wisp of stool in the esprojector control room, Cornelius realized that Viken had been soft-pedaling the truth.

Anglesey ate as he talked, gracelessly, letting the chair's tentacles wipe up after him. "Got to," he explained. "This stupid place is officially on Earth time, GMT. Jupiter isn't. I've got to be here whenever Joe wakes, ready to take him over."

"Couldn't you have someone spell you?" asked Cornelius.

"Bah!" Anglesey stabbed a piece of prot and waggled it at the other man. Since it was native to him, he could spit out English, the common language of the station, with unmeasured ferocity. "Look here. You ever done therapeutic esping? Not just listening in, or even communication, but actual pedagogic control?"

"No, not I. It requires a certain natural talent, like yours." Cornelius smiled. His ingratiating little phrase was swallowed without being noticed by the scored face opposite him. "I take it you mean cases like, oh, reeducating the nervous system of a palsied child?"

"Yes, yes. Good enough example. Has anyone ever tried to suppress the child's personality, take him over in the most literal sense?"

"Good God, no!"

"Even as a scientific experiment?" Anglesey grinned. "Has any esprojector operative ever poured on the juice and swamped the child's brain with his own thoughts? Come on, Cornelius, I won't snitch on you."

"Well . . . it's out of my line, you understand." The psionicist looked carefully away, found a bland meter face, and screwed his eyes to that. "I have, uh, heard something about . . . well, yes, there were attempts made in some pathological cases to, uh, bull through . . . break down the patient's delusions by sheer force—"

"And it didn't work," said Anglesey. He laughed. "It *can't* work, not even on a child, let alone an adult with a fully developed personality. Why, it took a decade of refinement, didn't it, before the machine was debugged to the point where a psychiatrist could even 'listen in' without the normal variation between his pattern of thought and the patient's . . . without that variation setting up an interference scrambling the very thing he wanted to study. The machine has to make automatic compensations for the differences between individuals. We still can't bridge the differences between species.

"If someone else is willing to cooperate, you can very gently guide his thinking. And that's all. If you try to seize control of another brain, a brain with its own background of experience, its own ego—you risk your very sanity. The other brain will fight back, instinctively. A fully developed, matured, hardened human personality is just too complex for outside control. It has too many resources, too much hell the subconscious can call to its defense if its integrity is threatened. Blazes, man, we can't even master our own minds, let alone anyone else's!"

Anglesey's cracked-voice tirade broke off. He sat brooding at the instrument panel, tapping the console of his mechanical mother.

"Well?" said Cornelius after a while.

He should not, perhaps, have spoken. But he found it hard to remain mute. There was too much silence—half a billion miles of it, from here to the sun. If you closed your mouth five minutes at a time, the silence began creeping in like a fog.

"Well," gibed Anglesey. "So our pseudojovian, Joe, has a physically adult brain. The only reason I can control him is that his brain has never been given a chance to develop its own ego. I *am* Joe. From the moment he was 'born' into consciousness, I have been there. The psibeam sends me all his sense data and sends him back my motor-nerve impulses. But nevertheless, he has that excellent brain, and its cells are recording every trace of experience, even as yours and mine; his synapses have assumed the topography which is my 'personality pattern.'

"Anyone else, taking him over from me, would find it was like an attempt to oust me myself from my own brain. It couldn't be done. To be sure, he doubtless has only a rudimentary set of Anglesey memories—I do not, for instance, repeat trigonometric theorems while controlling him—but he has enough to be, potentially, a distinct personality.

"As a matter of fact, whenever he wakes up from sleep—there's usually a lag of a few minutes, while I sense the change through my normal psi faculties and get the amplifying helmet adjusted—I have a bit of a struggle. I feel almost a . . . a resistance

. . . until I've brought his mental currents completely into phase with mine. Merely dreaming has been enough of a different experience to—"

Anglesey didn't bother to finish the sentence.

"I see," murmured Cornelius. "Yes, it's clear enough. In fact, it's astonishing that you can have such total contact with a being of such alien metabolism."

"I won't for much longer," said the esman sarcastically, "unless you can correct whatever is burning out those K-tubes. I don't have an unlimited supply of spares."

"I have some working hypotheses," said Cornelius, "but there's so little known about psibeam transmission—is the velocity infinite or merely very great, is the beam strength actually independent of distance? How about the possible effects of transmission . . . oh, through the degenerate matter in the Jovian core? Good Lord, a planet where water is a heavy mineral and hydrogen is a metal? What do we know?"

"We're supposed to find out," snapped Anglesey. "That's what this whole project is for. Knowledge. Bull!" Almost, he spat on the floor. "Apparently what little we have learned doesn't even get through to people. Hydrogen is still a gas where Joe lives. He'd have to dig down a few miles to reach the solid phase. And I'm expected to make a scientific analysis of Jovian conditions!"

Cornelius waited it out, letting Anglesey storm on while he himself turned over the problem on K-tube oscillation.

"They don't understand back on Earth. Even here they don't. Sometimes I think they refuse to understand. Joe's down there without much more than his bare hands. He, I, we started with no more knowledge than that he could probably eat the local life. He has to spend nearly all his time hunting for food. It's a miracle he's come as far as he has in these few weeks—made a shelter, grown familiar with the immediate region, begun on metallurgy, hydrurgy, whatever you want to call it. What more do they want me to do, for crying in the beer?"

"Yes, yes—" mumbled Cornelius. "Yes, I—"

Anglesey raised his white bony face. Something filmed over in his eyes.

"What—?" began Cornelius.

"Shut up!" Anglesey whipped the chair around, groped for the helmet, slapped it down over his skull. "Joe's waking. Get out of here."

"But if you'll only let me work while he sleeps, how can I—"

Anglesey snarled and threw a wrench at him. It was a feeble toss, even in low-gee. Cornelius backed toward the door. Anglesey was tuning in the esprojector. Suddenly he jerked.

"Cornelius!"

"Whatisit?" The psionicist tried to run back, overdid it, and skidded in a heap to end up against the panel.

"K-tube again." Anglesey yanked off the helmet. It must have hurt like blazes, having a mental squeal build up uncontrolled and amplified in your own brain, but he said merely: "Change it for me. Fast. And then get out and leave me alone. Joe didn't wake up of himself. Something crawled into the dugout with me—I'm in trouble down there!"

It had been a hard day's work, and Joe slept heavily. He did not wake until the hands closed on his throat.

For a moment, then, he knew only a crazy smothering wave of panic. He thought he was back on Earth Station, floating in null-gee at the end of a cable while a thousand frosty stars haloed the planet before him. He thought the great I-beam had broken from its moorings and started toward him, slowly, but with all the inertia of its cold tons, spinning and shimmering in the Earth light, and the only sound himself screaming and screaming in his helmet trying to break from the cable the beam nudged him ever so gently but it kept on moving he moved with it he was crushed against the station wall nuzzled into it his mangled suit frothed as it tried to seal its wounded self there was blood mingled with the foam his blood *Joe roared.*

His convulsive reaction tore the hands off his neck and sent a black shape spinning across the dugout. It struck the wall, thunderously, and the lamp fell to the floor and went out.

Joe stood in darkness, breathing hard, aware in a vague fashion that the wind had died from a shriek to a low snarling while he slept.

The thing he had tossed away mumbled in pain and crawled along the wall. Joe felt through light-lessness after his club.

Something else scrabbled. The tunnel! They were coming through the tunnel! Joe groped blindly to meet them. His heart drummed thickly and his nose drank an alien stench.

The thing that emerged, as Joe's hands closed on it, was only about half his size, but it had six mon-strously taloned feet and a pair of three-fingered hands that reached after his eyes. Joe cursed, lifted it while it writhed, and dashed it to the floor. It screamed, and he heard bones splinter.

"Come on, then!" Joe arched his back and spat at them, like a tiger menaced by giant caterpillars.

They flowed through his tunnel and into the room, a dozen of them entered while he wrestled one that had curled around his shoulders and anchored its sinuous body with claws. They pulled at his legs, trying to crawl up on his back. He struck out with claws of his own, with his tail, rolled over and went down beneath a heap of them and stood up with the heap still clinging to him.

They swayed in darkness. The legged seething of them struck the dugout wall. It shivered, a rafter cracked, the roof came down. Anglesey stood in a pit, among broken ice plates, under the wan light of a sinking Ganymede.

He could see, now, that the monsters were black in color and that they had heads big enough to accommodate some brains, less than human but probably more than apes. There were a score of them or so; they struggled from beneath the wreckage and flowed at him with the same shrieking malice.

Why?

Baboon reaction, thought Anglesey somewhere in the back of himself. See the stranger, fear the stranger, hate the stranger, kill the stranger. His chest heaved, pumping air through a raw throat. He yanked a whole rafter to him, snapped it in half, and twirled the iron-hard wood.

The nearest creature got its head bashed in. The next had its back broken. The third was hurled with shattered ribs into a fourth; they went down together. Joe began to laugh. It was getting to be fun.

"Yeee-ow! Ti-i-i-iger!" He ran across the icy ground, toward the pack. They scattered, howling. He hunted them until the last one had vanished into the forest.

Panting, Joe looked at the dead. He himself was bleeding, he ached, he was cold and hungry, and his shelter had been wrecked . . . but, he'd whipped them! He had a sudden impulse to beat his chest and howl. For a moment, he hesitated—why not? Anglesey threw back his head and bayed victory at the dim shield of Ganymede.

Thereafter he went to work. First build a fire, in the lee of the spaceship—which was little more by now than a hill of corrosion. The monster pack cried in darkness and the broken ground; they had not given up on him, they would return.

He tore a haunch off one of the slain and took a bite. Pretty good. Better yet if properly cooked. Heh! They'd made a big mistake in calling his attention to their existence! He finished breakfast while Ganymede slipped under the western ice mountains. It would be morning soon. The air was almost still, and a flock of pancake-shaped skyskimmers, as Anglesey called them, went overhead, burnished copper color in the first pale dawn-streaks.

Joe rummaged in the ruins of his hut until he had recovered the water-smelting equipment. It wasn't harmed. That was the first order of business, melt some ice and cast it in the molds of ax, knife, saw, hammer he had painfully prepared. Under Jovian conditions, methane was a liquid that you drank and water was a dense hard mineral. It would make good tools. Later on he would try alloying it with other materials.

Next—yes. To hell with the dugout; he could sleep in the open again for a while. Make a bow, set traps, be ready to massacre the black caterpillars when they attacked him again. There was a chasm not far from here, going down a long way toward the bitter cold of the metallic-hydrogen strata: a natural icebox, a place to store the several weeks' worth of meat his enemies would supply. This would give him leisure to— Oh, a hell of a lot!

Joe laughed, exultantly, and lay down to watch the sunrise.

It struck him afresh how lovely a place this was. See how the small brilliant spark of the sun swam up out of eastern fogbanks colored dusky purple and veined with rose and gold; see how the light strengthened until the great hollow arch of the sky became one shout of radiance; see how the light spilled warm and living over a broad fair land, the million square miles of rustling low forests and wave-blinking lakes and feather-plumed hydrogen geysers; and see, see, see how the ice mountains of the west flashed like blued steel!

Anglesey drew the wild morning wind deep into his lungs and shouted with a boy's joy.

"I'm not a biologist myself," said Viken carefully. "But maybe for that reason I can better give you the general picture. Then Lopez or Matsumoto can answer any questions of detail."

"Excellent," nodded Cornelius. "Why don't you assume I am totally ignorant of this project? I very nearly am, you know."

"If you wish," laughed Viken.

They stood in an outer office of the xenobiology section. No one else was around for the station's clocks said 1730 GMT and there was only one shift. No point in having more, until Anglesey's half of the enterprise had actually begun gathering quantitative data.

The physicist bent over and took a paperweight off a desk. "One of the boys made this for fun," he said, "but it's a pretty good model of Joe. He stands about five feet tall at the head."

Cornelius turned the plastic image over in his hands. If you could imagine such a thing as a feline centaur with a thick prehensile tail— The torso was squat, long-armed, immensely muscular; the hairless head was round, wide-nosed, with big deep-set eyes and heavy jaws, but it was really quite a human face. The overall color was bluish gray.

"Male, I see," he remarked.

"Of course. Perhaps you don't understand. Joe is the complete pseudojovian: as far as we can tell, the final model, with all the bugs worked out. He's the answer to a research question that took fifty

years to ask." Viken looked sideways at Cornelius.
"So you realize the importance of your job, don't
you?"

"I'll do my best," said the psionicist. "But if . . .
well, let's say that tube failure or something causes
you to lose Joe before I've solved the oscillation
problem. You do have other pseudos in reserve,
don't you?"

"Oh, yes," said Viken moodily, "But the cost—
We're not on an unlimited budget. We do go through
a lot of money, because it's expensive to stand up
and sneeze this far from Earth. But for that same
reason our margin is slim."

He jammed hands in pockets and slouched toward the inner door, the laboratories, head down
and talking in a low, hurried voice:

"Perhaps you don't realize what a nightmare planet
Jupiter is. Not just the surface gravity—a shade
under three gees, what's that? But the gravitational
potential, ten times Earth's. The temperature. The
pressure . . . above all, the atmosphere, and the
storms, and the darkness!

"When a spaceship goes down to the Jovian surface, it's a radio-controlled job; it leaks like a sieve,
to equalize pressure, but otherwise it's the sturdiest,
most utterly powerful model ever designed; it's loaded
with every instrument, every servomechanism, every safety device the human mind has yet thought
up to protect a million-dollar hunk of precision
equipment.

"And what happens? Half the ships never reach
the surface at all. A storm snatches them and throws
them away, or they collide with a floating chunk of
Ice VII—small version of the Red Spot—or, so help
me, what passes for a flock of *birds* rams one and
stoves it in!

"As for the fifty percent which do land, it's a
one-way trip. We don't even try to bring them

back. If the stresses coming down haven't sprung
something, the corrosion has doomed them anyway.
Hydrogen at Jovian pressure does funny things to
metals.

"It cost a total of—about five million dollars—to
set Joe, one pseudo, down there. Each pseudo to
follow will cost, if we're lucky, a couple of million
more."

Viken kicked cpen the door and led the way
through. Beyond was a big room, low-ceilinged,
coldly lit, and murmurous with ventilators. It reminded Cornelius of a nucleonics lab; for a moment
he wasn't sure why, then recognized the intricacies
of remote control, remote observation, walls enclosing forces which could destroy the entire moon.

"These are required by the pressure, of course,"
said Vicken, pointing to a row of shields. "And the
cold. And the hydrogen itself, as a minor hazard.
We have units here duplicating conditions in the
Jovian, uh, stratosphere. This is where the whole
project really began."

"I've heard something about that," nodded Cornelius, "Didn't you scoop up airborne spores?"

"Not I." Viken chuckled. "Totti's crew did, about
fifty years ago. Proved there was life on Jupiter. A
life using liquid methane as its basic solvent, solid
ammonia as a starting point for nitrate synthesis—
the plants use solar energy to build unsaturated
carbon compounds, releasing hydrogen; the animals
eat the plants and reduce those compounds again to
the saturated form. There is even an equivalent of
combustion. The reactions involve complex enzymes
and . . . well, it's out of my line."

"Jovian biochemistry is pretty well understood,
then."

"Oh, yes. Even in Totti's day, they had a highly
developed biotic technology: Earth bacteria had already been synthesized and most gene structures

pretty well mapped. The only reason it took so long to diagram Jovian life processes was the technical difficulty, high pressure and so on."

"When did you actually get a look at Jupiter's surface?"

"Gray managed that, about thirty years ago. Set a televisor ship down, a ship that lasted long enough to flash him quite a series of pictures. Since then, the technique has improved. We know that Jupiter is crawling with its own weird kind of life, probably more fertile than Earth. Extrapolating from the airborne microorganisms, our team made trial syntheses of metazoans and—"

Viken sighed. "Damn it, if only there were intelligent native life! Think what they could tell us, Cornelius, the data, the— Just think back how far we've gone since Lavoisier, with the low-pressure chemistry of Earth. Here's a chance to learn a high-pressure chemistry and physics at least as rich with possibilities!"

After a moment, Cornelius murmured slyly: "Are you certain there *aren't* any Jovians?"

"Oh, sure, there could be several billion of them," shrugged Viken. "Cities, empires, anything you like. Jupiter has the surface area of a hundred Earths, and we're only seen maybe a dozen small regions. But we do know there aren't any Jovians using radio. Considering their atmosphere, it's unlikely they ever would invent it for themselves—imagine how thick a vacuum tube has to be, how strong a pump you need! So it was finally decided we'd better make our own Jovians."

Cornelius followed him through the lab, into another room. This was less cluttered, it had a more finished appearance: the experimentor's haywire rig had yielded to the assured precision of an engineer.

Viken went over to one of the panels which lined the walls and looked at its gauges. "Beyond this lies another pseudo," he said. "Female, in this instance. She's at a pressure of two hundred atmospheres and a temperature of 194 Absolute. There's a . . . an umbilical arrangement, I guess you'd call it, to keep her alive. She was grown to adulthood in this, uh, fetal stage—we patterned our Jovians after the terrestrial mammal. She's never been conscious, she won't ever be till she's 'born.' We have a total of twenty males and sixty females waiting here. We can count on about half reaching the surface. More can be created as required.

"It isn't the pseudos that are so expensive, it's their transportation. So Joe is down there alone till we're sure that his kind *can* survive."

"I take it you experimented with lower forms first," said Cornelius.

"Of course. It took twenty years, even with forced-catalysis techniques, to work from an artificial airborne spore to Joe. We've used the psibeam to control everything from pseudoinsects on up. Interspecies control is possible, you know, if your puppet's nervous system is deliberately designed for it, and isn't given a chance to grow into a pattern different from the esman's."

"And Joe is the first specimen who's given trouble?"

"Yes."

"Scratch one hypothesis." Cornelius sat down on a workbench, dangling thick legs and running a hand through thin sandy hair. "I thought maybe some physical effort of Jupiter was responsible. Now it looks as if the difficulty is with Joe himself."

"We've all suspected that much," said Viken. He struck a cigarette and sucked in his cheeks around the smoke. His eyes were gloomy. "Hard to see how. The biotics engineers tell me *Pseudocentaurus sapiens* has been more carefully designed than any product of natural evolution."

"Even the brain?"

"Yes. It's patterned directly on the human, to make psibeam control possible, but there are improvements—greater stability."

"There are still the psychological aspects, though," said Cornelius. "In spite of all our amplifiers and other fancy gadgets, psi is essentially a branch of psychology, even today . . . or maybe it's the other way around. Let's consider traumatic experiences. I take it the . . . the adult Jovian's fetus has a rough trip going down?"

"The ship does," said Viken. "Not the pseudo itself, which is wrapped up in fluid just like you were before birth."

"Nevertheless," said Cornelius, "the two hundred atmospheres pressure here is not the same as whatever unthinkable pressure exists down on Jupiter. Could the change be injurious?"

Viken gave him a look of respect. "Not likely," he answered. "I told you the J-ships are designed leaky. External pressure is transmitted to the, uh, uterine mechanism through a series of diaphragms, in a gradual fashion. It takes hours to make the descent, you realize."

"Well, what happens next?" went on Cornelius. "The ship lands, the uterine mechanism opens, the umbilical connection disengages, and Joe is, shall we say, born. But he has an adult brain. He is not protected by the only half-developed infant brain from the shock of sudden awareness."

"We thought of that," said Viken. "Anglesey was on the psibeam, in phase with Joe, when the ship left this moon. So it wasn't really Joe who emerged, who perceived. Joe has never been much more than a biological waldo. He can only suffer mental shock to the extent that Ed does, because it *is* Ed down there!"

"As you will," said Cornelius. "Still, you didn't plan for a race of puppets, did you?"

"Oh, heavens, no," said Viken. "Out of the question. Once we know Joe is well established, we'll import a few more esmen and get him some assistance in the form of other pseudos. Eventually females will be sent down, and uncontrolled males, to be educated by the puppets. A new generation will be born normally— Well, anyhow, the ultimate aim is a small civilization of Jovians. There will be hunters, miners, artisans, farmers, housewives, the works. They will support a few key members, a kind of priesthood. And that priesthood will be esp-controlled, as Joe is. It will exist solely to make instruments, take readings, perform experiments, and tell us what we want to know!"

Cornelius nodded. In a general way, this was the Jovian project as he had understood it. He could appreciate the importance of his own assignment.

Only, he still had no clue to the cause of that positive feedback in the K-tubes.

And what could he do about it?

His hands were still bruised. *Oh, God,* he thought with a groan, for the hundredth time, *does it affect me that much? While Joe was fighting down there, did I really hammer my fists on metal up here?*

His eyes smoldered across the room, to the bench where Cornelius worked. He didn't like Cornelius, fat cigar-sucking slob, interminably talking and talking. He had about given up trying to be civil to the Earthworm.

The psionicist laid down a screwdriver and flexed cramped fingers. *"Whuff!"* he smiled. "I'm going to take a break."

The half-assembled esprojector made a gaunt backdrop for his wide soft body, where it squatted toad-fashion on the bench. Anglesey detested the whole idea of anyone sharing this room, even for a few hours a day. Of late he had been demanding his meals brought here, left outside the door of his adjoining bedroom-bath. He had not gone beyond for quite some time now.

And why should I?

"Couldn't you hurry it up a little?" snapped Anglesey.

Cornelius flushed. "If you'd had an assembled spare machine, instead of loose parts—" he began. Shrugging, he took out a cigar stub and relit it carefully; his supply had to last a long time.

Anglesey wondered if those stinking clouds were blown from his mouth on malicious purpose. *I don't like you, Mr. Earthman Cornelius, and it is doubtless quite mutual.*

"There was no obvious need for one, until the other esmen arrive," said Anglesey in a sullen voice. "And the testing instruments report this one in perfectly good order."

"Nevertheless," said Cornelius, "at irregular intervals it goes into wild oscillations which burn out the K-tube. The problem is why. I'll have you try out this new machine as soon as it is ready, but, frankly, I don't believe the trouble lies in electronic failure at all—or even in unsuspected physical effects."

"Where, then?" Anglesey felt more at ease as the discussion grew purely technical.

"Well, look. What exactly is the K-tube? It's the heart of the esprojector. It amplifies your natural psionic pulses, uses them to modulate the carrier wave, and shoots the whole beam down at Joe. It also picks up Joe's resonating impulses and amplifies them for your benefit. Everything else is auxiliary to the K-tube."

"Spare me the lecture," snarled Anglesey.

"I was only rehearsing the obvious," said Cornelius, "because every now and then it is the obvious answer which is hardest to see. Maybe it isn't the K-tube which is misbehaving. Maybe it is you."

"What?" The white face gaped at him. A dawning rage crept red across its thin bones.

"Nothing personal intended," said Cornelius hastily. "But you know what a tricky beast the subconscious is. Suppose, just as a working hypothesis, that way down underneath you don't *want* to be on Jupiter. I imagine it is a rather terrifying environment. Or there may be some obscure Freudian element involved. Or, quite simply and naturally, your subconscious may fail to understand that Joe's death does not entail your own."

"Um-m-m—" *Mirabile dictu,* Anglesey remained calm. He rubbed his chin with one skeletal hand. "Can you be more explicit?"

"Only in a rough way," replied Cornelius. "Your conscious mind sends a motor impulse along the psibeam to Joe. Simultaneously, your subconscious mind, being scared of the whole business, emits the glandular-vascular-cardiac-visceral impulses associated with fear. These react on Joe, whose tension is transmitted back along the beam. Feeling Joe's somatic fear symptoms, your subconscious gets still more worried, thereby increasing the symptoms— Get it? It's exactly similar to ordinary neurasthenia, with this exception: that since there is a powerful amplifier, the K-tube, involved, the oscillations can build up uncontrollably within a second or two. You should be thankful the tube does burn out— otherwise your brain might do so!"

For a moment Anglesey was quiet. Then he laughed. It was a hard, barbaric laughter. Cornelius started as it struck his eardrums.

"Nice idea," said the esman. "But I'm afraid it won't fit all the data. You see, I like it down there. I like being Joe."

He paused for a while, then continued in a dry impersonal tone: "Don't judge the environment from my notes. They're just idiotic things like estimates of wind velocity, temperature variations, mineral properties—insignificant. What I can't put in is how Jupiter looks through a Jovian's infrared-seeing eyes."

"Different, I should think," ventured Cornelius after a minute's clumsy silence.

"Yes and no. It's hard to put into language. Some of it I can't, because man hasn't got the concepts. But . . . oh, I can't describe it. Shakespeare himself couldn't. Just remember that everything about Jupiter which is cold and poisonous and gloomy to us is *right* for Joe."

Anglesey's tone grew remote, as if he spoke to himself:

"Imagine walking under a glowing violet sky, where great flashing clouds sweep the earth with shadow and rain strides beneath them. Imagine walking on the slopes of a mountain like polished metal, with a clean red flame exploding above you and thunder laughing in the ground. Imagine a cool wild stream, and low trees with dark coppery flowers, and a waterfall, methane-fall . . . whatever you like, leaping off a cliff, and the strong live wind shakes its mane full of rainbows! Imagine a whole forest, dark and breathing, and here and there you glimpse a pale-red wavering will-o'-the-wisp, which is the life radiation of some fleet shy animal, and . . . and—"

Anglesey croaked into silence. He stared down at his clenched fists, then he closed his eyes tight and tears ran out between the lids.

"Imagine being *strong!*"

Suddenly he snatched up the helmet, crammed it on his head, and twirled the control knobs. Joe had been sleeping, down in the night, but Joe was about to wake up and—roar under the four great moons till all the forest feared him?

Cornelius slipped quietly out of the room.

* * *

In the long brazen sunset light, beneath dusky cloud banks brooding storm, he strode up the hillslope with a sense of the day's work done. Across his back, two woven baskets balanced each other, one laden with the pungent black fruit of the thorntree and one with cable-thick creepers to be used as rope. The axe on his shoulder caught the waning sunlight and tossed it blindingly back.

It had not been hard labor, but weariness dragged at his mind and he did not relish the household chores yet to be performed, cooking and cleaning and all the rest. Why couldn't they hurry up and get him some helpers?

His eyes sought the sky, resentfully. The moon Five was hidden—down here, at the bottom of the air ocean, you saw nothing but the sun and the four Galilean satellites. He wasn't even sure where Five was just now, in relation to himself . . . *wait a minute, it's sunset here, but if I went out to the viewdome I'd see Jupiter in the last quarter, or would I? Oh, hell, it only takes us half an Earth-day to swing around the planet anyhow—*

Joe shook his head. After all this time, it was still damnably hard, now and then, to keep his thoughts straight. *I, the essential I, am up in heaven, riding Jupiter V between coldstars. Remember that. Open your eyes, if you will, and see the dead control room superimposed on a living hillside.*

He didn't though. Instead, he regarded the boulders strewn wind-blasted gray over the tough mossy vegetation of the slope. They were not much like Earth rocks, nor was the soil beneath his feet like terrestrial humus.

For a moment Anglesey speculated on the origin of the silicates, aluminates, and other stony compounds. Theoretically, all such materials should be inaccessibly locked in the Jovian core, down where the pressure got vast enough for atoms to buckle and collapse. Above the core should lie thousands of miles of allotropic ice, and then the metallic hydrogen layer. There should not be complex minerals this far up, but there were.

Well, possibly Jupiter had formed according to theory, but had thereafter sucked enough cosmic dust, meteors, gases, and vapors down its great throat of gravitation to form a crust several miles thick. Or more likely the theory was altogether wrong. What did they know, what *would* they know, the soft pale worms of Earth?

Anglesey stuck his—Joe's—fingers in his mouth and whistled. A baying sounded in the brush, and two midnight forms leaped toward him. He grinned and stroked their heads; training was progressing faster than he'd hoped with these pups of the black caterpillar beasts he had taken. They would make guardians for him, herders, servants.

On the crest of the hill, Joe was building himself a home. He had logged off an acre of ground and erected a stockade. Within the grounds there now stood a lean-to for himself and his stores, a methane well, and the beginnings of a large comfortable cabin.

But there was too much work for one being. Even with the half-intelligent caterpillars to help, and with cold storage for meat, most of his time would still go to hunting. The game wouldn't last forever, either; he had to start agriculture within the next year or so—Jupiter year, twelve Earth years, thought Anglesey. There was the cabin to finish and furnish; he wanted to put a waterwheel, no, methane wheel in the river to turn any of a dozen machines he had in mind, he wanted to experiment with alloyed ice and—

And, quite apart from his need of help, why should he remain alone, the single thinking creature on an entire planet? He was a male in this body, with male instincts—in the long run, his health was bound to suffer if he remained a hermit, and right now the whole project depended on Joe's health.

It wasn't right!

But I am not alone. There are fifty men on the satellite with me. I can talk to any of them, any time I wish. It's only that I seldom wish it, these days. I would rather be Joe.

Nevertheless . . . I, cripple, feel all the tiredness, anger, hurt, frustration, of that wonderful biological machine called Joe. The others don't understand. When the ammonia gale flays open his skin, it is I who bleed.

Joe lay down on the ground, sighing. Fangs flashed in the mouth of the black beast which humped over to lick his face. His belly growled with hunger, but he was too tired to fix a meal. Once he had the dogs trained—

Another pseudo would be so much more reward-ing to educate.

He could almost see it, in the weary darkening of his brain. Down there, in the valley below the hill, fire and thunder as the ship came to rest. And the steel egg would crack open, the steel arms—already crumbling, puny work of worms!—lift out the shape within and lay it on the earth.

She would stir, shrieking in her first lungful of air, looking about with blank mindless eyes. And Joe would come carry her home. And he would feed her, care for her, show her how to walk—it wouldn't take long, an adult body would learn those things very fast. In a few weeks she would even be talking, be an individual, a soul.

Did you ever think, Edward Anglesey, in the days when you also walked, that your wife would be a gray, four-legged monster?

Never mind that. The important thing was to get

others of his kind down here, female *and* male. The station's niggling little plan would have him wait two more Earth-years, and then send him only another dummy like himself, a contemptible human mind looking through eyes which belonged rightfully to a Jovian. It was not to be tolerated!

If he weren't so tired—

Joe sat up. Sleep drained from him as the realization entered. *He* wasn't tired, not to speak of. Anglesey was. Anglesey, the human side of him, who for months had only slept in catnaps, whose rest had lately been interrupted by Cornelius—it was the human body which drooped, gave up, and sent wave after soft wave of sleep down the psibeam to Joe.

Somatic tension traveled skyward; Anglesey jerked awake.

He swore. As he sat there beneath the helmet, the vividness of Jupiter faded with his scattering concentration, as if it grew transparent; the steel prison which was his laboratory strengthened behind it. He was losing contact— Rapidly, with the skill of experience, he brought himself back into phase with the neutral current of the other brain. He willed sleepiness on Joe, exactly as a man wills it on himself.

And, like any other insomniac, he failed. The Joe-body was too hungry. It got up and walked across the compound toward its shack.

The K-tube went wild and blew itself out.

The night before the ships left, Viken and Cornelius sat up late.

It was not truly a night, of course. In twelve hours the tiny moon was hurled clear around Jupiter, from darkness back to darkness, and there might well be a pallid little sun over its crags when the clocks said witches were abroad in Greenwich. But most of the personnel were asleep at this hour.

Viken scowled. "I don't like it," he said. "Too sudden a change of plans. Too big a gamble."

"You are only risking—how many?—three male and a dozen female pseudos," Cornelius replied.

"And fifteen J-ships. All we have. If Anglesey's notion doesn't work, it will be months, a year or more, till we can have others built and resume aerial survey."

"But if it does work," said Cornelius, "you won't need any J-ships, except to carry down more pseudos. You will be too busy evaluating data from the surface to piddle around in the upper atmosphere."

"Of course. But we never expected it so soon. We were going to bring more esmen out here, to operate some more pseudos—"

"But they aren't *needed*," said Cornelius. He struck a cigar to life and took a long pull on it, while his mind sought carefully for words. "Not for a while, anyhow. Joe has reached a point where, given help, he can leap several thousand years of history—he may even have a radio of sorts operating in the fairly near future, which would eliminate the necessity of much of your esping. But without help, he'll just have to mark time. And it's stupid to make a highly trained human esman perform manual labor, which is all that the other pseudos are needed for at this moment. Once the Jovian settlement is well established, certainly, then you can send down more puppets."

"The question is, though," persisted Viken, "can Anglesey himself educate all those pseudos at once? They'll be helpless as infants for days. It will be weeks before they really start thinking and acting for themselves. Can Joe take care of them meanwhile?"

"He has food and fuel stored for months ahead," said Cornelius. "As for what Joe's capabilities are, well, hm-m-m . . . we just have to take Anglesey's judgment. He has the only inside information."

"And once those Jovians do become personalities," worried Viken, "are they necessarily going to string along with Joe? Don't forget, the pseudos are not carbon copies of each other. The uncertainty principle assures each one a unique set of genes. If there is only one human mind on Jupiter, among all those aliens—"

"One *human* mind?" It was barely audible. Viken opened his mouth inquiringly. The other man hurried on.

"Oh, I'm sure Anglesey can continue to dominate them," said Cornelius. "His own personality is rather—tremendous."

Viken looked startled. "You really think so?"

The psionicist nodded. "Yes. I've seen more of him in the past weeks than anyone else. And my profession naturally orients me more toward a man's psychology than his body or his habits. You see a waspish cripple. I see a mind which has reacted to its physical handicaps by developing such a hellish energy, such an inhuman power of concentration, that it almost frightens me. Give that mind a sound body for its use and nothing is impossible to it."

"You may be right, at that," murmured Viken after a pause. "Not that it matters. The decision is taken, the rockets go down tomorrow. I hope it all works out."

He waited for another while. The whirring of ventilators in his little room seemed unnaturally loud, the colors of a girlie picture on the wall shockingly garish. Then he said, slowly:

"You've been rather close-mouthed yourself, Jan. When do you expect to finish your own esprojector and start making the tests?"

Cornelius looked around. The door stood open to an empty hallway, but he reached out and closed it before he answered with a slight grin: "It's been ready for the past few days. But don't tell anyone."

"How's that?" Viken started. The movement, in low-gee, took him out of his chair and halfway across the table between the men. He shoved himself back and waited.

"I have been making meaningless tinkering motions," said Cornelius, "but what I waited for was a highly emotional moment, a time when I can be sure Anglesey's entire attention will be focused on Joe. This business tomorrow is exactly what I need."

"Why?"

"You see, I have pretty well convinced myself that the trouble in the machine is psychological, not physical. I think that for some reason, buried in his subconscious, Anglesey doesn't want to experience Jupiter. A conflict of that type might well set a psionic amplifier circuit oscillating."

"Hm-m-m." Viken rubbed his chin. "Could be. Lately Ed has been changing more and more. When he first came here, he was peppery enough, and he would at least play an occasional game of poker. Now he's pulled so far into his shell you can't even see him. I never thought of it before, but . . . yes, by God, Jupiter must be having some effect on him."

"Hm-m-m," nodded Cornelius. He did not elaborate: did not, for instance, mention that one altogether uncharacteristic episode when Anglesey had tried to describe what it was like to be a Jovian.

"Of course," said Viken thoughtfully, "the previous men were not affected especially. Nor was Ed at first, while he was still controlling lower-type pseudos. It's only since Joe went down to the surface that he's become so different."

"Yes, yes," said Cornelius hastily. "I've learned that much. But enough shop talk—"

"No. Wait a minute." Viken spoke in a low, hurried tone, looking past him. "For the first time,

I'm starting to think clearly about this . . . never really stopped to analyze it before, just accepted a bad situation. There *is* something peculiar about Joe. It can't very well involve his physical structure, or the environment, because lower forms didn't give this trouble. Could it be the fact that—Joe is the first puppet in all history with a potentially human intelligence?"

"We speculate in a vacuum," said Cornelius. "Tomorrow, maybe, I can tell you. Now I know nothing."

Viken sat up straight. His pale eyes focused on the other men and stayed there, unblinking. "One minute," he said.

"Yes?" Cornelius shifted, half rising. "Quickly, please. It is past my bedtime."

"You know a good deal more than you've admitted," said Viken. "Don't you?"

"What makes you think that?"

"You aren't the most gifted liar in the universe. And then—you argued very strongly for Anglesey's scheme, this sending down the other pseudos. More strongly than a newcomer should."

"I told you, I want his attention focused elsewhere when—"

"Do you want it that badly?" snapped Viken.

Cornelius was still for a minute. Then he sighed and leaned back.

"All right," he said. "I shall have to trust your discretion. I wasn't sure, you see, how any of you old-time station personnel would react. So I didn't want to blabber out my speculations, which may be wrong. The confirmed facts, yes, I will tell them; but I don't wish to attack a man's religion with a mere theory."

Viken scowled. "What the devil do you mean?"

Cornelius puffed hard on his cigar; its tip waxed and waned like a miniature red demon star. "This

Jupiter V is more than a research station," he said gently. "It is a way of life, is it not? No one would come here for even one hitch unless the work was important to him. Those who reenlist, they must find something in the work, something which Earth with all her riches cannot offer them. No?"

"Yes," answered Viken. It was almost a whisper. "I didn't think you would understand so well. But what of it?"

"Well, I don't want to tell you, unless I can prove it, that maybe this has all gone for nothing. Maybe you have wasted your lives and a lot of money and will have to pack up and go home."

Viken's long face did not flicker a muscle. It seemed to have congealed. But he said calmly enough: "Why?"

"Consider Joe," said Cornelius. "His brain has as much capacity as any adult human's. It has been recording every sense datum that came to it, from the moment of 'birth'—making a record in itself, in its own cells, not merely in Anglesey's physical memory bank up here. Also, you know, a thought is a sense datum too. And thoughts are not separated into neat little railway tracks; they form a continuous field. Every time Anglesey is in rapport with Joe, and thinks, the thought goes through Joe's synapses as well as his own—and every thought carries its own associations, and every associated memory is recorded. Like if Joe is building a hut, the shape of the logs might remind Anglesey of some geometric figure, which in turn would remind him of the Pythagorean theorem—"

"I get the idea," said Viken in a cautious way. "Given time, Joe's brain will have stored everything that ever was in Ed's."

"Correct. Now a functioning nervous system with an engrammatic pattern of experience—in this case, a *non-human* nervous system—isn't that a pretty good definition of a personality?"

"I suppose so—Good Lord!" Viken jumped. "You mean Joe is—taking over?"

"In a way. A subtle, automatic, unconscious way." Cornelius drew a deep breath and plunged into it. "The pseudojovian is so nearly perfect a life form: your biologists engineered into it all the experiences gained from nature's mistakes in designing *us*. At first, Joe was only a remote-controlled biological machine. Then Anglesey and Joe became two facets of a single personality. Then, oh, very slowly, the stronger, healthier body . . . more amplitude to its thoughts . . . do you see? Joe is becoming the dominant side. Like this business of sending down the other pseudos—Anglesey only thinks he has logical reasons for wanting it done. Actually, his 'reasons' are mere rationalizations for the instinctive desires of the Joe-facet.

"Anglesey's subconscious must comprehend the situation, in a dim reactive way; it must feel his human ego gradually being submerged by the steamroller force of *Joe's* instincts and *Joe's* wishes. It tries to defend its own identity, and is swatted down by the superior force of Joe's own nascent subconscious.

"I put it crudely," he finished in an apologetic tone, "but it will account for that oscillation in the K-tubes."

Viken nodded slowly, like an old man. "Yes, I see it," he answered. "The alien environment down there . . . the different brain structure . . . good God! Ed's being swallowed up in Joe! The puppet master is becoming the puppet!" He looked ill.

"Only speculation on my part," said Cornelius. All at once, he felt very tired. It was not pleasant to do this to Viken, whom he liked. "But you see the dilemma, no? If I am right, then any esman will gradually become a Jovian—a monster with two bodies, of which the human body is the unimportant auxiliary one. This means no esman will ever agree to control a pseudo—therefore the end of your project."

He stood up. "I'm sorry, Arne. You made me tell you what I think, and now you will lie awake worrying, and I am quite wrong and you worry for nothing."

"It's all right," mumbled Viken. "Maybe you're not wrong."

"I don't know." Cornelius drifted toward the door. "I am going to try to find some answers tomorrow. Good night."

The moon-shaking thunder of the rockets, crash, crash, crash, leaping from their cradles, was long past. Now the fleet glided on metal wings, with straining secondary ramjets, through the rage of the Jovian sky.

As Cornelius opened the control-room door, he looked at his telltale board. Elsewhere a voice tolled the word to all the stations, *one ship wrecked, two ships wrecked,* but Anglesey would let no sound enter his presence when he wore the helmet. An obliging technician had haywired a panel of fifteen red and fifteen blue lights above Cornelius' esprojector, to keep him informed, too. Ostensibly, of course, they were only there for Anglesey's benefit, though the esman had insisted he wouldn't be looking at them.

Four of the red bulbs were dark and thus four blue ones would not shine for a safe landing. A whirlwind, a thunderbolt, a floating ice meteor, a flock of mantalike birds with flesh as dense and hard as iron—there could be a hundred things which had crumpled four ships and tossed them tattered across the poison forests.

Four ships, hell! Think of four living creatures, with an excellence of brain to rival your own, damned first to years in unconscious night and then, never awakening save for one uncomprehending instant, dashed in bloody splinters against an ice mountain. The wasteful callousness of it was a cold knot in Cornelius' belly. It had to be done, no doubt, if there was to be any thinking life on Jupiter at all; but then let it be done quickly and minimally, he thought, so the next generation could be begotten by love and not by machines!

He closed the door behind him and waited for a breathless moment. Anglesey was a wheelchair and a coppery curve of helmet, facing the opposite wall. No movement, no awareness whatsoever. Good!

It would be awkward, perhaps ruinous, if Anglesey learned of this most intimate peering. But he needn't, ever. He was blindfolded and ear-plugged by his own concentration.

Nevertheless, the psionicist moved his bulky form with care, across the room to the new esprojector. He did not much like his snooper's role; he would not have assumed it at all if he had seen any other hope. But neither did it make him feel especially guilty. If what he suspected was true, then Anglesey was all unawares being twisted into something not human; to spy on him might be to save him.

Gently, Cornelius activated the meters and started his tubes warming up. The oscilloscope built into Anglesey's machine gave him the other man's exact alpha rhythm, his basic biological clock. First you adjusted to that, then you discovered the subtler elements by feel, and when your set was fully in phase you could probe undetected and—

Find out what was wrong. Read Anglesey's tortured subconscious and see what there was on Jupiter that both drew and terrified him.

Five ships wrecked.

But it must be very nearly time for them to land. Maybe only five would be lost in all. Maybe ten would get through. Ten comrades for—Joe?

Cornelius sighed. He looked at the cripple, seated blind and deaf to the human world which had crippled him, and felt a pity and an anger. It wasn't fair, none of it was.

Not even to Joe. Joe wasn't any kind of soul-eating devil. He did not even realize, as yet, that he *was* Joe, that Anglesey was becoming a mere appendage. He hadn't asked to be created, and to withdraw his human counterpart from him would be very likely to destroy him.

Somehow, there were always penalties for everybody, when men exceeded the decent limits.

Cornelius swore at him, voicelessly. Work to do. He sat down and fitted the helmet on his own head. The carrier wave made a faint pulse, inaudible, the trembling of neurones low in his awareness. You couldn't describe it.

Reaching up, he turned to Anglesey's alpha. His own had a somewhat lower frequency. It was necessary to carry the signals through a heterodyning process. Still no reception . . . well, of course, he had to find the exact wave form, timbre was as basic to thought as to music. He adjusted the dials, slowly, with enormous care.

Something flashed through his consciousness, a vision of clouds rolled in a violet-red sky, a wind that galloped across horizonless immensity—he lost it. His fingers shook as he turned back.

The psibeam between Joe and Anglesey broadened. It took Cornelius into the circuit. He looked through Joe's eyes, he stood on a hill and stared into the sky above the ice mountains, straining for sign of the first rocket; and simultaneously, he was still Jan Cornelius, blurrily seeing the meters, prob-

ing about for emotions, symbols, any key to the
locked terror in Anglesey's soul.

The terror rose up and struck him in the face.

Psionic detection is not a matter of passive listening in. Much as a radio receiver is necessarily also a
weak transmitter, the nervous system in resonance
with a source of psionic-spectrum energy is itself
emitting. Normally, of course, this effect is unimportant; but when you pass the impulses, either
way, through a set of heterodyning and amplifying
units, with a high negative feedback—

In the early days, psionic psychotherapy vitiated
itself because the amplified thoughts of one man,
entering the brain of another, would combine with
the latter's own neural cycles according to the ordinary vector laws. The result was that both men felt
the new beat frequencies as a nightmarish fluttering
of their very thoughts. An analyst, trained into self-
control, could ignore it; his patient could not, and
reacted violently.

But eventually the basic human wave-timbres were
measured, and psionic therapy resumed. The modern esprojector analyzed an incoming signal and
shifted its characteristics over to the "listener's"
pattern. The *really* different pulses of the transmit-
ting brain, those which could not possibly be mapped
onto the pattern of the receiving neurones—as an
exponential signal cannot very practicably be mapped
onto a sinusoid—those were filtered out.

Thus compensated, the other thought could be
apprehended as comfortably as one's own. If the
patient were on a psibeam circuit, a skilled operator
could tune in without the patient being necessarily
aware of it. The operator could neither probe the
other man's thoughts or implant thoughts of his own.

Cornelius' plan, an obvious one to any psionicist,
had depended on this. He would receive from an

unwitting Anglesey-Joe. If his theory were right, and the esman's personality was being distorted into that of a monster—his thinking would be too alien to come through the filters. Cornelius would receive spottily or not at all. If his theory was wrong, and Anglesey was still Anglesey, he would receive only a normal human stream-of-consciousness, and could probe for other trouble-making factors.

His brain roared!

What's happening to me?

For a moment, the interference which turned his thoughts to saw-toothed gibberish struck him down with panic. He gulped for breath, there in the Jovian wind, and his dreadful dogs sensed the alienness in him and whined.

Then, recognition, remembrance, and a blaze of anger so great that it left no room for fear. Joe filled his lungs and shouted it aloud, the hillside boomed with echoes:

"Get out of my mind!"

He felt Cornelius spiral down toward unconsciousness. The overwhelming force of his own mental blow had been too much. He laughed, it was more like a snarl, and eased the pressure.

Above him, between thunderous clouds, winked the first thin descending rocket flare.

Cornelius' mind groped back toward the light. It broke a watery surface, the man's mouth snapped after air, and his hands reached for the dials, to turn his machine off and escape.

"Not so fast, you." Grimly, Joe drove home a command that locked Cornelius' muscles rigid. "I want to know the meaning of this. Hold still and let me look!" He smashed home an impulse which could be rendered, perhaps, as an incandescent question mark. Remembrance exploded in shards through the psionicist's forebrain.

"So. That's all there is? You thought I was afraid

to come down here and be Joe, and wanted to know why? But I *told* you I wasn't!"

I should have believed—whispered Cornelius.

"Well, get out of the circuit, then." Joe continued growling it vocally. "And don't ever come back in the control room, understand? K-tubes or no, I don't want to see you again. And I may be a cripple, but I can still take you apart cell by cell. Now—sign off—leave me alone. The first ship will be landing in minutes."

You a cripple . . . you, Joe-Anglesey?

"What?" The great gray being on the hill lifted his barbaric head as if to sudden trumpets. "What do you mean?"

Don't you understand? said the weak, dragging thought. *You know how the esprojector works. You know I could have probed Anglesey's mind in Anglesey's brain without making enough interference to be noticed. And I could not have probed a wholly nonhuman mind at all, nor could it have been aware of me. The filters would not have passed such a signal. Yet you felt me in the first fractional second. It can only mean a human mind in a nonhuman brain.*

You are not the half-corpse on Jupiter V any longer, You're Joe—Joe-Anglesey.

"Well, I'll be damned," said Joe. "You're right."

He turned Anglesey off, kicked Cornelius out of his mind with a single brutal impulse, and ran down the hill to meet the spaceship.

Cornelius woke up minutes afterwards. His skull felt ready to split apart. He groped for the main switch before him, clashed it down, ripped the helmet off his head and threw it clanging on the floor. But it took a little while to gather the strength to do the same for Anglesey. The other man was not able to do anything for himself.

They sat outside sickbay and waited. It was a harshly lit barrenness of metal and plastic, smelling of antiseptics: down near the heart of the satellite, with miles of rock to hide the terrible face of Jupiter.

Only Viken and Cornelius were in that cramped little room. The rest of the station went about its business mechanically, filling in the time till it could learn what had happened. Beyond the door, three biotechnicians, who were also the station's medical staff, fought with death's angel for the thing which had been Edward Anglesey

"Nine ships got down," said Viken dully. "Two males, seven females. It's enough to start a colony."

"It would be genetically desirable to have more," pointed out Cornelius. He kept his own voice low, in spite of its underlying cheerfulness. There was a certain awesome quality to all this.

"I still don't understand," said Viken.

"Oh, it's clear enough—now. I should have guessed it before, maybe. We had all the facts, it was only that we couldn't make the simple, obvious interpretation of them. No, we had to conjure up Frankenstein's monster."

"Well," Viken's words grated, "we have played Frankenstein, haven't we? Ed is dying in there."

"It depends on how you define death." Cornelius drew hard on his cigar, needing anything that might steady him. His tone grew purposely dry of emotion:

"Look here. Consider the data. Joe, now: a creature with a brain of human capacity, but without a mind—a perfect Lockean *tabula rasa,* for Anglesey's psibeam to write on. We deduced, correctly enough— if very belatedly—that when enough had been written, there would be a personality. But the question was: whose? Because, I suppose, of normal human fear of the unknown, we assumed that any personality in so alien a body had to be monstrous. Therefore it must be hostile to Anglesey, must be swamping him—"

The door opened. Both men jerked to their feet

The chief surgeon shook his head. "No use. Typical deep-shock traumata, close to terminus now. If we had better facilities, maybe—"

"No," said Cornelius. "You cannot save a man who has decided not to live anymore."

"I know." The doctor removed his mask. "I need a cigarette. Who's got one?" His hands shook a little as he accepted it from Viken.

"But how could he—decide—anything?" choked the physicist. "He's been unconscious ever since Jan pulled him away from that . . . that thing."

"It was decided before then," said Cornelius. "As a matter of fact, that hulk in there on the operating table no longer has a mind. I know. I was there." He shuddered a little. A stiff shot of tranquilizer was all that held nightmare away from him. Later he would have to have that memory exorcised.

The doctor took a long drag of smoke, held it in his lungs a moment, and exhaled gustily. "I guess this winds up the project," he said. "We'll never get another esman."

"I'll say we won't." Viken's tone sounded rusty. "I'm going to smash that devil's engine myself."

"Hold on a minute," exclaimed Cornelius. "Don't you understand? This isn't the end. It's the beginning!"

"I'd better get back," said the doctor. He stubbed out his cigarette and went through the door. It closed behind him with a deathlike quietness.

"What do you mean?" Viken said it as if erecting a barrier.

"*Won't* you understand?" roared Cornelius. "Joe has all Anglesey's habits, thoughts, memories, prejudices, interests . . . oh, yes, the different body and the different environment, they do cause some changes—but no more than any man might undergo on Earth. If you were suddenly cured of a wasting disease, wouldn't you maybe get a little boisterous and rough? There is nothing abnormal in it. Nor is it abnormal to want to stay healthy—no? Do you see?"

Viken sat down. He spent a while without speaking.

Then, enormously slow and careful: "Do you mean Joe is Ed?"

"Or Ed is Joe. Whatever you like. He calls himself Joe now, I think—as a symbol of freedom—but he is still himself. What *is* the ego but continuity of existence?

"He himself did not fully understand this. He only knew—he told me, and I should have believed him—that on Jupiter he was strong and happy. Why did the K-tube oscillate? An hysterical symptom? Anglesey's subconscious was not afraid to stay on Jupiter—it was afraid to come back!

"And then, today, I listened in. By now, his whole self was focused on Joe. That is, the primary source of libido was Joe's virile body, not Anglesey's sick one. This meant a different pattern of impulses—not too alien to pass the filters, but alien enough to set up interference. So he felt my presence. And he saw the truth, just as I did—

"Do you know the last emotion I felt, as Joe threw me out of his mind? Not anger anymore. He plays rough, him, but all he had room to feel was joy.

"I *knew* how strong a personality Anglesey has! Whatever made me think an overgrown child-brain like Joe's could override it? In there, the doctors— bah! They're trying to salvage a hulk which has been shed because it is useless!"

Cornelius stopped. His throat was quite raw from talking. He paced the floor, rolled cigar smoke around his mouth but did not draw it any farther in.

When a few minutes had passed, Viken said cautiously: "All right. You should know—as you said, you were there. But what do we do now? How do we get in touch with Ed? Will he even be interested in contacting us?"

"Oh, yes, of course," said Cornelius. "He is still himself, remember. Now that he has none of the cripple's frustrations, he should be more amiable. When the novelty of his new friends wear off, he will want someone who can talk to him as an equal."

"And precisely who will operate another pseudo?" asked Viken sarcastically. "I'm quite happy with this skinny frame of mine, thank you!"

"Was Anglesey the only hopeless cripple on Earth?" asked Cornelius quietly.

Viken gaped at him.

"And there are aging men, too," went on the psionicist, half to himself. "Someday, my friend, when you and I feel the years close in, and so much we would like to learn—maybe we, too, would enjoy an extra lifetime in a Jovian body." He nodded at his cigar. "A hard, lusty, stormy kind of life, granted—dangerous, brawling, violent—but life as no human, perhaps, has lived it since the days of Elizabeth the First. Oh, yes, there will be small trouble finding Jovians."

He turned his head as the surgeon came out again.

"Well!" croaked Viken.

The doctor sat down. "It's finished," he said.

They waited for a moment, awkwardly.

"Odd," said the doctor. He groped after a cigarette he didn't have. Silently, Viken offered him one. "Odd. I've seen these cases before. People who simply resign from life. This is the first one I ever saw that went out smiling—smiling all the time."

YOU KNOW WILLIE

THEODORE R. COGSWELL (1918–1987)

THE MAGAZINE OF FANTASY AND SCIENCE FICTION
MAY

Born in Coatesville, Pennsylvania, Theodore R. Cogswell drove an ambulance during the Spanish Civil War and later served with the United States Army Air Corps, rising to the rank of Captain. After World War II he embarked on a career in higher education, teaching at several colleges and universities. From 1965 until his death he was Professor of English at Keystone Junior College in Pennsylvania.

As a science fiction writer he is remembered as the author of many outstanding short stories and novellas, the best of which can be found in his collections The Wall Around the World *(1962) and* The Third Eye *(1968). He also served as Secretary to the Science Fiction Writers of America from 1973 to 1974, and he holds a legendary status in the history of the field as the editor and chief conspirator of the* Proceedings of the Institute for 21st Century Studies, *a hilarious forum for sf writers.*

A man with a deep social conscience, his "You Know Willie" represents a fine example of how social issues found expression in the sf magazines of the 1950s. (MHG)

*This is still 1957. The fight for civil rights has not yet
been fought. The United States had fought Hitler in
the name of democracy but with a segregated army
and with over a hundred thousand people of Japanese origin in concentration camps.*

*We've improved since, but I like to think that
science fiction writers did their bit now and then to
make American reality live up to the American dream.*

*Ted's story "You Know Willie" is a powerful dis-
play of the obvious fact (well, it should be obvious)
that if you judge by outer appearance only then no
one is safe. (IA)*

In the old days there wouldn't have been any fuss
about Willie McCracken shooting a Negro, but these
weren't the old days. The judge sat sweating, listening to the voice from the state capital that roared
through the telephone receiver.

"But you can't hang no white man for shooting
no nigger!"

"Who said anything about hanging?" said the
voice impatiently. "I want it to look good, that's all.
So don't make it any half hour job—take two weeks
if you have to."

The judge obediently took two weeks. There was
a long parade of witnesses for the defense and an
equally long one for the prosecution, and through it
all the jury, having been duly instructed before-
hand, sat gravely, happy for a respite from the hot
sun and fields—and the cash money that was accru-
ing to each of them at the rate of three dollars a
day. A bright young man was down from the capital
to oversee all major matters, and as a result, the
trial of Willie McCracken was a model of juridical
propriety.

The prosecution made as strong a case against
Willie as it could without bringing in such prejudi-
cial evidence as that the little garage the dead man

had opened after he came back from Korea had been taking business away from the one Willie ran at an alarming rate, or that it was common knowledge that Willie was the Thrice High Warlock of the local chapter of The Knights of the Flaming Sword and in his official capacity had given the deceased one week to get out of town or else.

There were two important witnesses. One was very old and very black, the other wasn't quite as young as she used to be but she was white. The first could technically be classed as a witch—though there was another and more sonorous name for what she was in the forgotten tribal language she used on ritual occasions—but contrary to the ancient injunction, she had not only been permitted to live, but to flourish in a modest fashion. There were few in the courtroom who had not at one time or another made secret use of Aunt Hattie's services. And although most of the calls had been for relatively harmless love potions or protective amulets, there were enough who had called with darker things in mind to cause her to be treated with unusual respect.

Aunt Hattie was the town's oldest inhabitant—legend had it that she was already a grown woman when Lincoln larcenously freed the slaves—and the deceased had been her only living blood relative.

Having been duly sworn, she testified that the defendant, Willie McCracken, had come to her cabin just as she was getting supper, asked for the deceased, and then shot him between the eyes when he came to the door.

She was followed by Willie's wife, a plumpish little blonde in an over-tight dress who was obviously enjoying all the attention she was getting. She in turn swore that Willie had been home in bed with her where he belonged at the time in question. From the expressions on the jurymen's faces, it was obvious that they were thinking that if he hadn't been, he was a darned fool.

There were eight Knights of the Flaming Sword sitting around the table in Willie's kitchen. Willie pulled a jug from the floor beside him, took a long swallow, and wiped his mouth nervously with the hairy back of his hand. He looked up at the battered alarm clock on the shelf over the sink and then lifted the jug again. When he set it down Pete Martin reached over and grabbed it.

"Buck up, Willie boy," he said as he shook the container to see how much was left in it. "Ain't nobody going to get at you with us here."

Willie shivered. "You ain't seen her squatting out under that cottonwood every night like I have." He reached out for the jug but Martin laughed and pulled it out of reach.

"You lay off that corn and you won't be seeing Aunt Hattie every time you turn around. The way you've been hitting the stuff since the trial it's a wonder you ain't picking snakes up off the table by now."

"I seen her, I tell you," said Willie sullenly. "Six nights running now I seen her plain as day just sitting out under that tree waiting for the moon to get full." He reached for the jug again but Martin pushed his hand away.

"You've had enough. Now you just sit there quiet like while I talk some sense. Aunt Hattie's dead and Jackson's dead and they're both safe six foot under. I don't blame you for getting your wind up after what she yelled in the courtroom afore she keeled over, but just remember that there ain't no nigger the Knights can't take care of, dead or alive. Now you go upstairs and get yourself a little shut-eye. You're plumb beat. I don't think you've had six hours good sleep since the finish of the trial.

You don't notice Winnie Mae losing any rest, do you?"

Willie kneaded his bald scalp with thick fingers. "Couldn't sleep," he said hoarsely. "Not with her out there. She said he'd come back first full moon rise and every night it's been getting rounder and rounder."

"He comes back, we'll fix him for you, Willie," said Martin in a soothing voice. "Now you do like I said. Moon won't be up for a good two hours yet. You go get a little sleep and we'll call you in plenty of time."

Willie hesitated and then got to his feet and lumbered up the stairs. He was so tired he staggered as he walked. When he got into the dark bedroom he pulled off his clothes and threw himself down on the brass bed beside Winnie Mae. He tried to keep awake but he couldn't. In a moment his heavy snores were blending with her light delicate ones.

The moonlight was strong and bright in the room when Willie woke. They hadn't called him! From the kitchen below he heard a rumble of voices and then drunken laughter. Slowly, as if hypnotized, he swung his fat legs over the side of the bed and stumbled to the window. He tried to keep from looking but he couldn't. She would be there, squatting beneath the old cottonwood, a shriveled little black mummy that waited . . . waited . . . waited. . .

Willie dug his knuckles suddenly into his eyes, rubbed hard, and then looked again. There was nothing! Nothing where the thick old trunk met the ground but a dusty clumb of crab grass. He stood trembling, staring down at the refuse-littered yard as if it was the most beautiful thing he had ever seen. There was something healing in the calm flood of moonlight. The hard knot he had been carrying inside his head dissolved and he felt strong and young again. He wanted to shout, to caper around the room.

Winnie Mae mumbled in her sleep and he turned to look at her. Her thin cotton nightgown was bunched up under her arms and she lay, legs astraddle, her plump body gleaming whitely in the moonlight. She whimpered as she pulled herself up out of her slumber and then closed her arms around the heavy body that was pressing down on her.

"Remember me," he whispered, "I'm Willie. You know Willie."

She giggled and pulled him tighter against her. Her breath began to come faster and her fingers made little cat clawings on his back. As she squirmed under him her hands crept higher, over his shoulders, up his neck . . .

There was a sudden explosion under him and a catterwauling scream of sheer horror. Willie jerked back as her nails raked across his face, and then he felt a sudden stabbing agony as she jabbed up with her knee. He staggered away from the bed, his hand cupped over his bleeding face.

His hands! Time slid to a nightmarish stop as his finger tips sent a message pulsing down through nerve endings that his bald scalp had somehow sprouted a thick mop of kinky hair. He jerked his hands down and held them cupped before him. The fresh blood was black in the moonlight, and not only the blood. He spun toward the cracked mirror and saw himself for the first time. The flabby body with its sagging belly was gone. In its place was that of a dark-skinned stranger . . . but not a stranger.

His fingers crept across his forehead looking for the small red bullet hole that was no longer there.

And then time started to rush forward again. Winnie Mae's screaming went on and on and there was a rushing of heavy feet up the stairs from the kitchen.

He tried to explain but there was a new softness to his speech that put the lie to his stumbling words. When the door burst open he stood for a moment, hands stretched out in supplication.

"No," he whimpered. "I'm Willie. You know Willie."

As they came slowly out of the shadows he broke. He took one slow step backward, and then two, and then when he felt the low sill press against his calves, turned and dove out the window onto the sloping roof. When he got to the ground he tried again to explain but somebody remembered his gun.

Willie as he had been would have been run to ground within the mile, but his new lithe body carried him effortlessly through the night. If it hadn't been for the dogs he might have got away.

Somebody had a deck of cards and they all drew. Pete Martin was low man so he had to go back after the gasoline.

HUNTING MACHINE

BY CAROL EMSHWILLER (1921–   )

SCIENCE FICTION STORIES
MAY

Carol Emshwiller debuted in the science fiction magazines in 1955 and has continued to publish in the field, but only sporadically. Her stories are frequently borderline sf or fantasy, and often experimental. Her one collection, Joy in Our Cause *(1974), contains both science fiction and mainstream work—dozens of other excellent stories still await collection. For my money, she is one of the most underrated and neglected writers in our field, capable of great beauty and lyricism, a quality also found in her poetry. She is married to the well-known sf illustrator (now film-maker) Ed Emshwiller.*

However, there is absolutely nothing lovely about "Hunting Machine," in its own way one of the most brutal stories I have ever read. (MHG)

I'll tell you right now that I'm an anti-hunting fanatic.

I don't mind hunting for food. We must all live and human beings are predators. I don't mind hunting in self-defense, when it is necessary to kill a predator that is feeding on human beings.

I do mind hunting for "sport," killing for the sake of killing.

All right, now I've said it as directly as I know how and I doubt that any of you, unless you are as fanatical about the matter as I am (I'd give anything to outfit animals with guns of their own and see how the hunters would feel if they were at the wrong end of the weapon), would be greatly moved by my statement.

But now read Carol's "Hunting Machine," in which she doesn't at all say what I say, in which she doesn't express her opinions or try to argue with you, in which she just tells a science fiction story— and see how you feel about it.

That may give you an idea of one reason why stories are written. They're not always "just to entertain." In fact, this story is anything but "entertaining." (IA)

It sensed Ruthie McAlister's rapid heartbeat, just as it sensed any other animal's. The palms of her hands were damp, and it felt that, too—it also felt the breathing, in and out. And it heard her nervous giggle.

She was watching her husband, Joe, as he leaned over the control unit of the thing that sensed heartbeats—the gray-green thing they called the hound, or Rover, or sometimes the bitch.

"Hey," she said. "I guess it's OK, huh?"

Joe turned a screw with his thumb nail and pulled out the wire attached to it. "Gimme a bobby pin."

Ruthie reached to the back of her head. "I mean it's not dangerous, is it?"

"Naw."

"I don't just mean about *it.*" She nodded at the gray-green thing. "I mean, I know you're good at fixing things like this, like the time you got beer for nothing out of the beer vendor and, golly, I guess we haven't paid for a TV show for years. I mean, I *know* you can fix things right, only won't they know when we bring it back to be checked out?"

"Look, these wardens are country boys, and besides, I can put this thing back so *nobody* knows."

The gray-green thing squatted on its six legs where Joe could lean over it; it sensed that Ruthie's heartbeat had slowed almost to normal, and it heard her sigh.

"I guess you're pretty good at this, huh, Joe?" She wiped her damp hands on her green tunic. "That's the weight dial, isn't it?" she asked, watching him turn the top one.

He nodded. "Fifteen hundred pounds," he said slowly.

"Oo, was he really and truly that big?"

"Bigger." And now the thing felt Joe's heart and breathing surge.

They had been landed day before yesterday, with their geodesic tent, pneumatic form beds, automatic camping stove, and pocket air tables, pocket TV set, four disposable hunting costumes apiece (one for each day), and two folding guns with power settings.

In addition, there was the bug-scat, go-snake, sun-stop, and the gray-green hunter, sealed by the warden and set for three birds, two deer and one black bear. They had only the bear to go; now, Joe McAlister had unsealed the controls, released the governor and changed the setting to brown bear, 1500 pounds.

"I don't care," he said, "I want that bear."

"Do you think he'll still be there tomorrow?"

Joe patted one of the long jointed legs of the thing. "If he's not, ol' bitch here will find him for us."

Next day was clear and cool, and Joe breathed big, expanding breaths and patted his beginning paunch. "Yes sir," he said, "this is the day for something big—something really big, that'll put up a real fight."

He watched the red of the sunrise fade out of the sky while Ruthie turned on the stove and then got out her makeup kit. She put sun-stop on her face, then powdered it with a tan powder. She blackened her eyelids and purpled her lips; after that, she opened the stove and took out two disposable plates with eggs and bacon.

They sat in the automatic blow-up chairs, at the automatic blow-up table. Joe said that there was nothing like North air to give you an appetite, and Ruthie said she bet they were sweltering back in the city. Then she giggled.

Joe leaned back in his chair and sipped his coffee. "Shooting deer is just like shooting a cow," he said. "No fight to 'em at all. Even when ol' hound here goads 'em, they just want to run off. But this bear's going to be different. Of course bears are shy too, but ol' hound knows what to do about that."

"They say it's getting to be so there aren't many of the big kind left."

"Yes, but one more won't hurt. Think of a skin and head that size in our living room. I guess anybody that came in there would sure sit up and take notice."

"It won't match the curtains," his wife said.

"I think what I'll do is pack the skin up tight and leave it somewhere up here, till the warden checks us through. Then, maybe a couple of days later, I'll come back and get it."

"Good idea." Ruthie had finished her coffee and was perfuming herself with bug-scat.

"Well, I guess we'd better get started." They hung their folded-up guns on their belts. They put their dehydrated, self-heating lunch in their pockets. They slung on their cold-unit canteens. They each took a packet containing chair, table and sun shade; then Joe fastened on the little mike that controlled the hunter. It fit on his shoulder where he could turn his head to the side and talk into it.

"All right, houn' dog," he said, shoulder hunched and head tilted, "get a move on, boy. Back to that spot where we saw him yesterday. You can pick up the scent from there."

The hunting machine ran on ahead of them. It went faster than anything it might have to hunt. Two miles, three miles—Joe and Ruthie were left behind. They followed the beam it sent back to them, walking and talking and helping each other over the rough spots.

About eleven o'clock, Joe stopped, took off his red hunting hat and mopped his balding forehead with the new bandanna he'd bought at Hunter's Outfitters in New York. It was then he got the signal. *Sighted, sighted, sighted . . .*

Joe leaned over his mike. "Stick on him boy. How far are you? Well, try to move him down this way if you can." He turned to his wife. "Let's see, about three miles . . . we'll take a half hour out for lunch. Maybe we'll get there a couple of hours from now. How's it going, kid?"

"Swell," Ruthie said.

The big bear sat on the rocks by the stream. His front paws were wet almost to the elbows. There were three torn fishheads lying beside him. He ate only the best parts because he was a good fisher; and he looked, now, into the clean cold water for another dark blue back that would pause on its way upstream.

It wasn't a smell that made him turn. He had a keen nose, but the hunting machine was made to have no smell. It was the gray dead lichen's crackle that made him look up. He stood still, looking in the direction of the sound and squinting his small eyes, but it wasn't until it moved that he saw it.

Three quarters of a ton, he was; but like a bird, or a rabbit, or a snake, the bear avoided things that were large and strange. He turned back the way he always took, the path to his rubbing tree and to his home. He moved quietly and rapidly, but the thing followed.

He doubled back to the stream again, then, and waded down it on the opposite side from the thing— but still it followed, needing no scent. Once the hunting machine sighted, it never lost its prey.

Heart beat normal, respiration normal, it sensed. Size almost 1600 pounds.

The bear got out on the bank and turned back, calling out in low growls. He stood up on his hind legs and stretched his full height. Almost two men tall, he stood and gave warning.

The hunting machine waited twenty yards away. The bear looked at it a full minute; then he fell back on all fours and turned south again. He was shy and he wanted no trouble.

Joe and Ruthie kept on walking north at their leisurely pace until just noon. Then they stopped for lunch by the side of the same stream the bear had waded, only lower down. And they used its cold water on their dehydrated meal—beef and onions, mashed potatoes, a lettuce salad that unfolded in the water like Japanese paper flowers. There were coffee tablets that contained a heating unit too, and fizzled in the water like firecracker fuses until the water was hot, creamy coffee.

The bear didn't stop to eat. Noon meant nothing to him. Now he moved with more purpose, looking back and squinting his small eyes.

The hunter felt the heart beat faster, the breathing heavy, pace increasing. Direction generally south.

Joe and Ruthie followed the signal until it suddenly changed. It came faster; that meant they were near.

They stopped and unfolded their guns. "Let's have a cup of coffee first," Ruthie said.

"OK, Hon." Joe released the chairs which blew themselves up to size. "Good to take a break so we can really enjoy the fight."

Ruthie handed Joe a fizzing cup of coffee. "Don't forget you want ol' Rover to goad some."

"Uh-huh. Bear's not much better than a deer without it. Good you reminded me." He turned and spoke softly into the little mike.

The hunting machine shortened the distance slowly. Fifteen feet, ten, five. The bear heard and turned. Again he rose up, almost two men tall, and roared his warning sound to tell the thing to keep back.

Joe and Ruthie shivered and didn't look at each other. They heard it less with their ears, and more with their spines—with an instinct they had forgotten.

Joe shook his shoulder to shake away the feeling of the sound. "I guess the ol' bitch is at him."

"Good dog," Ruthie said. "Get 'im, boy."

The hunter's arm tips drew blood, but only in the safe spots—shoulder scratches at the heavy lump behind his head, thigh punctures. It never touched the veins, or arteries.

The bear swung at the thing with his great paw. His claws screeched down the body section but didn't so much as make a mark on the metal. The blow sent the thing thirty feet away, but it came back every time. The muscles, claws and teeth were nothing to it. It was made to withstand easily more than what one bear could do, and it knew with its built-in knowledge how to make a bear blind-angry.

Saliva came to the bear's mouth and flew out over his chin as he moved his heavy head sideways and back. It splashed, gummy on his cheeks, and made dark, damp streaks across his chest. Only his rage was real to him now, and he screamed a deep rasp of frustration again and again.

Two hundred yards away, Joe said, "Some roar!"

"Uh-huh. If noise means anything, it sounds like he's about ready for a real fight."

They both got up and folded up the chairs and cups. They sighted along their gun barrels to see that they were straight. "Set 'em at medium," Joe said. "We want to start off slow."

They came to where the bear was, and took up a good position on a high place. Joe called in his mike to the hunter thing. "Stand by, houn' dog, and slip over here to back us up." Then he called to the bear. "Hey, boy. This way, boy. This way."

The gray-green thing moved back and the bear saw the new enemy, two of them. He didn't hesitate; he was ready to charge anything that moved. He was only five feet away when their small guns popped. The force knocked him down, and he rolled out of the way, dazed; he turned again for another charge, and came at them, all claws and teeth.

Joe's gun popped again. This time the bear staggered, but still came on. Joe backed up, pushing at his gun dial to raise the power. He bumped into Ruthie behind him and they both fell. Joe's voice was a crazy scream. "Get him."

The hunting machine moved fast. Its sharp forearm came like an uppercut, under the jaw, and into the brain.

He lay, looking smaller, somehow, but still big, his ragged fur matted with blood. Fleas were alive on it, and flies already coming. Joe and Ruthie looked down at him and took big breaths.

"You shouldna got behind me," Joe said as soon as he caught his breath. "I coulda kept it going longer if you'da just stayed out of the way."

"You told me to," Ruthie said. "You told me to stay right behind you."

"Well, I didn't mean *that* close."

Ruthie sniffed. "Anyway," she said, "how are you going to get the fur off it?"

"Hmmmph."

"I don't think that moth-eaten thing will make much of a rug. It's pretty dirty, too, and probably full of germs."

Joe walked around the bear and turned its head sideways with his toe. "Be a big messy job, all right, skinning it. Up to the elbows in blood and gut, I guess."

"I didn't expect it to be like *this* at all," Ruthie said. "Why don't you just forget it? You had your fun."

Joe stood, looking at the bear's head. He watched a fly land on its eye and then walk down to a damp nostril.

"Well come *on*." Ruthie took her small pack. "I want to get back in time to take a bath before supper."

"OK." Joe leaned over his mike. "Come on ol' Rover, ol' hound dog. You did fine."

WORLD OF A THOUSAND COLORS

BY ROBERT SILVERBERG (1934–   )

SUPER SCIENCE FICTION
JUNE

Here's a warm welcome to this series for the amazingly talented and prolific Robert Silverberg, a man who has enriched the science fiction field immeasurably over the last nearly thirty-five years. He began publishing in 1954 at the ripe age of twenty, while still an undergraduate at Columbia University in New York, and quickly became a regular contributor to many of the sf magazines of the day—in fact, he was so prolific that he used a bevy of pen names throughout the 1950s, and he was soon producing close to 1,000,000 (that's six zeros, folks) words a year of solid, commercial fiction.

We will be documenting his development as a writer, his many awards, and his contributions to the development of modern science fiction in later volumes in this series. "World of a Thousand Colors," from Super Science Fiction, *a typical magazine of its time, is evidence that even in those early days he was capable of producing one of the best stories of its year. (MHG)*

One of the great science fiction themes of all time is surely that of Heaven. Think about it! Heaven offers us a society utterly different from any that we actually know—immortality, ineffable happiness, reunion with loved ones, and so on. Isn't that what science fiction is supposed to do; construct a different society?

And as in science fiction, the different society is not really known to us. The comments in the Bible are not at all detailed or specific. I think most people believe Heaven consists of wings, haloes, and harps, and that we will all sit around on clouds and sing hymns. (Mark Twain thought this was about as accurate a description of Hell as anyone could think up.)

One thing we can be certain of where Heaven is concerned is that not everyone gets there. Some people (maybe even most people, maybe even almost everybody—depending on how narrow your sectarian faith is) go to Hell instead and suffer indescribable torments. No one has ever seen Hell either and the descriptions in the Bible are lacking in detail—when compared with the drama and descriptive verve of Dante, for instance.

Well, then, why shouldn't science fiction borrow the themes of Heaven and Hell and why shouldn't writers prepare their own versions?

Well, then, here is the young Silverberg doing just that. (IA)

When Jolvar Hollinrede discovered that the slim, pale young man opposite him was journeying to the World of a Thousand Colors to undergo the Test, he spied a glittering opportunity for himself. And in that moment was the slim, pale young man's fate set.

Hollinrede's lean fingers closed on the spun-fiber drinkflask. He peered across the burnished tabletop. "The *Test*, you say?"

The young man smiled diffidently. "Yes, I think I'm ready. I've waited years—and now's my big chance." He had had a little too much of the cloying liqueur he had been drinking; his eyes shone glassily, and his tongue was looser than it had any right to be.

"Few are called and fewer are chosen," Hollinrede mused. "Let me buy you another drink."

"No, I—"

"It will be an honor. Really. It's not every day I have a chance to buy a Testee a drink."

Hollinrede waved a jeweled hand and the servomech brought them two more drinkflasks. Lightly Hollinrede punctured one, slid it along the tabletop, kept the other in his hand unopened. "I don't believe I know your name," he said.

"Derveran Marti. I'm from Earth. You?"

"Jolvar Hollinrede. Likewise. I travel from world to world on business, which is what brings me to Niprion this day."

"What sort of business?"

"I trade in jewels," Hollinrede said, displaying the bright collection studding his fingers. They were all morphosims, not the originals, but only careful chemical analysis would reveal that. Hollinrede did not believe in exposing millions of credits' worth of merchandise to anyone who cared to lop off his hand.

"I was a clerk," Marti said. "But that's all far behind me. I'm on to the World of a Thousand Colors to take the Test! The Test!"

"The Test!" Hollinrede echoed. He lifted his unpunctured drinkflask in a gesture of salute, raised it to his lips, pretended to drain it. Across the table Derveran Marti coughed as the liqueur coursed down his throat. He looked up, smiling dizzily, and smacked his lips.

"When does your ship leave?" Hollinrede asked.

"Tomorrow midday. It's the *Star Climber*. I can't wait. This stopover at Niprion is making me fume with impatience."

"No doubt," Hollinrede agreed. "What say you to an afternoon of whist, to while away the time?"

An hour later Derveran Marti lay slumped over the inlaid cardtable in Hollinrede's hotel suite, still clutching a handful of waxy cards. Arms folded, Hollinrede surveyed the body.

They were about of a height, he and the dead man, and a chemotherm mask would alter Hollinrede's face sufficiently to allow him to pass as Marti. He switched on the playback of the room's recorder to pick up the final fragments of their conversation.

" . . . care for another drink, Marti?"

"I guess I'd better not, old fellow. I'm getting kind of muzzy, you know. No, please don't pour it for me. I said I didn't want it, and—well, all right. Just a little one. There, that's enough. Thanks."

The tape was silent for a moment, then recorded the soft thump of Marti's body falling to the table as the quick-action poison unlatched his synapses. Smiling, Hollinrede switched the recorder to *record* and said, mimicking Marti, *"I guess I'd better not, old fellow. I'm getting kind of muzzy, you know."*

He activated the playback, listened critically to the sound of his voice, then listened to Marti's again for comparison. He was approaching the light, flexible quality of the dead man's voice. Several more attempts and he had it almost perfect. Producing a vocal homologizer, he ran off first Marti's voice, then his own pronouncing the same words.

The voices were alike to three decimal places. That would be good enough to fool the most sensitive detector; three places was the normal range of variation in any man's voice from day to day.

In terms of mass there was a trifling matter of some few grams which could easily be sweated off in the gymnasium the following morning. As for the dead man's gesture-complex, Hollinrede thought he could manage a fairly accurate imitation of Marti's manner of moving; he had studied the young clerk carefully for nearly four hours, and Hollinrede was a clever man.

When the preparations were finished, he stepped away and glanced at the mirror, taking a last look at his own face—the face he would not see again until he had taken the Test. He donned the mask. Jolvar Hollinrede became Derveran Marti.

Hollinrede extracted a length of cotton bulking from a drawer and wrapped it around Marti's body. He weighed the corpse, and added four milligrams more of cotton so that Marti would have precisely the mass Jolvar Hollinrede had had. He donned Marti's clothes finally, dressed the body in his own, and smiling sadly at the convincing but worthless morphosim jewels on his fingers, transferred the rings to Marti's already-stiffening hands.

"Up with you," he grunted, and bundled the body across the room to the disposal.

"Farewell, old friend," he exclaimed feelingly, and hoisted Marti feet-first to the lip of the chute. He shoved, and the dead man vanished, slowly, gracefully, heading downward toward the omnivorous maw of the atomic converter buried in the deep levels of Stopover Planet Niprion.

Reflectively Hollinrede turned away from the disposal unit. He gathered up the cards, put away the liqueur, poured the remnant of the poisoned drink in the disposal chute.

An atomic converter was a wonderful thing, he thought pleasantly. By now the body of Marti had been efficiently reduced to its component molecules, and those were due for separation into atoms shortly after, and from atoms into subatomic particles. Within an hour the prime evidence to the crime would be nothing but so many protons, electrons, and neutrons—and there would be no way of

telling which of the two men in the room had entered the chute, and which had remained alive.

Hollinrede activated the tape once more, rehearsed
for the final time his version of Marti's voice, and
checked it with the homologizer. Still three decimal
places; that was good enough. He erased the tape.

Then, depressing the communicator stud, he said,
"I wish to report a death."

A cold robot face appeared on the screen. "Yes?"

"Several minutes ago my host, Jolvar Hollinrede,
passed on of an acute embolism. He requested immediate dissolution upon death and I wish to report
that this has been carried out."

"Your name?"

"Derveran Marti. Testee."

"A Testee? You were the last to see the late
Hollinrede alive?"

"That's right."

"Do you swear that all information you might
give will be accurate and fully honest?"

"I so swear," Hollinrede said.

The inquest was brief and smooth. The word of a
Testee goes without question; Hollinrede had reported the details of the meeting exactly as if he
had been Marti, and after a check of the converter
records revealed that a mass exactly equal to the
late Hollinrede's had indeed been disposed of at
precisely the instant witness claimed, the inquest
was at its end. The verdict was natural death.
Hollinrede told the officials that he had not known
the late jeweltrader before that day, and had no
interest in his property, whereupon they permitted
him to depart.

Having died intestate, Hollinrede knew his property became that of the Galactic Government. But,
as he pressed his hand, clad in its skintight chemotherm, against the doorplate of Derveran Marti's

room, he told himself that it did not matter. Now he *was* Derveran Marti, Testee. And once he had taken and passed the Test, what would the loss of a few million credits in baubles matter to him?

Therefore it was with a light heart that the pseudo-Derveran Marti quitted his lodgings the next day and prepared to board the *Star Climber* for the voyage to the World of a Thousand Colors.

The clerk at the desk peered at him sympathetically as he pressed his fingers into the checkout plate, thereby erasing the impress from the doorplate upstairs.

"It was too bad about that old fellow dying on you yesterday, wasn't it, sir? I do hope it won't affect your Test result."

Hollinrede smiled blankly. "It was quite a shock to me when he died so suddenly. But my system has already recovered; I'm ready for the Test."

"Good luck to you, sir," the clerk said as Hollinrede left the hotel and stepped out on the flaring skyramp that led to the waiting ship.

The steward at the passenger hatch was collecting identiplates. Hollinrede handed his over casually. The steward inserted it tip-first in the computer near the door, and motioned for Hollinrede to step within the beam while his specifications were being automatically compared with those on the identiplate.

He waited, tensely. Finally the chattering of the machine stopped and a dry voice said, "Your identity is in order. Testee Derveran Marti. Proceed within."

"That means you're okay," the steward told him. "Yours is Compartment Eleven. It's a luxury job, you know. But you Testees deserve it. Best of luck, sir."

"Thanks," Hollinrede grinned. "I don't doubt I'll need it."

He moved up the ramp and into the ship. Com-

partment Eleven *was* a luxury job; Hollinrede, who
had been a frugal man, whistled in amazement when
he saw it. It was nearly eight feet high and almost
twelve broad, totally private with an opaquer attached to the doorscope. Clinging curtains of ebony
synthoid foam from Ravensmusk VIII had been
draped lovingly over the walls, and the acceleration
couch was trimmed in golden bryozone. The rank
of Testee carried with it privileges that the late
Derveran Marti certainly would never have mus-
tered in private life—nor Jolvar Hollinrede either.

At 1143 the doorscope chimed; Hollinrede leaped
from the soft couch a little too nervously and
transluced the door. A crewman stood outside.

"Everything all right, sir? We blast in seventeen
minutes."

"I'm fine," Hollinrede said. "Can't wait to get
there. How long do you think it'll take?"

"Sorry, sir. Not at liberty to reveal. But I wish
you a pleasant trip, and should you lack for aught
hesitate not to call on me."

Hollinrede smiled at the curiously archaic way
the man had of expressing himself. "Never fear; I'll
not hesitate. Many thanks." He opaqued the doorscope and resumed his seat.

At precisely 1200 the drive-engines of the *Star
Climber* throbbed heavily; the pale green light over
the door of Hollinrede's compartment glowed brightly
for an instant, signaling the approaching blastoff.
He sank down on the acceleration couch to wait.

A moment later came the push of acceleration,
and then, as the gravshields took effect, the 7g
escape force dwindled until Hollinrede felt comfortable again. He increased the angle of the couch in
order to peer out the port.

The world of Niprion was vanishing rapidly in the
background: already it was nothing but a mottled

gray-and-gold ball swimming hazily in a puff of atmosphere. The sprawling metal structure that was the stopover hotel was invisible.

Somewhere back on Niprion, Hollinrede thought, the atoms that once had been Testee Derveran Marti were now feeding the plasma intake of a turbine or heating the inner shell of a reactor.

He let his mind dwell on the forthcoming Test. He knew little about it, really, considering he had been willing to take a man's life for a chance to compete. He knew the Test was administered once every five years to candidates chosen by Galaxywide search. The world where the Test was given was known only as the World of a Thousand Colors, and precisely where this world was no member of the general public was permitted to know.

As for the Test itself, by its very nature it was unknown to the Galaxy. For no winning Testee had ever returned from the World of a Thousand Colors. Some losers returned, their minds carefully wiped clean of any memories of the planet—but the winners never came back.

The Test's nature was unknown; the prize, inconceivable. All anyone knew was that the winners were granted the soul's utmost dream. Upon winning, one neither returned to his home world nor desired to return.

Naturally many men ignored the Test—it was something for "other people" to take part in. But millions, billions throughout the Galaxy competed in the preliminaries. And every five years, six or seven were chosen.

Jolvar Hollinrede was convinced he would succeed in the Test—but he had failed three times running in the preliminaries, and was thus permanently disqualified. The preliminaries were simple; they consisted merely of an intensive mental scanning. A flipflop circuit would flash YES or NO after that.

If YES, there were further scannings, until word was beamed through the Galaxy that the competitors for the year had been chosen.

Hollinrede stared moodily at the blackness of space. He had been eliminated unfairly, he felt; he coveted the unknown prize the Test offered, and felt bitter at having it denied him. When chance had thrown Testee Derveran Marti in his path, Hollinrede had leaped to take advantage of the opportunity.

And now he was on his way.

Surely, he thought, they would allow him to take the Test, even if he were discovered to be an impostor. And once he took it, he knew he would succeed. He had always succeeded in his endeavors. There was no reason for failure now.

Beneath the false mask of Derveran Marti, Hollinrede's face was tensely set. He dreamed of the Test and its winning—and of the end to the long years of wandering and toil.

The voice at the door said, "We're here, Testee Derveran. Please open up."

Hollinrede grunted, pulled himself up from the couch, threw open the door. Three dark-faced spacemen waited there for him.

"Where are we?" he asked nervously. "Is the trip over?"

"We have come to pilot you to the Test planet, sir," one of the spacemen told him. "The *Star Climber* is in orbit around it, but will not make a landing itself. Will you follow us?"

"Very well," Hollinrede said.

They entered a lifeship, a slim gray tube barely thirty meters long, and fastened acceleration cradles. There were no ports. Hollinrede felt enclosed, hemmed in.

The lifeship began to slide noiselessly along the ejection channel, glided the entire length of the *Star Climber*, and burst out into space. A preset orbit was operating. Hollinrede clung to the acceleration cradle as the lifeship spun tightly inward toward a powerful gravitational field not far away.

The ship came to rest. Hollinrede lay motionless, flesh cold with nervousness, teeth chattering.

"Easy does it, sir. Up and out."

They lifted him and gently nudged him through a manifold compression lock. He moved forward on numb feet.

"Best of luck, sir!" an envious voice called behind him.

Then the lock clanged shut, and Hollinrede was on his own.

A riotous blaze of color swept down at him from every point of the compass.

He stood in the midst of what looked like a lunar crater; far in the distance on all sides was the massive upraised fissured surface of a ringwall, and the ground beneath him was barren red-brown rock, crumbling to pumice here and there but bare of vegetation.

In the sky was a solitary sun, a blazing Type A blue-white star. That sun alone was incapable of accounting for this flood of color.

Streamers of every hue seemed to sprout from the rocks, staining the ringwall olive-gray and brilliant cerise and dark, lustrous green. Pigments of every sort bathed the air; now it seemed to glow with currents of luminous pink, now a flaming red, now a pulsing pure white.

His eyes adjusted slowly to the torrent of color. World of a Thousand Colors, they called this place? That was an underestimate. *Hundred thousand. Million. Billion.* Shades and near-shades mingled to form new colors.

"Are you Derveran Marti?" a voice asked.

Startled, Hollinrede looked around. It seemed as if a band of color had spoken: a swirling band of rich brown that spun tirelessly before him.

"Are you Derveran Marti?" the voice repeated, and Hollinrede saw that it had indeed come from the band of brown.

It seemed a desecration to utter the lie here on this world of awesome beauty, and he felt the temptation to claim his true identity. But the time for that was later.

"Yes," he said loudly. "I am Derveran Marti."

"Welcome, Derveran Marti. The Test will soon begin."

"Where?"

"Here."

"Right out here? Just like this?"

"Yes," the band of color replied. "Your fellow competitors are gathering."

Hollinrede narrowed his eyes and peered toward the far reaches of the ringwall. Yes; he saw tiny figures located at great distances from each other along the edge of the crater. One, two, three . . . there were seven all told, including himself. Seven, out of the whole Galaxy!

Each of the other six was attended by a dipping, bobbing blotch of color. Hollinrede noticed a squareshouldered giant from one of the Inner Worlds surrounded by a circlet of violent orange; to his immediate left was a sylphlike female, probably from one of the worlds of Dubhe, wearing only the revealing token garment of her people but shielded from inquisitive eyes by a robe of purest blue light. There were others; Hollinrede wished them well. He knew it was possible for all competitors to win, and now that he was about to attain his long-sought goal he held no malice for anyone. His mind was suffused with pity for the dead Derveran Marti, sacrificed that Jolvar Hollinrede might be in this place at this time.

"Derveran Marti," the voice said, "you have been chosen from among your fellow men to take part in the Test. This is an honor that comes to few; we of this world hope you appreciate the grace that has fallen upon you."

"I do," Hollinrede said humbly.

"We ourselves are winners of the prize you seek," the voice went on. "Some of us are members of the first expedition that found this world, eleven hundred years ago. As you see, life has unlimited duration in our present state of matter. Others of us have come more recently. The band of pale purple moving above you to the left was a winner in the previous competition to this.

"We of the World of a Thousand Colors have a rare gift to offer: total harmony of mind. We exist divorced of body, as a stream of photons only. We live in perfect freedom and eternal delight. Once every five years we find it possible to increase our numbers by adding to our midst such throughout the Galaxy as we feel would desire to share our way of life—and whom we would feel happy to welcome to us."

"You mean," Hollinrede said shakily, "that all these beams of light—were once *people?*"

"They were that—until welcomed into us. Now they are men no more. This is the prize you have come to win."

"I see."

"You are not required to compete. Those who, after reaching our world, decide to remain in the material state, are returned to their home worlds with their memories cleared of what they have been told here and their minds free and happy to the end of their lives. Is this what you wish?"

Hollinrede was silent, letting his dazzled eyes take

in the flamboyant sweep of color that illuminated the harsh, rocky world. Finally he said: "I will stay."

"Good. The Test will shortly begin."

Hollinrede saw the band of brown swoop away from him upward to rejoin its never-still comrades in the sky. He waited, standing stiffly, for something to happen.

Then this is what I killed a man for, he thought. His mind dwelled on the words of the band of brown.

Evidently many hundreds of years ago an exploratory expedition had come upon some unique natural phenomenon here at a far end of the universe. Perhaps it had been an accident, a stumbling into a pool of light perhaps, that had dematerialized them, turned them into bobbing immortal streaks of color. But that had been the beginning.

The entire Test system had been developed to allow others to enter this unique society, to leave the flesh behind and live on as pure energy. Hollinrede's fingers trembled; this was, he saw, something worth killing for!

He could see why some people might turn down the offer—those would be the few who cautiously would prefer to remain corporeal and so returned to their home worlds to live out their span.

But not me!

He faced upward and waited for the Test to begin. His shrewd mind was at the peak of its agility; he was prepared for anything they might throw at him. He wondered if anyone yet had come to the World of a Thousand Colors so determined to succeed.

Probably not. For most, the accolade was the result of luck—a mental scanning that turned up whatever mysterious qualities were acceptable to the people of this world. They did not have to *work* for their nomination. They did not have to kill for it.

But Hollinrede had clawed his way here—and he was determined to succeed.

He waited.

Finally the brown band descended from the mass of lambent color overhead and curled into a tight bowknot before him.

"The test is about to begin, Jolvar Hollinrede."

Use of his own name startled him. In the past week he had so thoroughly associated his identity with that of Derveran Marti that he had scarcely let his actual name drift through his mind.

"So you know," he said.

"We have known since the moment you came. It is unfortunate; we would have wanted Derveran Marti among us. But now that you are here, we will test you on your own merits, Jolvar Hollinrede."

It was just as well that way, he thought. The pretense had to end sooner or later, and he was willing to stand or fall as himself rather than under an assumed identity.

"Advance to the center of the crater, Jolvar Hollinrede," came the command from the brown band.

Leadenly Hollinrede walked forward. Squinting through the mist of color that hazed the view, he saw the other six competitors were doing the same. They would meet at the center.

"The Test is now under way," a new and deeper voice said.

Seven of them. Hollinrede looked around. There was the giant from the Inner World—Fondelfor, he saw now. Next to him, the near-nude sylph of Dubhe, and standing by her side, one diamond-faceted eye glittering in his forehead, a man of Alpheraz VII.

The selectors had cast their nets wide. Hollinrede

saw another Terran, dark of skin and bright of eye; a being of Deneb IX, squat and muscular. The sixth Testee was a squirming globule from Spica's tenth world; the seventh was Jolvar Hollinrede, itinerant; home world, Terra.

Overhead hung a circular diadem of violet light. It explained the terms of the Test.

"Each of you will be awarded a characteristic color. It will project before you into the area you ring. Your object will be to blend your seven colors into one; when you have achieved this, you will be admitted into us."

"May I ask what the purpose of this is?" Hollinrede said coldly.

"The essence of our society is harmony—total harmony among us all, and inner harmony within those groups which were admitted at the same temporal juncture. Naturally if you seven are incapable even of this inner harmony, you will be incapable of the greater harmony of us all—and will be rejected."

Despite the impatient frowns of a few of his fellow contestants, Hollinrede said, "Therefore we're to be judged as a unit? An entity?"

"Yes and no," the voice replied. "And now the Test."

Hollinrede saw to his astonishment a color spurt from his arm and hang hovering before him—a pool of inky blackness deeper in hue than the dark of space. His first reaction was one of shock; then he realized that he could control the color, make it move.

He glanced around. Each of his companions similarly faced a hovering mass of color. The giant of Fondelfor controlled red; the girl of Debhe, orange. The Alpherazian stared into a whirling bowl of deep yellow, the Terran green, the Spican radiant violet, the Denebian pearly gray.

Hollinrede stared at his globe of black. A voice

above him seemed to whisper, *"Marti's color would have been blue. The spectrum has been violated."*

He shrugged away the words and sent his globe of black spinning into the area between the seven contestants ringed in a color. At the same time each of the others directed his particular color inward.

The colors met. They clashed, pinwheeled, seemed to throw off sparks. They began to swirl in a hovering arc of radiance.

Hollinrede waited breathlessly, watching the others. His color of black seemed to stand in opposition to the other six. Red, orange, yellow, green, violet. The pearl-gray of the Denebian seemed to enfold the other colors warmly—all but Hollinrede's. The black hung apart.

To his surprise he saw the Dubhian girl's orange beginning to change hue. The girl herself stood stiffly, eyes closed, her body now bare. Sweat poured down her skin. And her orange hue began to shift toward the gray of the Denebian.

The others were following. One by one, as they achieved control over their Test color. First to follow was the Spican, then the Alpherazian.

Why can't I do that? Hollinrede thought wildly.

He strained to alter the color of his black, but it remained unchanged. The others were blending, now, swirling around; there was a predominantly gray cast, but it was not the gray of the Denebian but a different gray tending toward white. Impatiently he redoubled his efforts; it was necessary for the success of the group that he get his obstinate black to blend with the rest.

"The black remains aloof," someone said near him.

"We will fail if the black does not join us."

His streak of color now stood out boldly against the increasing milkiness of the others. None of the original colors were left now but his. Perspiration streamed down him; he realized that his was the only obstacle preventing the seven from passing the test.

"The black still will not join us," a tense voice said.

Another said, "The black is a color of evil."

A third said, "Black is not a color at all. Black is the absence of color; white is the totality of color."

A fourth said, "Black is holding us from the white."

Hollinrede looked from one to the other in mute appeal. Veins stood out on his forehead from the effort, but the black remained unchanging. He could not blend it with the others.

From above came the voice of their examiner, suddenly accusing: "Black is the color of *murder*."

The girl from Dubhe, lilting the ugly words lightly, repeated it. "Black is the color of murder."

"Can we permit a murderer among us?" asked the Denebian.

"The answer is self-evident," said the Spican, indicating the recalcitrant spear of black that marred the otherwise flawless globe of near-white in their midst.

"The murderer must be cast out ere the Test be passed," muttered the giant of Fondelfor. He broke from his position and moved menacingly toward Hollinrede.

"Look!" Hollinrede yelled desperately. "Look at the red!"

The giant's color had split from the gray and now darted wildly toward Hollinrede's black.

"This is the wrong way, then," the giant said, halting. "We must all join in it or we all fail."

"Keep away from me," Hollinrede said. "It's not my fault if—"

Then they were on him—four pairs of hands, two rough claws, two slick tentacles. Hollinrede felt himself being lifted aloft. He squirmed, tried to break from their grasp, but they held him up—

And dashed him down against the harsh rock floor.

He lay there, feeling his life seep out, knowing he had failed—and watched as they returned to form their circle once again. The black winked out of being.

As his eyes started to close, Hollinrede saw the six colors again blend into one. Now that the murderer had been cast from their midst, nothing barred the path of their harmony. Pearly gray shifted to purest white—the totality of color—and as the six merged into one, Hollinrede, with his dying glance, bitterly saw them take leave forever of their bodies and slip upward to join their brothers hovering brightly above.

LET'S BE FRANK

BY BRIAN W. ALDISS (1925–)

SCIENCE FICTION (GREAT BRITAIN)
JUNE

Brian W. Aldiss began publishing science fiction in 1954 and quickly emerged as one of the field's great innovators, stylists, and critics. We will be meeting him again and again as this series moves through the years.

I've always been tempted to write long headnotes for very short stories, but frankly, I'm not going to do it in this case. (MHG)

It's always a pleasure to read a story that doesn't fall into an easy classification.

This starts in the reign of England's Henry VIII (very popular in his time but one of the least-admired English monarchs now) and is only partly finished at the present time. It keeps on going.

It is an impossible story scientifically speaking, but it makes a weird kind of sense with a socko last paragraph. And do take another look at the title when you're done. (IA)

Four years after pretty little Anne Boleyn was executed in the Tower of London, a child was born into the Gladwebb family—an unusual child.

That morning, four people stood waiting in the draughty antechamber to milady's bedroom, where the confinement was taking place—her mother, an aunt, a sister-in-law and a page. The husband, young Sir Frank Gladwebb, was not present; he was out hunting. At length the midwife bustled out to the four in the antechamber and announced that the Almighty (who had recently become a Protestant) had seen fit to bless milady with a son.

"Why, then, do we not hear the child crying, woman?" milady's mother, Cynthia Chinfont St. Giles, demanded, striding into the room to her daughter. There the reason for the child's silence became obvious: it was asleep.

It remained in the "sleep" for nineteen years.

Young Sir Frank was not a patient man; he suffered, in an ambitious age, from ambition, and anything which stood between him and his advancement got short shrift. Returning from the hunt to find his first-born comatose, he was not pleased. The situation, however, was remedied by the birth of a second son in the next year, and of three more children in the four years thereafter. All of these offspring were excessively normal, the boy taking Holy Orders and becoming eventually the Abbot of St. Duckwirt, where simony supplemented an already generous income.

The sleeping child grew as it slept. It stirred in its sleep, sometimes it yawned, it accepted the bottle. Sir Frank kept it in an obscure room in the manor, appointing an old harridan called Nan to attend it. In moments of rage, or when he was in his cups, Sir Frank would swear to run a sword through the child; yet the words were idle, as those about him soon perceived. There was a strange bond between Sir Frank and the sleeping child. Though he visited it rarely, he never forgot it.

On the child's third birthday, he went up to see

it. It lay in the center of a four-poster, its face calm. With an impulse of tenderness, Sir Frank picked it up, cradling it, limp and helpless in his arms.

"It's a lovely lad, sire," Nan commented. And at that moment the sleeping child opened its eyes and appeared to focus them on its father. With a cry, Sir Frank staggered back dizzily, overwhelmed by an indescribable sensation. He sprawled on the bed, holding the child tightly to keep it from harm. When the giddy feeling had gone, he looked and found the child's eyes shut again, and so they remained for a long time.

The Tudor springs and winters passed, the sleeping child experiencing none of them. He grew to be a handsome young boy, and a manservant was engaged for him; still his eyes never opened, except on the rare occasions when his father—now engrossed in the affairs of court—came to see him. Because of the weakness which took him at these times, Sir Frank saw to it that they were few.

Good King Harry died, the succession passed to women and weaklings, Sir Frank came under the patronage of Robert Devereaux, Earl of Essex. And in the year of the coronation of Elizabeth, the sleeping child awoke.

Sir Frank, now a prosperous forty-one, had gone in to see his first-born for the first time in thirty months. On the four-poster lay a handsome, pale youth of nineteen, his straggling growth of beard the very shade of his father's more luxuriant crop. The manservant was out of the room.

Strangely perturbed, as if something inexpressible lay just below the surface of his thoughts, Sir Frank went over to the bed and rested his hands on the boy's shoulders. He seemed to stand on the brink of a precipice.

"Frank," he whispered—for the sleeping child

had been given his own name—"Frank, why don't you wake up?"

In answer to the words, the youth's eyes opened. The usual wash of dizziness came and went like a flash; Sir Frank found himself looking up into his own eyes.

He found more than that.

He found he was a youth of nineteen whose soul had been submerged until now. He found he could sit up, stretch, run a hand marveling through his hair and exclaim, "By our Lady!" He found he could get up, look long at the green world beyond his window and finally turn back to stare at himself.

And all the while "himself" had watched the performance with his own eyes. Shaking, father and son sat down together on the bed.

"What sorcery is this?" Sir Frank muttered.

But it was no sorcery, or not in the sense Sir Frank meant. He had merely acquired an additional body for his ego. It was not that he could be in either as he pleased; he was in both at the same time. When the son came finally to consciousness, it was to his father's consciousness.

Warily, experimenting that day and the next few days—when the whole household rejoiced at this awakening of the first-born—Sir Frank found that his new body could do all he could do: could ride, could fence, could make love to a kitchen wench: could indeed do these things better than the old body, which was beginning, just a little, to become less pliant under approaching middle age. His experience, his knowledge, all were resources equally at the command of either body. He was, in fact, two people.

A later generation could have explained the miracle to Sir Frank—though explaining in terms he would not have understood. Though he knew well enough the theory of family traits and likeness, it would have been impossible then to make him comprehend the intricacy of a chromosome which carries inside it—not merely the stereotypes of parental hair or temperament—but the secret knowledge of how to breathe, how to work the muscles to move the bones, how to grow, how to remember, how to commence the process of thought . . . all the infinite number of secret "how to's" that have to be passed on for life to stay above jelly level.

A freak chromosome in Sir Frank ensured he passed on, together with these usual secrets, the secret of his individual consciousness.

It was extraordinary to be in two places at once, doing two different things—extraordinary, but not confusing. He merely had two bodies which were as integrated as his two hands had been.

Frank II had a wonderful time; youth and experience, foresight and a fresh complexion, were united as never before. The combination was irresistible. The Virgin Queen, then in her late twenties, summoned him before her and sighed deeply. Then, catching Essex's eye, she put him out of reach of temptation by sending him off to serve the ambassador at the court of her brother-in-law, Philip.

Frank II liked Spain. Philip's capital was gayer, warmer and more sanitary than London. It was intoxicating to enjoy the best of both courts. It proved also extremely remunerative: the shared consciousness of Frank I and II was by far the quickest communicational link between the two rival countries, and as such was worth money. Not that Frank revealed his secret to a soul, but he let it be known he had a fleet of capable spies who moved without risk of detection between England and Spain. Burly Lord Burleigh beamed upon him. So did the Duke of Medina Sidonia.

So fascinating was it being two people at once,

that Frank I was slow to take any systematic survey
of other lurking advantages. An unfortunate tumble
from a horse, however, gave him leisure for medita-
tion. Even then, he might have missed the vital
point, were it not for something that happened in
Madrid.

Frank III was born.

Frank II had passed on the renegade chromosome via a little Spanish courtesan. The child was
called Sancha. There was no coma about him! As if
to defy the extreme secrecy under which the birth
took place, he wailed lustily from the start. And he
had the shared consciousness of his father and
grandfather.

It was an odd feeling indeed, opening this new
annex to life and experiencing the world through all
the child's weakness and helplessness. There were
many frustrations for Frank I, but compensations
too—not the least being closeted so intimately with
the babe's delightful mother.

The birth made Frank realize one striking, blinding fact: as long as the chromosome reproduced
itself in sufficient dominance, he was immortal! To
him, in an unscientific age, the problem did not
present itself quite like that; but he realized that
here was a trait to be kept in the family.

It happened that Frank had married one of his
daughters off to an architect called Tanyk. This
union produced a baby daughter some two weeks
after the secret birth of Frank III (they hardly thought
of him as Sancha). Frank I and II arranged that III
should come to England and marry Miss Tanyk just
as soon as both were old enough; the vital chromosome ought to be latent in her and appear in her
children.

Relations between England and Spain deteriorat-
ing, Frank II came home shortly with the boy Frank

III acting as his page. The fruits of several other liaisons had to be left behind with their mothers; they had no shared consciousness, only ordinary good red English blood.

Frank II had been back in the aptly named Mother Country for only a few months when a lady of his acquaintance presented him with Frank IV. Frank IV was a girl, christened Berenice. The state of coma which had ensnared Frank II for so long did not afflict Berenice, or any other of his descendants.

Another tremendous adjustment in the shared consciousness had to be made. That also had its conpensations; Frank was the first man ever relly to appreciate the woman's point of view.

So the eventful years rolled on. Sir Frank's wife died; the Abbey of St. Duckwirt flourished; Frank II sailed over to Hispaniola; the Armada sailed against England and was repulsed. And in the next year, Frank III (Sancha), with his Spanish looks and English money, won the hand of Rosalynd Tanyk, as prearranged. When his father returned from the New World (with his English looks and Spanish money), it was in time to see in person his daughter, Berenice, alias Frank IV, also taken in wedlock.

By this year, Frank I was old and gray and retired in the country. While he was experiencing old age in that body, he was experiencing active middle age in his son's and the delights of matrimony in his grandson's and granddaughter's.

He awaited anxiously the issue of Frank III (Sancha)'s marriage to his cousin Rosalynd. There were offspring enough. One in 1590. Twins in 1591. Three lovely children—but, alas, ordinary mortals, without shared consciousness. Then, while watching an indifferent and bloody play called "Titus Andronicus," two years later, Rosalynd came into la-

bor, and was delivered—at a tavern in Cheapside—of
Frank V.

In the succeeding years, she delivered Franks VI
and VIII. Frank VII sprang from Berenice (Frank
IV)'s union. So did Frank IX. The freak chromosome was getting into its stride.

Full of years, Sir Frank's body died. The diphthe-
ria which carried him off caused him as much suf-
fering as it would have done an ordinary man; dying
was not eased by his unique gift. He slid out into
the long darkness—but his consciousness continued
unabated in eight other bodies.

It would be pleasant to follow the history of these
Franks (who, of course, really bore different sur-
names and Christian names): but space forbids. Suf-
fice it to say that there were vicissitudes—the old
queen shut Frank II in the Tower, Frank VI had a
dose of the clap, Frank IX ruined himself trying to
grow asparagus, then newly discovered from Asia.
Despite this, the shared consciousness spread; the
five who shared it in this third generation prospered
and produced children with the same ability.

The numbers grew. Twelve in the fourth generation, twenty-two in the fifth, fifty in the sixth, and
in the seventh, by the time William and Mary came
to the throne, one hundred and twenty-four.

These people, scattered all over the country, a
few of them on the continent, were much like normal people. To outsiders, their relationship was not
apparent; they certainly never revealed it; they never
met. They became traders, captains of ships that
traded with the Indies, soldiers, parliamentarians,
agriculturalists; some plunged into, some avoided,
the constitutional struggles that dogged most of the
seventeenth century. But they were all—male or
female—Franks. They had the inexpressible benefit
of their progenitor's one hundred and seventy-odd

years' experience, and not only of his, but of all the other Franks. It was small wonder that, with few exceptions, whatever they did they prospered.

By the time George III came to the throne and rebellion broke out in the British colonies in America the tenth generation of Franks numbered 2,160.

The ambition of the original Frank had not died; it had grown subtler. It had become a wish to sample everything. The more bodily habitations there were with which to sample, the more tantalizing the idea seemed: for many experiences, belonging only to one brief era, are never repeated, and may be gone before they are perceived and tasted.

Such an era was the Edwardian decade from 1901 to 1911. It suited Frank's Elizabethan spirit, with its bounce and vulgarity and the London streets packed tight with horse vehicles. His manifestations prospered; by the outbreak of World War I they numbered over three and a half million.

The war, whose effect on the outlook and technology of the whole world was to be incalculable, had a terrific influence on the wide-spread shared consciousness of Frank. Many Franks of the sixteenth generation were killed in the muck of the trenches, he died not once but many times, developing an obsessive dread of war which never left him.

By the time the Americans entered the war, he was turning his many thoughts to politics.

It was not an easy job. Until now, he had concentrated on diversity in occupations, savoring them all. He rode the fiery horses of the Camargue; he played in the orchestras of La Scala, Milan; he farmed daffodils in the Scilly Isles; he built dikes along the Zuyder Zee; filmed with Réné Clair; preached in Vienna cathedral; operated in Bart's; fished in the bilious Bay of Biscay; argued with the founder of the Bauhaus. Now he turned the members of his consciousness among the rising generation into official posts, compensating for the sameness and grayness of their jobs with the thought that the change was temporary.

His plans had not gone far enough before the Second World War broke out. His consciousness, spread over eleven million people, suffered from Plymouth and Guernsey to Siam and Hong Kong. It was too much. By the time the war ended, world domination had become his aim.

Frank's chromosome was now breeding as true as ever. Blood group, creed, color of skin—nothing was proof against it. The numbers with shared consciousness, procreating for all they were worth, trebled with every generation.

Seventeenth generation: eleven millions in 1940.

Eighteenth generation: thirty-three millions in 1965.

Nineteenth generation: a hundred million in 1990.

Twentieth generation: three hundred million in 2015.

Frank was well placed to stand as Member of Parliament, for all his alter egos could vote for him. He stood as several members, one of whom eventually became Prime Minister; but the intricacies of office proved a dismal job. There was, after all, a simpler and far more thorough way of ruling the country: by simple multiplication.

At this task, all the Franks set to with a will.

By the beginning of the twenty-first century, Great Britain consisted only of Franks. Like a great multiplicity of mirrors, they faced each other across counter and club; young or old, fat or thin, rich or poor, all shared one massive consciousness.

Many modifications in private and public life took place. Privacy ceasing to exist, all new houses were glass-built, curtains abolished, walls pulled down. Police went, the entire legal structure vanished overnight—a man does not litigate against himself. A parody of Parliament remained, to deal with foreign affairs, but party politics, elections, leaders in newspapers (even newspapers themselves) were scrapped.

Most of the arts went. One manifestation of Frank did not care to see another manifestation of Frank performing. TV, publishing, Tin Pan Alley, film studios . . . out like lights.

The surplus Franks, freed from all these dead enterprises and many more, went abroad to beget more Franks.

All these radical changes in the habits of the proverbially conservative British were noticed elsewhere, particularly by the Americans and Canadians. They sent observers over to report on the scene.

Before long, the same radical changes were sweeping Europe. Frank's chromosome conquered everywhere. Peace was guaranteed.

By the end of another century's ruthless intermarriage, Russia and Asia were engulfed as thoroughly as Europe, and by the same loving methods. Billions of people: one consciousness.

And then came Frank's first set-back in all the centuries of his polydextrous existence. He turned his reproductive powers toward the Americas. He was repulsed.

From Argentine to Alaska, and all ports in between, the conqueror chromosome failed to conquer.

The massive, massed intellect set itself to work on the problem, soon arriving at the answer. Another chromosome had got there first. Evidence of the truth of this came when the drastic modifications in domestic and public life which had swept the rest of the world swept the linked continents of

North and South America. There was a second shared consciousness.

By various deductions, Frank concluded that the long-dead Frank II's visit to Hispaniola had scattered some of the vital chromosome there. Not properly stable at that time, it had developed its own separate shared consciousness, which had spread through the Americas much as the Frank chromosome had spread around the rest of the world.

It was a difficult situation. The Franks and the Hispaniolas shared the globe without speaking to each other. After a decade of debate, the Franks took an obvious way out of the impasse: they built themselves a fleet of space ships and headed into the solar system.

That, ladies, gentlemen and neuters, is a brief account of the extraordinary race which recently landed on our planet, Venus, as they call it. I think we may congratulate ourselves that our method of perpetuating our species is so vastly different from theirs; nothing else could have saved us from that insidious form of conquest.

THE CAGE

BY A. BERTRAM CHANDLER (1912–1984)

THE MAGAZINE OF FANTASY AND SCIENCE FICTION
JUNE

*The late Australian Ship's Master and action-adventure
science fiction writer returns to this series (see his
wonderful "Giant Killer" in our 1945 volume) with
his finest story. Now don't peek, but for my money
"The Cage" has one of the finest last lines in the
history of the short story.*

*Chandler has always been a bit of a problem for
me—the two above mentioned stories show what excellent work he was capable of, a level he simply
never reached with the bulk of his work, which is
rapidly fading from print. Nevertheless, this story
contains that wonderful flash of insight that charac-
terizes science fiction at its best, a flash that struck
this then sixteen-year-old reader like a bullet in the
late spring of 1957. (MHG)*

This is another puzzle story. (I told you I like them.)

*"The Cage" also demonstrates another interesting
point about science fiction. Science fiction, by allowing you to discuss a situation that does not and
cannot occur in "straight" fiction, also allows you to
make a point very neatly and powerfully that cannot
be made so clearly otherwise.*

It is a sardonic point that you won't forget in a hurry—if ever. And it is something that is worth thinking about.

Oh, before I forget—I have said at times that the best kind of title a story can have is one that clearly refers to something about the story in a straightforward and unmistakable manner. And then, when you are done with the story and happen to note the title again, it suddenly means something else. It's just beautiful when it's done well. (IA)

Imprisonment is always a humiliating experience, no matter how philosophical the prisoner. Imprisonment by one's own kind is bad enough—but one can, at least, talk to one's captors, one can make one's wants understood; one can, on occasion, appeal to them man to man.

Imprisonment is doubly humiliating when one's captors in all honesty, treat one as a lower animal.

The party from the survey ship could, perhaps, be excused for failing to recognize the survivors from the interstellar liner *Lode Star* as rational beings. At least two hundred days had passed since their landing on the planet without a name—an unintentional landing made when *Lode Star*'s Ehrenhaft generators, driven far in excess of their normal capacity by a breakdown of the electronic regulator, had flung her far from the regular shipping lanes to an unexplored region of Space. *Lode Star* had landed safely enough; but shortly thereafter (troubles never come singly) her Pile had got out of control and her Captain had ordered his First Mate to evacuate the passengers and such crew members not needed to cope with the emergency, and to get them as far from the ship as possible.

Hawkins and his charges were well clear when there was a flare of released energy, a not very violent explosion. The survivors wanted to turn to watch, but Hawkins drove them on with curses and, at times, blows. Luckily they were up wind from the ship and so escaped the fall-out.

When the fireworks seemed to be over Hawkins, accompanied by Dr. Boyle, the ship's surgeon, returned to the scene of the disaster. The two men, wary of radioactivity, were cautious and stayed a safe distance from the shallow, still smoking crater that marked where the ship had been. It was all too obvious to them that the Captain, together with his officers and technicians, was now no more than an infinitesimal part of the incandescent cloud that had mushroomed up into the low overcast.

Thereafter the fifty-odd men and women, the survivors of *Lode Star,* had degenerated. It hadn't been a fast process—Hawkins and Boyle, aided by a committee of the more responsible passengers, had fought a stout rearguard action. But it had been a hopeless sort of fight. The climate was against them, for a start. Hot it was, always in the neighborhood of 85° Fahrenheit. And it was wet—a thin, warm drizzle falling all the time. The air seemed to abound with the spores of fungi—luckily these did not attack living skin but throve on dead organic matter, on clothing. They throve to an only slightly lesser degree on metals and on the synthetic fabrics that many of the castaways wore.

Danger, outside danger, would have helped to maintain morale. But there were no dangerous animals. There were only little smooth-skinned things, not unlike frogs, that hopped through the sodden undergrowth, and, in the numerous rivers, fishlike creatures ranging in size from the shark to the tadpole, and all of them possessing the bellicosity of the latter.

Food had been no problem after the first few hungry hours. Volunteers had tried a large, succulent fungus growing on the boles of the huge fernlike trees. They had pronounced it good. After a lapse of five hours they had neither died nor even complained of abdominal pains. That fungus was to become the staple diet of the castaways. In the weeks that followed other fungi had been found, and berries, and roots—all of them edible. They provided a welcome variety.

Fire—in spite of the all-pervading heat—was the blessing most missed by the castaways. With it they could have supplemented their diet by catching and cooking the little frog-things of the rain forest, the fishes of the streams. Some of the hardier spirits did eat these animals raw, but they were frowned upon by most of the other members of the community. Too, fire would have helped to drive back the darkness of the long nights, would, by its real warmth and light, have dispelled the illusion of cold produced by the ceaseless dripping of water from every leaf and frond.

When they fled from the ship most of the survivors had possessed pocket lighters—but the lighters had been lost when the pockets, together with the clothing surrounding them, had disintegrated. In any case, all attempts to start a fire in the days when there were still pocket lighters had failed— there was not, Hawkins swore, a single dry spot on the whole accursed planet. Now the making of fire was quite impossible: even if there had been present an expert on the rubbing together of two dry sticks he could have found no material with which to work.

They made their permanent settlement on the crest of a low hill. (There were, so far as they could discover, no mountains.) It was less thickly wooded there than the surrounding plains, and the ground was less marshy underfoot. They succeeded in wrenching fronds from the fernlike trees and built for themselves crude shelters—more for the sake of privacy than for any comfort that they afforded. They clung, with a certain desperation, to the governmental forms of the worlds that they had left, and elected themselves a council. Boyle, the ship's surgeon, was their chief. Hawkins, rather to his surprise, was returned as a council member by a majority of only two votes—on thinking it over he realized that many of the passengers must still bear a grudge against the ship's executive staff for their present predicament.

The first council meeting was held in a hut—if so it could be called—especially constructed for the purpose. The council members squatted in a rough circle. Boyle, the president, got slowly to his feet. Hawkins grinned wryly as he compared the surgeon's nudity with the pomposity that he seemed to have assumed with his elected rank, as he compared the man's dignity with the unkempt appearance presented by his uncut, uncombed gray hair, his uncombed and straggling gray beard.

"Ladies and gentlemen," began Boyle.

Hawkins looked around him at the naked, pallid bodies, at the stringy, lusterless hair, the long, dirty fingernails of the men and the unpainted lips of the women. He thought, I don't suppose I look much like an officer and a gentleman myself.

"Ladies and gentlemen," said Boyle, "we have been, as you know, elected to represent the human community upon this planet. I suggest that at this, our first meeting, we discuss our chances of survival— not as individuals, but as a race—"

"I'd like to ask Mr. Hawkins what our chances are of being picked up," shouted one of the two women members, a dried-up, spinsterish creature with prominent ribs and vertebrae.

"Slim," said Hawkins. "As you know, no communication is possible with other ships, or with planet stations when the Interstellar Drive is operating. When we snapped out of the Drive and came in for our landing we sent out a distress call—but we couldn't say where we were. Furthermore, we don't know that the call was received—"

"Miss Taylor," said Boyle huffily, "Mr. Hawkins, I would remind you that I am the duly elected president of this council. There will be time for a general discussion later.

"As most of you may already have assumed, the age of this planet, biologically speaking, corresponds roughly with that of Earth during the Carboniferous Era. As we already know, no species yet exists to challenge our supremacy. By the time such a species does emerge—something analogous to the giant lizards of Earth's Triassic Era—we should be well established—"

"*We* shall be dead!" called one of the men.

"We shall be dead," agreed the doctor, "but our descendants will be very much alive. We have to decide how to give them as good a start as possible. Language we shall bequeath to them—"

"Never mind the language, Doc," called the other woman member. She was a small blonde, slim, with a hard face. "It's just this question of descendants that I'm here to look after. I represent the women of childbearing age—there are, as you must know, fifteen of us here. So far the girls have been very, very careful. We have reason to be. Can you, as a medical man, guarantee—bearing in mind that you have no drugs, no instruments—safe deliveries? Can you guarantee that our children will have a good chance of survival?"

Boyle dropped his pomposity like a worn-out garment.

"I'll be frank," he said. "I have not, as you, Miss Hart, have pointed out, either drugs or instruments. But I can assure you, Miss Hart, that your chances of a safe delivery are far better than they would have been on Earth during, say, the Eighteenth Century. And I'll tell you why. On this planet, so far as we know (and we have been here long enough now to find out the hard way), there exist no microorganisms harmful to Man. Did such organisms exist, the bodies of those of us still surviving would be, by this time, mere masses of suppuration. Most of us, of course, would have died of septicemia long ago. And that, I think, answers *both* of your questions."

"I haven't finished yet," she said. "Here's another point. There are fifty-three of us here, men and women. There are ten married couples—so we'll count them out. That leaves thirty-three people, of whom twenty are men. Twenty men to thirteen (aren't we girls always unlucky?) women. All of us aren't young—but we're all of us women. What sort of marriage set-up do we have? Monogamy? Polyandry?"

"Monogamy, of course," said a tall, thin man sharply. He was the only one of those present who wore clothing—if so it could be called. The disintegrating fronds lashed around his waist with a strand of vine did little to serve any useful purpose.

"All right, then," said the girl. "Monogamy. I'd rather prefer it that way myself. But I warn you that if that's the way we play it there's going to be trouble. And in any murder involving passion and jealousy the woman is as liable to be a victim as either of the men—and I don't want *that*."

"What do you propose, then, Miss Hart?" asked Boyle.

"Just this, Doc. When it comes to our matings we leave love out of it. If two men want to marry the same woman, then let them fight it out. The best man gets the girl—and keeps her."

"Natural selection . . ." murmured the surgeon. "I'm in favor—but we must put it to the vote."

*   *   *

At the crest of the low hill was a shallow depression, a natural arena. Round the rim sat the castaways—all but four of them. One of the four was Dr. Boyle—he had discovered that his duties as president embraced those of a referee; it had been held that he was best competent to judge when one of the contestants was liable to suffer permanent damage. Another of the four was the girl Mary Hart. She had found a serrated twig with which to comb her long hair, she had contrived a wreath of yellow flowers with which to crown the victor. Was it, wondered Hawkins as he sat with the other council members, a hankering after an Earthy wedding ceremony, or was it a harking back to something older and darker?

"A pity that those blasted molds got our watches," said the fat man on Hawkins' right. "If we had any means of telling the time we could have rounds, make a proper prizefight of it."

Hawkins nodded. He looked at the four in the center of the arena—at the strutting, barbaric woman, at the pompous old man, at the two dark-bearded young men with their glistening white bodies. He knew them both—Fennet had been a Senior Cadet of the ill-fated *Lode Star;* Clemens, at least seven years Fennet's senior, was a passenger, had been a prospector on the frontier worlds.

"If we had anything to bet with," said the fat man happily, "I'd lay it on Clemens. That cadet of yours hasn't a snowball's chance in hell. He's been brought up to fight clean—Clemens has been brought up to fight dirty."

"Fennet's in better condition," said Hawkins. "He's been taking exercise, while Clemens has just been lying around sleeping and eating. Look at the paunch on him!"

"There's nothing wrong with good, healthy flesh

and muscle," said the fat man, patting his own paunch.

"No gouging, no biting!" called the doctor. "And may the best man win!"

He stepped back smartly away from the contestants, stood with the Hart woman.

There was an air of embarrassment about the pair of them as they stood there, each with his fists hanging at his sides. Each seemed to be regretting that matters had come to such a pass.

"Go *on!*" screamed Mary Hart at last. "Don't you want me? You'll live to a ripe old age here— and it'll be lonely with no woman!"

"They can always wait around until your daughters grow up, Mary!" shouted one of her friends.

"If I ever have any daughters!" she called. "I shan't at this rate!"

"Go on!" shouted the crowd. "Go on!"

Fennet made a start. He stepped forward almost diffidently, dabbed with his right fist at Clemens' unprotected face. It wasn't a hard blow, but it must have been painful. Clemens put his hand up to his nose, brought it away and stared at the bright blood staining it. He growled, lumbered forward with arms open to hug and crush. The cadet danced back, scoring twice more with his right.

"Why doesn't he *hit* him?" demanded the fat man.

"And break every bone in his fist? They aren't wearing gloves, you know," said Hawkins.

Fennet decided to make a stand. He stood firm, his feet slightly apart, and brought his right into play once more. This time he left his opponent's face alone, went for his belly instead. Hawkins was surprised to see that the prospector was taking the blows with apparent equanimity—he must be, he decided, much tougher in actuality than in appearance.

The cadet sidestepped smartly . . . and slipped on the wet grass. Clemens fell heavily on to his opponent; Hawkins could hear the *whoosh* as the air was forced from the lad's lungs. The prospector's thick arms encircled Fennet's body—and Fennet's knee came up viciously to Clemens' groin. The prospector squealed, but hung on grimly. One of his hands was around Fennet's throat now, and the other one, its fingers viciously hooked, was clawing for the cadet's eyes.

"No gouging!" Boyle was screaming. "No gouging!"

He dropped down to his knees, caught Clemens' thick wrist with both his hands.

Something made Hawkins look up then. It may have been a sound, although this is doubtful; the spectators were behaving like boxing fans at a prizefight. They could hardly be blamed—this was the first piece of real excitement that had come their way since the loss of the ship. It may have been a sound that made Hawkins look up, it may have been the sixth sense possessed by all good spacemen. What he saw made him cry out.

Hovering above the arena was a helicopter. There was something about the design of it, a subtle oddness, that told Hawkins that this was no Earthy machine. Suddenly, from its smooth, shining belly, dropped a net, seemingly of full metal. It enveloped the struggling figures on the ground, trapped the doctor and Mary Hart.

Hawkins shouted again—a wordless cry. He jumped to his feet, ran to the assistance of his ensnared companions. The net seemed to be alive. It twisted itself around his wrists, bound his ankles. Others of the castaways rushed to aid Hawkins.

"Keep away!" he shouted. "Scatter!"

The low drone of the helicopter's rotors rose in pitch. The machine lifted. In an incredibly short space of time the arena was to the First Mate's eyes no more than a pale green saucer in which little white ants scurried aimlessly. Then the flying machine was above and through the base of the low clouds, and there was nothing to be seen but drifting whiteness.

When, at last, it made its descent Hawkins was not surprised to see the silvery tower of a great spaceship standing among the low trees on a level plateau.

The world to which they were taken would have been a marked improvement on the world they had left had it not been for the mistaken kindness of their captors. The cage in which the three men housed duplicated, with remarkable fidelity, the climatic conditions of the planet upon which *Lode Star* had been lost. It was glassed in, and from sprinklers in its roof fell a steady drizzle of warm water. A couple of dispirited tree ferns provided little shelter from the depressing precipitation. Twice a day a hatch at the back of the cage, which was made of a sort of concrete, opened, and slabs of a fungus remarkably similar to that on which they had been subsisting were thrown in. There was a hole in the floor of the cage; this the prisoners rightly assumed was for sanitary purposes.

On either side of them were other cages. In one of them was Mary Hart—alone. She could gesture to them, wave to them, and that was all. The cage on the other side held a beast built on the same general lines as a lobster, but with a strong hint of squid. Across the broad roadway they could see other cages, but could not see what they housed.

Hawkins, Boyle and Fennet sat on the damp floor and stared through the thick glass and the bars at the beings outside who stared at them.

"If only they were humanoid," sighed the doctor.

"If only they were the same shape as we are we might make a start towards convincing them that we, too, are intelligent beings."

"They aren't the same shape," said Hawkins. "And we, were the situations reversed, would take some convincing that three six-legged beer barrels were men and brothers. . . . Try Pythagoras' Theorem again," he said to the cadet.

Without enthusiasm the youth broke fronds from the nearest tree fern. He broke them into smaller pieces, then on the mossy floor laid them out in the design of a right-angled triangle with squares constructed on all three sides. The natives—a large one, one slightly smaller and a little one—regarded him incuriously with their flat, dull eyes. The large one put the tip of a tentacle into a pocket—the things wore clothing—and pulled out a brightly colored packet, handed it to the little one. The little one tore off the wrapping, started stuffing pieces of some bright blue confection into the slot on its upper side that, obviously, served it as a mouth.

"I wish they were allowed to feed the animals," sighed Hawkins. "I'm sick of that damned fungus."

"Let's recapitulate," said the doctor. "After all, we've nothing else to do. We were taken from our camp by the helicopter—six of us. We were taken to the survey ship—a vessel that seemed in no way superior to our own interstellar ships. You assure us, Hawkins, that the ship used the Ehrenhaft Drive or something so near to it as to be its twin brother . . ."

"Correct," agreed Hawkins.

"On the ship we're kept in separate cages. There's no ill treatment, we're fed and watered at frequent intervals. We land on this strange planet, but we see nothing of it. We're hustled out of cages like so many cattle into a covered van. We know that we're being driven *somewhere,* that's all. The van stops, the door opens and a couple of those animated beer barrels poke in poles with smaller editions of those fancy nets on the end of them. They catch Clemens and Miss Taylor, drag them out. We never see them again. The rest of us spend the night and following day and night in individual cages. The next day we're taken to this . . . zoo . . ."

"Do you think they were vivisected?" asked Fennet. "I never liked Clemens, but . . ."

"I'm afraid they were," said Boyle. "Our captors must have learned of the difference between the sexes by it. Unluckily there's no way of determining intelligence by vivisection—"

"The filthy brutes!" shouted the cadet.

"Easy, son," counseled Hawkins. "You can't blame them, you know. We've vivisected animals a lot more like us than we are to these things."

"The problem," the doctor went on, "is to convince these things—as you call them, Hawkins—that we are rational beings like themselves. How would they define a rational beings? How would *we* define a rational being?"

"Somebody who knows Pythagoras' Theorem," said the cadet sulkily.

"I read somewhere," said Hawkins, "that the history of Man is the history of the fire-making, tool-using animal . . ."

"Then make fire," suggested the doctor. "Make us some tools, and use them."

"Don't be silly. You know that there's not an artifact among the bunch of us. No false teeth even— not even a metal filling. Even so . . ." He paused. "When I was a youngster there was, among the cadets in the interstellar ships, a revival of the old arts and crafts. We considered ourselves in a direct line of descent from the old windjammer sailormen, so we learned how to splice rope and wire, how to make sennit and fancy knots and all the rest of it.

Then one of us hit on the idea of basketmaking. We were in a passenger ship, and we used to make our baskets secretly, daub them with violent colors and then sell them to passengers as genuine souvenirs from the Lost Planet of Arcturus VI. There was a most distressing scene when the Old Man and the Mate found out . . ."

"What are you driving at?" asked the doctor.

"Just this. We will demonstrate our manual dexterity by the weaving of baskets—I'll teach you how."

"It might work. . . ." said Boyle slowly. "It might just work. . . . On the other hand, don't forget that certain birds and animals do the same sort of thing. On Earth there's the beaver, who builds quite cunning dams. There's the bower bird, who makes a bower for his mate as part of the courtship ritual . . ."

The Head Keeper must have known of creatures whose courting habits resembled those of the Terran bower bird. After three days of feverish basketmaking, which consumed all the bedding and stripped the tree ferns, Mary Hart was taken from her cage and put in with the three men. After she had got over her hysterical pleasure at having somebody to talk to again she was rather indignant.

It was good, thought Hawkins drowsily, to have Mary with them. A few more days of solitary confinement must surely have driven the girl crazy. Even so, having Mary in the same cage had its drawbacks. He had to keep a watchful eye on young Fennet. He even had to keep a watchful eye on Boyle—the old goat!

Mary screamed.

Hawkins jerked into complete wakefulness. He could see the pale form of Mary—on this world it was never completely dark at night—and, on the other side of the cage, the forms of Fennet and

Boyle. He got hastily to his feet, stumbled to the girl's side.

"What is it?" he asked.

"I . . . I don't know . . . Something small, with sharp claws . . . It ran over me . . ."

"Oh," said Hawkins, "that was only Joe."

"*Joe?*" she demanded.

"I don't know exactly what he—or she—is," said the man.

"I think he's definitely *he,*" said the doctor.

"What is Joe?" she asked again.

"He must be the local equivalent to a mouse," said the doctor, "although he looks nothing like one. He comes up through the floor somewhere to look for scraps of food. We're trying to tame him—"

"You encourage the brute?" she screamed. "I demand that you do something about him—at once! Poison him, or trap him. Now!"

"Tomorrow," said Hawkins.

"Now!" she screamed.

"Tomorrow," said Hawkins firmly.

The capture of Joe proved to be easy. Two flat baskets, hinged like the valves of an oyster shell, made the trap. There was bait inside—a large piece of the fungus. There was a cunningly arranged upright that would fall at the least tug at the bait. Hawkins, lying sleepless on his damp bed, heard the tiny click and thud that told him that the trap had been sprung. He heard Joe's indignant chitterings, heard the tiny claws scrabbling at the stout basket-work.

Mary Hart was alseep. He shook her.

"We've caught him," he said.

"Then kill him," she answered drowsily.

But Joe was not killed. The three men were rather attached to him. With the coming of daylight they transferred him to a cage that Hawkins had fashioned. Even the girl relented when she saw the harmless ball of multicolored fur bouncing indignantly up and down in its prison. She insisted on feeding the little animal, exclaimed gleefully when the thin tentacles reached out and took the fragment of fungus from her fingers.

For three days they made much of their pet. On the fourth day beings whom they took to be keepers entered the cage with their nets, immobilized the occupants, and carried off Joe and Hawkins.

"I'm afraid it's hopeless," Boyle said. "He's gone the same way . . ."

"They'll have him stuffed and mounted in some museum," said Fennet glumly.

"No," said the girl. "They couldn't!"

"They could," said the doctor.

Abruptly the hatch at the back of the cage opened.

Before the three humans could retreat to the scant protection supplied by a corner a voice called, "It's all right, come on out!"

Hawkins walked into the cage. He was shaved, and the beginnings of a healthy tan had darkened the pallor of his skin. He was wearing a pair of trunks fashioned from some bright red material.

"Come on out," he said again. "Our hosts have apologized very sincerely, and they have more suitable accommodation prepared for us. Then, as soon as they have a ship ready, we're to go to pick up the other survivors."

"Not so fast," said Boyle. "Put us in the picture, will you? What made them realize that we were rational being?"

Hawkins' face darkened.

"Only rational beings," he said, "put other beings in cages."

THE EDUCATION OF TIGRESS MCCARDLE

BY C. M. KORNBLUTH (1923-1958)

VENTURE SCIENCE FICTION
JULY

Here's a very personal story by the talented Cyril Kornbluth, published during the year before his untimely death at 35 shocked the science fiction world. He remains an underappreciated writer, largely because the bulk of his novels were done in collaboration with Frederik Pohl and Judith Merril, but The Syndic *(1953) and especially the stories contained in* The Best of C. M. Kornbluth *(1976) proved what a true master he was, and give an indication of what he might have become.*

"The Education of Tigress McCardle" was, according to Fred Pohl, most likely written when the Kornbluths lived in a tract house on Long Island, with Cyril writing in the living room with their two kids in a playpen, screaming their heads off—and it shows!

This is the first of two fine stories by him in this volume. (MHG)

Cyril Kornbluth, as Marty has just pointed out and as I wish to emphasize, died about nine months after this story was published—quite prematurely, too, for he was only 35 years old. It was a great loss to the field, for he turned out some great stories in his writing career.

Think of all the subtle points considered and dealt with by Cyril in this one, quite short, story.

There is the matter of the delight of having children, something every parent has found out for himself ever since Eve said to Cain, "By the way, have you seen your kid-brother anywhere?"

There is the problem of how to reduce the birthrate in a society that labors under the constant and growing pressures of overpopulation. Is there any way of humanely persuading people not to have so many children? I'm not sure Cyril's method is humane, to be sure.

And there is a question of world conquest without the necessity of blood and mayhem. It would work better, too, because the conquest would be permanent.

Well, here, the story is all yours. (IA)

With the unanimity that had always characterized his fans, as soon as they were able to vote, they swept him into office as President of the United States. Four years later the 28th Amendment was ratified, republican institutions yielded gracefully to the usages of monarchy, and King Purvis I reigned in the land.

Perhaps even then all would have gone well if it had not been for another major entertainment personage, the insidious Dr. Fu Manchu, that veritable personification of the Yellow Peril, squatting like some great evil spider in the center of his web of intrigue. The insidious doctor appeared to have so much fun on his television series, what with a lovely concubine to paw him and a dwarf to throw knives, that it quite turned the head of Gerald Wang, a hitherto-peaceable antique dealer of San Francisco. Gerald decided that he too would become a veritible personification of the Yellow Peril, and that he too would squat like some great evil spider in the center of a web of intrigue, and that he would *really* accomplish something. He found it remarkably easy since nobody believed in the Yellow Peril any more. He grew a mandarin mustache, took to uttering cryptic quotations from the sages, and was generally addressed as "doctor" by the members of his organization, though he made no attempt to practice medicine. His wife drew the line at the concubine, but Gerald had enough to keep him busy with his personifying and squatting.

His great coup occurred in 1978 when after patient years of squatting and plotting one of his most insidious ideas reached the attention of His Majesty via a recommendation ridered onto the annual population-resources report. The recommendation was implemented as the Parental Qualifications Program, or P.Q.P., by royal edict. "Ow rackon thet'll make um mahnd they P's and Q's," quipped His Majesty, and everybody laughed heartily—but no one more heartily than the insidious Dr. Wang, who was present in disguise as Tuner of the Royal Git-tar.

A typical P.Q.P. operation (at least when judged typical by the professor of Chronoscope History Seminar 201 given by Columbia University in 2756 A.D., who ought to know) involved George Macardle. . . .

George Macardle had a *good* deal with his girl friend, Tigress Moone. He dined her and bought her pretties and had the freedom of the bearskin rug in front of her wood-burning fireplace. He had beaten the game; he had achieved a delightful combination of bachelor irresponsibility and marital gratification.

"George," Tigress said thoughtfully one day . . . so they got married.

With prices what they were in 1998 she kept her job, of course—at least until she again said thoughtfully: "George. . ."

She then had too much time on her hands; it was absurd for a healthy woman to pretend that taking care of a two-room city apartment kept her occupied . . . so she thoughtfully said, "George?" and they moved to the suburbs.

George happened to be a rising young editor in the Civil War Book-of-the-Week Club. He won his spurs when he got MIGHTIER THAN THE SWORD: A STUDY OF PENS AND PENCILS IN THE ARMY OF THE POTOMAC, 1863–1865 whipped into shape for the printer. They then assigned him to the infinitely more difficult and delicate job of handling writers. A temperamental troll named Blount was his special trial. Blount was writing a novelized account of Corporal Piggott's Raid, a deservedly obscure episode which got Corporal Piggott of the 104th New York (Provisional) Heavy Artillery Regiment deservedly court-martialed in the summer of '63. It was George's responsibility to see that Blount novelized the verdict of guilty into a triumphant acquittal followed by an award of the Medal of Honor, and Blount was being unreasonable about it.

It was after a hard day of screaming at Blount, and being screamed back at, that George dragged his carcass off the Long Island Railroad and into the family car. "Hi, dear," he said to Mrs. Macardle, erstwhile tigress-Diana, and off they drove, and so far it seemed like the waning of another ordinary day. But in the car Mrs. Macardle said thoughtfully: "George . . ."

She told him what was on her mind, and he refrained from striking her in the face because they were in rather tricky traffic and she was driving.

She wanted a child.

It was necessary to have a child, she said. Inexo-

rable logic dictated it. For one thing, it was absurd
for just the two of them to live in a great barn of a
six-room house.

For another thing, she needed a child to fulfill
her womanhood. For a third, the brains and beauty
of the Moone-Macardle strain should not die out; it
was their duty to posterity.

*(The students in Columbia's Chronoscope History
Seminar 201 retched as one man at the words.)*

For a fourth, everybody was having children.

George thought he had her there, but no. The
statement was perfectly correct if for "everybody"
you substituted "Mrs. Jacques Truro," their next-
door neighbor.

By the time they reached their great six-room
barn of a place she was consolidating her victory
with a rapid drumfire of simple declarative senten-
ces which ended with "Don't you?" and "Won't
we?" and "Isn't it?" to which George, hanging
onto the ropes, groggily replied: "We'll see . . .
we'll see . . . we'll see. . . ."

A wounded thing inside him was soundlessly
screaming: *youth! joy! freedom! gone beyond recall,
slain by wedlock, coffined by a mortgage, now to be
entombed beneath a reeking Everest of diapers!*

"I believe I'd like a drink before dinner," he
said. "Had quite a time with Blount today," he said
as the martini curled quietly in his stomach. He was
pretending nothing very bad had happened. "Kept
talking about his integrity. Writers! They'll never
learn . . . Tigress? Are you with me?"

His wife noticed a slight, complaining note in his
voice, so she threw herself on the floor, began to
kick and scream, went on to hold her breath until
her face turned blue, and finished by letting George
know that she had abandoned her Career to as-
suage his bachelor misery, moved out to this dreary
wasteland to satisfy his whim, and just once in her

life requested some infinitesimal consideration in return for her ghastly drudgery and scrimping.

George, who was a kind and gentle person except with writers, dried her tears and apologized for his brutality. They would have a child, he said contritely. "Though," he added, "I hear there are some complications about it these days."

"For Motherhood," said Mrs. Macardle, getting off the floor, "no complications are too great." She stood profiled like a statue against their picture window, with its view of the picture window of the house across the street.

The next day George asked around at his office.

None of the younger men, married since the P.Q.P. went into effect, seemed to have had children.

A few of them cheerily admitted they had not had children and were not going to have children, for they had volunteered for D-Bal shots, thus doing away with a running minor expense and, more importantly, ensuring a certain peace of mind and unbroken continuity during tender moments.

"Ugh," thought George.

(*The Columbia University professor explained to his students: "It is clearly in George's interest to go to the clinic for a painless, effect D-Bal shot and thus resolve his problem, but he does not go; he shudders at the thought. We cannot know what fear of amputation stemming from some early traumatic experience thus prevents him from action, but deep-rooted psychological reasons explain his behavior, we can be certain." The class bent over the chronoscope.*)

And some of George's co-workers slunk away and would not submit to questioning. Young MacBirney, normally open and incisive, muttered vaguely and passed his hand across his brow when George asked him how one went about having a baby—redtape-wise, that is.

It was Blount, coming in for his afternoon scream-ing match, who spilled the vengeful beans. "You and your wife phone P.Q.P. for an appointment," he told George with a straight face. "They'll issue you—everything you need." George in his inno-cence thanked him, and Blount turned away and grinned the twisted, sly grin of an author.

A glad female voice answered the phone on be-half of the P.Q.P. It assured George that he and Mrs. Macardle need only drop in any time at the Empire State Building and they'd be well on their way to parenthood.

The next day Mr. and Mrs. Macardle dropped in at the Empire State Building. A receptionist in the lobby was buffing her nails under a huge portrait of His Majesty. A beautifully lettered sign displayed the words with which His Majesty had decreed that P.Q.P. be enacted: "Ow Racken Theah's a Raht Smaht Ah-dee, Boys."

"Where do we sign up, please?" asked George.

The receptionist pawed uncertainly through her desk. "I *know* there's some kind of book," she said as she rummaged, but she did not find it. "Well, it doesn't matter. They'll give you everything you need in Room 100."

"Will I sign up there?" asked George nervously, conditioned by a life-time of red tape and uncom-fortable without it.

"No," said the receptionist.

"But for the tests—"

"There aren't any tests."

"Then the interviews, the deep probing of our physical and psychological fitness for parenthood, our heredity—"

"No interviews."

"But the evaluation of our financial and moral standing without which no permission can be—"

"No evaluation. Just Room 100." She resumed buffing her nails.

In Room 100 a cheerful woman took a Toddler out of a cabinet, punched the non-reversible activating button between its shoulder blades, and handed it to Mrs. Macardle with a cheery: "It's all yours, madame. Return with it in three months and depending on its condition you will, or will not, be issued a breeding permit. Simple, isn't it?"

"The little darling!" gurgled Mrs. Macardle, looking down into the Toddler's pretty face.

It spit in her eye, punched her in the nose and sprang a leak.

"Gracious!" said the cheerful woman. "Get it out of our nice clean office, *if* you please."

"How do you work it?" yelled Mrs. Macardle, juggling the Toddler like a hot potato. "How do you turn it off?"

"Oh, you *can't* turn it off," said the woman. "And you'd better not swing it like that. Rough handling goes down on the tapes inside it and we read them in three months and now if you *please*, you're getting our nice office *all wet—*"

She shepherded them out.

"Do something, George!" yelled Mrs. Macardle. George took the Toddler. It stopped leaking and began a ripsaw scream that made the lighting fixtures tremble.

"Give the poor thing to me!" Mrs. Macardle shouted. "You're hurting it holding it like that—"

She took the Toddler back. It stopped screaming and resumed leaking.

It quieted down in the car. The sudden thought seized them both—*too* quiet? Their heads crashed together as they bent simultaneously over the glassy-eyed little object. It laughed delightedly and waved its chubby fists.

"Clumsy oaf!" snapped Mrs. Macardle, rubbing her head.

"Sorry, dear," said George. "But at least we

must have got a good mark out of *it* on the tapes. I suppose it scores us good when it laughs."

Her eyes narrowed. "Probably," she said. "George, do you think if you fell heavily on the sidewalk—?"

"No," said George convulsively. Mrs. Macardle looked at him for a moment and held her peace.

"Note, young gentlemen," said the history professor, "the turning point, the seed of rebellion." They noted.)

The Macardles and the Toddler drove off down Sunrise Highway, which was lined with filling stations; since their '98 Landscruiser made only two miles to the gallon, it was not long before they had to stop at one.

The Toddler began its ripsaw shriek when they stopped. A hollow-eyed attendant shambled over and peered into the car. "Just get it?" he asked apathetically.

"Yes," said Mrs. Macardle, frantically trying to joggle the Toddler, to change it, to burp it, to do anything that would end the soul-splitting noise.

"Half pint of white 90-octane gas is what it needs," mumbled the attendant. "Few drops of SAE 40 oil. Got one myself. Two weeks to go. I'll never make it. I'll crack. I'll—I'll . . ." He tottered off and returned with the gasoline in a nursing bottle, the oil in an eye-dropper.

The Toddler grabbed the bottle and began to gulp the gas down contentedly.

"Where do you put the oil?" asked Mrs. Macardle.

He showed her.

"Oh," she said.

"Fill her up," said George. "The car, I mean. I . . . ah . . . I'm going to wash my hands, dear."

He cornered the attendant by the cash register. "Look," he said. "What, ah, would happen if you just let it run out of gas? The Toddler, I mean?"

The man looked at him and put a compassionate

hand on his shoulder. "It would *scream,* buddy," he said. "The main motors run off an atomic battery. The gas engine's just for a sideshow and for having breakdowns."

"Breakdowns? Oh, my God! How do you fix a breakdown?"

"The best way you can," the man said. "And buddy, when you burp it, watch out for the fumes. I've seen some ugly explosions . . ."

They stopped at five more filling stations along the way when the Toddler wanted gas.

"It'll be better-behaved when it's used to the house," said Mrs. Macardle apprehensively as she carried it over the threshold.

"Put it down and let's see what happens," said George.

The Toddler toddled happily to the coffee table, picked up a large bronze ashtray, moved to the picture window and heaved the ashtray through it. It gurgled happily at the crash.

"You little—!" George roared, making for the Toddler with his hands clawed before him.

"George!" Mrs. Macardle screamed, snatching the Toddler away. "It's only a machine!"

The machine began to shriek.

They tried gasoline, oil, wiping with a clean lint-free rag, putting it down, picking it up and finally banging their heads together. It continued to scream until it was ready to stop screaming, and then it stopped and gave them an enchanting grin.

"Time to put it to—away for the night?" asked George.

It permitted itself to be put away for the night.

From his pillow George said later: "Think we did pretty well today. Three months? Pah!"

Mrs. Macardle said: "You were wonderful, George."

He knew that tone. "My Tigress," he said.

Ten minutes later, at the most inconvenient time in the world, bar none, the Toddler began its ripsaw screaming.

Cursing, they went to find out what it wanted. They found out. What it wanted was to laugh in their faces.

(*The professor explained: "Indubitably, sadism is at work here, but harnessed in the service of human-ity. Better a brutal and concentrated attack such as we have been witnessing than long-drawn-out tor-ments." The class nodded respectfully.*)

Mr. and Mrs. Macardle managed to pull them-selves together for another try, and there was an exact repeat. Apparently the Toddler sensed some-thing in the air.

"Three months," said George, with haunted eyes.

"You'll live," his wife snapped.

"May I ask *just* what kind of crack that was supposed to be?"

"If the shoe fits, my good *man*—"

So a fine sex quarrel ended the day.

Within a week the house looked as if it had been liberated by a Mississippi National Guard division. George had lost ten pounds because he couldn't digest anything, not even if he seasoned his food with powdered Equanil instead of a salt. Mrs. Macardle had gained fifteen pounds by nervous gob-bling during the moments when the Toddler left her unoccupied. The picture window was boarded up. On George's salary, and with the glaziers' wages what they were, he couldn't have it replaced twice a day.

Not unnaturally, he met his next-door neighbor, Jacques Truro, in a bar.

Truro was rye and soda, he was dry martini; otherwise they were identical.

"It's the little whimper first that gets me, when you know the big screaming's going to come next. I could jump out of my skin when I hear that whimper."

"Yeah. The waiting. Sometimes one second, sometimes five. I count."

"I forced myself to stop. I was throwing up."

"Yeah. Me too. And nervous diarrhea?"

"All the time. Between me and that goddam thing the house is awash. Cheers."

They drank and shared hollow laughter.

"My stamp collection. Down the toilet."

"My fishing pole. Three clean breaks and peanut butter in the reel."

"One thing I'll never understand, Truro. *What* decided you two to have a baby?"

"Wait a minute, Macardle," Truro said. "Marguerite told me that *you* were going to have one, so *she* had to have one—"

They looked at each other in shared horror.

"Suckered," said Macardle in an awed voice.

"Women," breathed Truro.

They drank a grim toast and went home.

"It's beginning to talk," Mrs. Macardle said listlessly, sprawled in a chair, her hand in a box of chocolates. "Called me 'old pig-face' this afternoon." She did look somewhat piggish with fifteen superfluous pounds.

George put down his briefcase. It was loaded with work from the office that these days he was unable to get through in time. He had finally got the revised court-martial scene from Blount, and would now have to transmute it into readable prose, emending the author's stupid lapses of logic, illiterate blunders of language and raspingly ugly style.

"I'll wash up," he said.

"Don't use the toilet. Stopped up again."

"Bad?"

"He said he'd come back in the morning with an eight-man crew. Something about jacking up a corner of the house."

The Toddler toddled in with a bottle of bleach, made for the briefcase, and emptied the bleach into it before the exhausted man or woman could comprehend what was going on, let alone do anything about it.

George incredulously spread the pages of the court-martial scene. His eyes bulged as he watched the thousands of typed words vanishing before his eyes, turned pale and then white as the paper.

Blount kept no carbons. Keeping carbons called for a minimal quantity of prudence and brains, but Blount was an author and so he kept no carbons. The court-martial scene, the product of six months' screaming, was *gone*.

The Toddler laughed gleefully.

George clenched his fists, closed his eyes and tried to ignore the roaring in his ears.

The Toddler began a whining chant:

> *"Da*-dy's an *au*-thor!
> *Da*-dy's an *au*-thor!"

"That did it!" George shrieked. He stalked to the door and flung it open.

"Where are you going?" Mrs. Macardle quavered.

"To the first doctor's office I find," said her husband in sudden icy calm. "There I will request a shot of D-Bal. When I have had a D-Bal shot, a breeding permit will be of no use whatever to us. Since a breeding permit will be useless, we need not qualify for one by being tortured for another eleven weeks by that obscene little monster, which we shall return to P.Q.P. in the morning. And unless it behaves, it will be returned in a basket, for them to reassemble at their leisure."

"I'm so glad," his wife sighed.

The Toddler said: "May I congratulate you on your decision. By voluntarily surrendering your right to breed, you are patriotically reducing the population pressure, a problem of great concern to His Majesty. We of the P.Q.P. wish to point out that your decision has been arrived at not through coercion but through education: i.e., by presenting you in the form of a Toddler with some of the arguments against parenthood."

"I didn't know you could talk that well," marveled Mrs. Macardle.

The Toddler said modestly: "I've been with the P.Q.P. from the very beginning, ma'am; I'm a veteran Toddler operator, I may say, working out of Room 4567 of the Empire State. And the improved model I'm working through has reduced the breakdown time an average thirty-five per cent. I foresee a time, ma'am, when we experienced operators and ever-improved models will do the job in one day!"

The voice was fanatical.

Mrs. Macardle turned around in sudden vague apprehension. George had left for his D-Bal shot.

(*"And thus we see," said the professor to the seminar, "the genius of the insidious Dr. Wang in full flower." He snapped off the chronoscope. "The first boatloads of Chinese landed in California three generations—or should I say non-generations?—later, unopposed by the scanty, elderly population." He groomed his mandarin mustache and looked out for a moment over the great rice paddies of Central Park. It was spring; blue-clad women stooped patiently over the brown water, and the tender, bright-green shoots were just beginning to appear.*

The seminar students bowed and left for their next lecture, "The Hound Dog as Symbol of Juvenile Aggression in Ancient American Folk Song." It was all that remained of the reign of King Purvis I.)

THE TUNESMITH

BY LLOYD BIGGLE, JR. (1923–   )

WORLDS OF IF
AUGUST

Lloyd Biggle, Jr. is, as far as I know, the only science fiction writer to possess a Ph.D. in musicology (from The University of Michigan, 1953), an expertise that is quite evident in this story. He began publishing in the sf magazines in 1956, and soon became a prolific and popular regular. The best of his shorter works can be found in the collections The Rule of the Door and Other Fanciful Regulations *(1967),* The Metallic Muse *(1972), and* A Galaxy of Strangers *(1976).*

His series character Jan Darzek, an intergalactic private eye, is especially appealing—his adventures can be found in All the Colors of Darkness *(1963),* Watchers of the Dark *(1966),* This Darkening Universe *(1975),* Silence Is Deadly *(1977), and* The Whirligig of Time *(1979). Dr. Biggle excels at depicting alien creatures and their environments, although "The Tunesmith" is an excellent example of social science fiction in its extrapolation of current trends to their logical and sometimes illogical conclusions. (MHG)*

Once when I was young and foolish I said to an editor-friend of mine, "I've written every kind of science fiction there is."

He promptly said, "You have never written a sexy science fiction story."

I said, "Only because I prefer not to."

"Prove it," he said.

So I wrote a sexy science fiction story not intending to publish it. But it turned out be so good (in my own opinion) that I did publish it. (It appeared in 1957, by the way, but Marty didn't choose it for this volume. I might have, but he's the one who makes the decisions in connection with my stories.)

In any case, I was wrong, very wrong. There are a million kinds of science fiction stories that I can't write if only because there are a million kinds of things I know nothing about.

For instance, I know virtually nothing about music. Oh, I listen to it and there are kinds of music I like and kinds I don't like, but I know nothing about what it is that I am listening to. I can't play an instrument. I can't compose a tune. I don't understand the language.

It follows then that I can't write a science fiction story with a musical theme. But thank goodness, writers such as Lloyd Biggle can. (IA)

Everyone calls it the Center. It has another name, a long one, that gets listed in government appropriations and has its derivation analyzed in encyclopedias, but no one uses it. From Bombay to Lima, from Spitsbergen to the mines of Antarctica, from the solitary outpost on Pluto to that on Mercury, it is—the Center. You can emerge from the rolling mists of the Amazon, or the cutting dry winds of the Sahara, or the lunar vacuum, elbow your way up to a bar, and begin, "When I was at the Center—" and every stranger within hearing will listen attentively.

It isn't possible to explain the Center, and it isn't necessary. From the babe in arms to the centenar-

ian looking forward to retirement, everyone has
been there, and plans to go again next year, and the
year after that. It is the vacation land of the Solar
System. It is square miles of undulating American
Middle West farm land, transfigured by ingenious
planning and relentless labor and incredible expense.
It is a monumental summary of man's cultural heri-
tage, and like a phoenix, it has emerged suddenly,
inexplicably, at the end of the twenty-fourth century, from the corroded ashes of an appalling cultural decay.

The Center is colossal, spectacular and magnifi-
cent. It is inspiring, edifying and amazing. It is
awesome, it is overpowering, it is—everything.

And though few of its visitors know about this, or
care, it is also haunted.

You are standing in the observation gallery of the
towering Bach Monument. Off to the left, on the
slope of a hill, you see the tense spectators who
crowd the Grecian Theater for Euripides. Sunlight
plays on their brightly-colored clothing. They watch
eagerly, delighted to see in person what millions are
watching on visiscope.

Beyond the theater, the tree-lined Frank Lloyd
Wright Boulevard curves into the distance, past the
Dante Monument and the Michelangelo Institute.
The twin towers of a facsimile of the Rheims Cathe-
dral rise above the horizon. Directly below, you see
the curious landscaping of an eighteenth-century
French *jardin* and, nearby, the Molière Theater.

A hand clutches your sleeve, and you turn suddenly, irritably, and find yourself face to face with
an old man.

The leathery face is scarred and wrinkled, the
thin strands of hair glistening white. The hand on
your arm is a gnarled claw. You stare, take in the
slumping contortion of one crippled shoulder and

the hideous scar of a missing ear, and back away in alarm.

The sunken eyes follow you. The hand extends in a sweeping gesture that embraces the far horizon, and you notice that the fingers are maimed or missing. The voice is a harsh cackle. "Like it?" he says, and eyes you expectantly.

Startled, you mutter, "Why, yes. Of course."

He takes a step forward, and his eyes are eager, pleading. "I say, do you like it?"

In your perplexity you can do no more than nod as you turn away—but your nod brings a strange response. A strident laugh, an innocent, childish smile of pleasure, a triumphant shout. "I did it! I did it all!"

Or you stand in resplendent Plato Avenue, between the Wagnerian Theater, where the complete *Der Ring des Nibelungen* is performed daily, and the reconstruction of the sixteenth-century Globe Theatre, where Shakespearean drama is presented morning, afternoon and evening.

A hand paws at you. "Like it?"

If you respond with a torrent of ecstatic praise, the old man eyes you impatiently and only waits until you have finished to ask again, "I say, do you like it?"

But a smile and a nod is met with beaming pride, a gesture, a shout.

In the lobby of one of the thousand spacious hotels, in the waiting room of the remarkable library where a copy of any book you request is reproduced for you free of charge, in the eleventh balcony of Beethoven Hall, a ghost shuffles haltingly, clutches an arm, asks a question.

And shouts proudly, "I did it!"

* * *

Erlin Baque sensed her presence behind him, but

he did not turn. Instead he leaned forward, his left hand tearing a rumbling bass figure from the multichord while his right hand fingered a solemn melody. With a lightning flip of his hand he touched a button, and the thin treble tones were suddenly fuller, more resonant, almost clarinetlike. ("But God, how preposterously unlike a clarinet!" he thought.)

"Must we go through all that again, Val?" he asked.

"The landlord was here this morning."

He hesitated, touched a button, touched several buttons, and wove weird harmonies out of the booming tones of a brass choir. (But what a feeble, distorted brass choir!)

"How long does he give us this time?"

"Two days. And the food synthesizer's broken down again."

"Good. Run down and buy some fresh meat."

"With what?"

Baque slammed his fists down and shouted above the shattering dissonance. "I will not rent a harmonizer. I will not turn my arranging over to hacks. If a Com goes out with my name on it, it's going to be *composed*. It may be idiotic, and it may be sickening, but it's going to be done right. It isn't much, God knows, but it's all I have left."

He turned slowly and glared at her, this pale, drooping, worn-out woman who'd been his wife for twenty-five years. Then he looked away, telling himself stubbornly that he was no more to be blamed than she. When sponsors paid the same rates for good Coms that they paid for hackwork . . .

"Is Hulsey coming today?" she asked.

"He told me he was coming."

"If we could get some money for the landlord—"

"And the food synthesizer. And a new visiscope. And new clothes. There's a limit to what can be done with one Com."

He heard her move away, heard the door open, and waited. It did not close. "Walter-Walter called," she said. "You're the featured tunesmith on today's *Show Case*."

"So? There's no money in that."

"I thought you wouldn't want to watch, so I told Mrs. Rennik I'd watch with her."

"Sure. Go ahead. Have fun."

The door closed.

Baque got to his feet and stood looking down at his chaos-strewn worktable. Music paper, Com-lyric releases, pencils, sketches, half-finished manuscripts were cluttered together in untidy heaps. Baque cleared a corner for himself and sat down wearily, stretching his long legs out under the table.

"Damn Hulsey," he muttered. "Damn sponsors. Damn visiscope. Damn Coms."

Compose something, he told himself. You're not a hack, like the other tunesmiths. You don't punch out silly tunes on a harmonizer's keyboard and let a machine complete them for you. You're a musician, not a melody monger. Write some music. Write a—a sonata, for multichord. Take the time now, and compose something.

His eyes fell on the first lines of a Com-lyric release. "If your flyer jerks and clowns, if it has its ups and downs—"

"Damn landlord," he muttered, reaching for a pencil.

The tiny wall clock tinkled the hour, and Baque leaned over to turn on the visiscope. A cherub-faced master of ceremonies smiled out at him ingratiatingly. "Walter-Walter again, ladies and gentlemen. It's Com time on today's *Show Case*. Thirty minutes of Commercials by one of today's most talented tunesmiths. Our Com spotlight is on—"

A noisy brass fanfare rang out, the tainted brass tones of a multichord.

"Erlin Baque!"

The multichord swung into an odd, dipsey melody Baque had done five years before, for Tamper Cheese, and a scattering of applause sounded in the background. A nasal soprano voice mouthed the words, and Baque groaned unhappily. "We age our cheese, and age it, age it, age it, age it, age it the old-fashioned way . . ."

Walter-Walter cavorted about the stage, moving in time with the melody, darting down into the audience to kiss some sedate housewife-on-a-holiday, and beaming at the howls of laughter.

The multichord sounded another fanfare, and Walter-Walter leaped back onto the stage, both arms extended over his head. "Now listen to this, all you beautiful people. Here's your Walter-Walter exclusive on Erlin Baque." He glanced secretively over his shoulder, tiptoed a few steps closer to the audience, placed his finger on his lips, and then called out loudly, "Once upon a time there was another composer named Baque, spelled B-A-C-H, but pronounced Baque. He was a real atomic propelled tunesmith, the boy with the go, according to them that know. He lived some five or six or seven hundred years ago, so we can't exactly say that that Baque and our Baque were Baque to Baque. But we don't have to go Baque to hear Baque. We like the Baque we've got. Are you with me?"

Cheers. Applause. Baque turned away, hands trembling, a choking disgust nauseating him.

"We start off our Coms by Baque with that little masterpiece Baque did for Foam Soap. Art work by Bruce Combs. Stop, look—and listen!"

Baque managed to turn off the visiscope just as the first bar of soap jet-propelled itself across the screen. He picked up the Com lyric again, and his mind began to shape the thread of a melody.

"If your flyer jerks and clowns, if it has its ups

and downs, ups and downs, ups and downs, you need a WARING!"

He hummed softly to himself, sketching a musical line that swooped and jerked like an erratic flyer. Word painting, it was called, back when words and tones meant something. Back when the B-A-C-H Baque was underscoring such grandiose concepts as Heaven and Hell.

Baque worked slowly, now and then trying a harmonic progression at the multichord and rejecting it, straining his mind for some fluttering accompaniment pattern that would simulate the sound of a flyer. But then—no. The Waring people wouldn't like that. They advertised that their flyers were noiseless.

Urgent-sounding door chimes shattered his concentration. He walked over to flip on the scanner, and Hulsey's pudgy face grinned out at him.

"Come on up," Baque told him. Hulsey nodded and disappeared.

Five minutes later he waddled through the door, sank into a chair that sagged dangerously under his bulky figure, plunked his briefcase onto the floor, and mopped his face. "Whew! Wish you'd get yourself a place lower down. Or into a building with modern conveniences. Elevators scare me to death!"

"I'm thinking of moving," Baque said.

"Good. It's about time."

"But it'll probably be somewhere higher up. The landlord has given me two days' notice."

Hulsey winced and shook his head sadly. "I see. Well, I won't keep you in suspense. Here's the check for the Sana-Soap Com."

Baque took the card, glanced at it, and scowled.

"You were behind in your guild dues," Hulsey said. "Have to deduct them, you know."

"Yes. I'd forgotten."

"I like to do business with Sana-Soap. Cash right

on the line. Too many companies wait until the end
of the month. Sana-Soap wants a couple of changes,
but they paid anyway." He unsealed the briefcase
and pulled out a folder. "You've got some sly bits
in this one, Erlin my boy. They like it. Particularly
this 'sudsy, sudsy, sudsy' thing in the bass. They
kicked on the number of singers at first, but not
after they heard it. Now right here they want a
break for a straight announcement."

Baque nodded thoughtfully. "How about keeping
the 'sudsy, sudsy' ostinato going as a background to
the announcement?"

"Sounds good. That's a sly bit, that—what'd you
call it?"

"Ostinato."

"Ah—yes. Wonder why the other tunesmiths don't
work in bits like that."

"A harmonizer doesn't produce effects," Baque
said dryly. "It just—harmonizes."

"You give them about thirty seconds of that 'sudsy'
for background. They can cut it if they don't like
it."

Baque nodded, scribbling a note on the manuscript.

"And the arrangement," Hulsey went on. "Sorry,
Erlin, but we can't get a French horn player. You'll
have to do something else with that part."

"No horn player? What's wrong with Rankin?"

"Blacklisted. The Performers' Guild nixed him
permanently. He went out to the West Coast and
played for nothing. Even paid his own expenses.
The guild can't tolerate that sort of thing."

"I remember," Baque said softly. "The Monu-
ments of Art Society. He played a Mozart horn
concerto for them. Their final concert, too. Wish I
could have heard it, even if it was with multichord."

"He can play it all he wants to now, but he'll
never get paid for playing again. You can work that
horn part into the multichord line, or I might be

able to get you a trumpet player. He could use a converter."

"It'll ruin the effect."

Hulsey chuckled. "Sounds the same to everyone but you, my boy. *I* can't tell the difference. We got your violins and a cello player. What more do you want?"

"Doesn't the London Guild have a horn player?"

"You want me to bring him over for one three-minute Com? Be reasonable, Erlin! Can I pick this up tomorrow?"

"Yes. I'll have it ready in the morning."

Hulsey reached for his briefcase, dropped it again, leaned forward scowling. "Erlin, I'm worried about you. I have twenty-seven tunesmiths in my agency. You're the best by far. Hell, you're the best in the world, and you make the least money of any of them. Your net last year was twenty-two hundred. None of the others netted less than eleven thousand."

"That isn't news to me," Baque said.

"This may be. You have as many accounts as any of them. Did you know that?"

Baque shook his head. "No, I didn't know that."

"You have as many accounts, but you don't make any money. Want to know why? Two reasons. You spend too much time on a Com, and you write it too well. Sponsors can use one of your Coms for months—or sometimes even years, like that Tamper Cheese thing. People like to hear them. Now if you just didn't write so damned well, you could work faster, and the sponsors would have to use more of your Coms, and you could turn out more."

"I've thought about that. Even if I didn't, Val would keep reminding me. But it's no use. That's the way I have to work. If there was some way to get the sponsors to pay more for a *good* Com—"

"There isn't. The guild wouldn't stand for it, because good Coms mean less work, and most tunesmiths couldn't write a really good Com. Now don't think I'm concerned about my agency. Of course I make more money when you make more, but I'm doing well enough with my other tunesmiths. I just hate to see my best man making so little money. You're a throwback, Erlin. You waste time and money collecting those antique—what do you call them?"

"Phonograph records."

"Yes. And those moldy old books about music. I don't doubt that you know more about music than anyone alive, and what does it get you? Not money, certainly. You're the best there is, and you keep trying to be better, and the better you get the less money you make. Your income drops lower every year. Couldn't you manage just an average Com now and then?"

"No," Baque said brusquely. "I couldn't manage it."

"Think it over."

"These accounts I have. Some of the sponsors really like my work. They'd pay more if the guild would let them. Supposing I left the guild?"

"You can't, my boy. I couldn't handle your stuff— not and stay in business long. The Tunesmith's Guild would turn on the pressure, and the Performers' and Lyric Writers' Guilds would blacklist you. Jimmy Denton plays along with the guilds and he'd bar your stuff from visiscope. You'd lose all your accounts, and fast. No sponsor is big enough to fight all that trouble, and none of them would want to bother. So just try to be average now and then. Think about it."

Baque sat staring at the floor. "I'll think about it."

Hulsey struggled to his feet, clasped Baque's hand briefly, and waddled out. Baque closed the door behind him and went to the drawer where he

kept his meager collection of old phonograph records. Strange and wonderful music.

Three times in his career Baque had written Coms
that were a full half-hour in length. On rare occasions he got an order for fifteen minutes. Usually he
was limited to five or less. But composers like the
B-A-C-H Baque wrote things that lasted an hour or
more—even wrote them without lyrics.

And they wrote for real instruments, among them
amazing-sounding things that no one played any
more, like bassoons, piccolos and pianos.

"Damn Denton. Damn visiscope. Damn guilds."

Baque rummaged tenderly among the discs until
he found one bearing Bach's name. *Magnificat*. Then,
because he felt too despondent to listen, he pushed
it away.

Earlier that year the Performers' Guild had blacklisted its last oboe player. Now its last horn player,
and there just weren't any young people learning to
play instruments. Why should they, when there were
so many marvelous contraptions that ground out
the Coms without any effort on the part of the
performer? Even multichord players were becoming
scarce, and if one wasn't particular about how well
it was done, a mutichord could practically play itself.

The door jerked open, and Val hurried in. "Did
Hulsey—"

Baque handed her the check. She took it eagerly,
glanced at it, and looked up in dismay.

"My guild dues," he said. "I was behind."

"Oh. Well, it's a help, anyway." Her voice was
flat, emotionless, as though one more disappoint-
ment really didn't matter. They stood facing each
other awkwardly.

"I watched part of *Morning with Marigold*," Val
said. "She talked about your Coms."

"I should hear soon on that Slo-Smoke Com,"
Baque said. "Maybe we can hold the landlord off

for another week. Right now I'm going to walk around a little."

"You should get out more—"

He closed the door behind him, slicing her sentence off neatly. He knew what followed. Get a job somewhere. It'd be good for your health to get out of the apartment a few hours a day. Write Coms in your spare time—they don't bring in more than a part-time income anyway. At least do it until we get caught up. All right, if you won't, I will.

But she never did. A prospective employer never wanted more than one look at her slight body and her worn, sullen face. And Baque doubted that he would receive any better treatment.

He could get work as a multichord player and make a good income—but if he did he'd have to join the Performers' Guild, which meant that he'd have to resign from the Tunesmiths' Guild. So the choice was between performing and composing, the guilds wouldn't let him do both.

"Damn the guilds! Damn Coms!"

When he reached the street, he stood for a moment watching the crowds shooting past on the swiftly moving conveyer. A few people glanced at him and saw a tall, gawky, balding man in a frayed, badly fitting suit. They would consider him just another derelict from a shabby neighborhood, he knew, and they would quickly look the other way while they hummed a snatch from one of his Coms.

He hunched up his shoulders and walked awkwardly along the stationary sidewalk. At a crowded restaurant he turned in, found a table at one side, and ordered beer. On the rear wall was an enormous visiscope screen where the Coms followed each other without interruption. Around him the other customers watched and listened while they ate. Some nodded their heads jerkily in time with the music. A few young couples were dancing on the small dance floor, skillfully changing steps as the music shifted from one Com to another.

Baque watched them sadly and thought about the way things had changed. At one time, he knew, there had been special music for dancing and special groups of instruments to play it. And people had gone to concerts by the thousands, sitting in seats with nothing to look at but the performers.

All of it had vanished. Not only the music, but art and literature and poetry. The plays he once read in his grandfather's school books were forgotten.

James Denton's *Visiscope International* decreed that people must look and listen at the same time, and that the public attention span wouldn't tolerate long programs. So there were Coms.

Damn Coms!

When Val returned to the apartment an hour later, Baque was sitting in the corner staring at the battered plastic cabinet that held the crumbling volumes he had collected from the days when books were still printed on paper—a scattering of biographies, books on music history, and technical books about music theory and composition. Val looked twice about the room before she noticed him, and then she confronted him anxiously, stark tragedy etching her wan face.

"The man's coming to fix the food synthesizer."

"Good," Baque said.

"But the landlord won't wait. If we don't pay him day after tomorrow—pay him everything—we're out."

"So we're out."

"Where will we go? We can't get in anywhere without paying something in advance."

"So we won't get in anywhere."

She fled sobbing into the bedroom.

The next morning Baque resigned from the Tunesmiths' Guild and joined the Performers' Guild.

Hulsey's round face drooped mournfully when he heard the news. He loaned Baque enough money to pay his guild registration fee and quiet the landlord, and he expressed his sorrow in eloquent terms as he hurried Baque out of his office. He would, Baque knew, waste no time in assigning Baque's clients to his other tunesmiths—to men who worked faster and not so well.

Baque went to the Guild Hall, where he sat for five hours waiting for a multichord assignment. He was finally summoned to the secretary's office and brusquely motioned into a chair. The secretary eyed him suspiciously.

"You belonged to the Performers' Guild twenty years ago, and you left it to become a tunesmith. Right?"

"Right," Baque said.

"You lost your seniority after three years. You knew that, didn't you?"

"I did, but I didn't think it mattered. There aren't many good multichord players around."

"There aren't many good jobs around, either. You'll have to start at the bottom." He scribbled on a slip of paper and thrust it at Baque. "This one pays well, but we have a hard time keeping a man there. Lankey isn't easy to work for. If you don't irritate him too much—well, then we'll see."

Baque rode the conveyer out to the New Jersey Space Port, wandered through a rattletrap slum area getting his directions hopelessly confused, and finally found the place almost within radiation distance of the port. The sprawling building had burned at some time in the remote past. Stubby remnants of walls rose out of the weed-choked rubble. A wall curved toward a dimly lit cavity at one corner, where steps led uncertainly downward. Overhead, an enormous sign pointed its flowing colors in the direction of the port. The LANKEY-PANK OUT.

Baque stepped through the door and faltered at the onslaught of extraterrestrial odors. Lavender-tinted tobacco smoke, the product of the enormous leaves grown in bot-domes in the Lunar Mare Crisium, hung like a limp blanket midway between floor and ceiling. The revolting, cutting fumes of *blast*, a whisky blended with a product of Martian lichens, staggered him. He had a glimpse of a scattered gathering of tough spacers and tougher prostitutes before the doorman planted his bulky figure and scarred caricature of a face in front of him.

"You looking for someone?"

"Mr. Lankey."

The doorman jerked a thumb in the direction of the bar and noisily stumbled back into the shadows. Baque walked toward the bar.

He had no trouble in picking out Lankey. The proprietor sat on a tall stool behind the bar. In the dim, smokestreaked light his taut pale face had a spectral grimness. He leaned an elbow on the bar, fingered his flattened stump of a nose with the two remaining fingers on his hairy hand, and as Baque approached he thrust his bald head forward and eyed him coldly.

"I'm Erlin Baque," Baque said.

"Yeah. The multichord player. Can you play that multichord, fellow?"

"Why, yes, I can play—"

"That's what they all say, and I've had maybe two in the last ten years that could really play. Most of them come out here figuring they'll set the thing on automatic and fuss around with one finger. I want that multichord *played*, fellow, and I'll tell you right now—if you can't play you might as well jet for home. There isn't any automatic on my multichord. I had it disconnected."

"I can play," Baque told him.

"All right. It doesn't take more than one Com to

find out. The guild rates this place as Class Four, but I pay Class One rates if you can play. If you can really play, I'll slip you some bonuses the guild won't know about. Hours are six P.M. to six A.M., but you get plenty of breaks, and if you get hungry or thirsty just ask for what you want. Only go easy on the hot stuff. I won't go along with a drunk multichord player no matter how good he is. Rose!''

He bellowed the name a second time, and a woman stepped from a door at the side of the room. She wore a faded dressing gown, and her tangled hair hung untidily about her shoulders. She turned a small, pretty face toward Baque and studied him boldly.

"Multichord," Lankey said. "Show him."

Rose beckoned, and Baque followed her toward the rear of the room. Suddenly he halted in amazement.

"What's the matter?" Rose asked.

"No visiscope!"

"No. Lankey says the spacers want better things to look at than soapsuds and flyers." She giggled. "Something like me, for example."

"I never heard of a restaurant without visiscope."

"Neither did I, until I came here. But Lankey's got three of us to sing the Coms, and you're to do the multichord with us. I hope you make the grade. We haven't had a multichord player for a week, and it's hard singing without one."

"I'll make out all right," Baque said.

A narrow platform stretched across the end of the room where any other restaurant would have had its visiscope screen. Baque could see the unpatched scars in the wall where the screen had been torn out.

"Lankey ran a joint at Port Mars back when the colony didn't have visiscope," Rose said. "He has his own ideas about how to entertain customers. Want to see your room?"

Baque was examining the multichord. It was a battered old instrument, and it bore the marks of more than one brawl. He fingered the filter buttons and swore softly to himself. Only the flute and violin filters clicked into place properly. So he would have to spend twelve hours a day with the twanging tones of an unfiltered multichord.

"Want to see your room?" Rose asked again. "It's only five. You might as well relax until we have to go to work."

Rose showed him a cramped enclosure behind the bar. He stretched out on a hard cot and tried to relax, and suddenly it was six o'clock and Lankey stood in the door beckoning to him.

He took his place at the multichord and fingered the keys impatiently. He felt no nervousness. There wasn't anything he didn't know about Coms, and he knew he wouldn't have trouble with the music, but the atmosphere disturbed him. The haze of smoke was thicker, and he blinked his smarting eyes and felt the whisky fumes tear at his nostrils when he took a deep breath.

There was still only a scattering of customers. The men were mechanics in grimy work suits, swaggering pilots, and a few civilians who liked their liquor strong and didn't mind the surroundings. The women were—women; two of them, he guessed, for every man in the room.

Suddenly the men began an unrestrained stomping of feet accented with yelps of approval. Lankey was crossing the platform with Rose and the other singers. Baque's first horrified impression was that the girls were nude, but as they came closer he made out their brief plastic costumes. Lankey was right, he thought. The spacers would much prefer that kind of scenery to animated Coms on a visiscope screen.

"You met Rose," Lankey said. "This is Zanna and Mae. Let's get going."

He walked away, and the girls gathered about the multichord. "What Coms do you know?" Rose asked.

"I know them all."

She looked at him doubtfully. "We sing together, and then we take turns. Are you sure you know them all?"

Baque flipped on the power and sounded a chord. "Sing any Com you want—I can handle it."

"Well—we'll start out with a Tasty-Malt Com. It goes like this." She hummed softly. "Know that one?"

"I wrote it," Baque said.

They sang better than he had expected. He followed them easily, and while he played he kept his eyes on the customers. Heads were jerking in time with the music, and he quickly caught the mood and began to experiment. His fingers shaped a rolling rhythm in the bass, fumbled with it tentatively, and then expanded it. He abandoned the melodic line, leaving the girls to carry on by themselves while he searched the entire keyboard to ornament the driving rhythm.

Feet began to stomp. The girls' bodies were swaying wildly, and Baque felt himself rocking back and forth as the music swept on recklessly. The girls finished their lyrics, and when he did not stop playing they began again. Spacers were on their feet, now, clapping and swaying. Some seized their women and began dancing in the narrow spaces between the tables. Finally Baque forced a cadence and slumped forward, panting and mopping his forehead. One of the girls collapsed onto the stage. The others hauled her to her feet, and the three of them fled to a frenzy of applause.

Baque felt a hand on his shoulder. Lankey. His ugly, expressionless face eyed Baque, turned to study

the wildly enthusiastic customers, turned back to
Baque. He nodded and walked away.

Rose returned alone, still breathing heavily. "How
about a Sally Ann Perfume Com?"

Baque searched his memory and was chagrined to
find no recollection of Sally Ann's Coms. "Tell me
the words," he said. She recited them tonelessly—a
tragic little story about the shattered romance of a
girl who did not use Sally Ann. "Now I remember,"
Baque told her. "Shall we make them cry? Just
concentrate on that. It's a sad story, and we're
going to make them cry."

She stood by the multichord and sang plaintively.
Baque fashioned a muted, tremulous accompaniment, and when the second verse started he improvised a drooping countermelody. The spacers sat in
hushed suspense. The men did not cry, but some of
the women sniffed audibly, and when Rose finished
there was a taut silence.

"Quick!" Baque hissed. "Let's brighten things
up. Sing another Com—anything!"

She launched into a Puffed Bread Com, and Baque
brought the spacers to their feet with the driving
rhythm of his accompaniment.

The other girls took their turns, and Baque
watched the customers detachedly, bewildered at
the power that surged in his fingers. He carried
them from one emotional extreme to the other and
back again, improvising, experimenting. And his
mind fumbled haltingly with an idea.

"Time for a break," Rose said finally. "Better
get something to eat."

An hour and a half of continuous playing had left
Baque drained of strength and emotion, and he
accepted his dinner tray indifferently and took it to
the enclosure they called his room. He did not feel
hungry. He sniffed doubtfully at the food, tasted

it—and ate ravenously. Real food, after months of synthetics!

When he'd finished he sat for a time on his cot, wondering how long the girls took between appearances, and then he went looking for Lankey.

"I don't like sitting around," he said. "Any objection to my playing?"

"Without the girls?"

"Yes."

Lankey planted both elbows on the bar, cupped his chin in one fist, and sat looking absently at the far wall. "You going to sing yourself?" he asked finally.

"No. Just play."

"Without any singing? Without words?"

"Yes."

"What'll you play?"

"Coms. Or I might improvise something."

A long silence. Then—"Think you could keep things moving while the girls are out?"

"Of course I could."

Lankey continued to concentrate on the far wall. His eyebrows contracted, relaxed, contracted again. "All right," he said. "I was just wondering why I never thought of it."

Unnoticed, Baque took his place at the multichord. He began softly, making the music an unobtrusive background to the rollicking conversation that filled the room. As he increased the volume, faces turned in his direction.

He wondered what these people were thinking as they heard for the first time music that was not a Com, music without words. He watched intently and satisfied himself that he was holding their attention. Now—could he bring them out of their seats with nothing more than the sterile tones of a multichord? He gave the melody a rhythmic snap, and the stomping began.

As he increased the volume again, Rose came stumbling out of a doorway and hurried across the stage, perplexity written on her pert face.

"It's all right," Baque told her. "I'm just playing to amuse myself. Don't come back until you're ready."

She nodded and walked away. A red-faced spacer near the platform looked up at the revealed outline of her young body and leered. Fascinated, Baque studied the coarse, demanding lust in his face and searched the keyboard to express it. This? Or—this? Or—

He had it. He felt himself caught up in the relentless rhythm. His foot tightened on the volume control, and he turned to watch the customers.

Every pair of eyes stared hypnotically at his corner of the room. A bartender stood at a half crouch, mouth agape. There was uneasiness, a strained shuffling of feet, a restless scraping of chairs. Baque's foot dug harder at the volume control.

His hands played on hypnotically, and he stared in horror at the scene that erupted below him. Lasciviousness twisted every face. Men were on their feet, reaching for the women, clutching, pawing. A chair crashed to the floor, and a table, and no one noticed. A woman's dress fluttered crazily downward, and the pursued were pursuers while Baque helplessly allowed his fingers to race onward, out of control.

With a violent effort he wrenched his hands from the keys, and the ensuing silence crashed the room like a clap of thunder. Fingers trembling, Baque began to play softly, indifferently. Order was restored when he looked again, the chair and table were upright, and the customers were seated in apparent relaxation except for one woman who struggled back into her dress in obvious embarrassment.

Baque continued to play quietly until the girls returned.

At 6 A.M., his body wracked with weariness, his hands aching, his legs cramped, Baque climbed down from the multichord. Lankey stood waiting for him. "Class One rates," he said. "You've got a job with me as long as you want it. But take it a little easy with that stuff, will you?"

Baque remembered Val, alone in their dreary apartment and eating synthetic food. "Would I be out of order to ask for an advance?"

"No," Lankey said. "Not out of order. I told the cashier to give you a hundred on your way out. Call it a bonus."

Weary from his long conveyer ride, Baque walked quietly into his dim apartment and looked about. There was no sign of Val—she would still be sleeping. He sat down at his own multichord and touched the keys.

He felt awed and humble and disbelieving. Music without Coms, without words, could make people laugh and cry, and dance and cavort madly.

And it could turn them into lewd animals.

Wonderingly he played the music that had incited such unconcealed lust, played it louder, and louder—

And felt a hand on his shoulder, and turned to look into Val's passion-twisted face.

He asked Hulsey to come and hear him that night, and later Hulsey sat slumped on the cot in his room and shuddered. "It isn't right. No man should have that power over people. How do you do it?"

"I don't know," Baque said. "I saw that young couple sitting there, and they were happy, and I felt their happiness. And as I played everyone in the room was happy. And then another couple came in quarreling, and the next thing I knew I had everyone mad."

"Almost started a fight at the next table," Hulsey said. "And what you did after that—"

"Yes. But not as much as I did last night. You should have seen it last night."

Hulsey shuddered again.

"I have a book about ancient Greek music," Baque said. "They had something they called *ethos*. They thought that the different musical scales affected people in different ways—could make them sad, or happy, or even drive them crazy. They claimed that a musician named Orpheus could move trees and soften rocks with his music. Now listen. I've had a chance to experiment, and I've noticed that my playing is most effective when I don't use the filters. There are only two filters that work on that multichord anyway—flute and violin—but when I use either of them the people don't react so strongly. I'm wondering if maybe the effects the Greeks talk about were produced by their instruments, rather than their scales. I'm wondering if the tone of an unfiltered multichord might have something in common with the tones of the ancient Greek *kithara* or *aulos*."

Hulsey grunted. "I don't think it's the instrument, or the scales either. I think it's Baque, and I don't like it. You should have stayed a tunesmith."

"I want you to help me," Baque said. "I want to find a place where we can put a lot of people—a thousand, at least—not to eat, or watch Coms, but just to listen to one man play on a multichord."

Hulsey got up abruptly. "Baque, you're a dangerous man. I'm damned if I'll trust any man who can make me feel the way you made me feel tonight. I don't know what you're trying to do, but I won't have any part of it."

He stomped away in the manner of a man about to slam a door, but the room of a male multichordist at the Lankey-Pank Out did not rate that luxury.

Hulsey paused uncertainly in the doorway, gave Baque a parting glare, and disappeared. Baque followed him as far as the main room and stood watching him weave his way impatiently past the tables to the exit.

From his place behind the bar, Lankey looked at Baque and then glanced after the disappearing Hulsey. "Troubles?" he asked.

Baque turned away wearily. "I've known that man for twenty years. I never thought he was my friend. But then—I never thought he was my enemy, either."

"Sometimes it works out that way," Lankey said.

Baque shook his head. "I'd like to try some Martian whisky. I've never tasted the stuff."

Two weeks made Baque an institution, and the Lankey-Pank Out was jammed to capacity from the time he went to work until he left the next morning. When he performed alone, he forgot about Coms and played whatever he wanted. He even performed short pieces by Bach for the customers, and received generous applause, but the reaction was nothing like the tumultuous enthusiasm that followed his improvisations.

Sitting behind the bar, eating his evening meal and watching the impacted mass of customers, Baque felt vaguely happy. He was enjoying the work he was doing. For the first time in his life he had more money than he needed.

For the first time in his life he had a definite goal and a vague notion of a plan that would accomplish it—would eliminate the Coms altogether.

As Baque pushed his tray aside, he saw Biff the doorman step forward to greet a pair of newcomers, halt suddenly, and back away in stupefied amazement. And no wonder—evening clothes at the Lankey-Pank Out!

The couple halted near the door, blinking uncertainly in the dim, smoke-tinted light. The man was bronzed and handsome, but no one noticed him. The woman's beauty flashed like a meteor against the drab surroundings. She moved in an aura of shining loveliness, with her hair gleaming golden, her shimmering, flowing gown clinging seductively to her voluptuous figure, and her fragrance routing the foul tobacco and whisky odors.

In an instant all eyes were fixed on her, and a collective gasp encircled the room. Baque stared with the others and finally recognized her: Marigold, of *Morning with Marigold*. Worshiped around the Solar System by the millions of devotees to her visiscope program. Mistress, it was said, to James Denton, the czar of visiscope. Marigold Manning.

She raised a hand to her mouth in mock horror, and the bright tones of her laughter dropped tantalizingly among the spellbound spacers. "What an odd place! Where'd you ever hear about a place like this?"

"I need some Martian whisky, damn it," the man said.

"So stupid of the port bar to run out. With all those ships from Mars coming in, too. Are you sure we can get back in time. Jimmy'll raise hell if we aren't there when he lands."

Lankey touched Baque's arm. "After six," he said, without taking his eyes from Marigold Manning. "They'll be getting impatient."

Baque nodded and started for the multichord. The tumult began the moment the customers saw him. They abandoned Marigold Manning, leaped to their feet, and began a stomping, howling ovation. When Baque paused to acknowledge it, Marigold and her escort were staring openmouthed at the nondescript man who could inspire such undignified enthusiasm.

Her exclamation rang out sharply as Baque seated himself at the multichord and the ovation faded to an expectant silence. "What the hell!"

Baque shrugged and started to play. When Marigold finally left, after a brief conference with Lankey, her escort still hadn't got his Martian whisky.

The next evening Lankey greeted Baque with both fists full of telenotes. "What a hell of a mess this is! You see this Marigold dame's program this morning?"

Baque shook his head. "I haven't watched visiscope since I came to work here."

"In case it interests you, you were—what does she call it?—a 'Marigold Exclusive' on visiscope this morning. Erlin Baque, the famous tunesmith, is now playing the multichord in a queer little restaurant called the Lankey-Pank Out. If you want to hear some amazing music, wander out to the New Jersey Space Port and listen to Baque. Don't miss it. The experience of a lifetime." Lankey swore and waved the telenotes. "Queer, she calls us. Now I've got ten thousand requests for reservations, some from as far away as Budapest and Shanghai. And our capacity is five hundred, counting standing room. Damn that woman! We already had all the business we could handle."

"You need a bigger place," Baque said.

"Yes. Well, confidentially, I've got my eye on a big warehouse. It'll seat a thousand, at least. We'll clean up. I'll give you a contract to take charge of the music."

Baque shook his head. "How about opening a big place uptown? Attract people that have more money to spend. You run it, and I'll bring in the customers."

Lankey caressed his flattened nose thoughtfully. "How do we split?"

"Fifty-fifty," Baque said.

"No," Lankey said, shaking his head slowly. "I

play fair, Baque, but fifty-fifty wouldn't be right on a deal like that. I'd have to put up all the money myself. I'll give you one-third to handle the music."

They had a lawyer draw up a contract. Baque's lawyer. Lankey insisted on that.

In the bleak gray of early morning Baque sleepily rode the crowded conveyer toward his apartment. It was the peak rush load, when commuters jammed against each other and snarled grumpily when a neighbor shifted his feet. The crowd seemed even heavier than usual, but Baque shrugged off the jostling and elbowing and lost himself in thought.

It was time that he found a better place to live. He hadn't minded the dumpy apartment as long as he could afford nothing better, but Val had been complaining for years. And now when they could move, when they could have a luxury apartment or even a small home over in Pennsylvania, Val refused to go. Didn't want to leave her friends, she said.

Mulling over this problem in feminine contrariness, Baque realized suddenly that he was approaching his own stop. He attempted to move toward a deceleration strip—he shoved firmly, he tried to step between his fellow riders, he applied his elbows, first gently and then viciously. The crowd about him did not yield.

"I beg your pardon," Baque said, making another attempt. "I get off here."

This time a pair of brawny arms barred his way. "Not this morning, Baque. You got an appointment uptown."

Baque flung a glance at the circle of hard, grinning faces that surrounded him. With a sudden effort he hurled himself sideways, fighting with all of his strength. The arms hauled him back roughly.

"Uptown, Baque. If you want to go dead, that's your affair."

"Uptown," Baque agreed.

At a public parking strip they left the conveyer. A flyer was waiting for them, a plush, private job that displayed a high-priority X registration number. They flew swiftly toward Manhattan, cutting across air lanes with a monumental contempt for regulations, and they veered in for a landing on the towering Visiscope International building. Baque was bundled down an anti-grav shaft, led through a labyrinth of corridors, and finally prodded none too gently into an office.

It was a huge room, and its sparse furnishings made it look more enormous than it was. It contained only a desk, a few chairs, a bar in the far corner, an enormous visiscope screen—and a multi-chord. The desk was occupied, but it was the group of men about the bar that caught Baque's attention. His gaze swept the blur of faces and found one that he recognized: Hulsey.

The plump agent took two steps forward and stood glaring at Baque. "Day of reckoning, Erlin," he said coldly.

A hand rapped sharply on the desk. "I take care of any reckoning that's done around here, Hulsey. Please sit down, Mr. Baque."

A chair was thrust forward, and Baque seated himself and waited nervously, his eyes on the man behind the desk.

"My name is James Denton. Does my fame extend to such a remote place as the Lankey-Pank Out?"

"No," Baque said. "But I've heard of you."

James Denton. Czar of Visiscope International. Ruthless arbiter of public taste. He was no more than forty, with a swarthy, handsome face, flashing eyes, and a ready smile.

He tapped a cigar on the edge of his desk and carefully placed it in his mouth. Men sprang forward with lighters extended, and he chose one without looking up, puffed deeply, and nodded.

"I won't bore you with introductions to this gathering, Baque. Some of these men are here for professional reasons. Some are here because they're curious. I heard about you for the first time yesterday, and what I heard made me want to find out whether you're a potential asset that might be made use of, or a potential nuisance that should be eliminated, or a nonentity that can be ignored. When I want to know something, Baque, I waste no time about it." He chuckled. "As you can see from the fact that I had you brought in at the earliest moment you were—shall we say—available."

"The man's dangerous, Denton!" Hulsey blurted.

Denton flashed his smile. "I like dangerous men, Hulsey. They're useful to have around. If I can use whatever it is Mr. Baque has, I'll make him an attractive offer. I'm sure he'll accept it gratefully. If I can't use it, I aim to make damned certain that he won't be inconveniencing me. Do I make myself clear, Baque?"

Baque, looking past Denton to avoid his eyes, said nothing.

Denton leaned forward. His smile did not waver, but his eyes narrowed and his voice was suddenly icy. "Do I make myself clear, Baque?"

"Yes," Baque muttered weakly.

Denton jerked a thumb toward the door, and half of those present, including Hulsey, solemnly filed out. The others waited, talking in whispers, while Denton puffed steadily on his cigar. Finally an intercom rasped a single word. "Ready!"

Denton pointed at the multichord. "We crave a demonstration of your skill, Mr. Baque. And take care that it's a good demonstration. Hulsey is listening, and he can tell us if you try to stall."

Baque nodded and took his place at the multichord. He sat with fingers poised, timidly looking up at a circle of staring faces. Overlords of business, they were, and of science and industry, and never in their lives had they heard real music. As for Hulsey—yes, Hulsey would be listening, but over Denton's intercom, over a communication system designed to carry voices.

And Hulsey had a terrible ear for music.

Baque grinned contemptuously, touched the violin filter, touched it again, and faltered.

Denton chuckled dryly. "I neglected to inform you, Mr. Baque. On Hulsey's advice, we've had the filters disconnected."

Anger surged within Baque. He jammed his foot down hard on the volume control, insolently tapped out a visiscope fanfare, and started to play his Tamper Cheese Com. Denton, his own anger evident in his flushed face, leaned forward and snarled something. The men around him stirred uneasily. Baque shifted to another Com, improvised some variations, and began to watch the circle of faces. Overlords of industry, science and business. It would be amusing, he thought, to make them stomp their feet. His fingers shaped a compelling rhythm, and they began to sway restlessly.

He forgot his resolution to play cautiously. Laughing silently to himself, he released an overpowering torrent of sound that set the men dancing and brought Denton to his feet. He froze them in ridiculous postures with an outburst of surging emotion. He made them stomp recklessly, he brought tears to their eyes, and he finished off with the pounding force that Lankey called, "Sex Music."

Then he slumped over the keyboard, terrified at what he had done.

Denton stood behind his desk, face pale, hands clenching and unclenching. "Good God!" he muttered.

He snarled a word at his intercom. "Reaction?"

"Negative," came the prompt answer.

"Let's wind it up."

Denton sat down, passed his hands across his face, and turned to Baque with a bland smile. "An impressive performance, Mr. Baque. We'll know in a few minutes —ah, here they are."

Those who had left earlier filed back into the room, and several men huddled together in a whispered conference. Denton left his desk and paced the floor meditatively. The other men in the room, including Hulsey, gravitated toward the bar.

Baque kept his place at the multichord and watched the conference uneasily. Once he accidentally touched a key, and the single tone shattered the poise of the conferees, halted Denton in midstride, and startled Hulsey into spilling his drink.

"Mr. Baque is getting impatient," Denton called. "Can't we finish this?"

"One moment, sir."

Finally they filed toward Denton's desk. The spokesman, a white-haired, scholarly-looking man with a delicate pink complexion, cleared his throat self-consciously and waited until Denton had returned to his chair.

"It is established," he said, "that those in this room were powerfully affected by the music. Those listening on the intercom experienced no reaction except a mild boredom."

"I didn't call you in here to state the obvious," Denton snapped. "How does he do it?"

"We can only offer a working hypothesis."

"So you're guessing. Let's have it."

"Erlin Baque has the ability to telepathetically project his emotional experience. When the projection is subtly reinforced by his multichord playing, those in his immediate presence share that experience intensely. The projection has no effect upon those listening to his music at a distance."

"And—visiscope?"

"He could not project his emotions by way of visiscope."

"I see," Denton said. A meditative scowl twisted his face. "What about his long-term effectiveness?"

"It's difficult to predict—"

"Predict, damn it!"

"The novelty of his playing would attract attention, at first. While the novelty lasted he might become a kind of fad. By the time his public lost interest he would probably have a small group of followers who would use the emotional experience of his playing as a narcotic."

"Thank you, gentlemen. That will be all."

The room emptied quickly. Hulsey paused in the doorway, glared hatefully at Baque, and then walked out meekly.

"Obviously you're no nonentity," Denton said, "but whatever it is you have is of no use to me. Unfortunately. If you could project on visiscope, you'd be worth a billion an hour in advertising revenue. Fortunately for you, your nuisance rating is fairly low. I know what you and Lankey are up to. If I say the word, you'll never in this lifetime find a place for your new restaurant. I could have the Lankey-Pank Out closed down within an hour, but it would hardly be worth the trouble. If you can develop a cult for yourself, why—perhaps it will keep the members out of worse mischief. I'm feeling so generous this morning that I won't even insist on a visiscope screen in your new restaurant. Now you'd better leave, Baque, before I change my mind."

Baque got to his feet. At that moment Marigold Manning swept into the room, radiantly lovely, exotically perfumed, her glistening blonde hair swept up into a new and tantalizing hair style.

"Jimmy, darling—oh!" She stared at Baque, stared at the multichord, and stammered, "Why, you're—you're—Erlin Baque! Jimmy, why didn't you tell me?"

"Mr. Baque has been favoring me with a private performance," Denton said brusquely. "I think we understand each other, Baque. Good morning."

"You're going to put him on visiscope!" Marigold exclaimed. "Jimmy, that's wonderful. May I have him first? I can work him in this morning."

Denton shook his head. "Sorry, darling. We've decided that Mr. Baque's talent is not quite suitable for visiscope."

"At least I can have him for a guest. You'll be my guest, won't you, Mr. Baque? There's nothing wrong with giving him a guest spot, is there, Jimmy?"

Denton chuckled. "No. After all the fuss you stirred up, it might be a good idea for you to guest him. It'll serve you right when he bombs."

"He won't bomb. He'll be wonderful on visiscope. Will you come in this morning, Mr. Baque?"

"Well—" Baque began. Denton was nodding at him emphatically. "We'll be opening a new restaurant soon. I wouldn't mind being your guest on opening day."

"A new restaurant? That's wonderful. Does anyone know? I'll give it out this morning as an exclusive!"

"It isn't exactly settled, yet," Baque said apologetically. "We haven't found a place yet."

"Lankey found a place yesterday," Denton said. "He's having a contractor check it over this morning, and if no snags develop he'll sign a lease. Just let Miss Manning know your opening date, Baque, and she'll arrange a spot for you. Now if you don't mind—"

It took Baque half an hour to find his way out of the building, but he plodded aimlessly along the corridors and disdained asking directions. He hummed happily to himself, and now and then he broke into a laugh.

The overlords of business and industry—and their scientists—knew nothing about overtones.

"So that's the way it is," Lankey said. "You seem to have no notion of how lucky you were—how lucky we were. Denton should have made his move when he had a chance. Now we know what to expect, and when he finally wises up it'll be too late."

"What could we do if he decided to put us out of business?"

"I have a few connections myself, Baque. They don't run in high society, like Denton, but they're every bit as dishonest, and Denton has a lot of enemies who'll be happy to back us. Said he could close me down in an hour, eh? Unfortunately there's not much we could do that would hurt Denton, but there's plenty we can do to keep him from hurting us."

"I think we're going to hurt Denton," Baque said.

Lankey moved over to the bar and came back with a tall glass of pink, foaming liquid. "Drink it," he said. "You've had a long day, and you're getting delirious. How could we hurt Denton?"

"Visiscope depends on Coms. We'll show the people they can have entertainment without Coms. We'll make our motto *NO COMS AT LANKEY'S!*"

"Great," Lankey drawled. "I invest a thousand in fancy new costumes for the girls—they can't wear those plastic things in our new place, you know—and you decide not to let them sing."

"Certainly they're going to sing."

Lankey leaned forward, caressing his nose. "And no Coms. Then *what* are they going to sing?"

"I took some lyrics out of an old school book my grandfather had. Back in those days they were called poems. I'm setting them to music. I was going to try them out here, but Denton might hear about it, and there's no use starting trouble before it's necessary."

"No. Save all the trouble for the new place—after opening day we'll be important enough to be able to handle it. And you'll be on *Morning with Marigold*. Are you certain about this overtones business, Baque? You really could be projecting emotions, you know. Not that it makes any difference in the restaurant, but on visiscope—"

"I'm certain. How soon can we open?"

"I got three shifts remodeling the place. We'll seat twelve hundred and still have room for a nice dance floor. Should be ready in two weeks. Baque, I'm not sure this visiscope thing is wise."

"I want to do it."

Lankey went back to the bar and got a drink for himself. "All right. You do it. If your stuff comes over, all hell is going to break loose, and I might as well start getting ready for it." He grinned. "Damned if it won't be good for business!"

Marigold Manning had changed her hair styling to a spiraled creation by Zann of Hong Kong, and she dallied for ten minutes in deciding which profile she would present to the cameras. Baque waited patiently, his awkward feeling wholly derived from the fact that his dress suit was the most expensive clothing he had ever owned. He kept telling himself to stop wondering if perhaps he really did project emotions.

"I'll have it this way," Marigold said finally, waving a hand screen in front of her face for a last, searching look. "And you, Mr. Baque? What shall we do with you?"

"Just put me at the multichord," Baque said.

"But you can't just play. You'll have to say *something*. I've been announcing this every day for a week, and we'll have the biggest audience in years, and you'll just *have* to say *something*."

"Gladly," Baque said, "if I can talk about Lankey's."

"But of course, you silly man. That's why you're here. You talk about Lankey's, and I'll talk about Erlin Baque."

"Five minutes," a voice announced crisply.

"Oh, dear," she said. "I'm always so nervous just before."

"Be happy you're not nervous during," Baque said.

"That's so right. Jimmy makes fun of me, but it takes an artist to understand another artist. Do you get nervous?"

"When I'm playing, I'm much too busy."

"That's just the way it is with me. Once my program starts, I'm much too busy."

"Four minutes."

"Oh, bother!" She seized the hand screen again. "Maybe I would be better the other way."

Baque seated himself at the multichord. "You're perfect the way you are."

"Do you really think so? It's a nice thing to say, anyway. I wonder if Jimmy will take the time to watch."

"I'm sure he will."

"Three minutes."

Baque switched on the power and sounded a chord. Now he *was* nervous. He had no idea what he would play. He'd intentionally refrained from preparing anything because it was his improvisations that affected people so strangely. The one thing he had to avoid was the Sex Music. Lankey had been emphatic about that.

He lost himself in thought, failed to hear the final warning, and looked up startled at Marigold's cheerful, "Good morning, everyone. It's *Morning with Marigold!*"

Her bright voice wandered on and on. Erlin Baque. His career as a tunesmith. Her amazing discovery of him playing in the Lankey-Pank Out. She asked the engineers to run the Tamper Cheese Com. Finally she finished her remarks and risked the distortion of her lovely profile to glance in his direction. "Ladies and gentlemen, with admiration, with pride, with pleasure, I give you a Marigold Exclusive, Erlin Baque!"

Baque grinned nervously and tapped out a scale with one finger. "This is my first speech. Probably it'll be my last. The new restaurant opens tonight. Lankey's, on Broadway. Unfortunately I can't invite you to join us, because thanks to Miss Manning's generous comments this past week all space is reserved for the next two months. After that we'll be setting aside a limited number of reservations for visitors from distant places. Jet over and see us!

"You'll find something different at Lankey's. There is no visiscope screen. Maybe you've heard about that. We have attractive young ladies to sing for you. I play the multichord. We know you'll enjoy our music. We know you'll enjoy it because you'll hear no Coms at Lankey's. Remember that—*no Coms at Lankey's*. No soap with your soup. No air cars with your steaks. No shirts with your deserts. *No Coms!* Just good food, with good music played exclusively for your enjoyment—like this."

He brought his hands down onto the keyboard.

Immediately he knew that something was wrong. He'd always had a throng of faces to watch, he'd paced his playing according to their reactions. Now he had only Miss Manning and the visiscope engineers, and he was suddenly apprehensive that his success had been wholly due to his audiences. People were listening throughout the Western Hemisphere. Would they clap and stomp, would they think awesomely, "So that's how music sounds without words, without Coms!" Or would they turn away in boredom?

Baque caught a glimpse of Marigold's pale face, of the engineers watching with mouths agape, and thought perhaps everything was all right. He lost himself in the music and played fervently.

He continued to play even after the pilot screen went blank. Miss Manning leaped to her feet and hurried toward him, and the engineers were moving about confusedly. Finally Baque brought his playing to a halt.

"We were cut off," Miss Manning said tearfully. "Who would do such a thing to me? Never, never, in all the time I've been on visiscope—George, who cut us off?"

"Orders."

"Whose orders?"

"My orders!" James Denton strode toward them, lips tight, face pale, eyes gleaming violence and sudden death. He spat words at Baque. "I don't know how you worked that trick, but no man fools James Denton more than once. Now you've made yourself a nuisance that has to be eliminated."

"Jimmy!" Miss Manning wailed. "My program—cut off. How could you?"

"Shut up, damn it! I just passed the word, Baque. Lankey's doesn't open tonight. Not that it'll make any difference to you."

Baque smiled gently. "I think you've lost, Denton. I think enough music got through to beat you. By tomorrow you'll have a million complaints. So

will the government, and then you'll find out who
really runs Visiscope International."

"I run Visiscope International."

"No, Denton. It belongs to the people. They've
let things slide for a long time, and they've taken
anything you'd give them. But if they know what
they want, they'll get it. I gave them at least three
minutes of what they want. That was more than I'd
hoped for."

"How'd you work that trick in my office?"

"That wasn't my trick, Denton—it was yours.
You transmitted the music on a voice intercom. It
didn't carry the overtones, the upper frequencies,
so the multichord sounded dead to the men in the
other room. Visiscope has the full frequency range
of live sound."

Denton nodded. "I'll have the heads of some
scientists for that. I'll also have your head, though I
regret the waste. If you'd played square with me I'd
have made you a live billionaire. The only alternative is a dead musician."

He stalked away, and as the automatic door closed
behind him, Marigold Manning clutched Baque's
arm. "Quick! Follow me!" Baque hesitated, and
she hissed, "Don't stand there like an idiot! He's
going to have you killed!"

She led him through a control room and out into
a small corridor. They raced the length of it, darted
through a reception room and passed a startled
secretary without a word, and burst through a rear
door into another corridor. She jerked Baque after
her into an anti-grav lift, and they shot upward. At
the top of the building she hurried him to an air car
strip and left him standing in a doorway. "When I
give you a signal, you walk out," she said. "Don't
run, just walk."

She calmly approached an attendant, and Baque

heard his surprised greeting. "Through early this morning, Miss Manning?"

"We're running a lot of Coms," she said. "I want the big Waring."

"Coming right up."

Peering around the corner, Baque saw her step into the flyer. As soon as the attendant's back was turned, she waved frantically. Baque walked carefully toward her, keeping the flyer between the attendant and himself. A moment later they were airborne, and far below them a siren was sounding faintly.

"We did it!" she gasped. "If you hadn't got away before that alarm sounded, you wouldn't have left the building alive."

"Well, thanks," Baque said, looking back at the Visiscope International building. "But surely this wasn't necessary. Earth is a civilized planet."

"Visiscope International is not civilized!" she snapped.

He looked at her wonderingly. Her face was flushed, her eyes wide with fear, and for the first Baque saw her as a human being, a woman, a lovely woman. As he looked, she turned away and burst into tears.

"Now Jimmy'll have me killed, too. And where can we go?"

"Lankey's," Baque said. "Look—you can see it from here."

She pointed the flyer at the freshly painted letters on the strip above the new restaurant, and Baque, looking backward, saw a crowd forming in the street by Visiscope International.

Lankey floated his desk over to the wall and leaned back comfortably. He wore a trim dress suit, and he'd carefully groomed himself for the role of a jovial host, but in his office he was the same ungainly Lankey that Baque had first seen leaning over a bar.

"I told you all hell would break loose," he said, grinning. "There are five thousand people over by Visiscope International, and they're screaming for Erlin Baque. And the crowd is growing."

"I didn't play for more than three minutes," Baque said. "I thought a lot of people might write in to complain about Denton cutting me off, but I didn't expect anything like this."

"You didn't, eh? Five thousand people—maybe ten thousand by now—and Miss Manning risks her neck to get you out of the place. Ask her why, Baque."

"Yes," Baque said. "Why go to all that trouble for me?"

She shuddered. "Your music does things to me."

"It sure does," Lankey said. "Baque, you fool, you gave a quarter of Earth's population three minutes of Sex Music!"

Lankey's opened on schedule that evening, with crowds filling the street outside and struggling through the doors as long as there was standing room. The shrewd Lankey had instituted an admission charge. The standees bought no food, and Lankey saw no point in furnishing free music, even if people were willing to stand to hear it.

He made one last-minute change in plans. Astutely reasoning that the customers would prefer a glamorous hostess to a flat-nosed elderly host, he hired Marigold Manning. She moved about gracefully, the deep blue of her flowing gown offsetting her golden hair.

When Baque took his place at the multichord, the frenzied ovation lasted for twenty minutes.

Midway through the evening Baque sought out Lankey. "Has Denton tried anything?"

"Nothing that I've noticed. Everything is running smoothly."

"That seems odd. He swore we wouldn't open tonight."

Lankey chuckled. "He's had troubles of his own to worry about. The authorities are on his neck about the rioting. I was afraid they'd blame you, but they didn't. Denton put you on visiscope, and then he cut you off, and they figure he's reponsible. And according to my last report, Visiscope International has had more than ten million complaints. Don't worry, Baque. We'll hear from Denton soon enough, and the guilds, too."

"The guilds? Why the guilds?"

"The Tunesmiths' Guild will be damned furious about your dropping the Coms. The Lyric Writers' Guild will go along with them on account of the Coms and because you're using music without words. The Performers' Guild already has it in for you because not many of its members can play worth a damn, and of course it'll support the other guilds. By tomorrow morning, Baque, you'll be the most popular man in the Solar System, and the sponsors, and the visiscope people, and the guilds are going to hate your guts. I'm giving you a twenty-four-hour bodyguard. Miss Manning, too. I want both of you to come out of this alive."

"Do you really think Denton would—"

"Denton would."

The next morning the Performers' Guild blacklisted Lankey's and ordered all the musicians, including Baque, to sever relations. Rose and the other singers joined Baque in respectfully declining, and they found themselves blacklisted before noon. Lankey called in an attorney, the most sinister, furtive, disreputable-looking individual Baque had ever seen.

"They're supposed to give us a week's notice,"

Lankey said, "and another week if we decide to appeal. I'll sue them for five million."

The Commissioner of Public Safety called, and on his heels came the Health Commissioner and the Liquor Commissioner. All three conferred briefly with Lankey and departed grimfaced.

"Denton's moving too late," Lankey said gleefully. "I got to all of them a week ago and recorded our conversations. They don't dare take any action."

A riot broke out in front of Lankey's that night. Lankey had his own riot squad ready for action, and the customers never noticed the disturbance. Lankey's informants estimated that more than fifty million complaints had been received by Visiscope International, and a dozen governmental agencies had scheduled investigations. Anti-Com demonstrations began to errupt spontaneously, and five hundred visiscope screens were smashed in Manhattan restaurants.

Lankey's finished its first week unmolested, entertaining capacity crowds daily. Reservations were pouring in from as far away as Pluto, where a returning space detachment voted to spend its first night of leave at Lankey's. Baque sent to Berlin for a multichordist to understudy him, and Lankey hoped by the end of the month to have the restaurant open twenty-four hours a day.

At the beginning of the second week, Lankey told Baque, "We've got Denton licked. I've countered every move he's made, and now we're going to make a few moves. You're going on visiscope again. I'm making application today. We're a legitimate business, and we've got as much right to buy time as anyone else. If he won't give it to us, I'll sue. But he won't dare refuse."

"Where do you get the money for this?" Baque asked.

Lankey grinned. "I saved it up—a little of it.

Mostly I've had help from people who don't like Denton."

Denton didn't refuse. Baque did an Earth-wide program direct from Lankey's, with Marigold Manning introducing him. He omitted only the Sex Music.

Quitting time at Lankey's. Baque was in his dressing room, wearily changing. Lankey had already left for an early-morning conference with his attorney. They were speculating on Denton's next move.

Baque was uneasy. He was, he told himself, only a dumb musician. He didn't understand legal problems or the tangled web of connections and influence that Lankey negotiated so easily. He knew James Denton was evil incarnate, and he also knew that Denton had enough money to buy Lankey a thousand times over, or to buy the murder of anyone who got in his way. What was he waiting for? Given enough time, Baque might deliver a death-blow to the entire institution of Coms. Surely Denton would know that.

So what *was* he waiting for?

The door burst open, and Marigold Manning stumbled in half undressed, her pale face the bleached whiteness of her plastic breast cups. She slammed the door and leaned against it, sobs shaking her body.

"Jimmy," she gasped. "I got a note from Carol—that's his secretary. She was a good friend of mine. She says Jimmy's bribed our guards, and they're going to kill us on the way home this morning. Or let Jimmy's men kill us."

"I'll call Lankey," Baque said. "There's nothing to worry about."

"No! If they suspect anything they won't wait. We won't have a chance."

"Then we'll just wait until Lankey gets back."

"Do you think it's safe to wait? They know we're getting ready to leave."

Baque sat down heavily. It was the sort of move he expected Denton to make. Lankey picked his men carefully, he knew, but Denton had enough money to buy any man. And yet—

"Maybe it's a trap. Maybe that note's a fake."

"No. I saw that fat little snake Hulsey talking with one of your guards last night, and I knew then that Jimmy was up to something."

"What do you want to do?" Baque asked.

"Could we go out the back way?"

"I don't know. We'd have to get past at least one guard."

"Couldn't we try?"

Baque hesitated. She was frightened—she was sick with fright—but she knew far more about this sort of thing than he did, and she knew James Denton. Without her help he'd never have got out of the Visiscope International building.

"If you think that's the thing to do, we'll try it."

"I'll have to finish changing."

"Go ahead. Let me know when you're ready."

She opened the door a crack and looked out cautiously. "No. You come with me."

Minutes later, Baque and Miss Manning walked leisurely along the corridor at the back of the building, nodded to the two guards on duty there, and with a sudden movement were through the door. Running. A shout of surprise came from behind them, but no one followed. They dashed frantically down an alley, turned off, reached another intersection, and hesitated.

"The conveyer is that way," she gasped. "If we can reach the conveyer—"

"Let's go!"

They ran on, hand in hand. Far ahead of them the alley opened onto a street. Baque glanced anxiously upward for air cars and saw one. Exactly where they were he did not know.

"Are we—being followed?" she asked.

"I don't think so," Baque panted. "There aren't any air cars, and I didn't see anyone behind us when we stopped."

"Then we got away!"

A man stepped abruptly out of the dawn shadows thirty feet ahead. As they halted, stricken dumb with panic, he walked slowly toward them. A hat was pulled low over his face, but there was no mistaking the smile. James Denton.

"Good morning, Beautiful," he said. "Visiscope International hasn't been the same without your lovely presence. And a good morning to you, Mr. Baque."

They stood silently, Miss Manning's hand clutching Baque's arm, her nails cutting through his shirt and into his flesh. He did not move.

"I thought you'd fall for that little gag, Beautiful. I thought you'd be just frightened enough, by now, to fall for it. I have every exit blocked, but I'm grateful to you for picking this one. Very grateful. I like to settle a double cross in person."

Suddenly he whirled on Baque, his voice an angry snarl. "Get going, Baque. It isn't your turn. I have other plans for you."

Baque stood rooted to the damp pavement.

"Move, Baque, before I change my mind."

Miss Manning released his arm. Her voice was a choking whisper. "Go!"

"Baque!" Denton snarled.

"Go, quickly!" she whispered again.

Baque took two hesitant steps.

"Run!" Denton shouted.

Baque ran. Behind him there was the evil crack of a gun, a scream, and silence. Baque faltered, saw Denton looking after him, and ran on.

*   *   *

"So I'm a coward," Baque said.

"No, Baque." Lankey shook his head slowly. "You're a brave man, or you wouldn't have got into this. Trying something there would have been foolishness, not bravery. It's my fault, for thinking he'd move first against the restaurant. I owe Denton something for this, and I'm a man who pays his debts."

A troubled frown creased Lankey's ugly face. He looked perplexedly at Baque. "She was a brave and beautiful woman, Baque," he said, absently caressing his flat nose. "But I wonder why Denton let you go."

The air of tragedy that hung heavily over Lankey's that night did not affect its customers. They gave Baque a thunderous ovation as he moved toward the multichord. As he paused for a halfhearted acknowledgement, three policemen closed in on him.

"Erlin Baque?"

"That's right."

"You're under arrest."

Baque faced them grimly. "What's the charge?" he asked.

"Murder."

The murder of Marigold Manning.

Lankey pressed his mournful face against the bars and talked unhurriedly. "They have some witnesses," he said. "Honest witnesses, who saw you run out of that alley. They have several dishonest witnesses who claim they saw you fire the shot. One of them is your friend Hulsey, who just happened to be taking an early-morning stroll along that alley—or so he'll testify. Denton would probably spend a million to convict you, but he won't have to. He won't even have to bribe the jury. The case against you is that good."

"What about the gun?" Baque asked.

"They'll have a witness who'll claim he sold it to you."

Baque nodded. Things were out of his hands, now. He'd worked for a cause that no one understood—perhaps he hadn't understood himself what he was trying to do. And he'd lost.

"What happens next?" he asked.

Lankey shook his head sadly. "I'm not one to hold back bad news. It means life. They're going to send you to the Ganymede rock pits for life."

"I see," Baque said. He added anxiously, "You're going to carry on?"

"Just what were you trying to do, Baque? You weren't only working for Lankey's. I couldn't figure it out, but I went along with you because I like you. And I like your music. What was it?"

"I don't know. Music, I suppose. People listening to music. Getting rid of the Coms, or some of them. Perhaps if I'd known what I wanted to do—"

"Yes. Yes, I think I understand. Lankey's will carry on, Baque, as long as I have any breath left, and I'm not just being noble. Business is tremendous. That new multichord player isn't bad at all. He's nothing like you were, but there'll never be another one like you. We could be sold out for the next five years if we wanted to book reservations that far ahead. The other restaurants are doing away with visiscope and trying to imitate us, but we have a big head start. We'll carry on the way you had things set up, and your one-third still stands. I'll have it put in trust for you. You'll be a wealthy man when you get back."

"When I get back!"

"Well—a life sentence doesn't necessarily mean life. See that you behave yourself."

"Val?"

"She'll be taken care of. I'll give her a job of some kind to keep her occupied."

"Maybe I can send you music for the restaurant," Baque said. "I should have plenty of time."

"I'm afraid not. It's music they want to keep you away from. So—no writing of music. And they won't let you near a multichord. They think you could hypnotize the guards and turn all the prisoners loose."

"Would they—let me have my record collection?"

"I'm afraid not."

"I see. Well, if that's the way it is—"

"It is. Now I owe Denton two debts."

The unemotional Lankey had tears in his eyes as he turned away.

The jury deliberated for eight minutes and brought in a verdict of guilty. Baque was sentenced to life imprisonment. There was some editorial grumbling on visiscope, because life in the Ganymede rock pits was frequently a very short life.

And there was a swelling undertone of whispering among the little people that the verdict had been bought and paid for by the sponsors, by visiscope. Erlin Baque was framed, it was said, because he gave the people music.

And on the day Baque left for Ganymede, announcement was made of a public exhibition, by H. Vail, multichordist, and B. Johnson, violinist. Admission one dollar.

Lankey collected evidence with painstaking care, rebribed one of the bribed witnesses, and petitioned for a new trial. The petition was denied, and the long years limped past.

The New York Symphony Orchestra was organized, with twenty members. One of James Denton's plush air cars crashed, and he was instantly killed. An unfortunate accident. A millionaire who once heard Erlin Baque play on visiscope endowed a dozen convervatories of music. They were to be called the Baque Conservatories, but a musical historian who had never heard of Baque got the name changed to Bach.

Lankey died, and a son-in-law carried on his efforts as a family trust. A subscription was launched to build a new hall for the New York Symphony, which now numbered forty members. The project gathered force like an avalanche, and a site was finally chosen in Ohio, where the hall would be within easier commuting distance of all parts of the North American continent. Beethoven Hall was erected, seating forty thousand people. The first concert series was fully subscribed forty-eight hours after tickets went on sale.

Opera was given on visiscope for the first time in two hundred years. An opera house was built on the Ohio site, and then an art institute. The Center grew, first by private subscription and then under governmental sponsorship. Lankey's son-in-law died, and a nephew took over the management of Lankey's—and the campaign to free Erlin Baque. Thirty years passed, and then forty.

And forty-nine years, seven months and nineteen days after Baque received his life sentence, he was paroled. He still owned a third interest in Manhattan's most prosperous restaurant, and the profits that had accrued over the years made him an extremely wealthy man. He was ninety-six years old.

* * *

Another capacity crowd at Beethoven Hall. Vacationists from all parts of the Solar System, music lovers who commuted for the concerts, old people who had retired to the Center, young people on educational excursions, forty thousand of them, stirred restlessly and searched the wings for the conductor. Applause thundered down from the twelve balconies as he strode forward.

Erlin Baque sat in his permanent seat at the rear of the main floor. He adjusted his binoculars and peered at the orchestra, wondering again what a contrabassoon sounded like. His bitterness he had left behind on Ganymede. His life at the Center was an unending revelation of miracles.

Of course no one remembered Erlin Baque, tune-smith and murderer. Whole generations of people could not even remember the Coms. And yet Baque felt that he had accomplished all of this just as assuredly as though he had built this building—built the Center—with his own hands. He spread his hands before him, hands deformed by the years in the rock pits, fingers and tips of fingers crushed off, his body maimed by cascading rocks. He had no regrets. He had done his work well.

Two ushers stood in the aisle behind him. One jerked a thumb in his direction and whispered, "Now *there's* a character for you. Comes to every concert. Never misses one. And he just sits there in the back row watching people. They say he was one of the old tunesmiths, years and years ago."

"Maybe he likes music," the other said.

"Naw. Those old tunesmiths never knew anything about music. Besides—he's deaf."

LOINT OF PAW

BY ISAAC ASIMOV (1920–   )

THE MAGAZINE OF FANTASY AND SCIENCE FICTION
AUGUST

We occasionally have more than one story by a particular author in one of our "Best of" books. After all, if a writer is on a roll and turns out two or three of the best stories of the year (in our opinion) which are not too long to be included, how can we avoid including them?

Having said that, I might as well tell you that in my opinion "A Loint of Paw" is not one of the best stories that appeared in 1957. However, it is Marty that picks my stories and I am not allowed to argue the point. He says he likes it and it is only 500 words long, so why not?

Well, I do have to admit it's got one of the cleverest last lines I have ever thought up. (No peeking! Read it from the start and outguess me if you can!) (IA)

There was no question that Montie Stein had, through clever fraud, stolen better than a hundred thousand dollars. There was also no question that he was apprehended one day after the statute of limitations had expired.

It was his manner of avoiding arrest during that interval that brought on the epoch-making case of the State of New York *vs.* Montgomery Harlow Stein, with all its consequences. It introduced law to the fourth dimension.

For, you see, after having committed the fraud and possessed himself of the hundred grand plus, Stein had calmly entered a time machine, of which he was in illegal possession, and set the controls for seven years and one day in the future.

Stein's lawyer put it simply. Hiding in time was not fundamentally different from hiding in space. If the forces of law had not uncovered Stein in the seven-year interval that was their hard luck.

The District Attorney pointed out that the statute of limitations was not intended to be a game between the law and the criminal. It was a merciful measure designed to protect a culprit from indefinitely prolonged fear of arrest. For certain crimes, a defined period of apprehension of apprehension (so to speak) was considered punishment enough. But Stein, the D.A. insisted, had not experienced any period of apprehension at all.

Stein's lawyer remained unmoved. The law said nothing about measuring the extent of a culprit's fear and anguish. It simply set a time limit.

The D.A. said that Stein had not lived through the limit.

Defense stated that Stein was seven years older now than at the time of the crime and had therefore lived through the limit.

The D.A. challenged the statement and the defense produced Stein's birth certificate. He was born in 2973. At the time of the crime, 3004, he was thirty-one. Now, in 3011, he was thirty-eight.

The D.A. shouted that Stein was not physiologically thirty-eight, but thirty-one.

Defense pointed out freezingly that the law, once the individual was granted to be mentally competent, recognized solely chronological age, which could be obtained only by subtracting the date of birth from the date of now.

The D.A., growing impassioned, swore that if Stein were allowed to go free half the laws on the books would be useless.

Then change the laws, said Defense, to take time travel into account, but until the laws are changed let them be enforced as written.

Judge Neville Preston took a week to consider and then handed down his decision. It was a turning point in the history of law. It is almost a pity, then, that some people suspect Judge Preston to have been swayed in his way of thinking by the irresistible impulse to phrase his decision as he did.

For that decision, in full, was:

"A niche in time saves Stein."

GAME PRESERVE

BY ROG PHILLIPS (ROGER P. GRAHAM: 1909–1965)

WORLDS OF IF
OCTOBER

Rog Phillips was a proficient and prolific commercial writer who filled many pages in the sf magazines from 1945 until the early 1960s. A former power plant engineer and shipyard welder, he made his living exclusively from writing after World War II. The bulk of his work in the science fiction field appeared in the Ziff-Davis publications, primarily Amazing *and* Fantastic.

He published at least two minor novels, Time Trap *(1949) and* Worlds Within *(1950) but he is remembered in science fiction as the author of two stunning short stories—"The Yellow Pill" (see Vol. 20 of this series, forthcoming) and "Game Preserve," a deceptively profound piece of work. (MHG)*

One of the games of science fiction, which Horace L. Gold (founding editor of Galaxy *used to emphasize in his day, was that of turning things upside down. He would say, "We get used to looking at things in one particular way, but what happens if we try to build a society in precisely the opposite way."*

This was not completely original, of course. William S. Gilbert (of Gilbert & Sullivan) wrote one play after another in which "topsy-turvydom" ruled the day; in which things were deliberately stood on their heads.

Sometimes I did it myself. I wrote a story (one of my minor efforts) in which mother-love was obscene. In a more subtle fashion, I wrote several books in which my chief robot character, while undeniably a robot and in service to humanity, was nevertheless nobler, wiser, more moral, and better in every way than the human beings he served—and tried to do it so gently that the reader was lured into accepting it without resenting it. (I think I managed.)

Well, then, as long as humanity has been dealing with animals we have carefully tried to select them so that there is "an improvement of the breed" at least in our terms and for our benefit, so that we breed cows that are all milk, hens that are all eggs, sheep that are all wool, and horses that are all work.

Suppose we stand that on its head. Just suppose— (IA)

"Hi-hi-hi!" Big One shouted, and heaved erect with the front end of It.

"Hi-hi-hi," Fat One and the dozen others echoed more mildly, lifting wherever they could get a hold on It.

It was lifted and borne forward in a half crouching trot.

"Hi-hi hi-hi-hihihi," Elf chanted, running and skipping alongside the panting men and their massive burden.

It was carried forward through the lush grass for perhaps fifty feet.

"Ah-ah-ah," Big One sighed loudly, slowly letting the front end of It down until it dug into the soft black soil.

"Ahhh," Fat One and the others sighed, letting go and standing up, stretching aching back muscles, rubbing cramped hands.

"Ah-ah-ah-ah-ah-ah," Elf sang, running around and in between the resting men. He came too close to Big One and was sent sprawling by a quick, good humored push.

Everyone laughed, Big One laughing the loudest. Then Big One lifted Elf to his feet and patted him on the back affectionately, a broad grin forming a toothy gap at the top of his bushy black beard.

Elf answered the grin with one of his own, and at that moment his ever present yearning to grow up to be the biggest and the strongest like Big One flowed through him with new strength.

Abruptly Big One leaped to the front end of It, shouting "Hi-hi-Hi!"

"Hi-hi-hi," the others echoed, scrambling to their places. Once again It was borne forward for fifty feet—and again and again, across the broad meadow-land.

A vast matting of blackberry brambles came into view off to one side. Big One veered his course toward it. The going was uphill now, so the forward surges shortened to forty feet, then thirty. By the time they reached the blackberries they were wet and glossy with sweat.

It was a healthy patch, loaded with large ripe berries. The men ate hungrily at first, then more leisurely, pointing to one another's stained beards and laughing. As they denuded one area they leaped to It, carried it another ten feet, and started stripping another section, never getting more than a few feet from It.

Elf picked his blackberries with first one then another of the men. When his hunger was satisfied he became mischievous, picking a handful of berries and squashing them against the back or the chest of the nearest man and running away, laughing. It was dangerous sport, he knew, because if one of them caught him he would be tossed into the brambles.

Eventually they all had their fill, and thanks to Elf looked as though they were oozing blackberry juice from every pore. The sun was in its mid-afternoon position. In the distance a line of white-barked trees could be seen—evidence of a stream.

"Hi-hi-hi!" Big One shouted.

The journey toward the trees began. It was mostly downhill, so the forward spurts were often as much as a hundred feet.

Before they could hear the water they could smell it. They grunted their delight at the smell, a rich fish odor betokening plenty of food. Intermingled with this odor was the spicy scent of eucalyptus.

They pushed forward with renewed zeal so that the sweat ran down their skins, dissolving the berry juices and making rivulets that looked like purple blood.

When less than a hundred yards from the stream, which was still hidden beyond the tall grasses and the trees lining its bank, they heard the sound of voices, high pitched—women's voices. They became uneasy and nervous. Their surges forward short-ened to ten feet, their rest periods became longer, they searched worriedly for signs of motion through the trees.

They changed their course to arrive a hundred yards downstream from the source of the women's voices. Soon they reached the edge of the tree belt. It was more difficult to carry It through the scatter-ings of bushes. Too, they would get part way through the trees and run into trees too close together to get It past them, and have to back out and try another place. It took almost two hours to work through the trees to the bank of the stream.

Only Elf recognized the place they finally broke through as the place they had left more than two days before. In that respect he knew he was differ-ent, not only from Big One and other grownups,

but also all other Elfs except one, a girl Elf. He had
known it as long as he could remember. He had
learned it from many little things. For example, he
had recognized the place when they reached it. Big
One and the others never remembered anything for
long. In getting It through the trees they blundered
as they always had, and got through by trial and
error with no memory of past blunderings.

Elf was different in another way, too. He could
make more sounds than the others. Sometimes he
would keep a little It with him until it gave him a
feeling of security almost as strong as the big It,
then wander off alone with It and play with making
sounds, "Bz-bz. Walla-walla-walla-rue-rue-la-lo-hi.
Da!" and all kinds of sounds. It excited him to be
able to make different sounds and put them together so that they pleased his hearing, but such
sounds made the others avoid him and look at him
from a safe distance, with worried expressions, so
he had learned not to make *different* sounds within
earshot of the others.

The women and Elfs were upstream a hundred
yards, where they always remained. From the way
they were milling around and acting alarmed it was
evident to Elf they could no more remember the
men having been here a few days before than the
men could remember it themselves. It would be two
or three days before they slowly lost their fear of
one another. It would be the women and their Elfs
who would cautiously approach, holding their portable Its clutched for security, until, finally losing all
fear, they would join into one big group for a while.

Big One and the others carried It right to the
water's edge so they could get into the water without ever being far from It. They shivered and shouted
excitedly as they bathed. Fat One screamed with
delight as he held a squirming fish up for the others

to see. He bit into it with strong white teeth, water dripping from his heavy brown beard. Renewed hunger possessed him. He gobbled the fish and began searching for another. He always caught two fish for any other man's one, which was why he was fat.

Elf himself caught a fish. After eating it he lay on the grassy bank looking up at the white billowing clouds in the blue sky. The sun was now near the horizon, half hidden behind a cloud, sending divergent ramps of light downward. The clouds on the western horizon were slowly taking on color until red, orange, and green separated into definite areas. The soft murmur of the stream formed a lazy background to the excited voices of the men. From upstream, faintly, drifted the woman and Elf sounds.

Here, close to the ground, the rich earthly smell was stronger than that of the stream. After a time a slight breeze sprang up, bringing with it other odors, that of distant pines, the pungent eucalyptus, a musky animal scent.

Big One and the others were out of the water finally. Half asleep, Elf watched them move It up to dry ground. As though that were what the sun had been waiting for, it sank rapidly below the horizon.

The clouds where the sun had been seemed now to blaze for a time with a smoldering redness that cooled to black. The stars came out, one by one.

A multitude of snorings erupted into the night Elf crept among the sleeping forms until he found Big One, and settled down for the night, his head against Big One's chest, his right hand resting against the cool smooth metal of It.

Elf awoke with the bright morning sun directly in his eyes. Big One was gone, already wading in the stream after fish. Some of the others were with him. A few were still sleeping.

Elf leaped to his feet, paused to stretch elaborately, then splashed into the stream. As soon as he caught a fish he climbed out onto the bank and ate it. Then he turned to his search for a little It. There were many lying around, all exactly alike. He studied several, not touching some, touching and even nudging others. Since they all looked alike it was more a matter of *feel* than any real difference that he looked for. One and only one seemed to be the It. Elf returned his attention to it several times.

Finally he picked it up and carried it over to the big It, and hid it underneath. Big One, with shouts of sheer exuberance, climbed up onto the bank dripping water. He grinned at Elf.

Elf looked in the direction of the women and other Elfs. Some of them were wandering in his direction, each carrying an It of some sort, many of them similar to the one he had chosen.

In sudden alarm at the thought that someone might steal his new It, Elf rescued it from its hiding place. He tried to hide it behind him when any of the men looked his way. They scorned an individual It and, as men, preferred an It too heavy for one person.

As the day advanced, women and Elfs approached nearer, pretending to be unaware at times that the men were here, at other times openly fleeing back, overcome by panic.

The men never went farther than twenty feet from the big It. But as the women came closer the men grew surly toward one another. By noon two of them were trying to pick a fight with anyone who would stand up to them.

Elf clutched his little It closely and moved cautiously downstream until he was twenty feet from the big It. Tentatively he went another few feet—farther than any of the men dared go from the big It. At first he felt secure, then panic overcame him and he ran back, dropping the little It. He touched the big It until the panic was gone. After a while he went to the little It and picked it up. He walked around, carrying it, until he felt secure with it again. Finally he went downstream again, twenty feet, twenty-five feet, thirty . . . He felt panic finally, but not overwhelmingly. When it became almost unendurable he calmly turned around and walked back.

Confidence came to him. An hour later he went downstream until he went out of sight of the big It and the men. Security seemed to flow warmly from the little It.

Excitement possessed Elf. He ran here and there, clutching It closely so as not to drop it and lose it. He felt *free*.

"Bdlboo," he said aloud, experimentally. He liked the sounds. "Bdlboo-bdlboo-bdlboo." He saw a berry bush ahead and ran to it to munch on the delicious fruit. "Riddle piddle biddle," he said. It sounded nice.

He ran on, and after a time he found a soft grassy spot and stretched out on his back, holding It carelessly in one hand. He looked up and up, at a layer of clouds going in one direction and another layer above it going in another direction.

Suddenly he heard voices.

At first he thought the wind must have changed so that it was carrying the voices of the men to him. He lay there listening. Slowly he realized these voices were different. They were putting sounds together like those he made himself.

A sense of wonder possessed him. How could there be anyone besides himself who could do that?

Unafraid, yet filled with caution, he clutched It closely to his chest and stole in the direction of the sounds.

After going a hundred yards he saw signs of movement through the trees. He dropped to the ground and lay still for a moment, then gained courage to rise cautiously, ready to run. Stooping low, he stole forward until he could see several moving figures. Darting from tree to tree he moved closer to them, listening with greater excitement than he had ever known to the smoothly flowing variety of beautiful sounds they were making.

This was something new, a sort of game they must be playing. One voice would make a string of sounds then stop, another would make a string of different sounds and stop, a third would take it up. They were good at it, too.

But the closer he got to them the more puzzled he became. They were shaped somewhat like people, they carried Its, they had hands and faces like people. That's as far as the similarity went. Their feet were solid, their arms, legs, and body were not skin at all but strangely colored and unliving in appearance. Their faces were smooth like women's, their hair short like babies', their voices deep like men's.

And the Its they carried were unlike any Elf had ever seen. Not only that, each of them carried more than one.

That was an *idea*! Elf became so excited he almost forgot to keep hidden. If you had more than one It, then if something happened to one you would still feel secure!

He resisted the urge to return to the stream and search for another little It to give him extra security. If he did that he might never again find these creatures that were so like men and yet so different. So instead, he filed the idea away to use at the earliest opportunity and followed the strange creatures, keeping well hidden from them.

Soon Elf could hear the shouts of the men in the distance. From the behavior of the creatures ahead, they had heard those shouts too. They changed their direction so as to reach the stream a hundred yards or more downstream at about the spot where Elf had left. They made no voice sounds now that Elf could hear. They clutched their strangely shaped long Its before them tensely as though feeling greater security that way, their heads turning this way and that as they searched for any movement ahead.

They moved purposefully. An overwhelming sense of kinship brought tears to Elf's eyes. These creatures were *his kind*. Their differences from him were physical and therefore superficial, and even if those differences were greater it wouldn't have mattered.

He wanted, suddenly, to run to them. But the thought of it sent fear through him. Also they might run in panic from him if he suddenly revealed himself.

It would have to be a mutual approach, he felt. He was used to seeing them now. In due time he would reveal himself for a brief moment to them. Later he would stay in the open and watch them, making no move to approach until they got used to his being around. It might take days, but eventually, he felt sure, he could join them without causing them to panic.

After all, there had been the time when he absented himself from the men for three whole days and when he returned they had forgotten him, and his sudden appearance in their midst had sent even Big One into spasms of fear. Unable to flee from the security of the big It, and unable to bear his presence among them without being used to him, they had all fallen on the ground in a fit. He had had to retreat and wait until they recovered. Then, slowly, he had let them get used to his being in sight before approaching again. It had taken two full days to get to the point where they would accept him once more.

That experience, Elf felt, would be valuable to

remember now. He wouldn't want to plunge these creatures into fits or see them scatter and run away.

Also, he was too afraid right now to reveal himself even though every atom of his being called for their companionship.

Suddenly he made another important discovery. Some of the Its these creatures carried had something like pliable vines attached to them so they could be hung about the neck! The thought was so staggering that Elf stopped and examined his It to see if that could be done to it. It was twice as long as his hand and round one way, tapering to a small end that opened to the hollow inside. It was too smooth to hold with a pliable vine unless— He visualized pliable vines woven together to hold It. He wasn't sure how it could be done, but maybe it could.

He set the idea aside for the future and caught up with the creatures again, looking at them with a new emotion, awe. The ideas he got just from watching them were so staggering he was getting dizzy!

Another new thought hit him. He rejected it at once as being too fantastic. It returned. Leaves are thin and pliable and can be wrapped around small objects like pebbles. Could it be that these creatures were really men of some sort, with bodies like men, covered with something thin like leaves are thin? It was a new and dizzy height in portable securities, and hardly likely. No. He rejected the idea with finality and turned his mind to other things.

He knew now where they could reach the stream. He decided to circle them and get ahead of them. For the next few minutes this occupied his full attention, leaving no room for crazy thoughts.

He reached the stream and hid behind some bushes where he would have a quick line of retreat if necessary. He clutched It tightly and waited. In a few moments he saw the first of the creatures emerge a hundred feet away. The others soon joined the first. Elf stole forward from concealment to concealment until he was only fifteen feet from them. His heart was pounding with a mixture of fear and excitement. His knuckles were white from clutching It.

The creatures were still carrying on their game of making sounds, but now in an amazing new way that made them barely audible. Elf listened to the incredibly varied sounds, enraptured.

"This colony seems to have remained pure."

"You never can tell."

"No, you never can tell. Get out the binoculars and look, Joe."

"Not just yet, Harold. I'm looking to see if I can spot one whose behavior shows intelligence."

Elf ached to imitate some of the beautiful combinations of sounds. He wanted to experiment and see if he could make the softly muted voices. He had an idea how it might be done, not make a noise in your throat but breathe out and form the sounds with your mouth just like you were uttering them aloud.

One of the creatures fumbled at an It hanging around his neck. The top of it hinged back. He reached in and brought out a gleaming It and held it so that it covered his eyes. He was facing toward the men upstream and stood up slowly.

"See something, Joe?"

Suddenly Elf was afraid. Was this some kind of magic? He had often puzzled over the problem of whether things were there when he didn't look at them. He had experimented, closing his eyes then opening them suddenly to see if things were still there, and they always were; but maybe this was magic to make the men not be there. Elf waited, watching upstream, but Big One and the others did not vanish.

The one called Joe chuckled. "The toy the adult males have would be a museum piece if it were intact. A 1960 Ford, I think. Only one wheel on it, right front."

Elf's attention jerked back. One of the creatures was reaching over his shoulder, lifting on the large It fastened there. The top of the It pulled back. He reached inside, bringing out something that made Elf almost exclaim aloud. It was shaped exactly like the little It Elf was carrying, but it glistened in the sunlight and its interior was filled with a richly brown fluid.

"Anyone else want a Coke?"

"This used to be a picnic area," the one called Joe said, not taking his eyes from the binoculars. "I can see a lot of pop bottles lying around in the general area of that wreck of a Ford."

While Elf watched, breathless, the creature reached inside the skin of his hip and brought out a very small It and did something to the small end of the hollow It. Putting the very small It back under the skin of his hip, he put the hollow It to his lips and tilted it. Elf watched the brown liquid drain out. Here was magic. Such an It—the very one he carried—could be filled with water from the stream and carried around to drink any time!

When the It held no more liquid the creature dropped it to the ground. Elf could not take his eyes from it. He wanted it more than he had ever wanted anything. They might forget it. Sometimes the women dropped their Its and forgot them, picking up another one instead, and these creatures had beardless faces like women. Besides, each of them carried so many Its that they would feel just as secure without this one.

So many Its! One of the creatures held a flat white It in one hand and a very slim It shaped like a straight section of a bush stem, pointed at one end, with which he scratched on the white It at times, leaving black designs.

"There're fourteen males," the one called Joe whispered. The other wrote it down.

The way these creatures did things, Elf decided, was very similar to the way Big One and the other men went at moving the big It. They were very much like men in their actions, these creatures.

"Eighty-five or six females."

"See any signs of intelligent action yet?"

"No. A couple of the males are fighting. Probably going to be a mating free-for-all tomorrow or next day. There's one! Just a minute, I want to make sure. It's a little girl, maybe eight or nine years old. Good forehead. Her eyes definitely lack that large marble-like quality of the submoron parent species. She's intelligent all right. She's drawing something in the sand with a stick. Give me your rifle, Bill, it's got a better telescope sight on it than mine, and I don't want her to suffer."

That little It, abandoned on the ground. Elf wanted it. One of the creatures would be sure to pick it up. Elf worried. He would never get it then. If only the creatures would go, or not notice him. If only—

The creature with the thing over his eyes put it back where he had gotten it out of the thing hanging from his shoulder. He had taken one of the long slim things from another of the creatures and placed the thick end against his shoulder, the small end pointed upstream. The others were standing, their backs to Elf, all of them looking upstream. If they would remain that way, maybe he could dart out and get the little It. In another moment they might lose interest in whatever they were watching.

Elf darted out from his concealment and grabbed the It off the ground, and in the same instant an ear-shattering sound erupted from the long slim thing against the creature's shoulder.

*   *   *

"Got her!" the creature said.

Paralyzed with fright, Elf stood motionless. One of the creatures started to turn his way. At the last instant Elf darted back to his place of concealment. His heart was pounding so loudly he felt sure they would hear it.

"You sure, Joe?"

"Right through the head. She never knew what happened."

Elf held the new It close to him, ready to run if he were discovered. He didn't dare look at it yet. It wouldn't notice if he just held it and felt it without looking at it. It was cold at first, colder than the water in the stream. Slowly it warmed. He dared to steal a quick glance at it. It gleamed at him as though possessed of inner life. A new feeling of security grew within him, greater than he had ever known. The other It, the one half filled with dried mud, and deeply scratched from the violent rush of water over it when the stream went over its banks, lay forgotten at his feet.

"Well, that finishes the survey trip for this time."

Elf paid little attention to the voice whispers now, too wrapped up in his new feelings.

"Yes, and quite a haul. Twenty-two colonies—three more than ten years ago. Fourteen of them uncontaminated, seven with only one or two intelligent offspring to kill, only one colony so contaminated we had to wipe it out altogether. And one renegade."

"The renegades are growing scarcer every time. Another ten or twenty years and they'll be extinct."

"Then there won't be any more intelligent offspring in these colonies."

"Let's get going. It'll be dark in another hour or so."

The creatures were hiding some of their Its under

their skin, in their carrying cases. There was a feeling about them of departure. Elf waited until they were on the move, back the way they had come, then he followed at a safe distance.

He debated whether to show himself now or wait. The sun was going down in the sky now. It wouldn't be long until it went down for the night. Should he wait until in the morning to let them get their first glimpse of him?

He smiled to himself. He had plenty of time. Tomorrow and tomorrow. He would never return to Big One and the other men. Men or creatures, he would join with these new and wonderful creatures. They were *his kind*.

He thought of the girl Elf. They were her kind, too. If he could only get her to come with him.

On sudden impulse he decided to try. These creatures were going back the same way they had come. If he ran, and if she came right with him, they could catch up with the creatures before they went so far they would lose them.

He turned back, going carefully until he could no longer see the creatures, then he ran. He headed directly toward the place where the women and Elfs stayed. They would not be so easily alarmed as the men because there were so many of them they couldn't remember one another, and one more or less of the Elfs went unnoticed.

When he reached the clearing he slowed to a walk, looking for her. Ordinarily he didn't have to look much. She would see him and come to him, smiling in recognition of the fact that he was the only one like her.

He became a little angry. Was she hiding? Then he saw her. He went to her. She was on her stomach, motionless as though asleep, but something was different. There was a hole in one side of her head, and on the opposite side it was torn open, red and grayish white, with— He knelt down and touched her. She had the same inert feel to her that others had had who never again moved.

He studied her head curiously. He had never seen anything like this. He shook her. She remained limp. He sighed. He knew what would happen now. It was already happening. The odor was very faint yet, but she would not move again, and day after day the odor would get stronger. No one liked it.

He would have to hurry or he would lose the creatures. He turned and ran, never looking back. Once he started to cry, then stopped in surprise. Why had he been crying, he wondered. He hadn't hurt himself.

He caught up with the creatures. They were hurrying now, their long slender Its balanced on one shoulder, the big end resting in the palm of the hand. They no longer moved cautiously. Shortly it was new country. Elf had never been this far from the stream. Big One more or less led the men, and always more or less followed the same route in cross-country trips.

The creatures didn't spend hours stumbling along impossible paths. They looked ahead of them and selected a way, and took it. Also they didn't have a heavy It to transport, fifty feet at a time. Elf began to sense they had a destination in mind. Probably the place they lived.

Just ahead was a steep bank, higher than a man, running in a long line. The creatures climbed the bank and vanished on the other side. Cautiously Elf followed them, heading toward a large stone with It qualities at the top of the bank from whose concealment he could see where they had gone without being seen. He reached it and cautiously peeked around it. Just below him were the creatures, but what amazed Elf was the sight of the big It.

It was very much like the big It the men had, except that there were differences in shape, and instead of one round thing at one corner, it had one at each corner and rested on them so that it was held off the ground. It glistened instead of being dull. It had a strange odor that was quite strong.

The creatures were putting some of their Its into it, two of them had actually climbed into it—something neither Elf nor the men had ever dared to do with their own big It.

Elf took his eyes off of it for a moment to marvel at the ground. It seemed made of stone, but such stone as he had never before seen. It was an even width with edges going in straight lines that paralleled the long narrow hill on which he stood, and on the other side was a similar hill, extending as far as the eye could see.

He returned his attention to the creatures and their big It. The creatures had all climbed into it now. Possibly they were settling down for the night, though it was still early for that . . .

No matter. There was plenty of time. Tomorrow and tomorrow. Elf would show himself in the morning, then run away. He would come back again after a while and show himself a little longer, giving them time to get used to him so they wouldn't panic.

They were playing their game of making voice sounds to one another again. It seemed their major preoccupation. Elf thought how much fun it would be to be one of them, making voice sounds to his heart's content.

"I don't see why the government doesn't wipe out the whole lot," one of them was saying. "It's hopeless to keep them alive. Feeble-mindedness is dominant in them. They can't be absorbed into the race again, and any intelligent offspring they get from mating with a renegade would start a long line of descendants, at least one fourth of whom would be mindless idiots."

"Well," another of them said, "it's one of those things where there is no answer. Wipe them out, and next year it would be all the blond-haired people to be wiped out to keep the race of dark-haired people pure, or something. Probably in another hundred years nature will take care of the problem by wiping them out for us. Meanwhile we game wardens must make the rounds every two years and weed out any of them we can find that have intelligence." He looked up the embankment but did not notice Elf's head, concealed partially by the grass around the concrete marker. "It's an easy job. Any of them we missed seeing this time, we'll probably get next time. In the six or eight visits we make before the intelligent ones can become adults and mate we always find them."

"What I hate is when they see us, those intelligent ones," a third voice said. "When they walk right up to us and want to be friends with us it's too much like plain murder, except that they can't talk, and only make moronic sounds like 'Bdl-bdl-bdl.' Even so, it gets me when we kill them." The others laughed.

Suddenly Elf heard a new sound from the big It. It was not a voice sound, or if it was it was one that Elf felt he could not possibly match exactly. It was a growling. "RRrr-RRrrRRrr." Suddenly it was replaced by still a different sound, a "p-p-p-p-p" going very rapidly. Perhaps it was the way these creatures snored. It was not unpleasant. Elf cocked his head to one side, listening to the sound, smiling. How exciting it would be when he could join with these creatures! He wanted to so much.

The big It began to move. In the first brief second Elf could not believe his senses. How could it move without being carried? But it was moving, and the creatures didn't seem to be aware of it! Or perhaps they were too overcome by fear to leap out!

Already the big It was moving faster than a walk, and was moving faster with every heartbeat. How could they remain unaware of it and not leap to safety?

Belatedly Elf abandoned caution and leaped down the embankment to the flat ribbon of rock, shouting. But already the big It was over a hundred yards away, and moving faster now than birds in flight!

He shouted, but the creatures didn't hear him—or perhaps they were so overcome with fright that they were frozen. Yes, that must be it.

Elf ran after the big It. If he could only catch up with it he would gladly join the creatures in their fate. Better to die with them than to lose them!

He ran and ran, refusing to believe he could never overtake the big It, even when it disappeared from view, going faster than the wind. He ran and ran until his legs could lift no more.

Blinded by tears, he tripped and sprawled full length on the wide ribbon of stone. His nose bled from hitting the hard surface. His knees were scraped and bleeding. He was unaware of this.

He was aware only that the creatures were gone, to what unimaginable fate he could not guess, but lost to him, perhaps forever.

Sobs welled up within him, spilled out, shaking his small naked body. He cried as he hadn't cried since he was a baby.

And the empty Coca Cola bottle, clutched forgotten in his hand, glistened with the rays of the setting sun . . .

SOLDIER

BY HARLAN ELLISON (1934–   )

FANTASTIC UNIVERSE (AS "SOLDIER FROM TOMORROW) OCTOBER

It's a particular pleasure to welcome Harlan Ellison to this series, because he is such a stunning and powerful writer, and because he has done so much to shape the course of modern speculative fiction. Unlike too many writers in this series he has received many of the awards due him—at last count three Nebulas, four Writers Guild of America Awards, an incredible ten and a half Hugos (including two "Special Hugos" as best editor), and two Edgar Allan Poe Awards from the Mystery Writers of America, most recently in 1988 for his story "Soft Monkey." He is one of very few writers who has built a major reputation based on short fiction.

"Soldier" was adapted by Ellison for television and ran on the legendary Outer Limits *on September 19, 1964. Mr. Ellison reportedly received a substantial out-of-court settlement from the folks who made the film* The Terminator, *and all television appearances and videocassettes carry the written statement, "The Producers wish to acknowledge the works of Harlan Ellison." (MHG)*

General William Tecumseh Sherman who, next to

Ulysses Simpson Grant, was the most effective of the generals of the Union forces in the American Civil War was addressing a convention of the Grand Army of the Republic at Columbus, Ohio on August 11, 1880. The G. A. R. was an organization of Civil War veterans and, presumably, the passing of time softened the hard edges of memory and lent a roseate hue to things that lacked them altogether at the time.

Sherman, however (whom I, somehow, have always considered a rather wild eccentric) had not forgotten. He spoke at the convention and one line in his speech was: "There is many a boy here today who looks on war as all glory, but, boys, it is all hell." This has been shortened to "War is hell."

Why is it so hard for human beings to learn this? Why, having experienced war, do human beings fight again—often with bands playing, and people shouting with gleeful excitement?

Perhaps that is because, according to a Latin proverb: "Dulce bellum inexpertis." Translated, that means, "Sweet is war to those who have never experienced it."

William Shakespeare has Othello mourn the fact that he has disqualified himself from his "occupation." He says:

"Farewell the neighing steed, and the shrill trump,
The spirit-stirring drum, the ear-piercing fife,
The royal banner, and all quality,
Pride, pomp and circumstance of glorious war!"

Very pretty—but Shakespeare never experienced war.
But I've had my say. Now read Harlan's story. (IA)

Qarlo hunkered down farther into the firmhole, gathering his cloak about him. Even the triple-lining of the cape could not prevent the seeping cold of the battlefield from reaching him; and even through one of those linings—lead impregnated—he could feel the faint tickle of dropout, all about him, eating at his tissues. He began to shiver again. The Push was going on to the South, and he had to wait, had to listen for the telepathic command of his superior officer.

He fingered an edge of the firmhole, noting he had not steadied it up too well with the firmer. He drew the small molecule-hardening instrument from his pouch, and examined it. The calibrater had slipped a notch, which explained why the dirt of the firmhole had not become as hard as he had desired.

Off to the left the hiss of an eighty-thread beam split the night air, and he shoved the firmer back quickly. The spiderweb tracery of the beam lanced across the sky, poked tentatively at an armor center, throwing blood-red shadows across Qarlo's crag-like features.

The armor center backtracked the thread beam, retaliated with a blinding flash of its own batteries. One burst. Two. Three. The eighty-thread reared once more, feebly, then subsided. A moment later the concussion of its power chambers exploding shook the Earth around Qarlo, causing bits of unfirmed dirt and small pebbles to tumble in on him. Another moment, and the shrapnel came through.

Qarlo lay flat to the ground, soundlessly hoping for a bit more life amidst all this death. He knew his chances of coming back were infinitesimal. What was it? Three out of every thousand came back? He had no illusions. He was a common footman, and he knew he would die out here, in the midst of the Great War VII.

As though the detonation of the eighty-thread had been a signal, the weapons of Qarlo's company opened up, full-on. The webbings crisscrossed the blackness overhead with delicate patterns—appearing, disappearing, changing with every second, ranging through the spectrum, washing the bands of colors outside the spectrum Qarlo could catalog. Qarlo slid into a tiny ball in the slush-filled bottom of the firmhole, waiting.

He was a good soldier. He knew his place. When those metal and energy beasts out there were snarling at each other, there was nothing a lone foot soldier could do—but die. He waited, knowing his time would come much too soon. No matter how violent, how involved, how pushbutton-ridden Wars became, it always simmered down to the man on foot. It had to, for men fought men still.

His mind dwelled limply in a state between reflection and alertness. A state all men of war came to know when there was nothing but the thunder of the big guns abroad in the night.

The stars had gone into hiding.

Abruptly, the thread beams cut out, the traceries winked off, silence once again descended. Qarlo snapped to instant attentiveness. This was the moment. His mind was now keyed to one sound, one only. Inside his head the command would form, and he would act; not entirely of his own volition. The strategists and psychmen had worked together on this thing: the tone of command was keyed into each soldier's brain. Printed in, probed in, sunken in. It was there, and when the Regimenter sent his telepathic orders, Qarlo would leap like a puppet, and advance on direction.

Thus, when it came, it was as though he had anticipated it; as though he knew a second before the mental rasping and the *Advance!* erupted within his skull, that the moment had arrived.

A second sooner than he should have been, he was up, out of the firmhole, hugging his Brandelmeier to his chest, the weight of the plastic bandoliers and his pouch reassuring across his stomach, back, and hips. Even before the mental word actually came.

Because of this extra moment's jump on the command, it happened, and it happened just that way. No other chance coincidences could have done it, but done just that way.

When the first blasts of the enemy's zeroed-in batteries met the combined rays of Qarlo's own guns, also pin-pointed, they met at a point that should by all rights have been empty. But Qarlo had jumped too soon, and when they met, the soldier was at the focal point.

Three hundred distinct beams latticed down, joined in a coruscating rainbow, threw negatively charged particles five hundred feet in the air, shorted out . . . and warped the soldier off the battlefield.

Nathan Schwachter had his heart attack right there on the subway platform.

The soldier materialized in front of him, from nowhere, filthy and ferocious-looking, a strange weapon cradled to his body . . . just as the old man was about to put a penny in the candy machine.

Qarlo's long cape was still, the dematerialization and subsequent reappearance having left him untouched. He stared in confusion at the sallow face before him, and started violently at the face's piercing shriek.

Qarlo watched with growing bewilderment and terror as the sallow face contorted and sank to the littered floor of the platform. The old man clutched his chest, twitched and gasped several times. His legs jerked spasmodically, and his mouth opened wildly again and again. He died with mouth open, eyes staring at the ceiling.

Qarlo looked at the body disinterestedly for a moment; death . . . what did one death matter . . . every day during the War, ten thousand died . . .

more horribly than this . . . this was as nothing to him.

The sudden universe-filling scream of an incoming express train broke his attention. The black tunnel that his War-filled world had become, was filled with the rusty wail of an unseen monster, bearing down on him out of the darkness.

The fighting man in him made his body arch, sent it into a crouch. He poised on the balls of his feet, his rifle levering horizontal instantly, pointed at the sound.

From the crowds packed on the platform, a voice rose over the thunder of the incoming train:

"*Him!* It was *him!* He shot that old man . . . he's crazy!" Heads turned; eyes stared; a little man with a dirty vest, his bald head reflecting the glow of the overhead lights, was pointing a shaking finger at Qarlo.

It was as if two currents had been set up simultaneously. The crowd both drew away and advanced on him. Then the train barreled around the curve, drove past, blasting sound into the very fibers of the soldier's body. Qarlo's mouth opened wide in a soundless scream, and more from reflex than intent, the Brandelmeier erupted in his hands.

A triple-thread of cold blue beams sizzled from the small bell mouth of the weapon, streaked across the tunnel, and blasted full into the front of the train.

The front of the train melted down quickly, and the vehicle ground to a stop. The metal had been melted like a coarse grade of plastic on a burner. Where it had fused into a soggy lump, the metal was bright and smeary—more like the gleam of oxidized silver than anything else.

Qarlo regretted having fired the moment he felt the Brandelmeier buck. He was not where he should be—*where* he was, that was still another, more pressing problem—and he knew he was in danger. Every movement had to be watched as carefully as possible . . . and perhaps he had gotten off to a bad start already. But that noise . . .

He had suffered the screams of the battlefield, but the reverberations of the train, thundering back and forth in that enclosed space, was a nightmare of indescribable horror.

As he stared dumbly at his handiwork, from behind him, the crowd made a concerted rush.

Three burly, charcoal-suited executives—each carrying an attaché case which he dropped as he made the lunge, looking like unhealthy carbon-copies of each other—grabbed Qarlo above the elbows, around the waist, about the neck.

The soldier roared something unintelligible and flung them from him. One slid across the platform on the seat of his pants, bringing up short, his stomach and face smashing into a tiled wall. The second spun away, arms flailing, into the crowd. The third tried to hang onto Qarlo's neck. The soldier lifted him bodily, arched him over his head—breaking the man's insecure grip—and pitched him against a stanchion. The executive hit the girder, slid down, and lay quite still, his back oddly twisted.

The crowd emitted scream after scream, drew away once more. Terror rippled back through its ranks. Several women, near the front, suddenly became aware of the blood pouring from the face of one of the executives, and keeled onto the dirty platform unnoticed. The screams continued, seeming echoes of the now-dead express train's squealing.

But as an entity, the crowd backed the soldier down the platform. For a moment Qarlo forgot he still held the Brandelmeier. He lifted the gun to a threatening position, and the entity that was the crowd pulsed back.

Nightmare! It was all some sort of vague, formless

*nightmare to Qarlo. This was not the War, where
anyone he saw, he blasted. This was something else,
some other situation, in which he was lost, disori-
ented. What was happening?*

Qarlo moved toward the wall, his back prickly
with fear sweat. He had expected to die in the War,
but something as simple and direct and expected as
that had not happened. He was *here*, not *there*—
wherever *here* was, and wherever *there* had gone—
and these people were unarmed, obviously civilians.
Which would not have kept him from murdering
them . . . but what was happening? Where was the
battlefield?

His progress toward the wall was halted momentarily as he backed cautiously around a stanchion.
He knew there were people behind him, as well as
the white-faced knots before him, and he was beginning to suspect there was no way out. Such confusion boiled up in his thoughts, so close to hysteria
was he—plain soldier of the fields—that his mind
forcibly rejected the impossibility of being somehow
transported from the War into this new—and in
many ways more terrifying—situation. He concentrated on one thing only, as a good soldier should:
Out!

He slid along the wall, the crowd flowing before
him, opening at his approach, closing in behind. He
whirled once, driving them back farther with the
black hole of the Brandelmeier's bell mouth. Again
he hesitated (not knowing why) to fire upon them.

He sensed they were enemies. But still they were
unarmed. And yet, that had never stopped him
before. The village in TetraOmsk Territory, beyond
the Volga somewhere. They had been unarmed there,
too, but the square had been filled with civilians he
had not hesitated to burn. Why was he hesitating
now?

The Brandelmeier continued in its silence.

Qarlo detected a commotion behind the crowd, above the crowd's inherent commotion. And a movement. Something was happening there. He backed tightly against the wall as a blue-suited, brass-buttoned man broke through the crowd.

The man took one look, caught the unwinking black eye of the Brandelmeier, and threw his arms back, indicating to the crowd to clear away. He began screaming at the top of his lungs, veins standing out in his temples, "Geddoudahere! The guy's a cuckaboo! Somebody'll get kilt! Beat it, run!"

The crowd needed no further impetus. It broke in the center and streamed toward the stairs.

Qarlo swung around, looking for another way out, but both accessible stairways were clogged by fighting commuters, shoving each other mercilessly to get out. He was effectively trapped.

The cop fumbled at his holster. Qarlo caught a glimpse of the movement from the corner of his eye. Instinctively he knew the movement for what it was; a weapon was about to be brought into use. He swung about, leveling the Brandelmeier. The cop jumped behind a stanchion just as the soldier pressed the firing stud.

A triple-thread of bright blue energy leaped from the weapon's bell mouth. The beam went out over the heads of the crowd, neatly melting away a five foot segment of wall supporting one of the stairways. The stairs creaked, and the sound of tortured metal adjusting to poor support and an overcrowding of people, rang through the tunnel. The cop looked fearfully above himself, saw the beams curving, then settle under the weight, and turned a wide-eyed stare back at the soldier.

The cop fired twice, from behind the stanchion, the booming of the explosions catapulting back and forth in the enclosed space.

The second bullet took the soldier above the wrist

in his left arm. The Brandelmeier slipped uselessly from his good hand, as blood stained the garment he wore. He stared at his shattered lower arm in amazement. Doubled amazement.

What manner of weapon was this, the blue-coated man had used? No beam, that. Nothing like anything he had ever seen before. No beam to fry him in his tracks. It was some sort of power that hurled a projectile . . . that had ripped his body. He stared stupidly as blood continued to flow out of his arm.

The cop, less anxious now to attack this man with the weird costume and unbelievable rifle, edged cautiously from behind his cover, skirting the edge of the platform, trying to get near enough to Qarlo to put another bullet into him, should he offer further resistance. But the soldier continued to stand, spraddle-legged, staring at his wound, confused at where he was, what had happened to him, the screams of the trains as they bulleted past, and the barbarian tactics of his blue-coated adversary.

The cop moved slowly, steadily, expecting the soldier to break and run at any moment. The wounded man stood rooted, however. The cop bunched his muscles and leaped the few feet intervening.

Savagely, he brought the barrel of his pistol down on the side of Qarlo's neck, near the ear. The soldier turned slowly, anchored in his tracks, and stared unbelievingly at the policeman for an instant. Then his eyes glazed, and he collapsed to the platform.

As a gray swelling mist bobbed up around his mind, one final thought impinged incongruously: *he struck me . . . physical contact? I don't believe it! What have I gotten into?*

Light filtered through vaguely. Shadows slithered and wavered, sullenly formed into solids.

"Hey, Mac. Got a light?"

Shadows blocked Qarlo's vision, but he knew he was lying on his back, staring up. He turned his head, and a wall oozed into focus, almost at his nose tip. He turned his head the other way. Another wall, about three feet away, blending in his sight into a shapeless gray blotch. He abruptly realized the back of his head hurt. He moved slowly, swiveling his head, but the soreness remained. Then he realized he was lying on some hard metal surface, and he tried to sit up. The pains throbbed higher, making him feel nauseated, and for an instant his vision receded again.

Then it steadied, and he sat up slowly. He swung his legs over the sharp edge of what appeared to be a shallow, sloping metal trough. It was a mattressless bunk, curved in its bottom, from hundreds of men who had lain there before him.

He was in a cell.

"Hey! I said you got a match there?"

Qarlo turned from the empty rear wall of the cell and looked through the bars. A bulb-nosed face was thrust up close to the metal barrier. The man was short, in filthy rags whose odor reached Qarlo with tremendous offensiveness. The man's eyes were bloodshot, and his nose was crisscrossed with blue and red veins. Acute alcoholism, reeking from every pore; *acne rosacea* that had turned his nose into a hideous cracked and pocked blob.

Qarlo knew he was in detention, and from the very look, the very smell of this other, he knew he was not in a military prison. The man was staring at him, oddly.

"Match, Charlie? You got a match?" He puffed his fat, wet lips at Qarlo, forcing the bit of cigarette stub forward with his mouth. Qarlo stared back; he could not understand the man's words. They were so slowly spoken, so sharp and yet unintelligible. But he knew what to answer.

He said: "Marnames Qarlo Clobregnny, pyrt, sizfifwunoh tootoonyn." The soldier muttered by rote, surly tones running together.

"Whaddaya mad at *me* for, buddy? I didn't putcha in here," argued the match-seeker. "All I wanted was a light for this here butt." He held up two inches of smoked stub. "How come they gotcha inna cell, and not runnin' around loose inna bull pen like us?" He cocked a thumb over his shoulder, and for the first time Qarlo realized others were in this jail.

"Ah, to hell wit ya," the drunk muttered. He cursed again, softly under his breath, turning away. He walked across the bull pen and sat down with the four other men—all vaguely similar in facial content—who lounged around a rough-hewn table-bench combination. The table and benches, all one piece, like a picnic table, were bolted to the floor.

"A screwloose," the drunk said to the others, nodding his balding head at the soldier in his long cape and metallic skintight suit. He picked up the crumpled remnants of an ancient magazine and leafed through it as though he knew every line of type, every girlie illustration, by heart.

Qarlo looked over the cell. It was about ten feet high by eight across, a sink with one thumb-push spigot running cold water, a commode without seat or paper, and metal trough, roughly the dimensions of an average-sized man, fastened to one wall. One enclosed bulb burned feebly in the ceiling. Three walls of solid steel. Ceiling and floor of the same, riveted together at the seams. The fourth wall was the barred door.

The firmer might be able to wilt that steel, he realized, and instinctively reached for his pouch. It was the first moment he had had a chance to think of it, and even as he reached, knew the satisfying weight of it was gone. His bandoliers also. His

Brandelmeier, of course. His boots, too, and there seemed to have been some attempt to get his cape off, but it was all part of the skintight suit of metallic-mesh cloth.

The loss of the pouch was too much. Everything that had happened, had happened so quickly, so blurrily, meshed, and the soldier was abruptly overcome by confusion and a deep feeling of hopelessness. He sat down on the bunk, the ledge of metal biting into his thighs. His head still ached from a combination of the blow dealt him by the cop, and the metal bunk where he had lain. He ran a shaking hand over his head, feeling the fractional inch of his brown hair, cut battle-style. Then he noticed that his left hand had been bandaged quite expertly. There was hardly any throbbing from his wound.

That brought back to sharp awareness all that had transpired, and the War leaped into his thoughts. The telepathic command, the rising from the firm-hole, the rifle at the ready . . .

. . . then a sizzling shusssss, and the universe had exploded around him in a billion tiny flickering novas of color and color and color. Then suddenly, just as suddenly as he had been standing on the battlefield of Great War VII, advancing on the enemy forces of Ruskie-Chink, he was *not* there.

He was here.

He was in some dark, hard tunnel, with a great beast roaring out of the blackness onto him, and a man in a blue coat had shot him, and clubbed him. Actually *touched* him! Without radiation gloves! How had the man known Qarlo was not booby-trapped with radiates? He could have died in an instant.

Where was he? What war was this he was engaged in? Were these Ruskie-Chink or his own Tri-Continenters? He did not know, and there was no sign of an explanation.

Then he thought of something more important. If

he had been captured, then they must want to question him. There was a way to combat *that*, too. He felt around in the hollow tooth toward the back of his mouth. His tongue touched each tooth till it hit the right lower bicuspid. It was empty. The poison glob was gone, he realized in dismay. *It must have dropped out when the blue-coat clubbed me,* he thought.

He realized he was at *their* mercy; who *they* might be was another thing to worry about. And with the glob gone, he had no way to stop their extracting information. It was bad. Very bad, according to the warning conditioning he had received. They could use Probers, or dyoxl-scopalite, or hypno-scourge, or any one of a hundred different methods, any one of which would reveal to them the strength of numbers in his company, the battery placements, the gun ranges, the identity and thought wave band of every officer . . . in fact, a good deal. More than he had thought he knew.

He had become a very important prisoner of War. He *had* to hold out, he realized!

Why?

The thought popped up, and was gone. All it left in its wake was the intense feeling: I despise War, all war and *the* War! Then, even that was gone, and he was alone with the situation once more, to try and decide what had happened to him . . . what secret weapon had been used to capture him . . . and if these unintelligible barbarians with the projectile weapons *could*, indeed, extract his knowledge from him.

I swear they won't get anything out of me but my name, rank, and serial number, he thought desperately.

He mumbled those particulars aloud, softly as reassurance: "Marnames Qarlo Clobregnny, pryt, sizfifwunohtootoonyn."

The drunks looked up from their table and their shakes, at the sound of his voice. The man with the rosedrop nose rubbed a dirty hand across fleshy chin folds, repeated his philosophy of the strange man in the locked cell.

"Screwloose!"

He might have remained in jail indefinitely, considered a madman or a mad rifleman. But the desk sergeant who had booked him, after the soldier had received medical attention, grew curious about the strangely shaped weapon.

As he put the things into security, he tested the Brandelmeier—hardly realizing what knob or stud controlled its power, never realizing what it could do—and melted away one wall of the safe room. Three inch plate steel, and it melted bluely, fused solidly.

He called the Captain, and the Captain called the F.B.I., and the F.B.I. called Internal Security, and Internal Security said, "Preposterous!" and checked back. When the Brandelmeier had been thoroughly tested—as much as *could* be tested, since the rifle had no seams, no apparent power source, and fantastic range—they were willing to believe. They had the soldier removed from his cell, transported along with the pouch, and a philologist named Soames, to the I.S. general headquarters in Washington, D.C. The Brandelmeier came by jet courier, and the soldier was flown in by helicopter, under sedation. The philologist named Soames, whose hair was long and rusty, whose face was that of a starving artist, whose temperament was that of a saint, came in by specially chartered plane from Columbia University. The pouch was sent by sealed Brinks truck to the airport, where it was delivered under heaviest guard to a mail plane. They all arrived in Washington within ten minutes of one another, and without

seeing anything of the surrounding countryside, were
whisked away to the subsurface levels of the I.S.
Buildings.

When Qarlo came back to consciousness, he found
himself again in a cell, this time quite unlike the
first. No bars, but just as solid to hold him in, with
padded walls. Qarlo paced around the cell a few
times, seeking breaks in the walls, and found what
was obviously a door, in one corner. But he could
not work his fingers between the pads, to try and
open it.

He sat down on the padded floor, and rubbed the
bristled top of his head in wonder. Was he *never* to
find out what had happened to himself? And *when*
was he going to shake this strange feeling that he
was being watched?

Overhead, through a pane of one-way glass that
looked like a ventilator grille, the soldier was being
watched.

Lyle Sims and his secretary knelt before the window in the floor, along with the philologist named
Soames. Where Soames was shaggy, ill-kept, hungry-
looking and placid . . . Lyle Sims was lean, collegiate-
seeming, brusque and brisk. He had been special
advisor to an unnamed branch office of Internal
Security, for five years, dealing with every strange
or offbeat problem too outré for regulation inquiry.
Those years had hardened him in an odd way; he
was quick to recognize authenticity, even quicker to
recognize fakery.

As he watched, his trained instincts took over
completely, and he knew in a moment of spying,
that the man in the cell below was out of the ordinary.
Not so in any fashion that could be labeled—"drunk-
ard," "foreigner," "psychotic"—but so markedly
different, so *other*, he was taken aback.

"Six feet three inches," he recited to the girl

kneeling beside him. She made the notation on her pad, and he went on calling out characteristics of the soldier below. "Brown hair, clipped so short you can see the scalp. Brown . . . no, black eyes. Scars. Above the left eye, running down to center of left cheek; bridge of nose; three parallel scars on the right side of chin; tiny one over right eyebrow; last one I can see, runs from back of left ear, into hairline.

"He seems to be wearing an all-over, skintight suit something like, oh, I suppose it's like a pair of what do you call those pajamas kids wear . . . the kind with the back door, the kind that enclose the feet?"

The girl inserted softly, "You mean snuggies?"

The man nodded, slightly embarrassed for no good reason, continued, "Mmm. Yes, that's right. Like those. The suit encloses his feet, seems to be joined to the cape, and comes up to his neck. Seems to be some sort of metallic cloth.

"Something else . . . may mean nothing at all, or on the other hand . . ." He pursed his lips for a moment, then described his observation carefully. "His head seems to be oddly shaped. The forehead is larger than most, seems to be pressing forward in front, as though he had been smacked hard and it was swelling. That seems to be everything."

Sims settled back on his haunches, fished in his side pocket, and came up with a small pipe, which he cold-puffed in thought for a second. He rose slowly, still staring down through the floor window. He murmured something to himself, and when Soames asked what he had said, the special advisor repeated, "I think we've got something almost too hot to handle."

Soames clucked knowingly, and gestured toward the window. "Have you been able to make out anything he's said yet?"

Sims shook his head. "No. That's why you're here. It seems he's saying the same thing, over and over, but it's completely unintelligible. Doesn't seem to be any recognizable language, or any dialect we've been able to pin down."

"I'd like to take a try at him," Soames said, smiling gently. It was the man's nature that challenge brought satisfaction; solution brought unrest, eagerness for a new, more rugged problem.

Sims nodded agreement, but there was a tense, strained film over his eyes, in the set of his mouth. "Take it easy with him, Soames. I have a strong hunch this is something completely new, something we haven't even begun to understand."

Soames smiled again, this time indulgently. "Come, come, Mr. Sims. After all . . . he *is* only an alien of some sort . . . all we have to do is find out what country he's from."

"Have you heard him talk yet?"

Soames shook his head.

"Then don't be too quick to think he's just a foreigner. The word *alien* may be more correct than you think—only not in the *way* you think."

A confused look spread across Soames's face. He gave a slight shrug, as though he could not fathom what Lyle Sims meant . . . and was not particularly interested. He patted Sims reassuringly, which brought an expression of annoyance to the advisor's face, and he clamped down on the pipestem harder.

They walked downstairs together; the secretary left them, to type her notes, and Sims let the philologist into the padded room, cautioning him to deal gently with the man. "Don't forget," Sims warned, "we're not sure *where* he comes from, and sudden movements may make him jumpy. There's a guard overhead, and there'll be a man with me behind this door, but you never know."

Soames looked startled. "You sound as though

he's an aborigine or something. With a suit like that, he *must* be very intelligent. You suspect something, don't you?"

Sims made a neutral motion with his hands. "What I suspect is too nebulous to worry about now. Just take it easy . . . and above all, figure out what he's saying, where he's from."

Sims had decided, long before, that it would be wisest to keep the power of the Brandelmeier to himself. But he was fairly certain it was not the work of a foreign power. The trial run on the test range had left him gasping, confused.

He opened the door, and Soames passed through, uneasily.

Sims caught a glimpse of the expression on the stranger's face as the philologist entered. It was even more uneasy than Soames's had been.

It looked to be a long wait.

Soames was white as library paste. His face was drawn, and the complacent attitude he had shown since his arrival in Washington was shattered. He sat across from Sims, and asked him in a quavering voice for a cigarette. Sims fished around in his desk, came up with a crumpled pack and idly slid them across to Soames. The philologist took one, put it in his mouth, then, as though it had been totally forgotten in the space of a second, he removed it, held it while he spoke.

His tones were amazed. "Do you know what you've got up there in that cell?"

Sims said nothing, knowing what was to come would not startle him too much; he had expected something fantastic.

"That man . . . do you know where he . . . that soldier—and by God, Sims, that's what he *is*—comes from, from—now you're going to think I'm insane to believe it, but somehow I'm convinced—he comes from the future!"

Sims tightened his lips. Despite himself, he *was* shocked. He knew it was true. It *had* to be true, it was the only explanation that fit all the facts.

"What can you tell me?" he asked the philologist.

"Well, at first I tried solving the communications problem by asking him simple questions . . . pointing to myself and saying 'Soames,' pointing to him and looking quizzical, but all he'd keep saying was a string of gibberish. I tried for hours to equate his tones and phrases with all the dialects and subdialects of every language I'd ever known, but it was no use. He slurred too much. And then I finally figured it out. He had to write it out—which I couldn't understand, of course, but it gave me a clue—and then I kept having him repeat it. Do you know what he's speaking?"

Sims shook his head.

The linguist spoke softly. "He's speaking English. It's that simple. Just English.

"But an English that has been corrupted and run together, and so slurred, it's incomprehensible. It must be the future trend of the language. Sort of an extrapolation of gutter English, just contracted to a fantastic extreme. At any rate, I got it out of him."

Sims leaned forward, held his dead pipe tightly. "What?"

Soames read it off a sheet of paper:

"My name is Qarlo Clobregnny. Private. Six-five-one-oh-two-two-nine."

Sims murmured in astonishment. "My God . . . name, rank and—"

Soames finished for him, "—and serial number. Yes, that's all he'd give me for over three hours. Then I asked him a few innocuous questions, like where did he come from, and what was his impression of where he was now."

The philologist waved a hand vaguely. "By that time, I had an idea what I was dealing with, though not where he had come from. But when he began telling me about the War, the War he was fighting when he showed up here, I knew immediately he was either from some other world—which is fantastic —or, or . . . well, I just don't know!"

Sims nodded his head in understanding. "From *when* do you think he comes?"

Soames shrugged. "Can't tell. He says the year he is in—doesn't seem to realize he's in the past—is K79. He doesn't know when the other style of dating went out. As far as he knows, it's been 'K' for a long time, though he's heard stories about things that happened during a time they dated 'GV.' Meaningless, but I'd wager it's more thousands of years than we can imagine."

Sims ran a hand nervously through his hair. This problem was, indeed, larger than he'd thought.

"Look, Professor Soames, I want you to stay with him, and teach him current English. See if you can work some more information out of him, and let him know we mean him no hard times.

"Though Lord knows," the special advisor added with a tremor, "*he* can give us a harder time than we can give him. What knowledge he must have!"

Soames nodded in agreement. "Is it all right if I catch a few hours' sleep? I was with him almost ten hours straight, and I'm sure *he* needs it as badly as I do."

Sims nodded also, in agreement, and the philologist went off to a sleeping room. But when Sims looked down through the window, twenty minutes later, the soldier was still awake, still looking about nervously. It seemed he did *not* need sleep.

Sims was terribly worried, and the coded telegram he had received from the President, in answer to his own, was not at all reassuring. The problem was in his hands, and it was an increasingly worrisome problem.

Perhaps a deadly problem.

He went to another sleeping room, to follow Soames's example. It looked like sleep was going to be scarce.

Problem:

A man from the future. An ordinary man, without any special talents, without any great store of intelligence. The equivalent of "the man in the street." A man who owns a fantastic little machine that turns sand into solid matter, harder than steel— but who hasn't the vaguest notion of how it works, or how to analyze it. A man whose knowledge of past history is as vague and formless as any modern man's. A soldier. With no other talent than fighting. What is to be done with such a man?

Solution:

Unknown.

Lyle Sims pushed the coffee cup away. If he ever had to look at another cup of the disgusting stuff, he was sure he would vomit. Three sleepless days and nights, running on nothing but dexedrine and hot black coffee, had put his nerves more on edge than usual. He snapped at the clerks and secretaries, he paced endlessly, and he had ruined the stems of five pipes. He felt muggy and his stomach was queasy. Yet there was no solution.

It was impossible to say, "All right, we've got a man from the future. So what? Turn him loose and let him make a life for himself in our time, since he can't return to his own."

It was impossible to do that for several reasons: (1) What if he *couldn't* adjust? He was then a potential menace, of *incalculable* potential. (2) What if an enemy power—and God knows there were enough powers around anxious to get a secret weapon as valuable as Qarlo—grabbed him, and *did* somehow manage to work out the concepts behind the rifle, the firmer, the mono-atomic anti-gravity device in the pouch? What then? (3) A man used to war, knowing only war, would eventually *seek* or foment war.

There were dozens of others, they were only beginning to realize. No, something had to be done with him.

Imprison him?

For what? The man had done no real harm. He had not intentionally caused the death of the man on the subway platform. He had been frightened by the train. He had been attacked by the executives— one of whom had a broken neck, but was alive. No, he was just "a stranger and afraid, in a world I never made," as Housman had put it so terrifyingly clearly.

Kill him?

For the same reasons, unjust and brutal . . . not to mention wasteful.

Find a place for him in society?

Doing what?

Sims raged in his mind, mulled it over and tried every angle. It was an insoluble problem. A simple dogface, with no other life than that of a professional soldier, what good was he?

All Qarlo knew was war.

The question abruptly answered itself: If he knows no other life than that of a soldier . . . why, make him a soldier. (But . . . who was to say that with his knowledge of futuristic tactics and weapons, he might not turn into another Hitler, or Genghis Khan?) No, making him a soldier would only heighten the problem. There could be no peace of mind were he in a position where he might organize.

As a tactician then?

It might work at that.

Sims slumped behind his desk, pressed down the key of his intercom, spoke to the secretary, "Get me General Mainwaring, General Polk and the Secretary of Defense."

He clicked the key back. It just might work at that. If Qarlo could be persuaded to detail fighting plans, now that he realized where he was, and that the men who held him were not his enemies, and that allies of Ruskie-Chink (and what a field of speculation *that* pair of words opened!).

It just might work . . .

. . . but Sims doubted it.

Mainwaring stayed on to report when Polk and the Secretary of Defense went back to their regular duties. He was a big man, with softness written across his face and body, and a pompous white moustache. He shook his head sadly, as though the Rosetta Stone had been stolen from him just before an all-important experiment.

"Sorry, Sims, but the man is useless to us. Brilliant grasp of military tactics, so long as it involves what he calls 'eighty-thread beams' and telepathic contacts.

"Do you know those wars up there are fought as much mentally as they are physically? Never heard of a tank or a mortar, but the stories he tells of brain-burning and spore-death would make you sick. It isn't pretty the way they fight.

"I thank God I'm not going to be around to see it; I thought *our* wars were filthy and unpleasant. They've got us licked all down the line for brutality and mass death. And the strange thing is, this Qarlo fellow *despises* it! For a while there—felt foolish as hell—but for a while there, when he was explaining it, I almost wanted to chuck my career, go out and start beating the drum for disarmament."

The General summed up, and it was apparent Qarlo was useless as a tactician. He had been brought up with one way of waging war, and it would take a lifetime for him to adjust enough to be of any tactical use.

But it didn't really matter, for Sims was certain the General had given him the answer to the problem, inadvertently.

He would have to clear it with Security, and the President, of course. And it would take a great deal of publicity to make the people realize this man actually *was* the real thing, an inhabitant of the future. But if it worked out, Qarlo Clobregnny, the soldier and nothing *but* the soldier, could be the most valuable man Time had ever spawned.

He set to work on it, wondering foolishly if he wasn't too much the idealist.

Ten soldiers crouched in the frozen mud. Their firmers had been jammed, had turned the sand and dirt of their holes only to icelike conditions. The cold was seeping up through their suits, and the jammed firmers were emitting hard radiation. One of the men screamed as the radiation took hold in his gut, and he felt the organs watering away. He leaped up, vomiting blood and phlegm—and was caught across the face by a robot-tracked triple beam. The front of his face disappeared, and the nearly decapitated corpse flopped back into the firmhole, atop a comrade.

That soldier shoved the body aside carelessly, thinking of his four children, lost to him forever in a Ruskie-Chink raid on Garmatopolis, sent to the bogs to work. His mind conjured up the sight of the three girls and the little boy with such long, long eyelashes—each dragging through the stinking bog, a mineral bag tied to the neck, collecting fuel rocks for the enemy. He began to cry softly. The sound and mental image of crying was picked up by a Ruskie-Chink telepath somewhere across the lines, and even before the man could catch himself, blank his mind, the telepath was on him.

The soldier raised up from the firmhole bottom, clutching with crooked hands at his head. He began to tear at his features wildly, screaming high and piercing, as the enemy telepath burned away his brain. In a moment his eyes were empty, staring shells, and the man flopped down beside his comrade, who had begun to deteriorate.

A thirty-eight thread whined its beam overhead, and the eight remaining men saw a munitions wheel go up with a deafening roar. Hot shrapnel zoomed across the field, and a thin, brittle, knife-edged bit of plasteel arced over the edge of the firmhole, and buried itself in one soldier's head. The piece went in crookedly, through his left earlobe, and came out skewering his tongue, half-extended from his open mouth. From the side it looked as though he were wearing some sort of earring. He died in spasms, and it took an awfully long while. Finally, the twitching and gulping got so bad, one of his comrades used the butt of a Brandelmeier across the dying man's nose. It splintered the nose, sent bone chips into the brain, killing the man instantly.

Then the attack call came!

In each of their heads, the telepathic cry came to advance, and they were up out of the firmhole, all seven of them, reciting their daily prayer, and knowing it would do no good. They advanced across the slushy ground, and overhead they could hear the buzz of leech bombs, coming down on the enemy's thread emplacements.

All around them in the deep-set night the varicolored explosions popped and sugged, expanding in all directions like fireworks, then dimming the scene, again the blackness.

One of the soldiers caught a beam across the belly, and he was thrown sidewise for ten feet, to land in a soggy heap, his stomach split open, the organs glowing and pulsing wetly from the charge of the threader. A head popped out of a firmhole before them, and three of the remaining six fired simultaneously. The enemy was a booby—rigged to backtrack their kill urge, rigged to a telepathic hookup—and even as the body exploded under their combined firepower, each of the men caught fire. Flames leaped from their mouths, from their pores, from the instantly charred spaces where their eyes had been. A pyrotic-telepath had been at work.

The remaining three split and cut away, realizing they might be thinking, might be giving themselves away. That was the horror of being just a dogface, not a special telepath behind the lines. Out here, here was nothing but death.

A doggie-mine slithered across the ground, entwined itself in the legs of one soldier, and blew the legs out from under him. He lay there clutching the shredded stumps, feeling the blood soaking into the mud, and then unconsciousness seeped into his brain. He died shortly thereafter.

Of the two left, one leaped a barbwall, and blasted out a thirty-eight thread emplacement of twelve men, at the cost of the top of his head. He was left alive, and curiously, as though the war had stopped, he felt the top of himself, and his fingers pressed lightly against convoluted, slick matter for a second before he dropped to the ground.

His braincase was open, glowed strangely in the night, but no one saw it.

The last soldier dove under a beam that zzzzzzzed through the night, and landed on his elbows. He rolled with the tumble, felt the edge of a leech-bomb crater, and dove in headfirst. The beam split up his passage, and he escaped charring by an inch. He lay in the hollow, feeling the cold of the battle-field seeping around him, and drew his cloak closer.

The soldier was Qarlo . . .

He finished talking, and sat down on the platform . . .

The audience was silent . . .

Sims shrugged into his coat, fished around in the
pocket for the cold pipe. The dottle had fallen out
of the bowl, and he felt the dark grains at the
bottom of the pocket. The audience was filing out
slowly, hardly anyone speaking, but each staring at
others around him. As though they were suddenly
realizing what had happened to them, as though
they were looking for a solution.

Sims passed such a solution. The petitions were
there, tacked up alongside the big sign—duplicate
of the ones up all over the city. He caught the
heavy black type on them as he passed through the
auditorium's vestibule:

> SIGN THIS PETITION!
> PREVENT WHAT YOU HAVE HEARD
> TONIGHT!

People were flocking around the petitions, but
Sims knew it was only a token gesture at this point:
the legislature had gone through that morning. No
more war . . . under any conditions. And intelligence
reported the long playing records, the piped broad-
casts, the p.a. trucks, had all done their jobs. Similar
legislation was going through all over the world.

It looked as though Qarlo had done it, single-handed.

Sims stopped to refill his pipe, and stared up at
the big black-lined poster near the door.

> HEAR QARLO, THE SOLDIER FROM THE
> FUTURE!
> SEE THE MAN FROM TOMORROW,
> AND HEAR HIS STORIES
> OF THE WONDERFUL WORLD OF THE
> FUTURE!
> FREE! NO OBLIGATIONS! HURRY!

The advertising had been effective, and it was a fine campaign.

Qarlo had been more valuable just telling about his Wars, about how men died in that day in the future, than he could ever have been as a strategist.

It took a real soldier, who hated war, to talk of it, to show people that it was ugly, and unglamorous. And there was a certain sense of foul defeat, of hopelessness, in knowing the future was the way Qarlo described it. It made you want to stop the flow of Time, say, "No. The future will *not* be like this! We will abolish war!"

Certainly enough steps in the right direction had been taken. The legislature was there, and those who had held back, who had tried to keep animosity alive, were being disposed of every day.

Qarlo had done his work well.

There was just one thing bothering special advisor Lyle Sims. The soldier had come back in time, so he was here. That much they knew for certain.

But a nagging worry ate at Sims's mind, made him say prayers he had thought himself incapable of inventing. Made him fight to get Qarlo heard by everyone . . .

Could the future be changed?

Or was it inevitable?

Would Qarlo's world inevitably come 'round?

Would all their work be for nothing?

It couldn't be. It dare not be.

He walked back inside, got in line to sign the petitions again, though it was his fiftieth time.

THE LAST MAN LEFT IN THE BAR

BY C. M. KORNBLUTH (1923–1958)

INFINITY SCIENCE FICTION
OCTOBER

Cyril Kornbluth's second contribution to the best of 1957 is this strange and powerful story that antici-pates several of the themes and concerns of the "New Wave" science fiction writers of the mid-to-late 1960s.

A truly complex story from a complex man. (MHG)

I'm not going to pretend. This story is not lumi-nously clear to me. It requires more than one read-ing, and those readings require a great deal of attention. I (unfortunately) have a great deal of work to do and I don't think I've given it quite the neces-sary attention. This, I imagine, is my loss.

Some stories, after all, are dense and consist of layers beneath layers. They aren't made easy for the readers, who must dig and poke and think and per-haps wake up in the middle of the night suddenly getting a new insight.

Now remember, it is 1957. It is not yet time for the "New Wave," a way of writing that broke with the past of science fiction to take up some of the more advanced literary styles of the mainstream. This story, however, is New Wave for sure, and we can only conclude that Cyril had anticipated what was to come,

*that he had explored it early, and that he then died
before he could experience its flowering and receive
the acclaim due a pioneer.*

*What might he have accomplished if he had lived a
normal lifetime? (IA)*

You know him, Joe—or Sam, Mike, Tony, Ben,
whatever your deceitful, cheaply genial name may
be. And do not lie to yourself, Gentle Reader; you
know him too.

A loner, he was.

You did not notice him when he slipped in; you
only knew by his aggrieved air when he (finally)
caught your eye and self-consciously said "Shot of
Red Top and a beer" that he'd ruffle your working
day. (Six at night until two in the morning is a day?
But ah, the horrible alternative is to work for a
living.)

Shot of Red Top and a beer at 8:35.

And unbeknownst to him, Gentle Reader, in the
garage up the street the two contrivers of his dilemma conspired; the breaths of tall dark stooped
cadaverous Galardo and the mouse-eyed lassie
mingled.

"Hyü shall be a religion-isst," he instructed her.

"I know the role," she squeaked and quoted:
" 'Woe to the day on which I was born into the
world! Woe to the womb which bare me! Woe to
the bowels which admitted me! Woe to the breasts
which suckled me! Woe to the feet upon which I sat
and rested! Woe to the hands which carried me and
reared me until I grew! Woe to my tongue and my
lips which have brought forth and spoken vanity,
detraction, falsehood, ignorance, derision, idle tales,
craft, and hypocrisy! Woe to mine eyes which have
looked upon scandalous things! Woe to mine ears
which have delighted in the words of slanderers!
Woe to my hands which have seized what did not

of right belong to them! Woe to my belly and my bowels which have lusted after food unlawful to be eaten! Woe to my throat which like a fire has consumed all that it found!' "

He sobbed with the beauty of it and nodded at last, tears hanging in his eyes: "Yess, that religion. It iss one of my fave-o-ritts."

She was carried away. "I can do others. Oh, I can do others. I can do Mithras and Isis and Marduk and Eddyism and Billsword and Pealing and Uranium, both orthodox and reformed."

"Mithras, Isis, and Marduk are long gone and the resst are sss-till tü come. Listen tü your master, dü not chatter, and we shall an artwork make of which there will be talk under the green sky until all food is eaten."

Meanwhile, Gentle Reader, the loner listened. To his left strong silent sinewy men in fellowship, the builders, the doers, the darers: "So I told the foreman where he should put his Bullard. I told him I run a Warner and Swasey, I run a Warner and Swasey good, I never even *seen* a Bullard up close in my life, and where he should put it. I know how to run a Warner and Swasey and why should he take me off a Warner and Swasey I know how to run and put me on a Bullard and where he should put it, ain't I right?"

"Absolutely."

To his right the clear-eyed virtuous matrons, the steadfast, the true-seeing, the loving-kind: "Oh, I don't know what I want, what do you want? I'm a Scotch drinker really but I don't feel like Scotch but if I come home with muscatel on my breath Eddie calls me a wino and laughs his head off. I don't know what I want. What do you want?"

In the box above the bar the rollicking raster raced.

VIDEO	AUDIO
Gampa smashes bottle over the head of *Bibby*.	*Gampa:* Young whipper-snapper!
Bibby spits out water.	*Bibby:* Next time put some flavoring in it, Gramps!
Gampa picks up sugar bowl and smashes it over *Bibby's* head. *Bibby* licks sugar from face.	*Bibby:* My, that's better! But what of Naughty Roger and his attempted kidnapping of Sis to extort the secret of the Q-Bomb?
cut to *Limbo Shot* of Reel-Rye bottle.	
	Announcer: Yes, kiddies! What of Roger? But first a word from the makers of Reel-Rye, that happy syrup that gives your milk grown-up flavor! YES! Grown-up flavor!

Shot of Red Top and a beer. At 8:50.

In this own unsecret heart: Steady, boy. You've got to think this out. Nothing impossible about it, no reason to settle for a stalemate; just a little time to think it out. Galardo said the Black Chapter would accept a token submission, let me return the Seal, and that would be that. But I mustn't count on that as a datum; he lied to me about the Serpentists. Token submission *sounds* right; they go in big for symbolism. Maybe because they're so stone-broke, like the Japs. Drinking a cup of tea, they gussie it all up until it's a religion;

that's the way you squeeze nourishment out of poverty—

Skip the Japs. Think. He lied to me about the Serpentists. The big thing to remember is, I have the Chapter Seal and they need it back, or think they do. All you need's a little time to think things through, place where he won't dare jump you and grab the Seal. And this is it.

"Joe. Sam, Mike, Tony, Ben, whoever you are. Hit me again."

Joe—Sam, Mike, Tony, Ben?—tilts the amber bottle quietly; the liquid's level rises and crowns the little glass with a convex meniscus. He turns off the stream with an easy roll of the wrist. The suntan line of neon tubing at the bar back twinkles off the curve of surface tension, the placid whiskey, the frothy beer. At 9:05.

To his left: "So Finkelstein finally meets Goldberg in the garment center and he grabs him like this by the lapel, and he yells, 'You louse, you rat, you no-good, what's this about you running around with my wife? I ought to—I ought to—say, you call *this* a *button*hole?' "

Restrained and apprehensive laughter; Catholic, Protestant, Jew (choice of one), what's the different I always say.

Did they have a Jewish Question still, or was all smoothed and troweled and interfaithed and brother-hoodooed—

Wait. Your formulation implies that they're in the future, and you have no proof of that. Think straighter; you don't know *where* they are, or *when* they are, or *who* they are. You *do* know that you walked into Big Maggie's resonance chamber to change the target, experimental iridium for old reliable zinc

and

"Bartender," in a controlled and formal voice.

Shot of Red Top and a beer at 9:09, the hand vibrating with remembrance of a dirty-green El Greco sky which *might* be Brookhaven's heavens a million years either way from now, or one second sideways, or (bow to Method and formally exhaust the possibilities) a hallucination. The Seal snatched from the greenlit rock altar could be a blank washer, a wheel from a toy truck, or the screw top from a jar of shaving cream but for the fact that it wasn't. It was the Seal.

So: they began seeping through after that. The Chapter wanted it back. The Serpentists wanted it, period. Galardo had started by bargaining and wound up by threatening, but how could you do anything but laugh at his best offer, a rusty five-pound spur gear with a worn keyway and three teeth missing? His threats were richer than his bribes; they culminated with The Century of Flame. "Faith, father, it doesn't scare me at all, at all; sure, no man could stand it." Subjective-objective (How you used to sling *them* around!), and Master Newton's billiard-table similes dissolve into sense-impressions of pointer-readings as you learn your trade, but Galardo had scared hell out of you, or into you, with The Century of Flame.

But you had the Seal of the Chapter and you had time to think, while on the screen above the bar:

VIDEO	AUDIO
Long shot down steep, cobblestoned French village street. *Pierre* darts out of alley in middle distance, looks wildly around and runs toward camera, pistol in hand. *Annette* and *Paul* appear from same alley and dash after him.	*Paul:* Stop, you fool! *Pierre:* A fool, am I? *Annette:* Darling! *Paul:* Don't mind me. Take my gun—after him. He's a mad dog, I tell you!

Cut to *Cu* of *Pierre's* face; beard stubble and sweat.

Cut to long shot; *Pierre* aims and fires; *Paul* grabs his left shoulder and falls.

Cut to two-shot, *Annette* and *Paul*.

Dolly back.
Annette takes his pistol.

Annette stands; we see her aim down at *Paul*, out of the picture. Then we dolly in to a *Cu* of her head; she is smiling triumphantly.

A hand holding a pistol enters the *Cu*; the pistol muzzle touches *Annette's* neck.

Dolly back to middle shot. *Harkrider* stands behind *Annette* as *Paul* gets up briskly and takes the pistol from her hand.

Cut to long shot of street, *Harkrider* and *Paul* walk away from the camera, *Annette* between them. Fadeout.

Annette: This, my dear, is as good a time as any to drop my little masquerade. Are you American agents really so stupid that you never thought I might be—a plant, as you call it?

Sound: click of cocking pistol.

Harkrider: Drop it, Madame Golkov.

Paul: No, Madame Golkov; we American agents were not really so stupid. Wish I could say the same for—your people. Pierre Tourneur *was* a plant, I am glad to say; otherwise he would not have missed me. He is one of the best pistol shots in Counterintelligence.

Harkrider: Come along, Madame Golkov.

Music: theme up and out.

Them and their neatly packaged problems, them and their neatly packaged shows with beginning middle and end. The rite of the low-budget shot-in-Europe spy series, the rite of pugilism, the rite of the dog-walk after dinner and the beer at the bar with co-celebrant worshipers at the high altar of Nothing.

9:30. Shot of Red Top and a beer, positively the last one until you get this figured out; you're beginning to buzz like a transformer.

Do they have transformers? Do they have vitamins? Do they have anything but that glaring green sky, and the rock altar and treasures like the Seal and the rusty gear with three broken teeth? "All smelling of iodoform. And all quite bald." But Galardo looked as if he were dying of tuberculosis, and the letter from the Serpentists was in a sick and straggling hand. Relics of mediaeval barbarism.

To his left—

"Galardo!" he screamed.

The bartender scurried over—Joe, Sam, Mike, Tony, Ben?—scowling. "What's the matter, mister?"

"I'm sorry. I got a stitch in my side. A cramp."

Bullyboy scowled competently and turned. "What'll you have, mister?"

Galardo said cadaverously: "Wodeffer my vriend hyere iss havfing."

"Shot of Red Top and a beer, right?"

"What are you doing here?"

"Drink-ing beferachiss . . . havf hyü de-site-it hwat tü dü?"

The bartender rapped down the shot glass and tilted the bottle over it, looking at Galardo. Some of the whiskey slopped over. The bartender started, went to the tap and carefully drew a glass of beer, slicing the collar twice.

"My vriend hyere will pay."

He got out a half-dollar, fumbling, and put it on the wet wood. The bartender, old-fashioned, rapped it twice on the bar to show he wasn't stealing it even though you weren't watching; he rang it up double virtuous on the cash register, the absent owner's fishy eye.

"What are you doing here?" again, in a low, reasonable, almost amused voice to show him you have the whip hand.

"Drink-ing beferachiss . .. it iss so cle-an hyere." Galardo's sunken face, unbelievably, looked wistful as he surveyed the barroom, his head swiveling slowly from extreme left to extreme right.

"Clean. Well. Isn't it clean there?"

"Sheh, not!" Galardo said mournfully. "Sheh, not! Hyere it iss so cle-an . . . hwai did yü outreach tü us? Hag-rid us, wretch-it, hag-rid us?" There were tears hanging in his eyes. "Haff yü de-site-it hwat tü dü?"

Expansively: "I don't pretend to understand the situation *fully*, Galardo. But you know and I know that I've got something you people [think you] need. Now there doesn't seem to be any body of law covering artifacts that appear [*plink!*] in a magnetron on accidental overload, and I just have your word that it's yours."

"Ah, that iss how yü re-member it now," said sorrowful Galardo.

"Well, it's the way it [but wasn't something green? I think of spired Toledo and three angled crosses toppling] happened. I don't want anything silly, like a million dollars in small unmarked bills, and I don't want to be bullied, to be bullied, no, I mean not by you, not by anybody. Just, just tell me who you are, what all this is about. This is nonsense, you see, and we can't have nonsense. I'm afraid I'm not expressing myself very well—"

And a confident smile and turn away from him,

which shows that you aren't afraid, you can turn your back and dare him to make something of it. In public, in the bar? It is laughable; you have him in the palm of your hand. "Shot of Red Top and a beer, please, Sam." At 9:48.

The bartender draws the beer and pours the whiskey. He pauses before he picks up the dollar bill fished from the pants pocket, pauses almost timidly and works his face into a friend's grimace. But you can read him; he is making amends for his suspicion that you were going to start a drunken brawl when Galardo merely surprised you a bit. You can read him because your mind is tensed to concert pitch tonight, ready for Galardo, ready for the Serpentists, ready to crack this thing wide open; strange!

But you weren't ready for the words he spoke from his fake apologetic friend's grimace as you delicately raised the heavy amber-filled glass to your lips: "Where'd your friend go?"

You slopped the whiskey as you turned and looked.

Galardo gone.

You smiled and shrugged; he comes and goes as he pleases, you know. Irresponsible, no manners at all—but *loyal*. A prince among men when you get to know him, a prince, I tell you. All this in your smile and shrug—why, you could have been an actor! The worry, the faint neurotic worry, didn't show at all, and indeed there is no reason why it should. You have the whip hand; you have the Seal; Galardo will come crawling back and explain everything. As for example:

"You may wonder why I've asked all of you to assemble in the libr'reh."

or

"For goodness' sake, Gracie. I wasn't going to go to Cuba! When you heard me on the extension phone I was just ordering a dozen Havana *cigars*!"

or

"In your notation, we were from 19,276 A.D. Our basic mathematic is a quite comprehensible subsumption of your contemporary statistical analysis and topology which I shall now proceed to explain to you."

And that was all.

With sorrow, Gentle Reader, you will have noticed that the marble did not remark: "I am chiseled," the lumber "I am sawn," the paint "I'm applied to canvas," the tea leaf "I am whisked about in an exquisite Korean bowl to brew while the celebrants of *cha no yu* squeeze this nourishment out of their poverty." Vain victim, relax and play your hunches; subconscious integration does it. Stick with your lit-tle old subconscious integration and all will go *swimmingly*, if only it weren't so damned noisy in here. But it was dark on the street and conceivably things could happen there; stick with crowds and stick with witnesses, but if only it weren't so . . .

To his left they were settling down; it was the hour of confidences, and man to man they told the secret of their success: "In the needle trade, I'm in the needle trade, I don't sell anybody a crooked needle, my father told me that. Albert, he said to me, don't never sell nobody nothing but a straight needle. And today I have four shops."

To his right they were settling down; freed of the cares of the day they invited their souls, explored the spiritual realm, theologized with exquisite distinctions: "Now *wait* a minute, I didn't say I was a *good* Mormon. I said I was a Mormon and that's what I am, a Mormon. I *never* said I was a *good* Mormon, I just said I was a Mormon, my mother was a Mormon and my father was a Mormon, and that makes me a Mormon but I *never* said I was a *good* Mormon—"

Distinguo, rolled the canonical thunder; *distinguo*.

Demurely a bonneted lassie shook her small-change tambourine beneath his chin and whispered, snarling: "Galardo lied."

Admit it; you were startled. But what need for the bartender to come running with raised hand, what need for needletrader to your left to shrink away, the L.D.S. to cower?

"Mister, that's twice you let out a yell, we run a quiet place, if you can't be good, begone."

Begob.

"I ash-assure you, bartender, it was—unintenable."

Greed vies with hate; greed wins; greed always wins: "Just keep it quiet, mister, this ain't the Bowery, this is a family place." Then, relenting: "The same?"

"Yes, please." At 10:15 the patient lassie jingled silver on the parchment palm outstretched. He placed a quarter on the tambourine and asked politely: "Did you say something to me before, Miss?"

"God bless you, sir. Yes, sir, I did say something. I said Galardo lied; the Seal is holy to the Serpent, sir, and to his humble emissaries. If you'll only hand it over, sir, the Serpent will somewhat mitigate the fearsome torments which are rightly yours for snatching the Seal from the Altar, sir."

[Snatchings from Altars? *Ma foi*, the wench is mad!]

"Listen, lady. That's only talk. What annoys me about you people is, you won't talk sense. I want to know who you are, what this is about, maybe just a little hint about your mathematics, and I'll do the rest and you can have the blooming Seal. I'm a passable physicist even if I'm only a technician. I bet there's something you didn't know. I bet you didn't know the tech shortage is tighter than the scientist shortage. You get a guy can tune a magnetron, he writes his own ticket. So I'm weak on quantum mechanics,

the theory side, I'm still a good all-around man and
be-*lieve* me, the Ph.D.'s would kiss my ever-loving
feet if I told them I got an offer from Argonne—

"So listen, you Janissary emissary. I'm happy right
here in this necessary comissary and here I *stay*."

But she was looking at him with bright frightened
mouse's eyes and slipped on down the line when he
paused for breath, putting out the parchment palm
to others but not ceasing to watch him.

Coins tapped the tambour. "God bless you. God
bless you. God bless you."

The raving-maniacal ghost of G. Washington Hill
descended then into a girdled sibyl; she screamed
from the screen: "It's *Hit* Pa-*rade*!"

"I like them production numbers."

"I like that Pigalle Mackintosh."

"I like them production numbers. Lotsa pretty
girls, pretty clothes, something to take your mind
off your troubles."

"I like that Pigalle Mackintosh. She don't just
sing, mind you, she plays the saxophone. Talent."

"I like them production numbers. They show you
just what the song is all about. Like last week they
did *Sadist Calypso* with this mad scientist cutting up
the girls, and then Pigalle comes in and whips him
to death at the last verse, you see just what the
song's all about, something to take your mind off
your troubles."

"I like that Pigalle Mackintosh. She don't just
sing, mind you, she plays the saxophone and cracks a
blacksnake whip, like last week in *Sadist Caylpso*—"

"Yeah. Something to take your mind off your
troubles."

Irritably he felt in his pocket for the Seal and
moved, stumbling a little, to one of the tables against
the knotty pine wall. His head slipped forward on
the polished wood and he sank into the sea of myth.

Galardo came to him in his dream and spoke

under a storm-green sky: "Take your mind off your troubles, Edward. It was stolen like the first penny, like the quiz answers, like the pity for your bereavement." His hand, a tambourine, was out.

"Never shall I yield," he declaimed to the miserable wretch. "By the *honneur* of a Gascon, I stole it fair and square; 'tis mine, knave! *En garde!*"

Galardo quailed and ran, melting into the sky, the altar, the tambourine.

A ham-hand manhandled him. "Light-up time," said Sam. "I let you sleep because you got it here, but I got to close up now."

"Sam," he says uncertainly.

"One for the road, mister. On the house. *Up-sy-daisy!*" meaty hooks under his armpits heaving him to the bar.

The lights are out behind the bar, the jolly neons, glittering off how many gems of amber rye and the tan crystals of beer? A meager bulb above the register is the oasis in the desert of inky night.

"Sam," groggily, "you don't understand. I mean I never explained it—"

"Drink up, mister," a pale free drink, soda bubbles lightly tinged with tawny rye. A small sip to gain time.

"Sam, there are some people after me—"

"You'll feel better in the morning, mister. Drink up, I got to close up, hurry up."

"These people, Sam [it's cold in here and scary as a noise in the attic; the bottles stand accusingly, the chrome globes that top them eye you] these people, they've got a thing, The Century of—"

"Sure, mister, I let you sleep because you got it here, but we close up now, drink up your drink."

"Sam, let me go home with you, will you? It isn't anything like that, don't misunderstand, I just can't be alone. These people—look, I've got money—"

He spreads out what he dug from his pocket.

"Sure, mister, you got lots of money, two dollars and thirty-eight cents. Now you take your money and get out of the store because I got to lock up and clean out the register—"

"Listen, bartender, I'm not drunk, maybe I don't have much money on me but I'm an important man! Important! They couldn't run Big Maggie at Brookhaven without me, I may not have a degree but what I get from these people if you'll only let me stay here—"

The bartender takes the pale one on the house you only sipped and dumps it in the sink; his hands are iron on you and you float while he chants:

> *Decent man. Decent place.*
> *Hold their liquor. Got it here.*
> *Try be nice. Drunken bum.*
> *Don't—come—back.*

The crash of your coccyx on the concrete and the slam of the door are one.

Run!

Down the black street stumbling over cans, cats, orts, to the pool of light in the night, safe corner where a standard sprouts and sprays radiance.

The tall black figure that steps between is Galardo.

The short one has a tambourine.

"Take it!" He thrust out the Seal on his shaking palm. "If you won't tell me anything, you won't. Take it and go away!"

Galardo inspects it and sadly says: "Thiss appearss to be a blank wash-er."

"Mistake," he slobbers. "Minute." He claws in his pockets, ripping. "Here! Here!"

The lassie squeaks: "The wheel of a toy truck. It will not do at all, sir." Her glittereyes.

"Then this! This is it! This must be it!"

Their heads shake slowly. Unable to look his fingers feel the rim and rolled threading of the jar cap.

They nod together, sad and glittereyed, and The Century of Flame begins.

DAW

Don't Miss These Exciting DAW Anthologies

ANNUAL WORLD'S BEST SF
Donald A. Wollheim, editor

DAW

NEW DIMENSIONS IN MILITARY SF

Charles Ingrid
THE SAND WARS
He was a soldier fighting against both mankind's alien foe and the evil at the heart of the human Dominion Empire, trapped in an alien-altered suit of armor which, if worn too long, could transform him into a sand warrior—a no-longer human berserker.

☐ SOLAR KILL (Book 1) (UE2209—$3.50)
☐ LASERTOWN BLUES (Book 2) (UE2260—$3.50)
☐ CELESTIAL HIT LIST (Book 3) (UE2306—$3.50)

W. Michael Gear
THE SPIDER TRILOGY
The Prophets of the lost colony planet called World could see the many pathways of the future, and when the conquering Patrol Ships of the galaxy-spanning Directorate arrived, they found the warriors of World ready, armed and waiting.
☐ THE WARRIORS OF SPIDER (Book 1) (UE2287—$3.95)
☐ THE WAY OF SPIDER (Book 2) (UE2318—$3.95)

John Steakley
☐ ARMOR
Impervious body armor had been devised for the commando forces who were to be dropped onto the poisonous surface of A-9, the home world of mankind's most implacable enemy. But what of the man inside the armor? This tale of cosmic combat will stand against the best of Gordon Dickson or Poul Anderson.
(UE2368—$4.50)

NEW AMERICAN LIBRARY
P.O. Box 999, Bergenfield, New Jersey 07621

Please send me the DAW BOOKS I have checked above. I am enclosing $_____
(check or money order—no currency or C.O.D.'s). Please include the list price plus
$1.00 per order to cover handling costs. Prices and numbers are subject to change
without notice. (Prices slightly higher in Canada.)

Name _____

Address _____

City _____ State _____ Zip _____
Please allow 4-6 weeks for delivery.